His Third Try

LIZ ISAACSON

AEJ
CREATIVE WORKS

His Third Try

One

BOONE WHETTSTEIN PULLED UP TO HIS BROTHER'S
house, and all the balloons in the cab of his truck flew
forward, booping him in the back of the head. He swatted at
them while his daughter, Gerty, giggled and did the same.

Boone could listen to her laughter all day, every day, and
he grinned at her. "You get the cake, and I'll get the
balloons?" he suggested.

"No way," Gerty said. "I want to take in the balloons. I'll
just drop the cake."

"Why would you drop the cake?" Boone put the truck in
park and looked up at Matt's front windows. He was getting
married in the morning, but tonight was his son's sixteenth
birthday. Boone loved living near his brother again, and he'd
missed Matt and his kids when they'd left Montana a couple
of years ago.

He'd never in his wildest dreams thought he'd follow
Matt to Ivory Peaks, Colorado, but he wasn't unhappy that

he had. In fact, Boone was happier now than he'd been in a long, long time—even when he'd been with Karley, before he'd known about her infidelity.

"Because I'm tripping over everything lately," Gerty said. "You get the cake, Daddy, please?"

"Yeah, sure," he said easily. He could carry a cake as easily as he could a bunch of balloons, and he opened the door to get out of the truck. Gerty did the same on her side, and she gathered all the blue, white, purple, and green ribbons together to get the bunch of balloons back together.

With all those floating orbs gone, he collected the big, pink pastry box. He'd been more than willing to stop in town and get all the things Matt needed for the party, because he had about fifteen hundred things on his plate right now.

Boone turned as a car engine filled the country silence on his brother's street. A pick-up truck full of cowboys pulled up to the curb, with another one not far behind. That one only held one person—Matt's fiancée—and Boone grinned at Gloria Munson.

"Need any help, Boone?" she asked as she got out of her truck. She stood back, and a golden retriever jumped down from the cab too.

"Yeah, my gift is still in there." He nodded toward the back seat as Gloria approached. Gerty had gone ahead to the front door, which now stood open, and Matt came down the front steps to welcome everyone.

"Did you get it?" Matt asked, arriving at Boone's truck too.

"Right there," Boone said, nodding to the wrapped package on the back seat. "Gloria was going to grab it for me."

"And we're a go for everything?" He looked at Gloria, slid his arm around her and kissed her. "Hey, sweetheart. You look fantastic."

"Hey, baby." She beamed up at him, and Boone's jealousy soared toward the sky.

He turned away from the truck, the weight of the enormous cake shifting in his hands. He steadied it and said, "Someone just needs to grab it, please."

"I'll get it," Gloria said. "We're a go for later, yes."

"Perfect," Matt said. "Thank you both." He turned toward the cowboys crossing his lawn and started greeting them. Boone knew them all too, because they all worked at the Hammond Family Farm, about fifteen minutes from downtown Ivory Peaks—if such a small town could have a downtown.

Ivory Peaks did, and it housed a Cowboy Church, a general store, a small grocery store, two gas stations, a barber and salon that shared the space—men on one side and women on the other—and a pet supply store. A couple of restaurants, a dollar store, and the elementary school rounded out Main Street, and Boone sure did like the town.

He liked the huge mountains to the west, even if he was used to seeing them in the east. Well, all around, if he was being honest. Montana seemed covered with hills and mountains and snow—and sky.

He looked up into the Colorado sky and drew a deep

breath before going up the steps to Matt's house. Since it was the height of summer, he had all the windows closed and the air conditioning pumping hard.

Thank you, Lord, Boone thought, because he spent far too many hours outside without the cooled air. He went past the men and women milling about in the living room, waiting for the party to start, and into the kitchen, where he slid the cake box onto the counter.

Keith stood there with his friends, and Boone grinned at him. "There you are. I haven't seen you yet today." He stole a hug from his nephew, clapping him heartily on the back.

"Thanks, Uncle Boone." Keith laughed, and it sure did Boone's heart good to see how happy Keith was. He hoped Gerty would achieve something similar after acclimating to her new school, a new house, and hopefully new friends.

They'd moved here at the end of the school year, and she'd spent the past couple of months with her cousins, a boy who lived at the farm next door to where they lived, adults, and horses. His daughter loved horses more than people, which actually worried Boone. He wanted her to fit in here; he'd been praying for seventy-two solid days and nights that Gerty would find just one friend in the junior high on the outskirts of Denver, another ten minutes past Ivory Peaks.

Just one, he thought as he released Keith.

"These are my friends," Keith said. "Jordy, Luis, Dalton, and Bennie."

"Nice to meet you fellas," Boone said. "Where's Kassidy?"

"She and Izzy are coming in a minute," Keith said, looking toward the front door. "My Uncle Boone. My dad's brother."

"Nice to meet you, sir," chorused around, and Boone looked at the kids.

"Any of you have siblings who'll be in eighth grade?"

"I got a brother who'll be in eighth grade," Luis said, and Boone didn't correct him on the grammar. "His name's Alberto."

Boone nodded.

"My sister is going into seventh," Jordy said. "Is Gerty going into eighth?"

"Yep." Boone looked around for the mass of balloons, and they started squeezing through the door a moment later. "There she is, behind that mass of balloons."

Keith's face lit up, and he went to help Gerty. He took some of them from her, and they started tying the balloons to the backs of chairs, rails on the lamps, and even the handle of the fridge.

"This is her," Boone said when Gerty came into the kitchen with Keith. He introduced her around to his friends, though they were all a few years older than her. Boone just watched, because Gerty was a pretty girl, and she'd liked a boy named Michael Hammond all summer. He'd be fourteen in November, and Gerty had turned thirteen several weeks ago.

Boone had spent more time on his knees this summer than any other, because he could see the changes in his daughter. She'd been wearing a bra before she needed one, but when she needed new undergarments now, she went with another woman.

Before they'd moved to Colorado, that had been Boone's steady girlfriend, Karley. This past summer, he'd let her go with Molly Hammond and Gloria, who both worked at the farm where Boone and Gerty lived.

Matt and Gloria finally came inside the house and closed the front door, leaving Boone to wonder what had taken them so long. He knew, because they were set to be married tomorrow. It wasn't hard to figure out that they'd snuck away to kiss for a few minutes.

"All right," his brother called into the chaos. "I think we're ready to start." He waited a couple of seconds while conversations finished and people turned their attention toward him. "We've got tables and chairs outside on the deck and in the yard. There's pizza and cheesy bread. Some of those garlic knots and the cinnamon twists. Keith set up the volleyball net, and Britt got out all the roller skates and long boards we own or could find. There's a big cement pad back there for that, and we can put the sprinkler on it."

He looked around at the group, and Boone could read the expression on his brother's face. He was overwhelmed with love and gratitude for all the people who'd come to celebrate this birthday with his son.

"Thank you all for coming," he said, his voice thick. "We'll eat first and do presents after that. Right, Keith?"

"Sounds good, Dad."

"Okay, let's pray first, and then you can lead us out."

Cowboy hats started getting removed, as most people had left theirs on as they'd all end up outside again anyway.

"Gray, would you pray?" Matt asked, and Boone's eyes flew to the tall cowboy who acted as patriarch at the family farm where he worked. Technically, Gray Hammond signed Boone's paychecks, but he'd been gone all summer. He and his family went to Wyoming for the summer months, and they'd only just returned yesterday. Apparently, he and his wife usually stayed until later in August, but they'd wanted to be here for Keith's birthday party and Matt's wedding.

That made sense, because Matt had been working for Gray as the caretaker and foreman of his farm for seventeen years now. For fifteen of those, he'd just come down in the summer and run the farm while Gray and Elise left town. Now, he lived here permanently and worked there full-time.

Gray didn't do much around the farm anymore, as he was close to sixty years old. His son, Hunter, had been living there all summer, and he and his wife had opened and currently operated Pony Power, a children's equine therapy unit.

"Of course," Gray said, and he bowed his head. "Dear Lord, we thank Thee for the opportunity to gather as friends and family. It's such a blessing to be able to get together, and please bless each of us to look for ways to serve those around us, some of whom might even be in attendance at this party. Bless this year for Keith Whettstein, that it'll be one of his best, and bless his family, especially Matt and Gloria, who are getting married tomorrow. Bless those who haven't arrived yet, that they'll do so safely, and bless us all with Thy spirit of guidance and the bravery to go where Thou leads us. Amen."

"Amen," echoed through the house, and the front door opened. Kassidy and her girlfriend entered the house, and instead of leading everyone out the back door to the deck, Keith went toward the front.

"This way," Boone said, his voice plenty loud enough to get people to follow him. He led the way out to the back deck, where the noise of conversation and laughter didn't get quite so trapped and reverberate around inside his head quite so much.

Outside, he started opening the pizza boxes as the line queued up behind him. He didn't actually take any food— until the end of the line and those delicious, buttery cinnamon twists. He did nab one of those and take a crunchy, sweet bite as he got out of the way.

A cheer went up inside the house, and he looked through the glass doors where people were still coming out. Wes Hammond had walked in, and he'd brought his wife and children with him. Boone immediately looked for Michael, and he found the boy right beside Gerty.

Of course.

He frowned, and then got over it. Michael would go home in three days, and Gerty would have to figure out her own friendships here in Colorado.

"Mike," he called, and the boy looked his way. "Your family is here."

"They are?" He swung his attention back toward the house, immediately starting that way. He pushed back through the crowd, and Boone watched through the glass as he ran toward his mom and dad, throwing himself into his father's arms first. Wes grinned as wide as the lake that used to sit outside Boone's front door, and Boone could admit that their relationship touched his heart.

Michael Hammond was a good boy. He'd worked tirelessly around the farm this summer, separated from his own family, and living with his cousin and his grandfather as his only support. He probably hadn't been any happier to be in Ivory Peaks than Gerty had been, and they'd probably been good for each other.

Boone switched his gaze back to his daughter, who now stood in line alone. She reached for a plate, definitely an island among the cowboys behind her and the smaller girls—Britt's friends—in front of her.

Boone's heart expanded once again, because Gerty was a good girl too. In that moment, he had the overwhelming impression that she'd be okay. The words actually flowed through his mind and everything.

She'll be okay, Boone. Stop worrying and start trusting.

Boone swallowed, because he didn't know how to do that. He needed a guide for how to trust in the Lord more completely. He heard pastors from here to Sugar Pond talk about it. It sounded good in a sermon.

Put your faith in God.

Trust in the Lord with your whole soul.

Learn to rely on the arm of Jehovah.

What he didn't know or understand was *how* to do that. The Lord was surely tired of Boone's constant pleadings and just wanted him to stop, but he found himself asking exactly that: *How, Lord? How can I trust You more?*

The Lord had moved on to someone else, and Boone didn't get an answer while standing there at his nephew's birthday party. He did feel loved and cared for, and he appreciated that so very much.

Gloria poked her head out of the house. "Boone, it's here. Could you...?"

"On my way," he said, turning to go down the steps and away from the party. He could sneak away without Keith noticing, and he did, easily slipping into the garage a moment later. The lack of light in there took a moment for his eyes to adjust to, and he blinked for a few seconds before continuing. He went up a couple of steps to hit the garage door opener, and then the evening light started to flood the garage from the front driveway.

As he walked toward the still-rising door, he heard a woman say, "...has to move. Who's the moron who parked here?"

The door made it all the way up, and Boone saw Cosette Brian standing there. She took his breath away in her denim pencil skirt and nearly sheer blouse with bright green stick bugs on it. She wore a camisole underneath that, the fine lines of the thin straps going over her shoulders he could clearly see.

Though she was beautiful, she had that forked tongue that always seemed to whip at him personally. "I am," he said, raising his hand. "Sorry, I had cake and balloons. I can move the truck."

Cosette spun toward him, her eyes widening. "Boone." She'd once looked terrified of him. She'd called him a rascal a few months ago, on the day he'd arrived on the farm to stay for good. Then she'd run away, and he'd had to ask Gloria for her number so he could apologize for whatever he'd done wrong. They'd worked it out, and they'd been dancing around one another since.

An easy hello there. A hand-off for a receipt there. Nothing major. Nothing to paint him in a bad light in her mind.

Until now.

"Sorry," he said, digging in his front pocket for his keys. "I'll be out of the way in two shakes."

Cosette reached up and tucked her hair behind her ear as Mission, the cowboy she'd been talking to, walked away. She watched him go, and Boone didn't dare move now that they stood on the front driveway alone. She switched her gaze back to his when Mission made it to the front porch, and Boone's mouth turned dry.

He wasn't ready to date again. He wasn't. He absolutely was not, and he absolutely would not.

Cosette, to his knowledge, did not have a boyfriend and had not gone on a date with a man all summer long. But he didn't know her that well, and she didn't live on-site at the farm, so anything was possible.

Except the lightning currently arcing between them. *That* wasn't possible, and Boone threw up every defense he had against the sizzling attraction, because he did not have time for it. He did not want it.

He did not—fine, he did, but he couldn't risk his heart again, and he one-hundred-percent would not subject Gerty to yet another disastrous relationship that would result in a woman walking out on her. Been there, done that. Twice, even if the death of her mother had not been anything any of them had wanted.

He swallowed, sure he was reading the situation all wrong anyway. Cosette had never liked him all that much.

"After you move your truck, would you stay and help me put the bow on Keith's present?" she asked, letting her hand drop to her side.

Boone said the first thing that came to his mind, the thing he said as easily as he breathed, the thing he said whenever anyone asked him for help. She wasn't special; he was just a nice guy.

"Sure."

Two

COSETTE BRIAN REACHED INTO THE BACK OF THE truck she'd just parked in the driveway, her fingers brushing the huge, red ribbon before it got pulled away from her. Boone had picked it up ahead of her, and he stared at the enormous bow.

"This is amazing," he said, finally looking across the bed of the truck to her. "Where did you get this?"

"I made it," Cosette said, feeling her defenses rise up. She told herself to relax, that Boone wasn't judging her. He'd already said the bow was amazing. She had to mentally remind herself to smile, and when she did, the gloriously handsome Boone Whettstein did the same.

My goodness, she thought. *He should not be allowed out in public with that smile.* It would blind drivers and send them right into the ditch on the side of the road. The brilliance of it would make women swoon from here to the state line. That had to be a crime, didn't it?

Cosette's heart started jack-hammering in her chest, despite her clear attempts at being kind to Boone. She thought of Louisa and what she would say, and she kept her smile hitched in place.

Cosette wasn't getting up at five a.m. because she liked it, though she had grown to love her early-morning walks with her neighbor. Louisa Knotts had quickly become Cosette's best friend, despite her living in the small town of Mountain Glen for the past fifteen years. Louisa had moved in at the beginning of June, and she'd claimed to be prediabetic. She'd asked Cosette if she'd like to go walking with her in the mornings, as she needed the exercise.

It had turned out that Louisa was a former psychiatrist for a university, specializing in young adults who'd been through trauma. She'd retired from that job and worked as a paralegal now, for a small law office on the outskirts of the city.

Cosette wasn't actually all that young, but she'd found Louisa really easy to talk to. She'd told her about Boone, and they'd been talking about him for months. They'd been talking about Cosette's trust issues for just as long, and Louisa had asked Cosette to think about what the worst thing that could happen if she spoke to Boone.

What would be the worst thing? The absolute worst? she'd asked.

The best Cosette had been able to come up with was: *He'll talk back.*

And that's bad? Louisa had asked.

To Cosette, speaking to a male—especially one as

handsome, as tall, and as obviously cowboy as Boone—was bad, yes. She had no good relationships with men her own age, and once she'd told Louisa that, the challenge had come.

What if he could be the first?

She brought herself back to the present when Boone cocked his right eyebrow. She'd missed something, if the confusion running through those dark eyes was any indication.

"What?" she asked.

He leveled his eyebrows. "I asked how you learned how to do this." He held up the multi-looped bow.

"I took a class one Christmas," she said. "They're usually about a hundred times smaller than that. I just went big for this. We're going to put it right on top of the truck."

Boone looked to the top of the truck, which stood about as tall as Cosette. Matthew Whettstein had bought a small truck for his son's sixteenth birthday from Cosette's sister, who owned a used car lot here in Ivory Peaks.

She'd picked up the truck that morning, as Raven had been holding it at the lot, and Cosette was getting a ride home with Gloria from this party. She glanced toward the open garage. This party. She normally wouldn't even attend a party like this, though she knew Matt, and she knew all the other cowboys, cowgirls, and staff from Pony Power had been invited and were likely in the backyard.

So she was doing a lot outside her comfort zone today. She couldn't wait until Monday morning so she could tell Louisa.

Boone stepped to the side and reached up to put the bow on top. "How are you going to keep it there?"

"I've always wanted to be able to cock one eyebrow," she said, moving to open the back door of the truck. It had four doors and a shorter bed, and it was the perfect little vehicle for a high school student. It was about ten years old, but didn't have a lot of miles, as the previous owner had kept it out on his ranch and only used it to get from his house out to the far fields on his property.

Raven had only had it on the lot for six hours before Matt had showed up and bought it. Once the connection had been made between Raven, Matt, and Cosette, the plan for her to pick up the truck and bring it to the party had come together.

"You have?" Boone asked, staring openly at her now.

"Yeah," she said. "I can't do anything like that." She opened the back door and took out a big roll of duct tape. She pulled out a long piece, ripped it with her teeth, and stepped up into the truck, boosting her height. "Lift it up."

She looped the tape around itself, making a circle with sticky stuff all around, and plopped it right in the middle of the roof. "Stick it to that."

Boone did, and not a moment too soon. Cosette fell backward off the truck, managing to catch herself against the open door, but hitting her elbow in the process. A cry flew from her mouth, and Boone must've been a superhero, because he arrived at her side in less than two seconds flat.

"You okay?" he asked, his voice the tender, kind timbre she'd heard men use with their loved ones before.

She clutched her elbow as humiliation ran through her. "Yeah, I just hit my funny bone."

"Nothing funny about that bone," he said with a smile.

"No," was all she could come up with. He really couldn't smile like that. It erased the female mind, and how unfair was that?

Maybe just yours, she thought as her brain started working again. She tried to move, but the door had been pushed open as far as it would go, and she couldn't back up. Boone did, and they shuffled out of the doorway enough for her to close it.

"That's all?" he asked.

"I think so," Cosette said. "I'd just splay out the ends...." She started doing that, pulling the longer ends of the ribbon down over the rearview mirror on the front of the truck while Boone did the same over the back. He tucked them into the bed of the truck, and Cosette smiled to herself, because that was what she'd have done.

With the six ends billowing slightly in the breeze, she faced Boone again. "Thank you, Boone," she said, really trying out his name in her throat. It seemed to fit...okay.

"Yep," he said. "Are you gonna come back and eat?" He indicated she should go in front of him. "They'd just started when I came out."

"Oh, I don't know," she said.

"There's tons," he said, and he obviously had no qualms about joining the fray of people she could hear in the back-yard. Of course he didn't. Boone Whettstein was a people person, and in Cosette's opinion, that was the worst type of person imaginable.

"It's pizza and salad," he said. "Have you eaten?"

"No," she said.

He paused, something marching across his face she couldn't identify. "If you don't want to stay here, we could just go grab something." He cocked that right eyebrow again, this time the smile coming with it.

Cosette dang near blacked out. Instead, with her pulse rioting and her cells buzzing at her, she laughed.

She *laughed.*

Cosette couldn't even remember the last time she'd laughed in mixed company. Sure, she did with Raven sometimes, but that was it. Never at work. Never if Raven's boyfriend-of-the-month was over to the house or she was with male employees. Never if even a male neighbor was nearby.

Boone joined her, and the harmony and melody of their voices mingling in happiness as they did made Cosette long for something she'd vowed she did not want.

Companionship.

Not only that, but *male* companionship.

"You should stay," she said, because she had no idea how to flirt. Panic started to build beneath her breastbone. She'd gone too far already, and her vision swam slightly. "It's your nephew."

Boone lifted one hand toward her face, slowly. Oh-so-slowly, almost like someone had made the world start to spin backward. Cosette lifted her chin in defiance and to brace herself, all traces of laughter vanishing.

He paused, something curious in those eyes now. He dropped his hand without touching her and backed up. "I only want to stay if you're staying," he said. Just like that. Right out loud.

She'd known the cowboy was confident and bold, but she'd had no idea men talked like that. There wasn't any hidden meaning in those words, was there? Was he playing some game she didn't know about?

"I don't know," she said, glancing over her shoulder and into the garage again. Matt's truck sat parked there, with the other half of the two-car garage filled with broken-down boxes, a lawn mower, weed-eater, and various other equipment and supplies.

Just the fact that she looked away from Boone when he stood so close to her told her how far she'd come. She hadn't realized it until that moment.

"I'm not really a party person," she said, facing him again.

"Then let's go grab something," he said. "No one's going to miss me, and I know they have these huge taco boxes on Friday nights at South of the Border." His eyes sparkled with mischief, and she wondered what a Friday night with Boone and a two-dozen pack of beef tacos would actually be like.

The fact that she wondered that baffled her.

"I've always wanted to get one," he said.

"You haven't yet?" She smiled at him again, reached up,

and tucked her hair behind her ear. Shyness and awkwardness combined inside her, the same way they always had around good-looking men.

"Honestly?" he asked, but he didn't wait for her to answer. "I'm bushed by Friday night. If I make it back to the cabin and put a frozen pizza in the oven, I call it a win." He chuckled again, the sound like heavenly music to Cosette's ears.

"So no driving to town for a taco box."

"No, ma'am." He rocked back onto the heels of his cowboy boots.

"You're not bushed tonight? It's Friday." Her mind screamed at her that there was no way she was going with him to South of the Border. That would require riding in a vehicle with him—alone. Nope. She wouldn't do that.

"I got off early to come pick up things for the party."

"I really can't make you miss your nephew's sixteenth birthday party," she said. "It's a big deal." He looked like he was going to argue again, so she quickly added, "Did you know we're partnered up for tomorrow's wedding?"

Surprise darted across his face. "We are?"

"You're the best man, right?"

"Yes."

"I'm not the Maid of Honor, but Molly is walking with her husband. Gloria put me with you." Cosette had known for about a week, and maybe that was why she hadn't been able to stop thinking about Boone Whettstein over the past several days.

Truth be told, she'd been thinking about him since she'd

run into him—literally—on the front porch of the farm-house, months ago. But she wasn't ready to admit that yet.

Boone looked down to her hand. "Are we gonna...you know?"

"What?" Cosette looked at her hands too, her skin suddenly tingling.

"Do you—?" He cleared his throat in a somewhat violent manner. "Link your arm through mine? Something like that?" A hint of redness crept into his neck and cheeks, and Cosette marveled at his embarrassment. "I don't want to make you uncomfortable."

A sigh filled her whole soul, but she only let it out in measured lengths. "You don't make me uncomfortable, Boone."

"You sure?" he challenged, all of that confidence on display. "It sure seemed like I did, when I touched you...before."

"I was just startled." Cosette had the distinct thought that she'd have to tell him everything if they honestly started a relationship. *Don't be ridiculous,* she told herself. *No one is starting a relationship.*

Certainly not her.

"Okay," Boone said, his higher-pitched tone indicating he didn't believe her.

"Okay," she said, as if the matter was now decided because she wanted it to be. "So...we'll walk down the aisle together tomorrow, and then, I don't know what your family responsibilities are after that, but I don't have anyone to sit by at dinner."

That smile spread across his face, and because he controlled it and it moved slowly, Cosette didn't swoon. Her knees only went weak for a moment, and she leaned her hip into the hood of the truck to mask it.

"I'm sure I can sit by you," Boone said.

"Great," she said. "Then I'll take a raincheck on the tacos."

Both eyebrows flew up now, and she grinned and shook her head. "You're an enigma, Cosette Brian," he said. "I'm not real good at mysteries or solving puzzles, but you...I want to figure you out."

"Do you just say whatever comes into your head?" she asked, straightening away from the truck. "If so, that's kind of unsettling."

"My daddy always said I didn't have a filter," Boone said with a laugh, as if that was a good thing. Cosette wasn't sure if it was or not, but she liked that he didn't play games.

"Dad, no way!"

Cosette turned at the excited yell of a teenager, and she got out of the way as Keith Whettstein came barreling toward her and Boone. She knew her place among a crowd, and it was definitely near the back of it. People came pouring through the front door and down the sidewalk, as well as through the garage, all of them coming to see Keith's gift.

Keith looked around wildly, his gaze finally landing on Matt and Gloria, who stood at the front of the crowd, their hands locked together. "This is insane," he said. "You said you weren't going to get me a car."

"I didn't get you a car," Matt said, his grin as bright as

and powerful as the sun. "I got you a mini-truck, and don't forget. You paid for half of it."

Keith whooped and threw himself into his father's arms. They laughed together, and then Keith faced the truck again.

"I have the key," Boone said, and he put his hand out in front of Cosette. She certainly didn't want the spotlight, and she quickly extracted it from the front pocket of her skirt and placed it in his palm. He lifted it high above his head. "You want it?"

Keith looked at that key the way a hungry man would eye a doughnut. Boone laughed, and he stepped through the crowd to hug his nephew too, and as Keith got behind the wheel of the mini-truck, everyone who'd come to the party began to applaud.

Cosette looked around, her hands coming up to clap too, and she felt...something. Something she hadn't felt in a long, long time. It took her a moment to understand, and another to give it a name, but when she did, tears pricked her eyes.

Belonging.

Everyone here belonged here—including her.

She couldn't be seen crying in a crowd, so she kept her composure. She'd cry later, when her knees hit the floor in prayer. Right now, she thought, *Thank you, Lord. Thank you for giving me a new place to belong. Thank you, thank you, thank you.*

Boone returned to her side as the truck's engine roared to life and the applause started to die. As the crowd broke up and people began to return to the food in the backyard, he leaned down and said, "I'm looking forward to tomorrow, Cosette. And to the tacos," in a voice half the volume he normally used, which only made his tone that much sexier.

With that, he left Cosette to shiver in the summer evening as he joined his brother and Gloria. The trio moved to the front sidewalk to watch Keith drive down the road in his new truck, and Cosette realized she didn't have a way to leave the party.

So she did something completely insane. She walked over to Boone's side and looked down the road at the mini-truck trundling away too. When Boone looked at her, she simply said, "Gloria's my ride home. Guess I'll have to stay after all."

Three

Boone looked at himself in the mirror, wondering when he'd started looking old. *Older*, he clarified. He should look older, because Gerty was thirteen now, and Boone was no spring chicken.

He adjusted the way his bow tie sat at his collar, making sure it was precisely straight. Matt was getting married today, and Boone knew his brother wanted everything to be just right. That extended to his children and his brother, so Boone reached for the dark brown cowboy hat sitting on the counter in front of him.

He and Matt had gone shopping and bought themselves matching hats for today, and Matt's son, Keith, had a new cowboy hat for the wedding as well.

"Daddy," Gerty drawled, and Boone turned from the mirror in the event center. The doorway framed his daughter, and Boone suddenly saw how much older she was too.

The girl wasn't straight up and down anymore, and Gloria had taken the girls to get new dresses for the wedding.

Boone liked his brother's fiancé a whole lot, especially for how welcome Gloria had made him and Gerty feel when they'd come to Ivory Peaks. Not only that, but Gloria had included Gerty in absolutely everything this summer, the same as Britt, Matt's daughter. That meant she'd gone shopping with Gloria and Molly, and she'd gotten new clothes, new underclothes, and this pretty new dress in a shade of blue Boone could only find in the purest of summer skies.

He whistled as he ran his eyes down to Gerty's feet. "Look at you, pumpkin."

"Daddy," she said, a frown appearing between her eyes. She smiled it away and stepped into the room. "You look handsome."

"You sure you won't walk down the aisle with me?" Boone gave her a wide smile, teasing her. She'd told him a dozen times a day over the summer how embarrassing he was, but she still showed up for dinner every night, talked to him until he thought his ears might fall off, and came to the stables to spend time with the horses.

If there was one thing about Gerty, it was that she adored horses. They sure liked her too, and some of Boone's calm energy with animals had transferred to her. That was about all, as she had wispy, light blonde hair like her mother. She did have the shape of his eyes, and he could see the blue fire in them when she got upset with him.

Right now, they twinkled like stars in a dark sky, and he

offered her his arm. "I can't," she said. "Gloria wants us kids to walk her down the aisle."

Boone dropped his elbow back to his side, then moved his eyes to her feet. She wore cowgirl boots with her dress, the stitching around the toes the same blue color. "You guys have something up your sleeve," he said, clearly hinting for her to tell him what.

"I'm not telling," she said. "Gloria wants it to be a surprise."

"I won't tell anyone."

Gerty cocked one hip, her hair swaying. She wore half of it up at the moment, with tiny white flowers woven throughout. "You'll run straight to Uncle Matt."

Boone laughed, because he did have a tendency to run to Matt when he had some juicy gossip. Or when he needed help. Or for anything, really. "He's getting married in fifteen minutes. I'm not gonna have time to tell him anything."

"Which is why I stopped by," Gerty said. "You're supposed to be lining up right now. Kaitlin looked like she might blow a gasket any second."

Boone looked toward the open door, and he didn't see or hear the wedding planner. "We don't want that to happen." He wasn't surprised Kaitlin hadn't come to get him, because over the past few months as Matt and Gloria had been planning their wedding, Kaitlin had made it pretty clear that she'd like Boone to take her to dinner.

Or something.

He'd avoided her as much as possible, and when she'd finally cornered him and asked him if he wanted to get coffee or something, he'd blurted out something about not dating right now. He honestly couldn't remember. He knew it had been an embarrassing situation on both sides, and Kaitlin had made sure she hadn't run into him again.

"Let's go," he said, stepping past his daughter. She fell into step beside him, pausing to let him go through the doorway first. He automatically started looking for Cosette, though he told himself not to. She was his date for the wedding, and if he was late lining up, she'd likely be anxious.

No, he told himself. *She's not your date.*

He was walking down the aisle with her. That was all. He'd asked her about getting some tacos, but nothing had been set up. He wasn't sure if anything ever would be. Cosette Brian seemed to have a hundred-foot wall erected around herself, and Boone certainly wasn't going to be the knight in shining armor to knock it down.

A couple of people moved, and Boone caught sight of Cosette. She too wore a gorgeous blue dress, and with her dark auburn hair, she made Boone's lungs seize right up. They forgot they were supposed to breathe on their own, and his feet slowed as the more vital functions of his body failed him.

"Daddy," Gerty said, and Boone blinked. "Come on." She could turn from warm to cold in less time than it took for the weather to change, and Boone didn't need her displeasure today. He really did want everything to be perfect for Matt.

So he somehow got his wooden legs to bend and move properly, and he approached the group of people who didn't seem anywhere near getting in a line. His heart skipped a beat, because he still felt very much like an outsider here in Colorado. He told himself not to. Everyone had accepted him and welcomed him, but he suspected that had something to do with Gerty, his dead wife, or Matt. Probably all three.

Everyone loved Matt, and he was definitely the calmer of the two when compared to Boone. He couldn't help it if he loved to laugh, loved to tease people, and loved to get them all riled up.

"Mister Whettstein," a crisp female voice said. "You're the leader. Up here, please." Kaitlin walked away before Boone could really look at her.

He did his brotherly duty and went to the front of the line. Cosette wasn't there either, and he'd passed her back a couple of people, buried behind Molly, Elise, Dani, and a couple of other women Boone couldn't name. He hadn't looked at her, and as far as he knew, she hadn't looked at him.

"Boone," someone hissed, and he turned to his left, the sound definitely coming from that way. Hunter Hammond gestured to him in an over-exaggerated way, and Boone cast a glance in Kaitlin's direction.

She'd bustled off to do something else, and Boone took his opportunity to escape. He strode toward Hunter, who clapped him on the back and said, "Matt needs you for a sec."

"He's risking my life," Boone muttered, but Hunter only chuckled.

Boone went down the hall to the groom's room, where he'd left his brother twenty minutes ago, dressed, cufflinked, tied, and ready. He'd been pacing, and Boone had needed a break from the tension and anxiety. As he opened the door, he got punched in the face with it all over again.

Matt turned from the back of the room, Gray Hammond at his side. Boone couldn't fault his brother. Getting married again was an enormously huge event. Boone couldn't imagine doing it himself, so he tamed his slight irritation and put a smile on his face. He looked at Gray. "What's he freaking out about?"

"Nothing," Matt said at the same time Gray said, "The music."

Matt threw Gray a dirty look, but the older cowboy simply smiled at him. "I told 'im it's going to be fine. They hired a wedding planner to take care of details like that."

"Gray's right," Boone said. Besides, what would Matt do about it? Hire a new band? Switch out the CD?

"Can you just go check on the music for Gloria? She and the kids want what she rollerblades to, and I swear they're going to play that blasted wedding march." He ran his hands through his hair, his cowboy hat lying on the counter. When he looked at Boone, he seemed about to unravel.

"I'm on it, bro," he said. "Don't worry." He met Gray's eyes, silently pleading for him to somehow tranquilize Matt so he could make it through his own wedding. They'd had a great birthday party last night. After everyone else had left, Boone had stayed to help Matt clean up. He was taking Britt and Keith for Matt while he went on his honeymoon. The two of them had always gotten along so well, and Boone really would do anything for his brother.

He'd talked about their dad, and then their mom, and Boone knew he wished they were here. Daddy had died a few years back, and Mom had left Montana a decade before that. Boone wasn't entirely sure where she lived right now, though he did have her phone number and could've found out.

Matt had asked him not to. Last night, he'd said he'd texted her to let her know he was getting married, and she'd congratulated him. That was all he needed. Now, looking at him, Boone didn't think so.

If their father could've been there, he would've been. Taking solace in that, Boone turned to go make sure the right track would play when Gloria came down the aisle.

"Boone," Kaitlin griped at him, but he just held up one palm and kept moving. Matt wasn't even at the altar yet. He wasn't going to miss anything.

"Boone," another woman said, and this voice made him stop in his tracks. He looked over to Cosette as she approached, the skirt on her dress billowing as her legs moved. He yanked his eyes up to hers, finding sunshine and smiles there. That was new, at least when she looked at him.

Not entirely, he reminded himself, his own smile stretching across his face. "I just have an errand for Matt."

Cosette's eyebrows went up. "Oh? What's that?" She glanced over her shoulder to where Kaitlin was physically manhandling Travis Thatcher to get him in line where she wanted him. His arms flopped like noodles, and he looked petrified. Boone almost started laughing, but when the wedding planner spun and glared a hole in his larynx, the sound died. "Because Kaitlin is about to blow her top."

"The music," Boone said. "Could you tell her? Cover for me? I know it's dumb. You know the music is right. But Matt needs the reassurance." He pressed both hands together in front of him in a praying gesture. "Tell her I need two minutes. Please."

Cosette's hands wound around one another once, then twice. She swallowed and nodded. "Okay. I'll tell her." She turned back the way she'd come, and Boone put some boogie in his step to get this ridiculous check done for his brother.

He strode outside, as the wedding was taking place on a gorgeous patio that had a wrought-iron railing around it. On the far end, it opened up to the altar, which was made of two saddles. Boone himself had crafted some of it, and the saddles would lift off and get placed on a horse each for Matt and Gloria. They were literally riding off into their future with the sun setting behind them after the ceremony.

They'd already served dinner, which was a bit unorthodox, but Boone had told them they should do what they wanted. And they wanted to leave immediately following the ceremony. So all of the formalities, the dancing, the cake-cutting, and the greeting and eating had already happened.

Relief streamed through Boone that this day was almost over. He detoured to the left to the sound booth and leaned over it. "Hey, fellas," he said. "I just need to double-check what's gonna play when the bride makes her entrance."

Gloria's father had died a couple of years ago too, and she didn't have anyone to walk her down the aisle. Boone had offered. So had Hunter and Gray. In the end, she'd asked the children to escort her and give her to Matt, and they'd been thrilled. Well, Britt and Gerty had been. Keith...the jury was still out on him.

"Let's see," one of the men said. He wore a headset that looked entirely too professional for a farm wedding. He rifled through a couple of CDs. "Looks like this." He handed Boone the disc, and it had *80s mix* scrawled on it in black marker. "Right?"

"Yep," Boone said. "Thanks." He turned, then whipped back to the booth. "Wait. It's gonna be loud, right?"

"I got the memo for loud," the man said, giving Boone a look. One that said he knew how to do his job.

"It's just my brother's nervous," Boone said, smiling for all he was worth. "Thanks a lot." He turned and skedaddled back the way he'd come, bracing himself to be skewered by Kaitlin when he got back inside.

Sure enough, she scalded him with a heated look, and he actually jogged toward the hallway that would take him back to his brother. He opened the door and poked his head in. "Music is set, Matt. 80s mix. Loud."

"Thank you." Matt had donned his cowboy hat. "I better get out there."

"Yep," Gray said. "Let's go." He led the way, and Boone held the door for them. Gray was probably only twenty years older than Matt, and Boone supposed he could've been their father with that age difference. No matter what, he'd been a good friend and a steadying influence in Matt's life, right when Matt had needed him.

Boone too, if he'd admit it to himself.

"Boone!" Kaitlin yelled. "Get out here!"

"Yes, ma'am," he said, hurrying to get in position. He watched Matt and Gray disappear outside, and he looked around, wondering where Gerty had gotten to. He couldn't see her, and he supposed she knew where to be. She was a bright and intelligent girl, even if she had turned thirteen. Matt had warned him that teenagers lost their brains and they just sat under their beds for a few years. Boone hadn't seen that in Gerty yet, but she'd been quite a few things in her short life.

"Cosette, your cowboy is finally here," Kaitlin said, glaring at Boone.

"Relax," he said. "Matt just barely went out. He's probably shaking hands with every single person."

"Do not tell me to relax," Kaitlin said through gritted teeth. Her dark hair had been twisted up into an elegant up-do as if she were the one tying the knot that day.

Boone opened his mouth to reply, but Cosette's hand slid over his arm, rendering him mute. He did manage to twist his head to look at her, and she gave him an almost imperceptible shake of her head.

He snapped his mouth shut and faced the double glass doors leading out to the patio and then the altar. In that moment, music blared, actually shaking the glass and the rafters with the heavy bass beat.

"My word," Kaitlin grumbled.

Boone grinned, because if he ever got married again, he'd want to do it exactly the way he wanted to as well. Matt and Gloria were living that dream, and he actually considered dancing down the aisle.

"Don't you dare," Cosette said as if she could read his mind.

"What?" he asked.

She nodded to his right foot, which was tapping out a rhythm to the beat of the muted music. "They specifically said to just walk."

"I'm gonna walk," Boone said, smiling at her. He tucked her closer to his side, really securing her hand in his arm. "Are you ready to walk, Miss Brian?"

Her eyes met his, and the whole world fell away. Fire and ash could've filled the sky, and the only person Boone would've seen was Cosette. Tonight, she wore false eyelashes that made her eyes seem bigger than they were and plenty of soft pink gloss that made her lips shiny and silky.

"Boone," someone said, and he blinked, trying to find his way back to reality.

"Daddy," Gerty said, and that got him to resume his normal human functions. He looked right at her, because he'd always been able to find his daughter. She waved at him to get going. "We're waitin' on you."

With heat and embarrassment filling his face, Boone squared his shoulders, took a deep breath, and took the first step toward the doors that would lead the wedding party outside and into the ceremony.

Four

COSETTE COULD FEEL THE DANCE INSIDE BOONE starting to grow. In front of them, the doors opened, letting in the full volume of the music, and she nearly got blown back. "My word," she whispered, confident no one could hear her. Sure enough, Boone didn't even look her way.

He kept walking, smooth as butter, his long legs eating up a lot of distance with every stride. Eyes landed on them. On her. Dozens of eyes. Then hundreds of them. Cosette had the very real urge to flee, but she gripped Boone's arm a little tighter and kept moving.

One step. Then another. Each foot in front of the other.

She coached herself all the way down the aisle, the faces on either side of it blurring a little as she focused only on the pair of saddles that made up the altar. Matt stood there, beaming like the sun, moon, and stars combined, and Cosette felt his joy when she looked at him. It infused inside her, almost like it was her own. She wondered what it would feel like if it was, and how she could pinpoint what or who it was which had made her feel that way.

She'd existed with fear and pain and misery for so long, she wasn't sure how to escape from them.

"You're over there, darlin'," Boone said, using his huge cowboy hat to nod toward the women's side of the altar.

Cosette stumbled, though she'd practiced this twice already. She knew where to stand, and how many steps it took to get there. Her cheeks heated as she separated from him and had to walk four or five steps on her own. Since she'd come down the aisle with Boone, she had to move the furthest along the side to make room for the others in the wedding party.

She didn't mind, because it kept her out of the limelight for the guests who'd gathered to witness this wedding, and she got to have a bird's eye view of the happy couple as they said I-do.

Really, she could see past the pastor to Boone, and boy oh boy, the man was a sight for sore eyes. Cosette couldn't believe she found him handsome, just like she couldn't believe she'd said she'd go get tacos with him either.

He hadn't asked again, but it had only been twenty-four hours since Keith's birthday party. Elise Hammond arrived next to her, and Cosette gave the woman a smile. She had four children and was married to Gray. Together, they owned the farm where Cosette worked as an administrative assistant for Pony Power, the equine therapy unit for children that their daughter-in-law, Molly, spearheaded and ran.

Molly stepped next to Elise, and they gripped each

other's hands for a couple of seconds, their faces filled with a glow Cosette found fascinating. Had she ever looked like that? Had she ever been so excited for someone else that she couldn't contain herself?

Heck, had she ever been so excited for herself that she couldn't contain herself?

Even when she'd married Joel, she wasn't sure this level of enthusiasm had been present. She'd been raised by a single father who Grams had always said knew how to communicate better with horses and cattle than humans. She and Raven had stuck close to one another, and without her sister, Cosette was sure she wouldn't still be on this earth.

Gratitude for Raven, Daddy, and Grams streamed through her, and with her family cemented solidly in her mind, Cosette took a deep breath and looked back over to Boone. He cocked one eyebrow at her, clearly asking her if she was okay. She liked—and disliked—that he seemed to be able to read her, and that he sure seemed interested in helping her.

Deep down, she knew it was more than just helping that Boone Whettstein had in mind. He'd been careful around her, which she appreciated, though it was probably done out of self-preservation more than anything else. She hadn't exactly been nice to him when they'd first met.

Now, though, Boone had Cosette's mind in a frenzy almost all the time. She thought of him on the way to work, on the way home, and all through making dinner and then getting out her romance novels or going over to Raven's car dealership if her sister had to work late.

Just thinking about her routine, normal, safe life calmed Cosette. She gave Boone a smile, and he switched his gaze to Matt. Cosette ducked her head, the loud music finally finishing. In the space between songs, a gasp rose through the crowd.

They'd all stood to watch the wedding party come down the aisle, and while Cosette wore heels and had a couple of inches of height over the average woman, she still couldn't see what had caused the ruckus.

Boone started to laugh, and Cosette tossed him a look that told him to stop. He wasn't watching her, because he didn't stop, and every man on the other side of the altar wore a smile or was chuckling too.

Even Matt.

Another song started to play, this one a tune Cosette had heard many times. Gloria sang this song almost every day, and she didn't care who was listening.

"It's the—eye of the tiger, it's the thrill of the fight, rising up—!"

"To the challenge of our rival," Matt sang along with the song. He did a step-touch dance move that sent horror through Cosette. On the other side of the aisle, back behind the preacher, where Boone stood, he pumped his fist.

Cosette's eyes widened and her mouth dropped open. This was no way to act at a wedding. The next thing she knew, everyone was singing along with the song and Gloria came into view with a stroller in front of her.

Britt, Matt's daughter, rode in the stroller, and Keith glided along at Gloria's side, his face radiant. Gerty, Boone's daughter, flanked Gloria's other side, and she too seemed to be floating on air.

Cosette knew instantly that they were all wearing rollerblades, and Gloria liked to take horses, dogs, and kids out into the Colorado countryside with her when she went blading.

"And the last known survivor stalks his prey in the night," everyone sang, even elderly Christopher Hammond, who had to be over eighty years old now.

To her great surprise, even Cosette chimed in with, "And he's watching us all with the *eye-ye-ye-yeee*—of the tiger."

Gloria slid to a stop right beside Matt, her face full of love and happiness. Cosette envied her powerfully in that moment, simply because she didn't seem to have anything negative in her life. She knew that wasn't true, because she'd been working with Gloria for over a year, and the woman had problems like everyone else.

Just the fact that she didn't have a parent or a sibling here to support her testified of that. But despite that —*despite it*—she had found the good. The happiness she needed. The man who was going to make all of her dreams come true, even after it had seemed like she'd lost everything.

Cosette felt herself clawing her way back toward the surface, one she'd slipped below and hadn't known it. Only after she'd managed to walk away from Joel for good did she realize how far beneath the ground he'd buried her.

Every day since had been a trial. Every hour a gift from the Good Lord above. She watched as Matt hugged his son heartily, pounding him on the back. He bent down and lifted his daughter from the stroller and she wrapped her skinny arms around his neck and her tiny legs around his midsection.

Gerty stepped over and hugged her uncle, and then together, the three children gave Gloria a little push toward Matt. Keith wheeled the stroller out of the way, and the kids went to sit in the first row.

Cosette breathed a sigh that everyone was in place now, and she looked at Matt and Gloria as they gazed at one another. The weight of Boone's eyes on her grew heavier, but Cosette really wanted to try to unravel all of the love streaming from Matt and Gloria.

It filled the air, the whole sky, and then snuck right into Cosette's heart. A part of her that had died long ago started to breathe again, and new life beat through her bloodstream. Perhaps she could have a second chance at the happiness she'd thought she was getting a decade ago. Perhaps even years of pain and abuse could be healed by true love.

With her heart pounding and sprinting and hammering all at the same time, she finally gave in to the fierceness of Boone's eyes. Hers met his, and it felt like someone had shot a flaming arrow from her to him, binding them and making her inch closer to him.

Perhaps he could be her cowboy prince, her knight in shining armor, the man who rode up on a white steed to save the maiden who'd been trapped in the tower for far too long.

Both of his eyebrows went up this time, and Cosette shook her head. She'd spent too much time in the pages of her fairy tales growing up, and now romance novels that she was older. She knew better than to believe that fictional heroes were real, and just because Boone was drop-dead gorgeous didn't mean he had the ability to save her.

No, if Cosette wanted the second chance she'd just caught a glimpse of, she was going to have to get herself above ground and into the tower first. Then, maybe, Boone might be able to rescue her and make all of her wildest dreams come true.

She swallowed, her way of forcing herself to focus on the ceremony. Gloria had already read her vows, and Matt held both of her hands. "I love you," he said, simply but with so much emotion that tears came to Cosette's eyes. There was no denying what he'd said, what he felt. She could feel it too.

"I love you as wide as the sky," he said. "As big as the moon, and as the day is long. I'm not perfect, but I'm going to do my best to make sure you're happy."

She pressed one palm to her erratically beating heart, because it sounded like a promise from a man that would be kept.

Rays of sunshine filled her soul, and Cosette believed for the first time since Joel had struck her that a man *could* keep his promises. That he *could* love and cherish a woman. That he *could* say *I love you* and mean it with everything he possessed.

She lost the battle to her tears, because there was so much more going on than just a wedding. Several broken parts of her had been miraculously healed, and the relief and gratitude of that had brought her tears of joy.

Thank you, she thought, hoping her silent prayer would make it to the Lord among all the other love and joy present.

The pastor pronounced Matt and Gloria husband and wife, and the crowd began to cheer. Cosette stood still and let all of the healing power of God wash through her, and when she blinked and looked up into the dark eyes of Boone, he said, "You can hold onto me."

A sob flew from her throat, and she did exactly that. This time, without worry. This time, with hope. This time, as a woman who wasn't afraid of a man.

She did wonder how many questions Boone would have, and she straightened quickly, wiping her eyes. "That was beautiful," she said.

Boone slipped his hand into hers and said nothing. Just the fact that he was there, at her side, supporting her, meant the world to Cosette. It meant that he didn't mind that she'd bent a little in the wind. He was going to tie her to himself and hold her steady. He was going to make sure her trunk continued to grow straight and strong *despite* the wind.

As she stood beside him, her fingers clutching his tightly, all she could do was pray that he wouldn't mind taking a fixer-upper of a woman out for tacos.

Soon.

Five

BOONE DID HIS BEST TO SMILE AT GERTY AND Michael as they approached the truck. They weren't holding hands, and Boone had never seen them do so. He knew what a crush looked like though, and he finally wiped the half-smile, half-grimace from his face before his daughter saw it.

"Ready?" he asked the two teenagers.

"Uncle Boone," Britt yelled as she got out of Keith's truck, her therapy dog right behind her. The golden retriever smiled everywhere she went, and Boone couldn't help grinning back at Pearl.

"Ready," Gerty said. "Did you get the barbecue chips, Dad?"

"Yes," Boone said, still focused on Britt as she half-ran, half-skipped toward him. Keith got out too, carrying two backpacks. He smiled and lifted his hand in a wave to Boone, who did the same back to him.

Then he laughed as he scooped Britt into his arms, the

tiny girl practically flying up into the stratosphere. "Look at you, Little Miss," he said. "I didn't know we wore dresses to go hiking."

"I have her cane," Keith said, lifting the backpacks over the back of the truck to put them in the bed. "Just a sec." He hurried back to his truck to get Britt's cane, and she frowned at him as he put it in Boone's truck. "And Pearl's leash."

"I don't need that," Britt said, turning to look at Boone.

"Yeah, I know," he said. "But it makes your daddy feel better if we bring it. I'll carry it, just in case." He gave her a bright smile, because she most likely would need the cane.

"Look," Gerty said, and Boone turned to see her holding up a walking stick. "Mike and I have them too. It's no big deal, Britt."

Boone's heart expanded with love right then and there. Britt slid down his body to the ground and ran to hug Gerty. "Yours is so colorful," she said. "Maybe we could paint mine too." She spun to look at Boone with big, wide eyes. How Matt ever said no to her, Boone would never know.

"Not right now," he said, which was a way of saying yes. "We're headed out right now. I've got the chips, the carrots, and the sandwiches."

"Did you get the macaroni salad from Elise?" Keith asked. "It's amazing, Uncle Boone."

"I got it all from Elise," Boone said, though he knew how to put together a picnic lunch for a day of hiking. He had been a widower for years now, and Gerty hadn't died of starvation yet.

"I'm gonna text Kassidy and tell her we're leaving now,"

Keith said as he opened the front passenger door to get in. "Come on, Pearl." He waited for the golden retriever to jump into the cab.

Boone grunted in agreement, though he wasn't overly thrilled to be chaperoning his nephew's date with his girlfriend. He had told Matt he'd keep an eye on his son, and he definitely gave Keith a glare as he opened the back door. Keith didn't even look up from his phone, and Boone sighed inwardly as he lifted Britt onto the back bench seat.

Gerty and Michael went around the back of the truck to the other door, and they climbed in too, with Gerty in the middle, and Mike sitting right behind where Boone would be driving. He closed Britt's door and walked a pace or two toward the tailgate. "Help me, Lord," he murmured, because he realized he was now on a triple date with his daughter and Mike, Keith and Kassidy, and him and Britt.

If the only woman he could get to go out with him was his nine-year-old niece...or a golden retriever....

Boone didn't even want to complete the thought. He balked at the thought of dating anyway, despite the image of Cosette's pretty face and big, hazel-green eyes entering his mind.

He got behind the wheel and reached to start the truck. School hadn't started yet, which meant the August sunshine still heated the Colorado Rockies plenty past comfortable. In Montana, the weather would've started to chill already, and Boone didn't hate the extended summer.

"She's on her way," Keith said, clearly having missed all

of Boone's glares. He gave his nephew another one while he adjusted the air conditioning and turned down the radio.

"Great," he said in a deadpan. "You're gonna be good with her today, right?"

Keith finally looked at him, a hint of surprise in his eyes. "Yeah. Why wouldn't I be?" He stroked Pearl's head, and the dog looked like she'd died and gone to heaven.

"Just because I'm not your dad doesn't mean I'm gonna let you sneak off into the forest to kiss."

"Uncle Boone." Keith shook his head, his whole face turning the shade of a beet in less time than it took to breathe. "I'm not gonna do that." His last sentence came out in a mumble.

"Good," Boone boomed, glaring into the rear-view mirror. "That goes for everyone in this truck. No kissing today."

"Dad," Gerty said with plenty of venom in her voice. "Stop it."

"I won't stop it," Boone said. "You two are too young for kissing."

"I haven't kissed her, sir," Michael said, meeting Boone's eyes in the mirror. "Honest."

"You're holding her hand right now," Boone said, putting the truck in reverse. He couldn't see their hands, but he knew. He wasn't sure how, but he did. Father's instinct, perhaps.

Michael's shoulder shifted, and his face colored too. He said nothing, and Gerty looked out Britt's window, her arms now folded across her chest. Fine with Boone. He backed out of the driveway in front of the cabin where he lived with Gerty and got the truck bumping down the mostly smooth dirt road.

"When did you kiss a girl for the first time?" Keith asked.

Boone dang near drove them right into the largest pine tree on the corner of the lot at the homestead. He jerked the wheel, a gasp coming from his mouth.

Gerty started to giggle in the back seat, and Boone didn't like that. The girl would tease him relentlessly if he said anything, and she'd pull out her forked tongue if he didn't. She didn't seem to know when to say something and when to not yet, and he glared at her while she leaned over and whispered something to Michael.

"No whispering," he practically shouted. "It's rude." Gerty rolled her eyes, and Boone pressed on the brake. "Do you want to stay home?"

"No, sir," she said quickly, her smile fading and her eyes widening as she pleaded with him silently.

"Whispering *is* rude," Britt said. "That's what my teacher says."

A beat of silence filled the truck before Boone got it moving again. "She's right," he said in a much more normal voice, tone and volume. "If you can't say something out loud to all of us, don't say it."

"I was just saying that you'd probably kissed a girl when you were thirteen," Gerty said. "Which is how old I am, Daddy."

"Yeah, well." Boone cleared his throat, tossing a look over to Keith. He sat there nonplussed, his flushed embar-

49

rassment from a few minutes ago gone. "Maybe I was thirteen, but she was older."

"Were you really thirteen?" Keith asked.

Boone shifted in his seat and decided not to deny it. "Yes."

"I can't believe you, Dad," Gerty said indignantly. "I'm totally sneaking off into the woods to kiss Michael today."

The teenager whipped his attention toward Gerty. "Really?"

"No," Boone said. "Not really." He rolled his eyes now. "Can we talk about something else? Wasn't there some show on last night that y'all were hyped about?" He went past the homestead, the long fence separating the horse pastures from the dirt road that ran along it coming into view. Barns and stables sat in front of him, and that was where he went to work every day.

No one said anything, and as he neared the big red barn that acted as the administration office for Pony Power, the door opened and Cosette came outside. Boone's first instinct was to pull over and ask her to go hiking with them. Then he'd have a date too.

Even as he slowed and came to a stop, he knew she wouldn't come. First, there wasn't any room for her in the truck. Second, she was working today.

"Howdy," he said, leaning toward Keith, who'd rolled down his window. "We're off to go hiking."

Cosette looked at Keith, then Boone, then the kids in the back seat, her smile growing with each moment. "That's great," she said. "I just came out to get some fresh air. They're staining the stalls in there, and it's full of fumes."

Boone nodded, feeling the weight of all the teenage eyes on him. "So you can't come hiking with us?"

"Not today," she said, still grinning.

"Too bad," he said, smiling back. "Well, call me if you need somethin' with the horses. Otherwise, Travis and Cody are here today."

"Mission's back today too," Cosette said. "We'll be fine. Gray and Wes are here too." She looked down the fence line toward the homestead. "Have fun." She offered a wave and another smile, and Boone forced himself to get his truck moving again.

No one said anything as he trundled along, past the pine trees and all the way to the stop sign. He barely slowed before taking the left turn that would take them away from the town of Ivory Peaks and further into the mountains.

Just when Boone was about to go crazy, he reached for the volume knob on the radio. Before he could turn it up, Keith said, "Are you gonna ask Cosette out?"

Boone nearly ran the truck off the road for a second time in the past five minutes. "No," he barked, though technically, he already had. "Why would you think that?" He added a half-scoff, half-laugh to the end of his question.

Keith shrugged and looked out his window. Boone focused on the road again, his throat suddenly too tight to swallow. Britt hummed to herself in the back seat while he kneaded the steering wheel, words piling up beneath his tongue. Gerty seemed to be drilling holes in the back of his head with her eyes, but he refused to look in the mirror to see if that was true or not.

There was no traffic out here, and he didn't need to check any of his mirrors. Not right now, at least. To alleviate the increasing tension, he reached over and managed to get the volume turned up before Keith could ask any more embarrassing-for-Boone questions.

Relief poured through him when the song playing was one all the kids knew from one of their social media apps, and the three teenagers started singing along with the lyrics. With that simple act, Boone's belief in God was reaffirmed, and he pressed his eyes closed as he thought, *Thank you, Lord.*

Then he added, *Some help today would be great, and if there's anything I'm doing with Cosette to make people think I like her, can you make me stop that, please?*

He drove casually, but his mind fired at him. *You do like Cosette. You said you wanted to figure her out. What about the tacos?*

Tacos, tacos, tacos.

"Dad, that's our turn."

"Right." He swung the truck at the same time he braked, and everyone protested except him. "Made it." He gave everyone a grin as he pulled into a spot at the trailhead, and they all looked blankly back at him. "Come on. Every-one's carrying their own pack and their own walking stick."

He bolted from the truck, jogging around the front to help Britt down. She didn't protest his help, nor did she frown at her cane now that Michael and Gerty had them too. "All set?" he asked, adjusting the straps on his pack. He carried all of the food, as well as his own water, and gladness crept through him.

Boone did love the outdoors with his whole heart, and he let Gerty and Michael take the lead while Keith went to help Kassidy with her car keys. He saw no evidence of kissing or even an attempted kiss while his nephew zipped her keys into her backpack, which she already wore.

He sent Britt behind Michael, then Keith and Kassidy went up the trail, and Boone followed them all. He took a deep breath of the mountain air, finally feeling centered and in control of the situation again.

Then he thought about kissing Cosette again, and everything inside his mind and everywhere his pulse existed went off the rails. This time, he didn't fight the feelings as they washed through him, but he entertained them.

What would it be like—really be like—to go out with her?

There's only one way to find out, he thought as the clouds shifted and the sunlight came raining down on them.

"COME ON," HE SAID A COUPLE OF HOURS LATER. He wadded up his trash and stuck it in the plastic grocery sack. "Time to get cleaned up and head back."

Keith and Kassidy sat several yards away on a boulder overlooking the valley, hand-in-hand. They hadn't snuck off to do any kissing, so Boone's lecture had worked. Likewise,

Gerty and Michael had stayed within his sight, and even if they hadn't held hands, he could sense their crushes for each other.

He supposed it wasn't a bad thing. Michael Hammond was a good boy, and he didn't even live in Ivory Peaks. Boone had already gone through this cycle, and he suspected he would again. Gerty was his only child, his little girl, and he couldn't stand the thought of her growing up and dating. Kissing boys. Getting married.

Boone wasn't supposed to have to go through these things alone. He sighed as he got to his feet, his thoughts running around his wife. *Wish you were here, Nik,* he thought. He touched two fingertips to the brim of his cowboy hat and then pointed them toward heaven, and his eyes met Gerty's as his hand came back down.

"I'll get it all, Daddy," she said, because she knew that gesture. Boone had told her when she was a little girl that they could always talk to her mother. All they had to do was give her a nod or a kiss, and then send it toward heaven.

Gerty kept her eyes on his as she approached, reached for the bag, and then paused. "Would Mom have liked this hike?"

"Yes," Boone said without hesitation. "Mama would've loved this place." Nikki had loved hiking, being outside, riding horses, and everything the mountains offered. The seasons, the way the leaves changed colors in the fall, and the way they renewed their life in the spring. She adored pine trees and had kept one in their house all year round, not just at Christmastime.

After she'd gotten ill, she'd told Boone that she loved them so much because they grew so straight and they remained true for decades. "They're evergreen," she'd whispered that night in bed. He'd held her as tightly as he could, knowing even then that he wouldn't have her forever. "Like my love for you and Gerty."

After she'd died, Boone had tried to make her evergreen too. He'd tried to make sure Gerty knew her and knew everything about her. He didn't shy away from talking about her, and he looked his daughter dead in the eye and asked, "What do you think she'd have liked best about Colorado?"

"How big the mountains are," Gerty said, turning to look out at them again. "How long they go on. How they pierce the sky."

Boone slung his arm around his daughter's shoulders, glad he could talk to her about kissing and about her mother in the same day. "She would've loved these mountains here," he said. "With all the pines."

"That's what we don't have here, Dad," Gerty said quietly as Keith approached. "A pine tree in our house."

Keith caught the last part of her sentence, and he looked from her to Boone. "We should get you one. For your mom." He smiled at Gerty, and they had always been close, despite the few years of age difference. "I remember you always had one at Saffron Lake."

"Yeah." Gerty nodded and stepped out from underneath Boone's arm. "At least a fake one, right, Dad?"

"Yep," Boone said. "Though I bet we could get a permit and come cut one down here." He bent to pick up his pack and Gerty collected the trash from Keith, Michael, and Kassidy. "Come on, Britt," he called, and the little girl turned from the edge of the woods where she stood.

"There's chipmunks here," she called.

"I'll get her," Keith said, already moving that way.

Gerty handed Boone the bag of trash, and he shoved it in his pack, her eyes wider and more wary now. "What's up, bumblebee?" he asked, forgetting that she hated the childhood nickname she'd once loved.

Today, she didn't flinch. She glanced over to Michael and then to Keith. "Daddy, can me and Mike ride back with Kassidy? Her and Keith are goin' to a movie this afternoon. We want to go too."

Boone's first instinct was to say no, of course not. She couldn't go on a double-date with her cousin and his girlfriend. No. Absolutely not.

"I'm a good driver, sir," Kassidy said, right there at Gerty's side. To their credit, they didn't exchange a glance, though this ask was clearly rehearsed.

"I have plenty of money from this summer," Gerty asked.

His eyebrows went up, and Michael stepped into the conversation right on cue. "I have money too, sir."

"Kassidy said she'd drive us back to the farm after," Gerty said. "Keith's truck is out there and all."

Keith and Britt were staying with Boone and Gerty until Matt and Gloria came home from their honeymoon, so they'd definitely have to get back out to the farm. He surveyed the three teenagers, trying to decide how to play this.

"Have you ever been in an accident?" he asked Kassidy.

"No, sir."

He narrowed his eyes, channeling his father from long ago. "Speeding ticket?"

"Nope."

"I've got a friend I can call, you know," Boone said, actually pulling his phone from his back pocket. "I'll know in less than five minutes."

"I've never gotten in any trouble on the road," Kassidy said, smiling at him like she knew this was just a game, and she'd already won.

"How long have you had your license?" In Colorado, anyone with a license less than six months old couldn't have passengers in the car without someone over age twenty-one.

"I'm seventeen, sir," she said. "I've had my license for a little over a year."

Boone's next question went out the window. He frowned at his phone as if it had shown him something terrible. "You'll be home by midnight?"

"Yes, sir," she said, actually giggling.

"The movie starts at three-twenty, Dad," Gerty said dryly. "Can we go or not?"

Boone looked at her and blinked a couple of times. "With that attitude, I—"

"I'm sorry, Daddy," she said, stepping into him and wrapping her arms around him in a hug. "I'd love to go, but maybe you have some chores for me to do? I can empty the dishwasher or come give Cotton a bath."

"I didn't think you had a dishwasher," Michael said, and that made Boone smile. He grinned at the boy, who grinned back.

Boone hugged his daughter tight and then let her go. She looked at him with wide, unassuming eyes, full of pleading. "Fine," he said. "But it is different with four teenagers in the car." He glanced at Kassidy, who nodded. "And the same rules we had out here apply in town, at the movie theater, anywhere you are."

"I know the rules," Gerty said.

"Tell 'em to me anyway."

She cut a look at Michael, who nodded slightly to encourage her. She half-rolled her eyes as she looked back at Boone. "Don't go off on your own. Stay with the group."

"Mm hm." Boone shouldered his pack and folded his arms.

"Call if I'm going to be later than I said."

He waited for more, because there was definitely more.

"Don't eat too much licorice," she said, her eyebrows going up. A question mark almost existed on the end of the sentence.

He burst out laughing, though that wasn't the one he was looking for. "Definitely don't do that, bumblebee," he said. "She really does like to just keep eating licorice, and then she has some—" He cut off at the horrified look on his daughter's face. He cleared his throat, his smile sliding off his face.

"You forgot a couple," he said.

"Tell 'em to me," she said, mimicking him.

He cocked one eyebrow at her, but she didn't back down this time. "I want a text about what movie you're seeing, what time it starts, and what time it's done. No R-rated movies."

"I know the movie," she said.

Boone kept going anyway. "Be safe. Remember who you are." He glanced at Michael, then Kassidy and Keith and Britt as they came up to the group. "No kissing."

None of the teens said anything, and Boone wouldn't be able to drive away with only Britt if they didn't agree to this. Even if they broke the rule, he would be able to rest assured that they'd agreed.

"Sounds like y'all are comin' back to the farm with me," he said, turning away.

"Daddy," Gerty said.

"Be safe," Keith said. "Remember who you are. No kissing. Got it, Uncle Boone." He practically kicked Michael, and the boy jumped.

"Be safe," he said. "Remember who you are. No kissing. Yes, sir."

"I can abide by all the rules," Kassidy said. "Just a tiny clarification."

Keith shook his head violently, and Boone laughed again. "No clarifications. We got it, Uncle Boone."

He sobered and met his daughter's eye. "Gerty?"

"No R-rated movies," she said. "I'll text you what we're watching, when it starts, when it ends. No kissing."

"Be safe," Boone said. "You remember the safe word?"

"Yes, Dad."

"Remember who you are."

"I know, Dad."

"If any of y'all has any trouble." He surveyed them. "Any at all. Who are you going to call?"

"You, Uncle Boone," Keith said at the same time Michael and Gerty said, "You."

"Me," Boone said. "All right? I can't be callin' my brother on his honeymoon and tellin' him that his only son is hurt or anything."

"No, sir," Keith said.

Boone looked at each of them again, seeing how much they wanted to go—and how much they respected him. "All right," he said.

Gerty squealed and launched herself back into his arms, where they both laughed. "Thank you, Daddy."

"I can fund the movie," he said gruffly. "Send me a bill, whoever pays for the tickets and treats."

"I will," Keith said. "Come on, guys, let's get going."

They all started back down the trail, and Boone kept pace with Britt. She seemed to grow more and more weary with every step, and he finally swept her off her feet and put her on his shoulders. "Should we catch up, honey?"

"Yes," she said, giggling.

Boone jogged down the trail, catching up to the teens in only a couple of minutes. When they were almost back to the truck, his phone bleeped out several notification chimes, practically right on top of each other.

"I must not have had service up there," he said. He slowed so he wouldn't trip over any roots or rocks and pulled his phone out again, one hand still holding Britt's legs against his chest.

Cosette had texted him four or five times, and as he swiped to read them, his heart beating in the back of his throat, she called.

"Hey," he said. "I was out of range. I just got your texts but haven't read them yet."

"How close are you to being back?" she asked, her voice on the outer edge of upset.

"Half-hour," he said. "Why?" What's goin' on?"

"I need you here. It's Peanut Brittle," she said. "His foot got caught in a door, and we think he may have broken his ankle."

Adrenaline spiked through Boone. "Did you call the vet?"

"They can't come until tonight," Cosette said, her voice growing quiet as she pulled her phone away from her mouth. "Okay, just a sec. It's Boone." She sighed and added in a louder voice, "Gray says if you can't fix it, we might have to put him down."

"I'm on the way," Boone said, unable to stomach the thought of a horse in pain. He felt it as if it was his own, and he quickly added, "Talk soon," and hung up so he could focus on getting down to the truck faster.

He hugged everyone—even Kassidy and Michael—in the parking lot, told them what Cosette had said, and put

Britt in the back seat. "All right," he said, exhaling. "Let's get back to the farm."

As he drove, he couldn't help hearing Cosette's voice in his head on a loop. *I need you here. I need you here. I need you.*

I need you.

Six

COSETTE HURRIED TO THE PASSENGER SIDE OF Boone's truck and reached for the door as the vehicle came to a stop. "I've got her," she said. "He's in Stable Three."

"Pearl's up here too." Boone flew from the truck without closing his door, and Cosette turned her attention to Britt while the golden retriever jumped out after him.

"Hey, Britt. How was the hike?"

"Great," Britt said in her usual cheerful fashion. "Can I see Peanut Brittle too?"

"Yep. Let's get you out." She helped the girl unbuckle and then she lifted her from the truck. Britt definitely limped as she followed her uncle at a slower pace, but her dog came right to her side. When they finally arrived in the stable, Cosette found Boone on the floor, making some low humming noise in the back of his throat.

Both hands touched Peanut Brittle, who wore a wild look in his eye. No matter what, Peanut adored and trusted

Boone. All of the horses here did, and it hadn't taken long for Molly to see his horse whispering qualities and pull him over to Pony Power. He worked with and trained all of their therapy horses now, right alongside Gloria.

When he wasn't doing that, he ran the after-school horseback riding lessons, which would be starting up next week once the kids went back to school.

"I'm gonna move it," he said to the horse, watching his face. "It might hurt, okay, Brittle? But you'll be okay. It's just for a second." He did a cracking, cranking chiropractic move on the last word, and the horse shrieked.

Cosette thought it was the most awful noise in the whole world, and she flinched and looked away. Pearl backed up and barked a couple of times, then inched forward and nuzzled Peanut Brittle's face, obviously trying to calm him.

"All right," Boone said, stroking both the dog and the horse. "Get 'im up." He stood too, dusting off his jeans and his hands. "It's not broken. Let's see if it's back in place."

Travis and Mission closed in and took the ends of the rope from Boone. They tugged, urging Peanut Brittle to get to his feet. The horse did, and Boone stood right in front of him, stroking both hands down the sides of his face. "See? All better." He grinned at the horse, and Cosette would have to be heartless not to swoon for the cowboy on the spot.

As she was the only woman in attendance, she didn't see anyone else reaching for the wall to steady themselves the way she did. Thankfully, she and Britt had stayed back, and no one looked her way.

"Is he puttin' weight on it?"

"No," Travis said.

"Let's see if he will." Boone took the rope again and backed up, bringing Peanut Brittle with him. "Let's go for a walk, Brittle. Just you and me." He turned then, his eyes landing on Cosette. He offered her a smile that held more than just friendliness, but he moved past her without saying anything.

Perhaps she'd invented what she wanted to see in his gaze, in that strong mouth.

"Can I come, Uncle Boone?" Britt asked.

"Sure can, honey. Can you catch up?"

Britt skipped after him, Pearl trotting at her side, and Cosette stayed out of the way while Mission and Travis went too. They still held plenty of anxiety in their eyes, and they'd stay close to Boone and Peanut Brittle to help if needed.

Cosette didn't need to do anything else. Well, besides get back to her desk and pick up where she'd left off in the invoicing for next week's riding lessons. Molly would be stopping by for a meeting about the schedule too, and Cosette had to figure out how to get the printer to work before that meeting.

She had experience with many a printer, but the one here seemed to have a vendetta against her at the most inopportune times. She ran her hands through her hair and went down the hall to get back to her office. Boone was back, and he'd fix everything.

Startled at her faith in him, she tried to push him and his gentle way with horses and kids alike from her mind. That so didn't work, but she wrestled with the printer, reinstalled the driver, and finally got the schedule for the next two weeks to print.

She marked the holes in it with a neon yellow highlighter and set it on the edge of her desk. Then she peered at her computer, trying to remember where she'd been before Travis had yelled and Mission had come running down the hall, shouting for someone to call the vet.

"How's the horse?"

She looked up at Gray, who'd poked his head into her office.

"Boone's walking him," she said. "I'm not sure."

"I'll go find him." With that, Gray left, his brother following him with a wave in Cosette's direction. She went back to her computer, proud of herself for not being startled at the sound of a male voice.

She felt like she'd improved by leaps and bounds since coming to this farm, and she'd never been happier about her career change than she was in that moment.

She'd just finished sending the last invoice when someone knocked on her doorframe. She glanced up, freezing when she found Boone standing there. She jumped to her feet, her body mimicking her heart as it leapt toward her skull. "How's Peanut Brittle?"

He smiled, though he definitely seemed tired. "He's great. Walking okay, if a bit limpy. I think he's just fakin', but we'll see when the vet gets here."

She nodded, her fingers knotting around one another. Boone looked at her hands, and she dropped them back to her sides.

"I don't still make you nervous, do I?" he asked, concern flashing through his eyes as he frowned.

"No," she said.

"You sure?"

"Yes."

Boone still looked doubtful. "I thought we had fun at the birthday party last week. And the wedding." He hadn't danced with her before the ceremony, but the birthday party had been fun. They'd sat together and eaten pizza, laughed as the kids tried to break the piñata, and then she'd left with Gloria.

He'd been a perfect escort at the wedding, and Cosette hadn't been able to stop thinking about him since. "Both of those were fun," she said.

He checked over his shoulder and then stepped fully into the office. "You know, Travis had the situation with Brittle handled."

"They told me to call you," she said, her throat a bit scratchy now. She wasn't nervous he was coming closer, she was...thrilled. Filled with anticipation. They almost felt like the same thing, except she didn't want to cower and hide. She wanted to stand her ground and see if he'd take her hand in his.

"You said you needed me here."

"I did."

He grinned at her. "Maybe you just wanted tacos."

"So what if I did?" She raised her chin, and for the first time in a long time, she wasn't afraid she'd get struck there.

In the past, she'd curled inward, ducked her head, protected her most vital parts.

Boone chuckled, and oh, the man must know what that sound did to a woman's stomach. Hers vibrated and sent zings through her whole body. Her fingers flinched toward his, and she only held them back by her sheer will.

"I can make that happen," he said, quieting and bringing his eyes up to hers. "Any night you want."

She tilted her head at him, wondering if this was flirting. To her, it sure felt like it. "Oh yeah? I thought you had three kids this week. Your nights are free?"

"Next week, then," he said, grinning again and clearly enjoying this game. "I can get Matt and Gloria to take Gerty once they're back." He pulled out his phone and started tapping. "In fact, I'll ask him right now."

Cosette watched in awe and slight horror as he legit sent a text to his brother on his honeymoon. He looked up when he was done. "You didn't just text him."

"I did," Boone said, looking up, clear surprise in his eyes. "Why?"

"He's on his *honeymoon*," Cosette said, swatting at his chest.

Boone flinched and backed up a step, his eyes shining with laughter. "I don't see the problem."

"You do too," she said, turning and going back around her desk. "If my brother texted me on my honeymoon, I'd never babysit for him."

"I thought you just had the one sister."

She gave him a piercing glare. "You know what I mean."

His phone beeped, and he returned his attention to it. "He said yes." He flashed the device in her direction, but he didn't leave it for long enough that she could read it. "So what night next week sounds like it could be a fiesta?"

Cosette had no idea how to answer. Did he really think she was a *fiesta* type of woman? Before she could inform him of such a thing, his phone rang, and she did catch Matt's name on the screen. "Oh, you're in trouble."

"I am not." He shook his head and turned his back as he answered. "Howdy, bro." He'd taken one step away from her desk before he froze. "Yes," he said. All of a sudden, he flew toward the door. "Of course I'm serious," he said, obviously trying to keep his voice low. "No, I don't have to tell you who it is."

She barely caught the last part of his sentence as he got further from her office. She sank back into her chair, both palms resting against the desktop. Then, slowly, she smiled at her computer screen, which had gone dark. She could just barely see her reflection in the blackness of the monitor, and she studied the half of her face she could see.

She looked happy. No, more than that. Content. Comfortable. And happy.

In the next moment, she realized she might have a date with a handsome cowboy. Her hand shot out, dislodging the receiver on her work telephone. She picked it up and called her sister, immediately hanging up and yanking open her desk drawer to get her phone. She didn't need to use the line for Pony Power to call Raven.

Her fingers shook as she tapped her sister's name, and

she took a couple of deep breaths while she listened to the line ring. "This is Raven," her much more trusting and outgoing sister's voice chirped.

"You know it's me," Cosette said. "Why can't you just answer with hello?"

"Oh, hello, *Miss Gregory*," she said. "Yes, I did call about that carpet cleaner."

Cosette had no idea what her sister was talking about, but she must be in some sort of pickle. Raven often found herself in such a situation. So she just sat there, suppressing a giggle lest the customer she was with could hear her.

"Mm hm, let me get to my office so I can look at that paperwork." Scratching and static came through the line as Raven covered her phone. Cosette still heard her say, "Excuse me, Mister Richfield. Linus here will take care of you and answer all your questions." A few more seconds passed, and then Raven said, "Praise the Lord you called. I thought I was going to be stuck in that meeting *forever*."

Cosette laughed then, feeling freer than she had the last time she'd done so. "I need your help," she said after she'd quieted.

"With what?"

Cosette twisted toward the big window that sat behind her desk. "Well, uh, I think a man asked me to dinner."

Silence filled the other end of the line, and Cosette knew the feeling. She reached out to touch the smooth glass, seeing only the water spots on the outside pane. If she didn't focus so closely, she could see the beauty of the pastures and sky beyond the spots. She hoped that whoever looked her way could look past all the blemishes on the surface to the real beauty within.

Boone seemed to do that, and it terrified and excited Cosette at the same time. An insane giggle spilled from her mouth. "Are you there? I'm dying here."

"Who asked you out?" Raven asked. "And what did you say?" Those would be the questions on the tip of the iceberg, but Cosette didn't care. She really did need help riddling through this situation, and all of her feelings.

That's why you have a therapist, she thought. She could make a single call and get in to see Michelle that afternoon if necessary. She also went walking with a friend in the mornings who'd once been a psychiatrist. Louisa could help her too, and Cosette would see her tomorrow morning bright and early.

"This cowboy named Boone Whettstein," Cosette said, tapping the icon to make the speaker turn on. She couldn't sit still and have this conversation. She got to her feet and ran her hands through her hair again. "I actually didn't answer him. I sort of...flirted with him about when we could go?" She paced toward the back corner, where she hung her coat in the winter. Right now, the rack stood empty, but she reached out to feel the wood texture of it.

"I don't like how unsure you sound about that."

"It's been a while since I flirted," Cosette admitted, turning away from the rack. Her eyes drifted up to the vent in the ceiling.

"So do you have a date or don't you?"

"I don't know. I—"

"She has a date," Boone said, and Cosette spun toward him, her heart throbbing in every cell in her body. He wore that devilish smile as he added, "At least if she can go on Tuesday, Wednesday, or Friday."

"Oh, Tuesday sounds good," Raven said while Cosette's mouth fished open and closed. "She's free on Tuesday. Taco Tuesday." Her sister practically yelled from the phone sitting on Cosette's desk.

Boone grinned like he'd just won a huge contest. "Tuesday sounds great." Someone down the hall called his name, and his attention got diverted that way. He raised one hand and looked back into the office. "We can work out the details later. 'Bye, Cosette." He grinned at the desk and yelled, "'Bye, Raven."

"Good-bye!" her sister called, and Boone lifted his hand in a farewell wave to Cosette, who'd stood there shell-shocked during the entire exchange. Only the humming of the air conditioning blowing through that blasted vent filled the air.

"Is he gone?" Raven whispered, and Cosette dove for her phone. She jabbed the speaker off and lifted the device to her ear.

"I can't believe you did that," she breathed into the phone. "I can't go out with him on Tuesday." Five days. There was no way she could be ready to go on a date with a man—a male!—in only five days.

"Of course you can," Raven said matter-of-factly. "He sounded nice, *and* he knew my name, which means you've talked to him before—about personal things."

Cosette scoffed and kept her eyes trained on the doorway. She wasn't making that mistake again. No siree. "You don't go out with someone because they sound nice."

"*You* don't," Raven said. "But I would, and you *know* him, Cosette. *You* called me to ask about this date. Why don't you want to go all of a sudden?"

She did want to go, but she had a hard time untangling the words in her throat to explain. It was really her scarred heart screaming at her not to let them get sliced and diced again. Her chin telling her not to let them get split open. Her hands and knees smarting at her not to get into a situation where she was trying to run and kept falling.

"I want to go," she whispered, the words catching against the dryness in her throat.

"What?"

She cleared her throat. "I want to go." Panic spiraled up and then down, and she did what Louisa had suggested a couple of months ago. She let it. She didn't try to hold onto any control, and after only a moment, when the anxiety and tension and panic couldn't control her, it ebbed away into nothing.

"Will you help me get ready?" she asked. "I'm going to need help."

"I'll be there," Raven said. "Let me just check to see if I have to work on Tuesday night...." Shuffling of papers came through the line, and then Raven nearly deafened Cosette when she said, "Nope. I'm off. I'll be at your house at four."

"I don't even get off until five," Cosette said. "You don't need to come at four."

"Oh, you need me to sign some papers?" Raven asked, her voice far too bright and way too loud to be real. "Gotta go, Cosy."

The line went dead, and Cosette scowled at her phone. "Don't call me Cosy," she griped as she sat down. The tension drained from her muscles, and she now stared at her half-reflection again. "I have a feeling she just used someone else to get out of talking to me."

The reflection nodded as she did, and Cosette sighed. At least she had a date in the near future, and she dang near squealed. But Molly entered the office with, "Afternoon, Cosette," and she hurriedly adopted her professional persona so she wouldn't burden her boss with the trivial details of her pathetic love life.

With Boone in it, her love life wouldn't be so pathetic anymore, and Cosette shelved her dreams of being whisked away from her boring, quiet house to an evening of maracas, salsa, and tacos. Mm, lots of tacos.

"ALL RIGHT," LOUISA SAID AS SHE PICKED UP THE pace. Cosette matched her stride for stride. "So your date is tonight." She glanced over to Cosette, but she kept her gaze on the horizon.

"Mm hm."

Louisa already knew the Taco Tuesday date with Boone was happening in only a few hours. Several hours. Fine, maybe twelve hours. Cosette's stomach clenched, and she almost pulled her phone from the pocket on her workout pants to cancel.

"I see that look," Louisa said, her voice so chipper. "You're not canceling on him."

"I didn't say I was."

"I *know* you, Cosette." Louisa laughed though her breathing had increased. They turned the corner and the hill they both dreaded came into view.

Cosette had almost died the first time she'd climbed it with her new best friend at her side. Now, she certainly didn't look forward to marching up the hill, especially so early in the morning, but she knew she could do it. She'd made it to the top many times before, and she would again.

She realized that her first date with Boone Whettstein was exactly like this approaching hill. If she didn't go, she still wouldn't know if she'd survive a first date with a handsome cowboy. Fear struck her right through the heart, but intellectually, she knew she'd leave her house tomorrow morning and find Louisa on the sidewalk, waiting for her.

"Any tips?" Cosette asked. "For tonight?" She looked at Louisa, who offered her a brilliant smile.

"Of course. I'd say...wear something you feel like a million bucks in."

Cosette's brain started to buzz. She had plenty of clothes that made her feel strong and confident. She could put an extra wave in her hair and make the point on her eyeliner the sharpest it had ever been.

"Then," Louisa said, her arms swinging back and forth

now as she picked up the pace again. "Be honest with him. If you don't want to go to a restaurant, tell him."

"He's planning tacos," Cosette said, her heart rate picking up too. "I don't think there will be a restaurant."

"I would still say you should tell him you don't want a big, loud restaurant." Louisa glanced over to her. "My bet is that he already knows, if he knows you at all."

Cosette nodded, though she wasn't sure how well Boone knew her. He only knew what she allowed him to know, and she hadn't told him specifically about her anxiety over large groups and loud situations.

"Okay," Louisa said as they neared the base of the hill. "Now, you've got your date—and it's going to be amazing, Cosette. I can't wait to see you tomorrow so I can hear all about it—so you've got to help me get Stan Wadley to set up a Taco Tuesday date with me."

She grinned for all she was worth, and Cosette giggled despite the increasing incline. "Stan Wadley?" she asked. "The choir director?"

"He's *cute*," Louisa said, panting now and her arms not swinging so wildly. "And boy, can he sing."

The two women looked at one another, and they both laughed. Cosette kept going up, up, up the hill, and she didn't reach for her phone to cancel with Boone.

She didn't, because she wanted to go out with him and see what life looked like on the other side of that first date.

"I'm not going out like this," Cosette said later that day. "I'm not." She met Raven's eye in the mirror, both of them in battle mode. Raven wasn't going to give in. Neither was Cosette.

Fortunately, the doorbell rang, and that broke the silent stare-fest between the sisters. "I'm not comfortable in this," Cosette said, eyeing her reflection in the mirror beyond her sister. The sequins on it made her dizzy. The emerald fabric and form-fitting gown rivaled the one she'd worn to a wedding.

"You'll never get a second date in jeans."

The goal wasn't a second date. The goal was to survive the first. "This will blind him," Cosette shot back. "Then I'll never get another date, period." She glanced over her shoulder, half-expecting to see Boone standing there. "You go get the door, and I'll change." She turned and added, "Unzip me."

Raven did what she asked, saying, "It's a lovely dress."

"It's a Taco Tuesday date," Cosette said. "I want to be comfortable, Raven. I already feel way out of my comfort zone."

"I know." Her sister spoke softly, her fingers along the zipper feather-light and loving. Cosette had once hidden everything from her sister, mentally and physically. Now, she didn't have to. "I'll get the door, but don't be surprised if he's in love with me by the time you change." Beaming, Raven left the bedroom, pulling the door closed behind her.

Cosette stepped out of the dress and left it puddled on the floor. She hurried to pull on her best pair of skinny jeans, a sweater with a fun, brown-based geometric pattern, and a pair of boots. Not cowgirl, but the regular kind that went up to her knee and zipped along the side of her calf.

She finger-combed her hair as her sister's bright laughter mingled with Boone's deeper chuckles. She would never wish the violence and fear she'd endured on anyone, least of all Raven. At the same time, her sister simply didn't understand what it was like to live in perpetual fear, and Cosette sometimes felt so alone.

She met her eyes in the mirror and said, "You've got this, Cosette. He obviously likes you, and it's okay to like him."

It was. She just hadn't had a man like her for a long time, at least not for the right reasons.

She took a deep breath and turned to open the door.

Seven

Boone kept glancing toward the mouth of the hallway while trying not to appear disinterested in Raven Brian. But he so wasn't interested in her. She was a pretty woman, and he could see how she belonged with Cosette.

Mountain Glen sat about ten minutes north of Ivory Peaks, and it had taken him fifteen to get to town from the farm. He'd left an hour early, so he'd been in the quaint mountain town for an extra half-hour.

They had a gas station and a simple, small grocery store and not much else. Some really cute houses and plenty of silence and open air. The town reminded him a lot of his former home in Montana, especially the land he'd owned with the lake.

Technically, he still owned Saffron Lake as he hadn't sold it and he didn't have any housing costs here. The cabin where he and Gerty lived came with the job on the farm, and Boone didn't live an extravagant life.

"Here she is," Raven said, and she moved to Cosette's side as she entered the front of the house.

Everything inside Boone lit up at the sight of her, and he'd always found it fascinating how attraction worked. Why did she tickle all of his hormones while her sister didn't? He had no idea, but he knew now that he felt something for Cosette that he couldn't—and didn't want to—deny.

She wore a pair of dark-wash jeans that seemed stitched onto her body. They disappeared into a pair of dark brown leather boots that stretched up to her knee. Her sweater said fall and furry and *touch-me-please-Boone*, and he fisted his fingers so he wouldn't lunge toward her.

"Hey," he said, clearing the frog from his throat immediately afterward. "I hope you're hungry, because we have a boatload of tacos waiting for us."

"A boatload?" Her eyebrows went up, giving him a better glimpse of the light in her eyes. "You already have them?"

"Yep," he said.

"Are we going back to your place then?"

He grinned at her and shook his head. "Nope." Feeling brave and bold, something he hadn't felt since leaving Montana several months ago, he extended his hand toward hers. "Shall we?"

"Go," Raven said as Cosette licked her lips. She definitely seemed nervous, and Boone forced himself to remain calm and smiling.

Cosette stepped smoothly toward Boone, and she slipped

her hand into his. Snaps, crackles, and pops moved up his arm, the warmth from her fingers making his feel like he'd stuck them in the freezer for a good long while before he'd arrived.

"You're a man of mysteries, Mister Whettstein," Cosette said, and he thought she was flirting with him. Karley hadn't really been flirty or fun with him in a while, and he should've been able to see the signs that she'd lost interest in him.

He hadn't, and he strengthened his resolve to go slow and be cautious with Cosette. Not only did she seem to need that, but Boone did too. No, not Boone. Gerty. His daughter deserved his protection, and he wasn't going to risk her getting attached to Cosette if things weren't going to work out between them.

He wasn't sure how he could possibly know for certain that the relationship would work, and Gerty already knew Cosette. He'd had this argument with himself for the past five days, and he'd deliberately left the farm before the horseback riding lessons were over so he could slip out while Gerty was still busy.

Matt would take her home with him, telling Gerty that he has a "meeting" to attend and Boone would pick her up on the way back to the farm. She was thirteen, not stupid, and she'd know his meeting was really a date the moment she smelled the cologne on him.

After all, he wouldn't spritz that stuff around to go talk to Gray or Hunter.

He pushed his daughter from his mind for now and led

Cosette toward the door. "I won't keep her out late," he said to Raven.

"Keep her as late as you want," Raven called.

They stepped outside, and Boone took a deep breath. "She's great," he said, glancing back to her. "Your sister."

"She is great," Cosette agreed.

Once they got to his truck, she paused and wouldn't get in. "I need to know where we're going." She looked at him. "I don't like busy restaurants," she added in a near-whisper.

Boone studied her for a moment, quickly dismissing the opportunity to tease her. She'd just revealed something difficult and personal to him, and he wouldn't make light of that. "When I found out you lived in Mountain Glen, I told Matt, and he has a friend here. They have a cute little barn, and I'm having the tacos delivered there."

Cosette started nodding about halfway through, then she got into the truck. Boone wrestled with himself as he went around to get behind the wheel. Once in place, he looked over to her. "Do I get to know why you're...nervous around me?"

Cosette met his eye, wariness there. "I once...." She sighed, folded her arms, and looked out the windshield. Boone gave her some space in the form of silence and pulled out of her driveway.

"Have you lived here long?" he asked when she didn't say anything else.

"Yes, quite a few years," she said.

"Five?" he pressed. "Ten?"

"Fourteen," she said. "Almost fifteen. Something like that."

"Wow, that's a long time," he said. "Matt's been coming down to Ivory Peaks and tending to the Hammond's farm in the summers for about that long."

"I just started there a year or so ago," Cosette said, her tongue forming the words exactly right. "I have a degree in business management, and I was working remotely for a company in Denver previously."

"Wow," he said. "Do you miss working from home?"

"Sometimes," she said. "Usually only when it snows." She gave him a smile, and Boone would take anything he could get at this point.

He glanced at his phone to know where to turn to get to the barn. Matt's friend, Jericho, had promised that he'd have it all set up. His phone chimed, and the food delivery app had just notified him that his driver was close.

They were also almost to the barn, and Boone thanked the Lord above that things were coming together so seamlessly.

"Are we going to Jericho Johnson's?" she asked.

"Yes," Boone said, glancing at her. "Is that okay?"

"Sure," Cosette said. "Jericho is a great guy."

"How do you know him?"

"We go to the same church," Cosette said. "He leads the choir."

"Oh," Boone said, swallowing his tongue. "Does he make you nervous?"

"He's almost eighty, so no."

"So it's just younger men."

"It's...men I'm interested in," she said, her voice almost a whisper. "Or men interested in me."

Boone opened his mouth to reply, but his brain took an extra beat or two to catch up to what she'd said. Then he said, "I am interested in you, Cosette."

"Why is that?" she asked, her voice stronger now.

"What do you mean?" He came to a stop in front of the house his map app told him to. He put the vehicle in park and turned toward her fully.

"I mean," she said, exhaling. "Why are you interested?"

Boone had no idea what to say. He hadn't dated a lot before meeting Nikki, and since she'd died, he'd kept their friends close by. He too blew out his breath and looked at the house. "My wife died almost seven years ago now. I didn't date much after her, and when I did decide to put myself out there again, I started going with her best friend."

Cosette didn't say anything, but her eyes never left his face. He couldn't look at her quite yet. "Her name was Karley. We dated for a while. A year or so. Eighteen months. Something."

"When you broke up, you moved here."

Boone swung his attention toward her. "Yeah, about that. So I don't know why I'm interested in you, only that I am. When I walk into your house and see Raven, it's fine. She's a nice woman. Pretty. Put together. Then you come out." He shook his head, the most embarrassing things ever in his head. There was no way he could say them out loud.

He did say, "And you're different. You make me...light up, and I'm interested."

He shrugged one shoulder and looked at her. "Why are you interested in me?" The first time they'd met, she'd called him a rascal for making sure she didn't fall down.

"You're handsome," she said. "Witty, hard-working, and really good with kids and horses." She shrugged too. "I don't know, it seems like you have something inside you I want to know about."

"I should've said that about you," Boone said with a smile.

"I'm sorry about your wife," Cosette said with a small, shy smile.

"Yeah." Boone reached to unbuckle his seat belt. "I should warn you that I'm super overprotective of Gerty because of...things. I didn't tell her about this date, and I'm not sure when I will."

Cosette nodded, her eyes serious and somber. "That's fine."

He got out of the truck and went around to open her door. She slid to the ground and took his hand in hers. "I was married once too," she said.

"Oh yeah?"

"Yeah," she said as they went up the sidewalk. The sun still hung above the horizon, casting plenty of gold light on the big brown barn at the end of the sidewalk. The doors opened and the taco delivery guy walked out.

"Ah, dinner's here," Boone said. He released Cosette's hand to shake the delivery man's. "Thank you."

"Yep." The man smiled at both of them and kept going. Boone made it to the barn door first and turned back to Cosette, grinning for all he was worth. He could only pray at this point that everything inside was perfect.

"Are you ready for this?"

"Tacos in a barn," she said, smoothing down her sweater. "I'm so ready." She glowed, and Boone laughed as he opened the door.

"C'mon in then." He stepped back, surveying the interior and finding it...absolutely perfect. Tea lights hung in the rafters, casting soft yellow light onto a single table only a few paces inside the door. The cement floor had been swept clean, and the barn didn't hold all the usual farm-barn things.

This was definitely a non-animal barn, and Cosette stepped past him and said, "Wow, Boone."

He entered the barn and let the door fall closed behind him. The scent of spicy salsa and grilled chicken met his nose, and his stomach rumbled at him. He ignored it and followed Cosette closer to the table.

Two plates sat there, with a trio of candles already burning in the center of the table. Beside them sat a box with cartoon tacos all over it, and Boone picked up half the stack of napkins and set it next to her plate.

"All right," he said, pulling back her chair for her. She sat, looking up at him. The firelight illuminated the side of her face, making her softer and sweeter than before. "I got a lot of tacos."

He opened the box and started pulling out the different

types of tacos. "Soft shell chicken, hard shell beef. Oh, this one is a cheesy quesadilla wrapped one. I only got a couple of those, so you only get one, sweetheart." He put the yellow-wrapped taco on her plate. The rest he simply sprinkled on the table.

By the time he'd gotten them all out of the box, tacos covered almost every inch of the table. He clapped his hands together and went around the table to his seat. As he sat, he met Cosette's eye and said, "Let's feast."

She took in the tacos, and Boone thought maybe he'd gotten too many. He hadn't been kidding when he'd said he'd ordered a lot of tacos. He'd eat them cold for days, so even if Cosette only ate one, he wouldn't be out anything.

When her eyes met his, she looked a bit baffled. "This is a lot of tacos."

"Too many choices?" He reached for the yellow-wrapped one and peeled the paper back. "Just start with one. I'm gonna go in with this one first." The paper crinkled as he took it the rest of the way off, and sure enough, a soft flour tortilla had been formed around a hard shell taco, the two pieces glued together by plenty of gooey cheddar cheese.

His mouth watered, but he watched as Cosette unwrapped her cheese quesadilla taco too. She smiled at him, and he swore the lights in the barn burned brighter. He lifted his quesadilla taco in a silent toast, and she did too.

They bit into their respective tacos at the same time, and Boone let a loud groan come out of his mouth. Cosette started to laugh, which meant Boone did too, and he nearly choked on the tortilla, cheese, chicken, and hard corn shell.

"Stop it," he said, trying to get the pointed shards of shell out of his throat.

"Me?" she teased. "You're the one who moaned like you'd been starving for years and this taco alone would save your life." She giggled again, and Boone could only beam at her.

"I have cuts on my throat," he said, still chuckling. As he sobered, he cocked his head at her. "I'm not sure I've ever heard you laugh." He reached across the mass of tacos on the table and covered her hand with his. "It's beautiful."

Cosette turned her hand over and threaded her slender fingers through his. Though they both worked for Pony Power, his hands definitely held more pigment than hers. He found the cream-tan-cream-tan pattern stunning, and he looked up, sure this date was a fantasy.

"I laughed at Keith's birthday party," she said.

Boone tilted his head, trying to remember. "I'd classify that as a giggle."

"Okay." She shook her head, a glow coming from her though she ducked her head, her smile slipping. "There's a reason why I called you a rascal," she said, not going back to her taco for another bite. "Why I'm nervous around you. Why I don't laugh very much."

Boone waited, his smile fading. "I'm all ears." He lowered his eyes and focused on his taco, hoping that would encourage her to start talking.

She still didn't, and Boone reached for his quesadilla taco, determined to wait her out this time.

Eight

COSETTE FLINCHED AT THE SOUND OF THE
crunchy taco shell. She watched Boone eat his whole taco as
they sat in silence, and she had the very real feeling if she
didn't start talking, the date would be over. Before she knew
it, they'd be back at her house, and he'd be scuffing his boots
against the porch, telling her he didn't think things would
work out between them.

"I was married once," she said as he reached for a napkin.
"To a man named—Joel." She pushed his name out of her
throat. She didn't have to fear him anymore, and as she
inhaled, she pushed away the fear, the humiliation, and all of
the victimization she'd worked through. "He abused me."

Boone didn't blink as he looked at her. "Cosette."

"Verbally," she said, swallowing. "And physically. That's
why I reacted the way I did when you—when *I* ran into *you*
when we first met. I don't...I'm not good with touching and

physical things. He could make things that should be soft and fun into pain and suffering."

Boone reached toward her and then pulled his hand back. She'd introduced tension and awkwardness into their relationship, and she regretted that. But Boone had to know all of this to understand her and hopefully, so they could continue to get to know one another over a heap of tacos.

"I'm so sorry," Boone said, putting his hands in his lap.

"You can hold my hand."

"Can I?"

She reached toward him. "Yes."

He took her hand in his, and there was no pain or suffering. His touch sent sparklers through her whole body, with the flames snapping out and disappearing as more appeared. She smiled at him, and his mouth curved upward too.

"I'm gonna need you to...." Boone cleared his throat. "Tell me what's okay with you and what's not."

"I will," Cosette said. "Okay? I'll just tell you."

He kept his eyes on hers, the flickering flames from the candles casting shadows and creating light on his face, as he brought her hand closer to him. She leaned forward, and she pulled in a slow breath as Boone pressed his lips to the inside of her wrist. "Okay?" he murmured.

Cosette hadn't been touched so sweetly in so long that she had no idea what feelings and emotions streamed through her. This man had completely captivated her, from his black jeans to his bright white cowboy hat to his blue-and-yellow plaid shirt.

His lips felt like stars shining against her skin, and she

couldn't comprehend kissing him. He released her hand, and it almost fell like dead weight to the table.

"You didn't say if that was okay," he said.

"It was okay," she whispered.

Boone gave her half a smile that fit his boyish face and he picked up another taco. "Thanks for telling me, Cosette. We don't have to go fast or anything. With Gerty and everything, I'm fine to go slow and take our time getting to know one another to see if this will work out between us."

Relief streamed through Cosette. "Thank you, Boone. That sounds ideal for me."

"Have you dated since your divorce?"

She shook her head. "No."

"How long has it been?"

"A little over fourteen years," she said.

Boone nodded and picked up a soft-shell taco. "I feel like Taco Tuesday is a bust. You've taken one bite."

Cosette looked back at the cheese-quesadilla-wrapped taco and picked it up. "I love tacos, so not a bust." She bit into her taco, and it really was delicious. "Did they give us any sour cream?"

"Sure." Boone reached into the box and pulled out a couple of sour cream packets. "There you go."

"Thank you." She grinned at him and reached for a packet. "What do you have planned after this?"

"Do we need more than a table full of tacos?" He spread his arm across the table, everything about him so full of light. Goodness. Spirit. He chuckled and leaned forward. "Don't worry, sweetheart. There's more."

A cozy, warm feeling moved through Cosette. She imagined herself snuggling up with this good man in front of a fireplace and letting him hold her until she fell asleep. She hadn't had such a fantasy in far too long, and she simply let her mind work through all of the barriers keeping her from achieving the things in her imagination.

"I can't wait," she said, squeezing out a healthy amount of sour cream onto her taco. Then she took a great big bite like Boone had done, moaning and letting her eyes drift closed in bliss.

But the really great thing was how loud and how instantaneously he laughed. Cosette laughed with him, her mouth full of food, something she would've never done with anyone else. Even her dad or Raven. Everything about Cosette had been so buttoned up, so closed off, until this very moment.

He finished another couple of tacos while she ate the quesadilla one and a single soft-shell chicken one. He started tossing them all back into the box, and then asked, "Do you want any for lunch this week?"

"Do you eat leftover fast-food tacos?" She stood, placing her napkin on the table. She assumed she could leave everything for someone else to come clean up.

Boone paused. "Of course. You don't?"

"Not everything is leftover-worthy," she said.

"Huh." He finished boxing and tucked in the flaps. "Like what?"

"French fries," she said, pushing in her chair and grinning at him. "Tell me you don't eat French fries leftover."

"They're really great in the air fryer," he said, his voice taking on a wounded note that made her giggle. "These tacos would be too, but I'm gonna eat them cold." He tucked the box under his right arm and reached for her hand with his left one. "If you want one for lunch or something, you let me know, and I'll bring it to your office."

"Just one? I only get one?"

He smiled at her, the gesture still oh-so-bright, but softer somehow. The moment lengthened between them, and neither of them made a move to leave the barn. She felt like someone had almost suspended time, so she could still see and hear and think—and move very slowly. But she couldn't actually do much.

She did reach up and run her fingers down the side of his face, his beard soft and tickling her fingertips.

"You can have as many as you want," Boone whispered. "Just let me know."

Her hand dropped back to her side as time zoomed forward again. "Okay." She faced the door, and he led her out of the barn. After he deposited the tacos onto the back seat of his truck, he exhaled mightily.

"I thought we'd walk over to Shepherd Pond," he said. "It's not far from here, and they have live music every night this week."

Cosette's spirits lifted once again, and she barely recognized herself or her life as Boone took her hand again and they started walking toward the corner. She didn't walk hand-in-hand with a man. She didn't go out in public after work. She didn't order food to be dropped off at her house, and she didn't tip her head back and laugh when a sexy cowboy told her he'd once reheated a mushroom stroganoff and it was "gloppy, with all this oil and wow. Gross."

LATER THAT NIGHT, COSETTE PUT HER FOOT ON the top step of her porch and immediately turned and backed up to make room for Boone, who followed her. "This was so fun," she said. She flew in the big, wide, dark sky right now, and only a thin kite string tethered her to the earth. The wind really whipped up here, but she enjoyed it. She'd enjoyed so much about this evening.

"Thank you for comin' out with me," he said. "Even if Raven did sort of push you into it." His hand in hers squeezed, and Cosette added more pressure to his hand too.

"She did," Cosette said. "But I've learned that sometimes I need a push in the right direction to get going."

"I think we all do," Boone said, ducking his head. When he dared to peek up at her again, Cosette's heart tap-danced against her ribs. Could he hear the clunking of it? It beat so loud in her ears, and she could physically feel her pulse in her chest where she normally didn't.

"Before you go," she said, her voice a tad higher than usual. "Would you...would you want to come to my house for dinner this weekend?" Her instincts told her to run into the house and slam the door behind her. Or wrap her fingers together. Something.

She stayed very still and maintained eye contact with

Boone. He searched her face for a couple of moments, then said, "Of course."

"You can bring Gerty."

"I probably won't," he said.

Cosette put her other hand over the back of his, effectively sandwiching his long, strong fingers between her palms. "What will you tell her?"

"I don't know." He ducked his head again. "You don't want to go out?" He raised his eyes back to hers. "Gray says there's a great hamburger place out here. I guess his brother funded it or something, and they have a bunch of Hammond stuff on the menu."

"The Burger Babe," Cosette said. "I've been there."

"So we can go somewhere else."

Cosette would go anywhere with him, and she wanted to tell him that. It felt too soon, so she held the words back. "If you don't care, I'd rather cook at home for you."

"I'm sure you have a reason," he said, quickly adding, "I don't have to know it right now."

Cosette slowly slid her hands away from his, already feeling colder and more lonely without his touch. She wasn't sure what that meant, because she hadn't ever wanted to be touched again after Joel. When she'd shown up on her father's porch at three-thirty in the morning, she hadn't even let him hug her. Number one, she'd had bruises she hadn't wanted disturbed, and number two, she literally could not stand the thought of anyone touching her ever again.

"It goes back to what I told you in the barn." She moved over to her front door, only a couple of paces from Boone.

He drifted with her, and she sure did like that. "I just need to go slow."

"And inviting me into your personal space and cooking for me is slow?"

"It's comfortable for me," she said quietly. She wasn't sure how to make him understand, so she simply looked into his eyes. He didn't understand, she could tell. How he'd planned the absolute perfect first date *for her*, she didn't know.

"You made this first date...comfortable for me. I guess I want the second to be within my comfort zone too, before we venture out to restaurants and whatnot."

The confusion and questions melted from his gaze and he nodded. "A private dinner with you sounds like a dream," he said. "Tell me what time, and I'll be here."

Cosette smiled at him and asked, "Seven? Does that give you enough time to shower, talk to Gerty, and drive here?"

"Yes, ma'am." He didn't lean down, and he'd already tucked his hands in his pockets. If Cosette wanted to touch him again before he left, she'd have to initiate it. Since she did want to feel the whispering warmth of his skin one more time, she went up on her tiptoes and balanced herself against his chest with one hand.

"I'll see you tomorrow then," she said, pressing her lips against that sexy beard.

"Tomorrow," he said, his mouth barely moving.

Cosette's face flamed with heat, and she let her hair fall down between them as she turned and opened the door. She stepped inside, turned back, and waved to him. It took almost all of her will power to get the door closed, and she stayed very still as the sound of his cowboy boots landed on the porch and then faded as he went back to his truck.

Her shoulders had just relaxed when Raven chirped, "You're back. How was it?"

Cosette jumped, pressing one palm against her pulse. "You're still here."

Her sister rose from the couch, where she'd been laying down. "Yep."

"Your car isn't here."

"Linus sold it," she said. "He came to pick it up."

Cosette didn't want to drive her sister home tonight, but she turned to go into the kitchen. "Do you want a ride home?"

"I was thinking I'd just stay here, and you can drop me at the dealership on the way to the farm tomorrow morning."

"Only if you make coffee and French toast in the morning." Cosette met her sister's eyes.

"Only if you start talking about your date. You must begin with the moment you left this house and keep talking until you reach the moment you came home." Raven gave her a saccharine-sweet smile, and Cosette was sure she thought she wouldn't be making breakfast in the morning.

Oh, she was wrong. So wrong.

"I held his hand," Cosette said, unable to meet her sister's eye. "And he has the nicest truck on the planet. And a great laugh. Oh, and guess how many tacos he bought for dinner?" Giddiness spread through her heart and mind, and Cosette couldn't believe she even wanted to talk about her date with Boone. Raven was surprised too, but Cosette set a tea kettle on the stove and Raven settled onto a barstool for more stories.

"COSETTE?"

She looked up as Gerty Whettstein entered the office. Cosette's heart instantly started to pound, and she got to her feet, her current task forgotten. "Hi, Gerty." She looked behind the teenager to see if her daddy was with her. Boone sure wasn't, and she hadn't gotten any rules from him on how to interact with Gerty.

She knew he hadn't told his daughter about their date a couple of nights ago, and that he didn't want to introduce Cosette into his daughter's life quite yet. At least not outside of Pony Power.

"What can I do for you?"

She glanced over her shoulder, as if she was expecting her father to be there too. "Uh, my daddy said something about an invoice for the Millers? I guess they asked about it, and they need one."

"Okay." Cosette sighed as she sat back down. Her chair squeaked, and she clicked away from the invoice she needed to pay for the roof repair last month. "I sent it to them digitally last week."

"She said they didn't get it."

"The twins, right?"

"Yes," Gerty said, coming all the way to Cosette's desk. "Talon and Porter Miller."

"Here it is," Cosette said, locating the Miller's account. "They're doing the beginning horseback riding lessons. Let me print it for you. Are they still here?"

"They just started," Gerty said. "I'll give it to their mom when she comes to pick them up."

The printer on Cosette's desk started to whir. "Great," she said. "It's right there."

"Thank you, ma'am." Gerty retrieved the page and turned to leave the office. Cosette watched her go, wondering if Boone braided that long, blonde hair every morning for his daughter.

Cosette had wanted to be a mother once. Now, she wasn't so sure. She only had a few child-bearing years left, and she honestly wasn't sure if she'd be able to get pregnant. When she'd been married to Joel, she had just one time, and she'd lost that baby.

"Cosette?" Gerty turned back, the doorway framing her now. She wore an apprehensive look on her face, and Cosette pushed away the dark cloud threatening to engulf her with memories of her past.

"Yeah, sweetie?"

"I didn't want to say anything, but my daddy said I should."

Cosette just waited, because she'd learned not to say anything if she didn't have to.

"I turned in a time card for all the stuff I did last week,

and I didn't get a check today." Her cheeks brightened with spots of red. "Maybe you didn't get it?"

A cascading feeling of guilt hit Cosette in the chest, right behind her heart. "I'm sorry, Gerty. Let me check." She'd spent the morning going through all of the weekly time cards and printing all of the checks. She'd only finished distributing them an hour ago, and she only needed to pay a few more farm bills before she left for the day.

Her date with Boone sat in only a few hours, and her hands shook as she reached to get the tray which held all the time cards and their attached payment receipts. Gerty migrated closer again as Cosette leafed through each salmon-colored card. She didn't see one with Gerty's name on it.

"It's not here," she said, reaching the last one. She looked up into the girl's beautiful blue eyes. She hadn't gotten those from her father, and Cosette thought her mother must've been beautiful. She'd lost her mother at a young age too— not as young as Gerty—and she wanted to tell Gerty she'd be okay. "Where did you put it?" she asked instead.

She waved to the open door behind her. "I put it in the slot there. On Saturday after I finished helpin' Travis shoe a horse."

Cosette looked past her to the door. "My door doesn't have a slot, Gerty."

Gerty turned and looked, clearly saw there was no mail slot in the door, and whipped back to Cosette. "Uh oh." She strode toward the exit and went out into the hall. "I swear it was right here," she called back.

Cosette smiled to herself, knowing exactly where Gerty

had put her time card. She'd just entered the hall when Gerty said, "I put it in here." She indicated a door a couple down from Cosette's, which had once been the front door on this administration barn.

She reached to open the door, and since nothing around here ever got locked for long, it swung open. "Here it is." She stooped and came up triumphant with the card. "Is it too late?" She came toward Cosette, a familiar look of worry in her eyes. She'd definitely gotten that from Boone, and Cosette gave her a friendly smile, a whole new door in her heart opening in that single breath of time.

Tears came to her eyes, and her first instinct told her to drop her gaze to the ground. She did for a second, and then forced it back to Gerty's.

"Of course not, honey," she said. "If you have five minutes, I'll do it right now."

"Okay," Gerty said, her face brightening. "Thank you, Cosette."

"Sure." She took the time card and headed back to her office. "How's the first week of school?"

Behind her, Gerty groaned and said, "I don't know. It's fine, I guess."

"You don't like school?" For some reason, that surprised Cosette.

"I like it fine," Gerty said. Cosette sat at her desk and started clicking again. "It's just...I think I'm too much like my daddy."

"Oh?" Cosette refused to look at her, choosing to focus on her payroll software.

"Yeah." Gerty slumped into the single chair in front of Cosette's desk, obviously unhappy. "He can't stand to be contained by walls, and I'm so much like that. I just want to be here, walking the horses to their next lesson or to the washing stall."

Cosette flashed a grin in her direction, then looked at the time card. "You do a great job around here."

"I'm just lucky Gray and Hunter let me get paid for helping."

Cosette put in the hours she'd worked last week, and hit enter. "All right. I'll get it printed in just a sec."

Gerty grinned and stood. "Thank you again, Cosette."

The printer hummed again, and she plucked the check from it. "I need this bottom part, and then you're good to go." Cosette ripped off the thing she needed to staple to Gerty's time card and handed the check to the teen.

Gerty looked at it, her eyes even bigger. "Thanks." She turned back in the doorway again. "Hey, are you going to that party tonight with my dad?"

Cosette's mind blanked, but somehow her neck got her head to nod.

"Awesome, will you tell him that I asked about my check?" She smiled and held it up. "Thanks again."

Cosette nodded, but Gerty had already left. She sank into her chair again, completely spent. She definitely needed to clarify with Boone what she should say to his daughter about their relationship.

She would tonight, on their date.

Nine

Boone pointed for Travis Thatcher, the cowboy who drove the side-by-side over the dirt road. It definitely wasn't as smooth out here, but the all-terrain vehicle which seated two didn't have any problem with the rocks and dirt.

"I see 'em," Travis yelled. Boone wasn't sure if he was upset or not. He'd been working with Travis for four months, but the only time he'd even looked a tiny bit alarmed was when Boone had said that the Colorado cowboys didn't know what winter ranching was. He smiled just thinking about that debate and how unglued Cody and Mission had become.

Boone stood by his statement, because no one understood cold until they'd been to Montana. And having to go outside and take care of animals every day? Even Boone had questioned his career more times than one.

Right now, the weather in Ivory Peaks was spectacular. A

golden afternoon, with a slight breeze and the trees highest up on the mountains to the west already turning red and orange. The kids had started school now, and Boone didn't feel quite so much pressure to make sure Gerty stayed out of trouble.

The girl never really got into trouble, though she had a stubborn streak a mile long. His thoughts wandered down a path he'd once been on with her and Nikki, and as it did, a new branch forked to the right. Could he go down that path and bring Gerty with him?

He knew who trod the other path. Cosette.

He sure had enjoyed his evening with her on Tuesday, and he couldn't wait to see her again tonight. He may have had a couple of very vivid dreams about kissing her, but he wasn't going to tell her that, nor was he going to try to make those dreams come true tonight.

He'd seen her around the farm every day this week, as usual, but she hadn't asked for a taco for lunch, and Boone had polished them all off that day for lunch. He wondered if he should stop by her office more regularly—outside of his normal job responsibilities—just to see her.

Probably, he told himself as Travis slowed the ATV.

"These goats," he said as the engine noise died into an idle. He got out of the side-by-side and surveyed the land beyond the fence. Poppy Harris owned the adjacent farm, and she too had a child she was raising alone. Matt had told Boone about her when he'd first moved in, because single parenting was hard work.

Steele, her son, was only ten, and he'd turned out to be a

pretty decent playmate for Gerty if Michael Hammond wasn't around. Of course, Gerty had cousins too, and she loved Keith and Britt and getting to spend more time with them.

On Tuesday night, when he'd picked up his daughter from Matt's, she hadn't said one word about where he'd been. Nothing about the cologne. No, she'd gone on and on about something Keith had said about barrel racing and how she couldn't wait to prove him wrong.

Boone could see so much of himself in Gerty, as well as so much of Nikki. Her mother had never let anyone get away with just saying something if it was wrong, and he'd simply been trying to coach Gerty for years to be as kind as she could be while still saying what was on her mind. The last thing he wanted to do was silence her. She already looked to outside sources for "girl things," and he wanted to be the one she came to when she needed something. He wanted to be the most involved person in her life.

He got out of the ATV too and said, "I can take them back to Poppy." That would get him off the farm for a half-hour, and when he came back, the therapy lessons would be winding down. Then he'd just need to check the horses and get them ready to go back in the stable. Travis had put out the pasture schedule, and they were rotating animals this weekend.

"I can do it," Travis said. "I know all these silly goats' names." He shook his head and called, "Laundry, don't eat that!" He vaulted the fence that marked the edge of the

Hammond Family Farm and scooped the goat into his arms with a definite "mmaa!" from the animal.

"Call me if you need me," Boone said as Travis dropped the goat on the other side of a second fence, one that Poppy had put in to try to keep her rogue goats from bothering the Hammonds. Or rather, from bothering Travis.

Boone suspected such a thing was impossible—both riling up Travis and keeping these goats on their side of the fence—but he chuckled to himself as he rounded the vehicle to get behind the wheel.

Back at the barns and stables, he took a moment to simply drink in all the activity there. Molly and Hunter Hammond had truly built something they should be very, very proud of. He and Gloria worked with eight therapy horses now, and they worked every other day. Four children on weekday afternoons came to the farm for exercises, therapy, and strength training. Pony Power had graduated seven children after they'd recovered from physical set-backs, and some of their clients had been coming since the day the facility had opened.

Molly had hired on four counselors, who worked with the same children each week. They worked five days a week, and they were required to understand and go through the equine therapy program before they could see a child.

As he stood there and watched a girl of ten years old work on saddling a horse with her trembling fingers, such a feeling of love, peace, and acceptance filled him. He loved this land. He loved that horse. He adored that little girl for her fighting spirit, for her tenacity in continuing to try even when she failed, for her parents who refused to give up on her.

"Hey," Molly said, stepping beside him. "I heard there were goats out again."

"Yep." Boone looked at her and smiled. She smelled like manure covered in flowers, and that wasn't a great combination. He said nothing about it though, because everyone on the farm carried some undesirable scents with them all the time, himself included. He actually liked that he didn't smell like ocean rain or cool water all the time. "Travis is taking care of it."

"He always does." Molly smiled out across the arena, where all of the children worked. "After this session, we'll rotate the horses."

"I saw the schedule," he said. Besides the equines who worked with children, the Hammonds had several horses simply to do their work around the farm. Matt had brought his personal horse too, and he and Gloria were making plans to buy another one. His brother had a nice place in town now, and it had a paddock for his horse. He'd opted to keep it out here so he could use it during the day, as Matt actually worked the farm, not inside the children's equine therapy unit.

"Is Gerty coming to help?"

"I bet she's already here," Boone said. "I haven't seen her. She was doin' something with Matt this afternoon, and then she had to check on her check from last week." At least he hoped she'd go talk to Cosette about that. She'd wanted him to do it, and Boone had refused. He'd told her she was thirteen years old now, and she could go talk to an adult like an adult.

"Send her over to me if you see her," Molly said. "I'm going to be down at the Gathering Spot."

"Yes, ma'am," he said as she walked away. The Gathering Spot was where the children went after their work with the horses. Then they had someone designated to walk them over to the counselor cabins. Gerty had been one of those walkers this summer, and she'd loved it.

Boone probably had something to do, but no one cracked a whip at him, so he leaned against the fence and watched the horses do their job. He'd been working with a particularly lively horse for a month now, and he wasn't in any hurry to get him therapy-ready. Sometimes it took a long time for an animal to settle into complete concentration, especially with a child.

The one in front of him—a gorgeous, deep brown horse named Lava Cake—never deviated from what she was supposed to be doing. Gloria had trained her, and the only person he'd ever met with more horse genes than him was his brother's wife.

"Hey," Matt said, and Boone turned toward his voice.

"Speak of the devil." Boone grinned and chuckled with his brother.

"You thinkin' about me?" Matt put one foot on the bottom rung of the fence and let his arms hang over the top one, just like Boone.

"Your wife," Boone said.

"Wow," Matt said, clear surprise in his voice. "I don't know what to do with that."

Boone tipped his head back and laughed. "Nothing, brother. I was just thinkin' about how she's better than me at training horses."

"It's because she lets them run free while she rollerblades," Matt said.

"Is that right?" Boone hadn't worn a pair of rollerblades in at least two decades. Probably longer. "Well, I can't do that."

"No one can," Matt said. "So..."

"Yes," Boone said, already knowing what his brother was going to say. "Okay? You don't need to say it out loud."

"You don't even know what I was gonna say."

"I do," Boone said, glancing to his left, where everyone walked to get past the paddocks and pastures. The barns and stables lined the other side of the walkway, and Boone didn't need to be overheard. "I told you, we're not advertising anything."

"You've been out with her once."

"And it was a big deal for both of us." Boone shot Matt a dirty look. "Can you just not?" He normally loved his older brother. Matt had always been the one safe place for Boone. The very solid rock that literally never cracked. When Nikki had died, Matt had been right there, and he'd stayed for days and weeks to make sure Boone had everything under control before he left.

"You haven't said two words about Tuesday," Matt said, his voice low. At least he was trying. "I just want two words."

"I just said it was a big deal."

"More than that. Did you have a good time?"

"Obviously," Boone said. "You're takin' Gerty home with you again tonight, aren't you?"

"Mm." Matt moved his foot to the ground. "I worry about you, Boone."

Boone faced him, trying to find the answers he needed in his brother's dark eyes. Everything about Matt was a couple of shades darker than Boone, including his personality. Boone loved to laugh and joke and he definitely took more of the spotlight from Matt at family functions. Here, and in Montana.

"Why's that?" he asked when he couldn't find anything in his brother's eyes.

"You've only been here a few months," Matt said. "I just worry that you might not be ready for another relationship."

Boone couldn't argue with him, especially after how the last one had ended. "Yeah, well, I worry about that too." He faced the arena again, and an airhorn sounded. "That's my cue." If he had any hope of arriving at Cosette's for dinner on time, he couldn't dawdle getting the horses cared for and moved where they needed to go.

"Mine too," Matt said. "We're switching everything up. I'm not sure what Travis is thinking."

"Travis is thinking that some of our horses have access to sweeter grass than others," Travis said as he walked by. "And we need to make it fair for everyone."

Boone grinned at the cowboy's back, meeting Cody's

eyes. The other cowboy laughed at their silent exchange, and Boone did too.

"I can hear you," Travis said.

"Did the goats get back home?" Boone called.

"He's gonna pour water in your bed," Matt said, and that only made Boone laugh harder.

"He will not," Boone said. "I'll lock my doors just to be safe."

"Do you actually know where the key is to your door?"

Boone shook his head, still grinning like a fool.

"That's what I thought," Matt said, giving him a playful shove. "You never lock up anything."

"I do too," Boone protested. "Remember when there were all those reports of wolves who could open doors in Montana? I locked my doors then."

"Oh, I remember," Matt said dryly, stepping past Boone. "You called me at midnight to read me the story out loud, and Janice was *so* mad."

"But you locked your doors," Boone said, going with him. "Right, brother?"

"I did," Matt admitted. "For maybe a night or two." He pointed to Lava Cake as if Boone couldn't see her. "There's your girlfriend, waitin' for you." He smiled at Boone. "When you pick Gerty up tonight, I want more than two words about the date."

"We'll see," Boone said, watching Travis enter the stable up ahead. "I'm not gettin' her until morning, remember? She and Britt are having a sleepover."

"So you'll come for breakfast and tell us all about it."

Boone nodded as if he really would, but he hadn't mentioned Cosette to Gerty yet. His brother started to walk away, and Boone spun toward him, leaving Lava Cake without a greeting. "Matt." He jogged toward him. "Listen, you can't tell Gerty about Cosette. I haven't, uh, told her yet."

His brother's eyebrows went up. "I thought you said she'd know after Tuesday night."

"I thought she would," Boone said. "But she didn't say anything, and I...didn't either."

Matt folded his arms and watched Boone for several moments past comfortable. "New deal then. You call me on your way home from Cosette's. I know she lives out in Mountain Glen, and that's a good thirty minutes for you. I get to know everything if I have to hide this from your daughter. And my kids."

Boone swallowed, because that was a steep deal. "Fine," he said, already working through solutions to this new problem. Perhaps his phone could mysteriously die.

"Fine." Matt turned and continued down the path. "Now get goin' so you're not late."

By the time Boone pulled up to Cosette's quaint little cottage at the end of the block, he was late. Not astronomically late, and he had texted her to let her know he was running behind. He took the steps up to the porch two at a time, and knocked loudly on the door before ringing the doorbell.

"It's open!" she called from inside, and Boone didn't hesitate to twist the knob and walk into her house.

"I'm so sorry," he said. "You'd have thought that farm was Grand Central Station this evening. People everywhere, and they all seemed to want to talk to me."

Cosette stood in the kitchen, a pair of tongs with bright blue handles in her hand. She wore a pair of shorts the color of driven snow and a blouse with plenty of pink and red flowers on it. Over that, she'd tied an apron around her waist that protected those shorts. It was black and said *medium rare or bust.*

His mouth watered at the sight of her. Or maybe that was the scent hanging in the air. Now that he'd slowed down, he realized he'd smelled something delicious outside too. "Are you grilling?" he asked.

"Yes, sir," she said, pointing with the tongs toward the back door. It slid open, and he could see her whole backyard through the glass. "I'm assuming you like steak?"

"Who doesn't like steak?"

"There are people who don't," she said.

"I don't believe it." He grinned at her, and while he told himself they both needed to go slow, she wasn't currently cooking. He walked right into the kitchen and right up to her. "You look amazing tonight, Cosette." He took her in his arms, glad she didn't flinch or blink or push him away. "Thanks for inviting me."

He leaned down and touched his cheek to hers, taking

another big breath of her goodness and purity. He then stepped back and smiled at her. "Anything I can do to help?" His stomach roared in that moment, loud enough for both of them to hear.

Embarrassed, he clapped his hand over his belt buckle. Cosette started to laugh, and she could wield tongs like a weapon. "Go sit. The food's almost ready."

Boone did what she said, because he didn't want to be teriyakied or glazed. He took in her dark gray countertops, noticing the bowl of salad there, as well as a pan of brownies.

"Cosette," he said, his mouth positively dripping now. "Did you make these?"

"Yes," she said just before she swept the square pan out of his reach. "And they're dessert, Boone." She slid the pan to the other end of the counter and gave him a look that said, *Touch these and die a slow death, Mister Whettstein.*

He blinked at her, at her strength, at her playfulness, at the way she'd somehow crawled into his heart already and made a place for herself. "Fine," he said, lifting his chin and going around the counter to the bar. "I don't even like chocolate."

Cosette burst out laughing again, this time shaking her head as she said, "You're such a liar."

Boone chuckled with her, and as they started to quiet, he said, "You know, some people eat dessert first. I've heard it tastes better if you're not stuffed full."

Cosette turned from the stove, that blue pair of tongs still gripped in her powerful fingers. "Is that what you want, Boone? Dessert first?"

Ten

COSETTE WAITED FOR BOONE TO ANSWER HER, BUT he just sat there, blinking. If she didn't pull the potatoes soon, the cheese would be fried on the sheet pan. Finally, he said, "Yes, Cosette. I'd love dessert first."

She should've been used to this man taking everything in her life and turning it upside down. For some reason, she still wasn't. "All right," she said. "We can have dessert first." She bent to open the oven and get the twice-baked potatoes out. "But the meat is going to be tough if we do that."

"You know what's amazing?" Boone asked, and Cosette could hear the tease in his tone.

"Do enlighten me," she said.

"A brownie-steak sandwich."

She turned toward him, pure horror running through her. Her taste buds rejected this flavor combination violently, even if the handsome cowboy sitting at her bar enticed her to do crazy things like eat dessert first. "No," she said, making an executive decision. "This is *my* house, and *my* meal, and I've grilled you an amazing medium-rare steak, and you are *not* sandwiching it between two brownies." She glared at him as she strode toward the door to go get the meat. She'd already put a plate out there and everything. It had been resting and should be perfect.

"Dessert first," she muttered as she left, just loud enough for him to hear. She hurried back to the counter and grabbed the pan of brownies. "I'm taking these with me."

Boone's loud laughter followed her outside, and Cosette delivered quite the juggling act by getting the steaks off the grill and onto the plate while holding the pan of brownies. She took everything back inside and laid it all out on the counter.

Memories flooded her mind, and she looked at Boone, who'd quieted while she'd retrieved their protein. "I have a couple of things I want to talk to you about tonight," she said.

"All right," he said easily. "Shoot."

She indicated the food in front of her. They stood on opposite sides of the bar, and the world narrowed to the meal she'd prepared and Boone. "My mother passed away when I was only twelve," she said. "This was her favorite meal. Raven and I would make it for her every summer, because her birthday was in July."

"That's amazing," Boone said, just as softly and just as seriously as Cosette had spoken. He came around the island and stepped to her side, his hand sliding carefully along her waist. "I'm sorry about your mom."

"She was a great mom."

"I'm sure she was." He picked up a plate and handed it to her. "How did she pass?"

"Car accident," she said. "She was a pedestrian, and she got hit." She looked at the white plate in her hand, so clean and pure. She switched her gaze to Boone. "Could we say grace? Would that be weird?"

"No," he said. "It wouldn't be weird." His hand, which had been reaching for the second plate she'd laid out on the countertop, moved to swipe his cowboy hat from his head. Tonight's was the color of fresh cream, more yellow than white, and Cosette liked how it matched his lighter features.

He smiled at her gently, and she liked that she could tell the different levels of Boone Whettstein already. "Do you want me to say it?"

"Would you?" Cosette asked, her insides feeling like they'd been encased in gelatin. Everything wobbled, especially with Boone standing so close to her.

He nodded and pressed his hat to his heart. His eyes drifted closed and he bowed his head. "Lord," he said in a clear voice. This man had obviously petitioned the Lord before. "We ask Thee for Thy blessing upon us here tonight." He paused, and Cosette liked that he let the silence into the house too. So much about Boone was so loud, and she liked knowing he had this side to him as well. "We're grateful for this food, and for the jobs that allow us to have it. We're grateful for family nearby who love us and help us when we need it."

He cleared his throat. "Please bless this food and the

hands that made it. Help Cosette to feel her worth and know of Thy love for her. Amen."

Cosette couldn't add her own "Amen," to the prayer, as dumbfounded as she was. She looked at Boone, who took long seconds to make sure his cowboy hat sat just right on his head. That was down low over his eyes. He finally couldn't stall any longer and asked, "Okay?"

She nodded, her emotions swirling and curling through her. She couldn't speak for fear she'd burst into tears.

"What is it?" he asked, his gentle side fully employed now.

"I haven't—" Her voice cracked, and she turned away from him. She mentally commanded herself to get control and stay strong.

"Hey, it's okay," he said, the warmth from his hand cascading down her arm as he moved it that way. His fingers took root between hers, and Cosette squeezed.

She found strength *in him*, and she had no idea why or what that meant. "I haven't had someone pray for me in a long time," she said.

"I'm sure that's not true," Boone said. "You have friends and neighbors. People at church. Your sister. Your daddy. They've all been prayin' for you."

"Not like that," she said, feeling the very thing Boone had prayed she would. God's love in her own life. For her. It was a wonderful gift he'd given her, and she turned back to him and offered him a weak, wobbly smile.

He reached up with his free hand and swiped his fingers under her left eye. "No cryin' tonight, okay? I can't be tellin'

Matt about how I made you cry." He smiled and released her hand. "This really looks amazing. I didn't know you could cook."

She drew in a breath, steadying herself. "A hidden talent." She picked up her plate again and started pinching salad onto it. "Any steak is fine, Boone. They're all the same."

"Yes, ma'am," he said, taking one and then using the same pair of tongs for a potato.

"After my dad retired from the military," Cosette said. "He started entering grilling contests. He taught both me and Raven about the finer points of meat and the most tender cuts. That kind of stuff."

Boone smiled, taking two potatoes. "That's great." He switched places with her, and she got her potato and steak while he put salad on his plate. "We're at the table?"

"Yes," she said. "Napkins and utensils are over there." She nodded to the eat-in-kitchen dining table, and Boone moved that way.

"I have soda or water," she said.

"Water's great," he said. "It was hot today, and I don't think I drank enough."

She got two bottles of water out of the fridge and took them to the table. She put one in front of him and sat down with her plate of food. He glanced at her and picked up his silverware. "Thanks, Cosette. This really is amazing."

"Surely you cook," she said, watching him slice through his meat with his steak knife.

"We get by," he said.

"Did your wife cook a lot?"

He looked at her, but she couldn't decipher his expression. "Sometimes," he said. "She worked some evenings, and since my mom...wasn't around much, Matt and I know how to cook."

Cosette nodded, not wanting to keep firing questions at him. "Have you taught Gerty to cook?"

"A little," he said. "She can make stuff like mac-and-cheese and frozen pizza." He indicated their full plates. "Nothing like this."

Cosette finally cut into her steak. "My mom loved to cook," she said. "She taught Raven and me as soon as we could stand on a stool and reach the counter."

Boone gave her a gorgeous smile, so much light streaming from him. She marveled at that, as he'd clearly been through some hard times in his life. A mom who wasn't around much, a wife who'd died early, and a broken relationship that had driven him out of his home state.

He'd been parenting his daughter alone for several years now. He didn't seem broken. He didn't hesitate to smile, nor did he seem averse to starting and maintaining a romantic relationship.

She dropped her eyes to her food and speared a bite of steak, then went for the end of her potato. She ate while Boone did, wondering if she'd killed the conversation.

"Was there something else you wanted to talk about?" he asked. "You said you had two things."

Cosette swallowed and reached for her water. "Yes. But I think we need dessert now." She got up and retrieved the pan of brownies, as well as a little serving spatula. She cut the brownies into only four pieces using the spatula and then dug under the edge of one.

"Whoa," Boone said, his face shining. "We need two plates."

Cosette looked at his plate, then hers, then the brownies. "You're right. Let's just eat them right out of the pan." That was what she usually did anyway, and she left the spatula stuck halfway under the brownie as she put the pan down. She picked up her fork and took the middle bite from all four brownies.

Boone watched her put the treat in her mouth, his eyes wide. "You just ate off all of them."

She smiled at him, the rich, dark chocolate in her mouth making everything happy inside her. "Yeah."

His eyebrows shot up. "That's all you have to say for yourself? Yeah?"

Cosette lifted one shoulder in a small shrug and went in for a second bite. "Yep." This time, she forked up a bite of brownie near the middle, but from only one square.

"You don't like the edge?" Boone asked, reaching for a bite. "It's the best part."

"Mm, I like the gooey middle," Cosette said as he stabbed through the harder outer edge.

He popped his bite into his mouth, and Cosette wasn't at all surprised to hear him groan in an exaggerated way. She giggled and ducked her head, so glad her hair had cooperated with her tonight. Everything about Boone seemed to cooperate with him, as he looked extra-amazing in a dark black shirt with tiny white boxes flecked across it.

They ate another few bites of brownie, and finally Cosette felt satiated enough to say, "So Gerty stopped by my office this afternoon."

Boone's gaze flew to hers. "Oh?"

"She was asking about her check and time card. We got it all worked out."

He grinned, his appetite back on real food as he cut into his twice-baked potato. "I'm glad. She was nervous about goin' to talk to you."

"She did seem so," Cosette said. "She told me to tell you if I saw you tonight at 'the party.'" She cocked her head and waited for him to explain. When he said nothing, she continued with, "I need to know what to say to her when she asks me things like that."

"What did you say?"

"I said I'd tell you she stopped by if I saw you."

"Oh, well, great," he said.

"I don't want to lie to her, Boone." Cosette spoke in a quiet voice, the shape and sound of his name in her mouth fitting perfectly.

"I know," he sighed out. "I don't want to either."

Cosette lifted her eyes from her salad to the man across the table from her. She could hardly believe he was here, or that she was there with him. "I don't see why she can't know you're dating someone. She doesn't have to know it's me until you're ready." Because he *was* fibbing to his daughter.

This wasn't a party, no matter how anyone sliced the situation.

"If I tell her that, I might as well tell her who."

"Then maybe you should." Cosette delivered the sentence evenly, refusing to look at Boone. The man would do what he wanted to do, she knew that. Most people did, despite what others said. She didn't want to be the one to boss him around, that was for sure, and she shook her hair over her shoulders and forced herself to perk up.

"All right," she said. "That's it. Those are the things I wanted to tell you or talk to you about tonight." She cut another bite of steak. "Your turn."

"My turn for what?"

"To talk."

He shook his head, his smile seemingly the easiest thing he produced. "*We're* talkin', Cosette. It's not one-sided."

"Don't you have anything to tell me or talk about?"

"Actually," he said, shifting in his chair. "I was wondering if you'd come help me pick out a tree for my cabin."

"A tree?"

"Yeah." He nodded, his countenance falling slightly. "My wife—Nikki—she had this pine tree in our house in Montana. She'd decorate it for different things, or sometimes it would just have lights on it. I think it would help Gerty remember her mama, and that's important to me."

"Boone," she said, her heartbeat vibrating like hummingbird wings. "Of course I will." She suddenly froze as he speared his last bite of steak and moved his fork toward the brownie pan. Surely he wouldn't. She'd made her opinion really clear about how steak didn't go with brownies.

His hand seemed to move in slow motion, and something like a yelping gasp came from her mouth as he dug a bite of brownie out of the pan. All she could see was that gooey brownie hanging onto the tines of his fork, with that perfectly pink square of steak above it.

Then he put the bite in his mouth, that now-annoying groan coming from his mouth. "Yeah," he said nice and loud. "That's *gooood.*"

His voice thawed her, and she said, "You're impossible."

"You're a great cook." He grinned at her, and Cosette had a vision of him coming home to her in this house every evening. She'd wear her grilling championship apron and make dinner for him and Gerty, and they'd talk about the farm, horses, school, homework, and other mundane things, the way husbands and wives and families did.

Cosette wanted that life, with a pine tree to remind them all of Gerty's mother and Boone's first wife.

She'd wanted it when she'd met and married Joel, and after everything in that relationship had turned sour, she'd thought she'd never have another chance at that type of happiness. As she sat with Boone and they talked, Cosette's world shifted.

God had given her a second chance. He'd provided a way for her to heal and grow and discover who she truly was. In a lull in the conversation, both of their dinners long gone, she said, "So I'll come with you to get a pine tree for your cabin.

Then...there's a pumpkin festival next month. I've never been. Would you take me?"

"Sure," Boone said without even asking when it was. "You've never been?"

She shook her head, realizing she still had so many things to tell him. "Raven runs the used car dealership in Ivory Peaks," she said. "My father lives in the suburbs of Denver. I needed...something a little quieter, so I moved here."

"Yeah, you said you've been here for a long time," he said, clearly fishing for more information as to why she hadn't been to a small-town festival in all the years she'd lived in Mountain Glen.

She got up and collected her plate and then his. "Do you want to go for a walk?"

"Yep."

She put their dishes in the sink and returned to him. He took both of her hands in his, and Cosette fought the urge to pull away. After the initial moment, the one where her brain shrieked at her to flee, she relaxed into the touch. "After I managed to get away from my ex-husband, I didn't go out much," she said. "Or ever. I needed a place of refuge, and that was my house. I barely left, even to get groceries."

Boone held very still, just as he had on Taco Tuesday. "Managed to get away?"

"A story for another time," she said, almost absently. She drew in a deep breath, clearing the cobwebs from her mind. "I'd love to go to the pumpkin festival. I know there's a flyer about it hanging in the grocer. Maybe we can walk by there and get all the details."

"Sounds good to me," Boone said, adding, "And we can get ice cream there too. There's nothing better than brownies, unless it's ice cream and brownies together."

She smiled with him, because he really was like a big little boy, and he brought such joy to her with the simplest of things—like ice cream and pumpkins and pine trees.

Eleven

"I don't care if you have until the tenth," Boone said, reaching for the file for the hoof he needed to shape. He couldn't reach it, and he waved his fingers at his daughter for her to hand it to him. "You're re-taking that math test tomorrow."

"Daddy," Gerty started, putting the tool he needed in his palm.

"Don't *Daddy* me," Boone said, rifling the file along the bottom of the hoof. "There's somethin' wrong with this frog." He straightened, his lower back pinching slightly. "You can't fail a test and then just do extra credit to try to make it up."

"I don't get fractions," she said.

"Then you get out your books at night and let me help you." He glared at his thirteen-year-old, who hadn't even told him she had a test. He asked her every evening about her schoolwork, and he couldn't have her lying to him. "I ask you every day about your stuff. You said you didn't have anything."

"I got all my homework done and turned in," she said.

"Then why'd you fail the test?" He met her eye, but she looked away really quickly. That wasn't good. Boone hadn't been around a ton of teens, but he knew when someone was lying to him.

"You can't come work over here if you're not going to get good grades," he said, turning away from her.

"Daddy, don't do that."

"I just said not to Daddy me," he said through clenched teeth. He walked over to the window and looked out into the blue sky. Mother Nature had been sending winds in the afternoon, which foretold of the autumn weather coming.

"I love working here," Gerty said from behind him, her voice smaller and without any attitude.

"Then you better get your math grade up," he said. "You're going to go talk to Mrs. Gyllenskogg in the morning and you're going to ask her how you can retake that test." He turned back to face his daughter. She stood next to the horse, one hand on his neck while she studied the ground.

"Yes, sir," she said.

"And if you don't get your grade up, you're gonna have to talk to Molly about why you can't work here."

Gerty looked up, obviously mortified. Boone saw so much of Nikki in his daughter's eyes, and his heart sang painfully at him.

"She said she'd go talk to her teacher."

He swung his attention to the doorway, finding Cosette

standing there. She wore fire in her eyes, and as his slipped down her body, he found her fingers in fists. Confusion riddled through him, and he kept his mouth closed.

Cosette moved toward Gerty, who looked at her with the same surprise on her face that Boone felt coursing through him. "Are you okay?"

He frowned and actually shook his head. Of course Gerty was okay. They'd just been having a conversation. He hadn't liked it, no, but his daughter was fine.

She nodded, her blonde braid pulling against the front of her shirt. Cosette reached for her and said something Boone didn't catch. The two of them went toward the hall Cosette had come down, and she glanced over to him at the last second. "She'll be right back."

They disappeared, and Boone had no idea what had just happened. "She'll be right back? Where is she going?" he wondered. He walked back over to the horse, who'd simply waited for him to finish the shoeing. He too ran his hand down the animal's neck, taking comfort from him the way Boone had many times over the years.

After Nikki's death, the first one he'd told besides Gerty, Matt, and his father had been his old horse named Ironsides. The horse hadn't lived much longer than Nikki had, and Boone barely remembered most of the next year.

"I don't know about this shoe," he said to Earl Gray. "I've got a leather pad for you, but I'm not gonna put any padding in it, okay?" Sometimes if he tried to do that, it put too much pressure on the already-weak frog, and then Earl Gray would be in even more pain when he walked.

He got to work trimming the leather to fit the shape of Earl's hoof, and he'd put that in place and had the horse mostly shod when Gloria asked, "How's it going, Boone?"

Boone didn't look up from the job in front of him. He'd been teaching Gerty how to take care of a lame horse, diagnose problems, and come up with solutions before he'd heard about the math test. His daughter had been gone for at least ten minutes, and she'd missed a crucial part of the lesson.

But Gloria hadn't inquired about his personal life.

"He's definitely going to be better with these shoes," Boone said. "But there is something goin' on with this frog on this side."

"I can have Brady look at him next time he comes around."

"I would." Boone pounded in the last nail and dropped Earl's leg. "He's still got some spring in him, I would say." He looked at his brother's wife, and he could see how perfect they were for each other without Matt even there. Some of his tension drained away, and he managed a smile for Gloria. "How'd the auction go?" She and Matt had gone to a rescue horse auction in Broomfield, a decent drive from Ivory Peaks. Almost an hour and a half one-way if Boone remembered right.

"Matt's unloading the horses now," Gloria said. "He sent me to get you, because we got a couple of skittish ones."

Boone looked at Earl and then Gloria, tired way down in his bones. And Gerty still hadn't returned. "All right."

"Cheer up, Boone. He thinks you're better than me,"

Gloria said with a grin. She turned to leave right as Gerty and Cosette came back into the big room where Boone had been working.

"He's done," Boone said, his voice turning harder without him meaning to. "Take him back to the pasture, Gerty." He watched his daughter as she approached, dumbstruck. "Have you been cryin'?"

"No," she said, ducking her head further from him.

"Yes, you have," he said, not really tactful in situations like this. Gloria had stalled near Cosette, and Boone whiplashed his attention between them and his daughter. He turned his back on the women and took a deep breath. "Gerty," he said in a much softer, calmer voice. "What's goin' on?"

She bent to get the reins, and as she straightened, she burst into tears. Boone didn't hesitate to wrap her up in his arms and hold on tight. "Hey, shh," he said, the way he had when she'd cried as a child. She was still a child, and Boone needed to remember that. "It's okay." He murmured reassurances that everything was fine; he wasn't mad at her; they could still have popcorn for dinner.

Gerty didn't cry too often, though there had been a spell in fifth grade where he'd thought she'd never *stop* crying. But once she'd made it past that, she'd been mature and actually fun for Boone to talk to.

She stepped back and wiped her eyes. "I'll take him out to the pasture."

"Uncle Matt needs my help for a bit," Boone said. "But

when I get home, we'll make the popcorn and put on that Korean drama you like."

Gerty nodded, still sniffling, and she led Earl Gray out the big door instead of back the way she'd come with Cosette. Boone had no choice but to face her and Gloria, and he found it hard to breathe as he did. Someone had definitely encased his chest in cement, and he couldn't crack it with just the expansion of his lungs.

Cosette wore sympathy on her face, with a dangerous edge underneath. Gloria looked from her to Boone. "I'll tell Matt you'll be a minute. They'll be fine in the trailer."

"Thanks, Gloria," Boone said. His stomach pinched and complained for food, and he couldn't wait to get home and collapse on the couch with a giant bowl of cheesy popcorn in both hands.

Gloria left, and Boone stayed right where he was. "What did I do wrong?" he asked, because he clearly had done something.

Cosette folded her arms across her chest, really hugging herself tight. "You seemed really upset with Gerty."

"I was," Boone said, frowning. "So what? She failed her math test, hid it from me, and then tried to tell me it didn't matter."

"She got the point."

"Did she?" Boone asked. "How would you know anyway, Cosette? I think I know her better than you do."

Her eyes widened, and Boone sighed. "Listen," he said. "I know Gerty and how much she can take. We have *rules* in our family, and one of them is she has to get good grades to work here at the farm. She lied to me, Cosette, and if I don't get after her, she'll keep doing it."

"Michael posted a picture of him and another girl at a dance," Cosette said. "She'd had enough, and you couldn't see it."

Boone took a step toward Cosette, his mind flying in a dozen directions. "I—"

"I didn't know you had a temper."

He paused, his thoughts scattering—all save one. "I *don't* have a temper. I was talking to my daughter in a normal, controlled voice. I was frustrated, sure, but she lied to me, and that's not how we do things with each other." His stomach squeezed, and his lungs tightened. "Me and her, we're all the other has. We *don't* lie to each other." He gestured toward the big door where she'd led Earl Gray outside. "That doesn't mean I have a temper. It means I was being her *father* and not her friend."

Cosette stared at him, blinking every few seconds.

"And you interrupted me in teaching her how to take care of a horse who has an injured frog," he said. "She missed the last part of the lesson."

"Boone." Cosette came toward him, but he wasn't in the mood to talk to her. He had to clean up in here and then go help his brother. He shoved his farrier tools in the leather bag, freezing when Cosette put her delicate hand on his forearm.

He looked first at it and then into her eyes. "I'm sorry," she said. "I could tell from a distance how upset Gerty was, and you didn't seem to see it. She broke down in my office when she showed me Michael's social media, and well, maybe I misjudged your temper."

"Maybe," he said softly, thinking that word could go toward any number of things right now. "I thought she was upset because she'd been caught."

"She was," Cosette said simply. "She loves you to the very core, Boone, and she doesn't want to disappoint you."

His eyebrows went up. "She told you that?"

"More or less." Cosette removed her hand from his arm, and he wanted to grab onto her and keep her close. Instead, he let her wander over to the big open door. "She's a good girl."

"I know she is." Boone resumed his clean-up. "She still can't lie to me."

"No," Cosette said. "I agree that she can't." She turned back. "Just...go easy on her tonight."

"I will," Boone said. "We're havin' popcorn for dinner, and I just told her she could put on her Korean dramas." He cocked one eyebrow at Cosette, whose face softened as she smiled. "Have you seen those? They're awful. So I'm really sacrificing."

"Yeah," Cosette said dryly. "I'm sure. You'll probably be asleep within ten minutes of eating—what was it? Popcorn?"

"Popcorn is a meal," Boone said, grinning at this beautiful woman in his life.

She giggled and shook her head no. "I don't think so."

"It is," he insisted. "Number one, it's a whole grain, so no one can accuse me of not thinking about my daughter's health. Number two, we put this cheese powder on it. That's dairy *and* protein."

Cosette folded her arms again, cocking one hip and keeping that smile on her face. "Cheese powder? Is that even real food?"

"Real food," Boone said, lunging toward her. He grabbed her as she squealed, and they laughed together as he swung her around. "It's real food," he said, almost yelling the words. He set her on her feet, so much joy and happiness streaming between the two of them. He looked down into her eyes, then his drifted south to her lips.

Oh, boy, he thought. He leaned closer, his heartbeat suddenly riding on a jackhammer. Cosette steadied herself in his arms, her hands sliding up his chest. Sparks ignited with the heat of her touch, and Boone let his eyes drift closed the closer he got to Cosette.

"Daddy?"

He jumped right out of his skin as his eyes shot open. He spun toward Gerty's voice, practically shoving Cosette behind him, as if his daughter wouldn't be able to see her that way. "Heya, baby," he said. "You got Earl put away already?"

"Yes," she said, something glinting in those blue eyes. "Uncle Matt needs you." She flicked a glance at Cosette, turned, and walked away.

Relief sagged through Boone, but his evening of relaxation, cheesy popcorn, and a nap before bedtime evaporated right before his eyes.

"You better go," Cosette said quietly. "And you better

get prepared to tell her something over your popcorn dinner."

Boone turned to get his tools, saying, "Yeah, you're right." When he turned back to her, she wore hope in her eyes.

"This is good," she said. "Then you won't have to fib to her about our date this weekend. She could even come. She might like the pumpkin patch."

Boone didn't know how to answer. He didn't want to bring his thirteen-year-old on a date with him. Not if there was any chance of kissing, and judging by the moment Gerty had just interrupted, there might be. "I'll talk to her," he said, making no promises.

He moved toward her and paused right at her side, him facing the exit and Cosette still facing the back of the barn. "Thank you for helping her this afternoon," he said. "I'm not good with the boy-thing."

"Sure," Cosette said.

He leaned down and touched his mouth to Cosette's cheek, and she pressed right into his lips, cementing their connection. "I'll call you later tonight," he whispered. "Have fun with your choir practice."

She barely nodded, and Boone headed for the exit, his phone ringing in his back pocket. He ignored it, because he knew who it would be. Matt.

"There you are," his brother griped only a few paces away from the barn, lowering his phone from his ear. "I've got two squirrelly and nervous rescues here, and I need you."

"Here I am," Boone said, refusing to look back to the

barn. The walk to where Matt and Gloria had parked the trailer wouldn't take long, and Boone slowed his steps. "Matt." His nerves fired at him, but he wasn't sure why. Matt knew he'd been going out with Cosette. "How did you tell your kids about you and Gloria?"

Matt studied him while they walked a pace or two. "I just asked them if they liked her," he said. "Then I said I did too, and we were going out."

Boone nodded, his jaw tightening as his teeth pressed together. "I think Gerty saw me almost kiss Cosette just now. I'm gonna have to tell her something."

"Yep," Matt said with a sigh. He faced the horse trailer too, just as it shook and a nervous whinny filled the air. "I'd go with the truth, Boone. Everyone just wants the truth."

"Amen, brother." Boone handed his tools to Matt and jogged toward the trailer where Gloria, Travis, Cody, and Mission all stood at the ready. "Ready, boys?" He didn't wait for them to affirm before he opened the back of the trailer and stepped into the space, filling it with his presence so the horses would know he wasn't going to let anything bad happen to them.

"Hey, hey," he said in a soothing, soft voice. Gloria joined him, because she was excellent with horses too. "Sh, sh, sh, ch, ch, ch." Boone made the noise with his mouth as he brought the first horse out. "There you go."

He ran a hand along the horse's back, finding flea bites and matted hair. "She needs a bath," he said. "Ointment and bandages, probably." The horse's ribs could be counted, and a fury Boone couldn't understand built beneath his breastbone.

"Go with Travis," Matt said. "Help him keep her calm."

"What's her name?" Boone asked, keeping one big hand on the horse's neck, calming her and reminding her she wouldn't be abused anymore.

"Jambalaya," Matt said.

"Oh, we're changin' that," Boone said as he walked with the horse. "Come on now, Ruby Rose. You come with me, and let's get you cleaned up."

BY THE TIME BOONE ARRIVED AT HIS CABIN, HE WAS soaking wet, chilled, and starving. The scent of various foods filled the lane in front of the cabins, as he wasn't the only one who lived out here. Yellow lights shone in his front windows, and as he climbed the front steps, he saw Gerty check through the window.

She opened the door before he arrived, and Boone smiled at her. "Howdy, bumblebee." He drew her into a hug and lifted her right up off her feet. "I'm sorry if I was on your case too hard this afternoon."

"You weren't, Daddy," she said, clinging to him with her arms and legs. "Did Cosette tell you about Michael?"

"Yes."

Gerty didn't say anything else, and Boone figured now was as good of a time as any to tell her about Cosette. "Did you see me and Cosette?"

"Yes," she said.

"I've been goin' out with her," he whispered. "I like her. She seems to like me."

Gerty wiggled and he set her down. She looked up at him, so much innocence and understanding in her face. "Why didn't you tell me?"

He sighed as he indicated she should go on inside. He didn't want to have this conversation on the porch. Once the front door closed behind him, he said, "I don't want you to get hurt again, Gerty. You're my top priority, and I don't know." He hung his cowboy hat on the rack by the front door. "I just want to know me and Cosette are going to work before you get involved. I know you miss Karley, and I know it's my fault we both got burned in Montana. I'm not going to put you through that again."

Gerty went into the kitchen and picked up the bag of popcorn she'd obviously gotten out already. "I don't miss Karley anymore," she said. "Gloria is here, and Miss Molly, and Elise." She looked up at him. "I like them, and they take me shopping and stuff the way Karley did."

Boone nodded as he ran his hands through his hair. "All right." He hated that he couldn't provide everything for his daughter, but he wasn't a woman. He didn't understand his daughter in a lot of the same ways he hadn't understood his wife. Nikki had taught him a lot about how she thought, but Boone hadn't had the blessing of his wife's tutelage for many years now. "I need us to talk to each other," he said. "Always. Hard things. Easy things. Good things. Bad things. Okay?"

Gerty nodded as she turned to put the popcorn in the microwave. "Okay."

"So tell me about Mike." Boone pulled out the barstool and sat on it, groaning as he did.

Gerty's shoulders slumped, and she kept her back to him. "I liked him, Dad."

"I know you did."

"I thought he liked me."

"I'm sure he did."

Gerty turned to face him. "You think so?"

"Gerty, let me tell you a little something about boys," Boone said, wishing with all the power of his soul that Nikki was here to do this. Maybe he could get Gloria or Molly to talk to Gerty.

But she held up her hand. "You don't have to, Daddy. Cosette told me."

His eyebrows shot up. "She did? What did she say?"

"She said boys are so dumb sometimes, and they really just want to hold a girl's hand and kiss them, and it doesn't matter if it's me or Emmalyn in Coral Canyon."

Boone blinked, not sure how to respond. "I mean...at Michael's age, probably," he said.

"What about you?" She cocked her left eyebrow the way he did sometimes. "I saw you with Cosette. You were going to kiss her."

Boone coughed and cleared his throat. "I mean, maybe."

"No maybe, Daddy. You were."

"Yeah, but I wasn't going out with someone else last week," he said. "And kissing them. It's totally different."

"I never kissed Michael," Gerty said.

She had told him that several times, and Boone believed her. "A teenage boy is kind of dumb," he admitted. "They have a lot of hormones and pretty girls like you intrigue them."

Gerty scoffed. "I'm not pretty."

"Yes, you are." Boone got up as the microwave beeped. "You look just like your mother, and she was gorgeous." He beamed down at Gerty. "Are you okay if I go out with Cosette? Really okay?"

Gerty looked into his eyes, searching for several seconds. "I think so," she said. "I just want you to be happy, Daddy. Mama wanted you to be happy too."

Boone's heart smashed itself into a tiny box. "I know." He was trying, and he said as much.

"Yeah, that's why you're going out with Cosette," Gerty said. "She's your third try, and you're going to get it right this time, Daddy. I just know it."

His third try. Boone hadn't thought of it like that, but he supposed Gerty was right.

"I don't want to be left out," Gerty said. "If you and Cosette do end up married or something, I don't want to be a stranger to her."

"So you want to tag along while we hold hands and flirt with each other?" he teased, knowing Gerty would blush and bark the word no at him.

She did exactly that, and Boone laughed as he mixed up the butter and cheese powder, then poured it over their popcorn. He tossed and stirred, split the popcorn in half, and handed Gerty her dinner. "I won't leave you out," he promised. "You're my number one priority."

"Mm hm," Gerty said, her mouth already full of popcorn. She went over to the couch and flipped on the TV. "When are you going out with her again?"

Twelve

TRAVIS THATCHER FLIPPED UP THE COLLAR ON HIS jacket so the wind couldn't whip down his back and chill him from the inside out. Ivory Peaks was going through a freak cold spell right now, and that brought a frown to his face.

He kept a garden behind the row of cabins on the lane behind the homestead, and this cold snap wouldn't be good for his squashes. The pumpkins, watermelons, butternuts, and eggplants would be squishy and soft, burned by the frost when it came and then baked by the sun when it returned.

All of his hard work across months this past summer would be ruined. He'd managed to get a few rows of his veggies covered, but with everything he had to do around the farm, he couldn't spend hours covering everything to try to save it from Jack Frost.

He also couldn't just do nothing, so he stood back and watched the morning wind try to rip off the plastic he'd just put over his bell peppers and eggplants. The squashes were too big to try to cover, and he'd left his beets, as they weathered cold spells fairly well.

Travis turned away from the garden as the sun brightened the day. With the plot of land he planted on the east side of the cabins, it got the best light and heat of the day, and avoided the scorching hot afternoons in July and August.

September had arrived in Ivory Peaks, and the tallest mountains to the west had snow on them already. He hoped it would melt in the next few days as the weather warmed again, but he'd lived in Colorado long enough to know it sometimes didn't.

It could snow in September or October, as well as all the way into May and June. Freak storms swept through the Rocky Mountains, dumping feet of snow in a single day and fouling up roads, schools, and Travis's mood.

He longed for a job on a ranch in California, but he'd never leave the Denver area again. His mother lived here, and she needed his help. He had a couple of half-sisters, but they'd both gotten married within the past couple of years, and Roberta lived in Albuquerque now, and Vivian was about to move to Pennsylvania for her husband to finish dental school.

They were both a decade younger than him, and the care of his mother had always fallen on his shoulders. He honestly didn't mind, because his mom was a great cook, sharp as a tack, and didn't bug him about getting married.

Besides, he'd tried that once in the city, and he much

preferred the country life. Most of the time. If he didn't let his loneliness creep up on him and cripple him. He tried to make sure he spoke to as many adults as possible during the day, because he lived alone right now—and had for a good, long while.

There weren't that many cowboys working at the Hammond Family Farm, and right now, Mission and Cody shared a cabin, Boone and his daughter lived in the one on the end, and Gloria's sat empty. She'd moved into town when she'd married Matt, and Travis wondered what it would be like to come home to someone at night.

He'd been divorced for a decade, but his bank account reminded him of his life in the city. He'd once been an investment banker, and gardening reminded him a lot of playing the stock market. *Always a risk*, he thought.

He got behind the wheel of his truck to get on over to the commercial side of the farm. Molly Hammond ran Pony Power from the row of barns and stables that lined the front pasture, which separated the homestead from that part of the farm. Gray Hammond had a family barn and livestock behind the homestead, and then the row of cowboy cabins before the fields took over.

Travis acted as Matt's second around the farm, which meant he had to check in with him to find out what the priorities were for the day. He did all of the rotations for the horses for both the farm and the equine therapy unit, and he scheduled the fields to be turned over too.

Right now, their focus was on harvesting and fence fixing, both chores Travis didn't particularly like but he didn't particularly hate them either. He'd been in a tractor all day yesterday, buffeted by the wind as he tried to mow the final cut of the hay the proper way, so he expected to be on fences today.

Sure enough, when he arrived in the back barn where everyone came to greet Matt for the day, he received a clipboard with a map of the farm attached to it. "The red section needs to be checked and cleared today," Matt said while Travis studied his map. "I'm putting you with Hunter."

"Hunter's working out here today?" Travis looked up, genuinely surprised.

"Said he'll be here by ten," Matt said.

Which was three hours away.

"So you'll need to take a walkie until he gets here," Matt said, moving over to Mission and handing him the keys to the tractor. "Cody, you're with me on horse care this morning, and then we'll get the cattle fed this afternoon."

"Yes, sir," Cody said, one of the more agreeable cowboys Travis had ever met. He looked back at his clipboard, unsurprised to be working alone. He'd been working at this ranch for the past five years, after a five-year job at one a bit further north in Golden. Matt and Gray both trusted him, and he'd take the walkie even though he didn't need it.

He studied the map for a minute or so, then tucked it under his arm so he could go get his horse saddled. Hunter would probably come out on an ATV, but Travis didn't want to deal with the guttural growl of the engine this morning.

Once he had a pretty bay horse named Peppermint Tea saddled, he set out for the northeast section of the ranch. Clearing it meant he'd have to check all of the fences. All the water lines. All the fields to make sure they hadn't left equipment, tools, or fencing materials out there. Matt wanted the farm cleared so they were ready for winter and could focus on bringing in the harvest. Travis had worked enough farms and ranches in Colorado conditions to know that things had to be checked and re-checked.

He kept his gloves on and his head down as he walked the field. He held the reins for Peppermint as they trod along the fence line. Nothing seemed amiss.

Then Travis heard the bleating of a goat. "No," came out of his mouth without him able to censor it. He looked back the way he'd come and saw nothing. He turned and surveyed the fence in front of him. Nothing.

Maybe he'd imagined it. He'd been out here far too many times to rescue Poppy Harris's goldarn goats. Every time he took them back, she apologized and said she'd keep them contained. Travis had stopped believing her after the third time.

Her goats were a rambunctious bunch, but he seemed to be some sort of goat Pied Piper, because they'd follow him back to her pens and barns and right on inside them. He'd latch them inside and then go tell her he'd done so. He honestly wasn't sure why she kept letting them out.

Another "maaa" filled the air, and Travis spun around. Sure enough, a gray goat stood about fifty feet away, on the wrong side of the fence. His distress call had alerted all of his hoofed buddies, and as Travis stood there and watched, caprine after caprine either jumped the fence or squeezed their billy goat gruff bodies underneath it to join Graybeard.

"No," Travis said again, striding toward them. He waved his arms above his head. "Not today, Satan!" He was already going to lose his melons and squashes. Did the Lord really have to send a herd of goats to torment him?

Several of the animals maa'ed and baa'ed at him, not really caring as he stomped closer to them, yelling at them to get back on their side of the fence. He looked over the two fences marking the property line between Harris Farms and the Hammond Family Farm. Perhaps Poppy was walking her goats today, and these...eleven had gotten away from her.

Travis held no real hope of spotting the woman. With the wind and the threat of rain, she wouldn't be out gallivanting around. He shouldn't be either, but as one baby goat bumped into him, he couldn't very well leave the animals out here.

"Fine," he said grumpily. "Come on, you silly things." He went back to his horse and swung into the saddle. He yipped and hollered at the goats, which was obviously some sort of formal bearded mammal language, because all of the trespassers started to follow him.

He went to the road to get past the fences, and then he clip-clopped down the lane to Harris Farms. He didn't see any movement near the picturesque farmhouse where Poppy lived with her son. Steele should be at school, as Elise and Poppy and Boone shared responsibility for carpooling. Her minivan sat in the driveway, but Travis didn't take the goats in that direction.

He knew right where to put them, and perhaps he could simply corral them back in their pen and skedaddle back to his side of the fence without talking to Poppy. She obviously didn't know her goats were out, and he didn't need to make her feel bad about it.

"Go on," he told them once they'd reached the pen where they were supposed to be. The gate swung open in the breeze, and he jumped down from his horse to hold it for the animals. "Get back in here, you fools. All of your food and water is here."

Why animals had to flee from their safety and security was beyond him. But they all did. A small break in the fence, and cows, chickens, goats, sheep, and horses could practically taste the freedom.

The last goat—a stubborn cream-colored nanny goat—finally waltzed into the pen, unconcerned about his continual yelling and yipping, and he swung the gate closed. He latched it, noting that it did that just fine. These goats weren't getting out on their own, unless one of them had grown an opposable thumb somehow.

He glared at them as if that might actually be true, his mood growing worse by the moment. Thunder cracked through the sky above, and Travis looked up. "No," he moaned.

The sky opened in the next moment, and he ran for Peppermint. He towed her toward the nearest barn, hoping the two of them could just stay there while the clouds emptied the worst of their rain.

He burst into the barn, the wind catching the door and flinging it against the wall. It sounded like thunder all over again, and Travis's pulse ran in a frenzied circle in his chest. He panted as the noise settled into driving rain against the roof.

"Great," he yelled. "Now I'm stuck over here." A drop of rain hit his hand. He looked up, sure he was living inside a nightmare. "In a barn with a leaking roof." He let his chin sag toward his chest as he shook his head. "What else can go wrong?"

In the rainy silence that followed his voice, he distinctly heard something. He looked up, searching for the source of the...breathing. "Hello?" he called. "Poppy?"

She stepped out from behind the corner of the wall that led down an aisle where she might keep horses. His irritation with the pretty strawberry blonde spiked. "Did you know your goats were out again?" He threw his hand up toward the roof. "And that this thing leaks?"

He might as well have blamed her for sending the downpour too.

Poppy simply gazed at him in one moment, her blue heeler appearing at her side, and in the next, she burst into tears.

Travis immediately backtracked, his insides icing over. "Poppy, I mean...." He didn't know how to finish that sentence.

She didn't turn away from him, and as her sobs

increased, Travis couldn't just stand there and do nothing. He hurried toward her and took the woman into his arms. "I'm sorry," he said. "I was just frustrated."

"Not...you...." she said, gasping for air. The dog at their feet whined, but she didn't even flinch toward him. "I'm fine."

She so wasn't fine, and Travis wasn't going to let her go until she calmed further. He caught the scent of apple-cinnamon in her hair, and for some reason, he reached up and stroked his hand down the back of her head. "It's okay," he said as gently as he could. "Whatever it is, it'll be okay."

How he could promise that, he wasn't sure. He simply didn't want her to hurt. Something told him not to say anything else, so he kept his mouth closed while he held Poppy tightly.

Thirteen

POPPY HARRIS TOLD HERSELF TO STOP CRYING. Over and over she told herself. Only when the storm had blown through her soul was she able to take a steadying breath and not sob it all out. She'd sniffle for a good long while, as that was how she operated.

Whatever it is, it's going to be okay.

No, it wasn't. The words screamed through her head, no matter how she tried to silence them. Another thread started about how warm Travis Thatcher made her. How strong he was. How good he smelled.

She honestly didn't know how her brain had room for all the thoughts inside it. She couldn't even keep up with what she had going on in her life, and she thought she could handle a boyfriend?

No.

Not only that, but Travis obviously didn't like her. He'd been cordial and kind when returning her goats in the past, but today, he'd been different. Heaven knew everyone had bad days, and Poppy herself knew that so, so well.

Better than she'd like for sure.

We'll have to foreclose, ma'am, if we don't get the payment by the end of the month.

A new kind of scream gathered in her soul, the same as it had in the house. She'd escaped to the open air, the farm, and the barns she loved so much, because she'd always been able to think out here.

If she lost this farm, she had no idea what she'd do. Where would she go? Where would she and Steele live? How could she afford another farm?

She couldn't, but she also couldn't stand the thought of getting rid of her animals or selling them to someone else.

Maybe Travis.

She stepped out of his arms, feeling calmer and quieter now. Her thoughts were made of insanity, and she didn't dare look at the handsome cowboy who lived next door. She'd met him plenty of times, and she'd never felt this spark of attraction before. Perhaps her embarrassment had always kept it at bay.

She'd literally just broken down into an emotional wreck right in front of him. *Can't get much more embarrassing than that,* she thought.

"Do you know how the goats keep getting out?" he asked.

Fire flew through her veins. "I have no idea," she said. In the past, she'd thanked him for bringing them back, but today, she couldn't force herself to do it.

Travis blinked and fell back a step, which was probably for the best. Poppy wasn't sure what showed on her face, but she'd always been terrible at hiding how she really felt.

"Do you...need anything?" he asked.

Poppy burst out laughing, the sound high and cruel and so not-funny. "Yes," she said, her smile disappearing as quickly as the maniacal laughter did. "I do need some help with a great many things." She indicated the still-dripping roof. "My barn is in disrepair to the point that the roof leaks. It's been doing that for a while, so the hay up in the loft? All moldy."

She turned as if she could see it through solid wood walls. "Can't use it. Can't sell it. It's just a whole ton of work to get rid of it. And it's not even free to do that. But that hardly matters, because I'm broke. So broke that I'm going to lose this place, then it'll just be the next owner's problem."

She took a deep breath and ignored Travis as he opened his mouth to say something. "They'll get a leaking barn, rotten hay, naughty goats, and a farmhouse that needs to be gutted and redone. Sounds like a real bargain, huh?"

Poppy turned in a full circle, nearly tripping over Cotton, the blue heeler who always stuck close to her. When she was upset, Cotton usually climbed right on top of her. "I'm honestly not sure why the bank cares if I pay the mortgage. This place is a wreck. It should be condemned. No one would *dare* live here, let alone *pay* to live here."

She sucked at the air, finding it cold and damp. Travis

stood there, his eyes wide, his pulse beating steadily in the vein in his neck.

She needed to get out of this barn, now. "Thanks for bringing the goats back. Maybe I can sell them and stay in my house for one more month." She brushed past him and his expensive horse—selling that animal would for-sure allow her to stay in her house and on her farm, probably for several months—and stepped out into the rain.

Poppy couldn't even feel it as it pelted her skin. She walked through the mud, wishing she could dodge the wind, until she made it to the back lawn. By the time she reached the deck, the mud had been wiped and washed from her boots.

Inside the house, she slammed the wind and weather out, her chest heaving. She pressed her back into the closed door and slid to the floor, another wave of emotion overcoming her.

Cotton whined and climbed onto her lap, and the wet, soggy dog licked her face. She usually hated that, but today, she simply let him.

This farm and this house were all she knew. She'd been here for the past thirteen years, first arriving with her boyfriend, Eli.

He'd had a job in the city, and Poppy had happily cleaned up the run-down farm. She had a degree in horticulture, and she adored working outside. Within a year, she and Eli had bought a couple of horses, then some milk cows, a coop full of chickens, and a whole herd of goats.

All she had left at this point was the run-down farmhouse, three horses, an unruly donkey, a handful of chickens who produced enough eggs for her to feed her son breakfast in the morning, and eleven goats. Plus Cotton, and she'd never get rid of him. Steele adored the dog, and Poppy did too. She'd sold everything else she could just to stay afloat.

She leaned her head back to face the ceiling, her eyes closed. "Lord," she prayed. "I need help. Please, send someone to help me."

Like most farms, Poppy had good years and bad. This year, because of some equipment issues, she hadn't been able to get in as much alfalfa. She made her living on selling it to other farms and ranches, and she'd only brought in half of what she normally did.

With it only being September, Poppy didn't see a way to generate income until next summer—unless she got a job off the farm.

With that light bulb idea in her mind, she got to her feet. She wasn't going to let a thunderstorm and a phone call ruin her day. The clock had barely struck ten in the morning, and Poppy had five hours before Steele would be out of school. Even then, Gray Hammond, who lived next door, was picking up the kids and bringing them home.

Poppy had time to go find a job.

After peeling her wet clothes from her body, showering, blowing out her hair, and putting on a coat of mascara and a quick slick of lip gloss, she sat down in front of her computer. With dry clothes on and the heat running through the farmhouse, she felt put together and capable.

"All right, Cotton," she said as the dog circled and laid on her feet.

She could do this. She'd delivered a baby all by herself, her mom and dad outside in the waiting room. She hadn't wanted them in the room, but she'd always known they'd be right at her side to help her.

Her first thought as she searched for jobs in the Denver area was to call her father. He'd transfer money into her account and she could buy herself some time to start earning money. The prideful part of herself refused to do it, because she'd asked her parents for help plenty of times in the past decade.

Poppy had gotten quite good at accepting service, but this time, she couldn't. She was thirty-five years old. It was time to be an adult.

She had a degree in horticulture, but moving into fall and winter wasn't a great time to get started in gardening and landscaping. A few jobs existed with city departments, and they'd have a lot of work cleaning up their parks and common areas, so Poppy applied to all three of them.

She searched for secretarial jobs and started filling out online applications, an open notebook at her side. Poppy loved writing things down to reference later, and this way, she'd know where she applied and on what day so she could follow-up in a week or so.

Desperation clogged her lungs, then her throat. She couldn't afford to wait a week to start working. She needed a job today.

She tipped back in her chair, noting how quiet the house

had become. The air had stopped blowing, and the clock above the computer tick-tick-ticked into the emptiness. She felt the same way inside, with only her heart to keep her going at the moment.

Her eyes drifted closed, and her first thought flew toward heaven. "Help me get a job really fast," she said aloud, her lips barely moving. She'd prayed for help while on the kitchen floor too, and that had been for the Lord to send someone to help her.

Travis had been in the barn, dumbfounded at her outburst.

"The Lord didn't send you a cowboy," she told herself firmly. She didn't want one of those anyway, and God surely wouldn't play such a cruel trick on her.

She sighed and leaned up closer to the computer screen again. She'd applied for...she checked the notebook—nine jobs. Who always needed help?

Housecleaning services. Farms. Ranches.

She performed that search next, and to her great surprise, a farm only point-four miles away needed help. *The Hammond Family Farm* stared at her from the computer screen, and Poppy had to blink a couple of times to make sure it didn't disappear.

One listing was for a counselor at Pony Power, the children's equine therapy unit housed at the farm. The other was for an additional "worker" for Elise Hammond's landscaping company.

Poppy reached for her phone with gusto, knocking her notebook to the floor in the process. The cup holding pens, paperclips, and other baubles went with it, and Poppy ignored the scattering of hard objects on her hardwood floor as she dove after the phone.

She retrieved it and dialed Elise. She'd known the woman for all of her thirteen years in Ivory Peaks, because Poppy and Eli had moved onto the farm only a few months after Elise and Gray Hammond had been married.

Poppy had attended holiday dinners there, and when unexpected, anonymous gifts arrived on the doorstep for her or Steele, she knew they came from Elise Hammond. The woman had a special touch she applied to everything, and she'd been the one to organize the church's youth group to come help Poppy with her yard and farm chores one summer when she'd broken her leg while riding her bike with her son.

"Poppy," Elise said pleasantly. "How are you?"

Tears gathered in Poppy's eyes, and her whole face went tight. She couldn't speak through the pressure and tension, and swallowing didn't happen either.

"Poppy?" Elise asked, concerned now. "Are you okay?"

She nodded, but Elise couldn't hear that. "I—" she started, but her voice came out too high. She drew in a deep breath and told herself this was not the hardest thing she'd ever had to do in her life. She cleared her throat. "I need a job, Elise," she said. "And I was looking online, and I saw that you need someone for your landscaping company."

"I do," Elise said. A pause went by before she said, "You'd be perfect, Poppy. Can I come over and go over everything with you? Are you home?"

Poppy got to her feet, realizing she'd been kneeling on the hard floor in her office. "You're just going to give it to me?" She steadied herself with a hand on the back of her desk chair.

"Yes," Elise said simply. "You have a degree in horticulture, if I remember right." She wore a smile in her voice. "I've overbooked myself for this summer and fall, and I still have an entire yard redesign to implement before it snows." She trilled out a laugh that held a lot of happiness, as well as some tension. "I was hoping to hire someone fast, and I just put the job up early this morning, praying for a miracle. And well, here you are, calling. You're my miracle."

Poppy burst into tears, because she hadn't felt needed or useful in such a long time.

"I'm coming over," Elise said firmly. "I know you're home."

"I'm home," Poppy squeaked out. "Just come in. I'll put some coffee on." She lowered the phone from her ear and let Elise end the call.

You're my miracle.

Poppy exhaled out her tears, her entire face hot. A wave of love filled her, first for Elise, and then for the Lord. He'd provided for her all of these years, and she was once again reminded that He had not abandoned her.

She tucked her phone into her pocket and bent to pat Cotton. "She's just going to give me the job."

Cotton seemed to smile, and he looked up at her with such love in his eyes. Feeling slightly stronger, Poppy went to brew a pot of coffee. She still couldn't stop weeping, and she prayed the Lord would strengthen her before Elise arrived. With the scent of coffee filling the house as it drip, drip, dripped into the pot, Poppy opened her Bible on the makeshift island she'd bought years ago at a second-hand furniture store.

The pages wisped underneath her fingers, their thinness like onion skins and soft to the touch. The leather on the outside was well loved and well used, and Poppy blinked back her tears as she flipped to the story where Jesus fed the five thousand with only a few loaves of bread and a few fishes.

She'd once listened to her pastor talk about what this story meant to him. "There were leftovers," he said. "There is enough of the Lord's love and grace and forgiveness for you. There will always be leftovers."

Poppy had loved that sermon so much, she'd come home and written down as much of it as she could remember. The index card tucked between the pages in her Bible reminded her of an often-used piece of cloth, and the pencil she'd written in had been gone over again in pen as it had started to fade.

She re-read the notes of the sermon, the well inside her starting to fill with strength and determination. She wasn't going to lose this farm. She was going to find a way to provide for herself and her son, no matter what.

Someone knocked on the back door, surprising Poppy. Elise should be using the front door, and she always rang the doorbell.

Cotton barked, his claws skittering across the hard floor

as he ran toward the back door. Poppy looked toward the door, which had a window in the top two-thirds. Travis Thatcher stood there, and he lifted one hand in an open-palm wave. She flew toward the door to open it as the wind nearly claimed his cowboy hat.

In fact, when she got the door open, he was looking to his left, his cowboy hat gone. "Come in," she said, nudging Cotton back with her foot. "It's freezing out there."

He looked at her, his dark-as-midnight eyes boring right into her. He lifted his gloved hands to his mouth and blew on them before taking a step inside. She hurried to close the door behind him, her emotions and hormones tangling in a way they hadn't in a very long time.

"I'm sorry about what I said in the barn earlier," she said, swallowing all of her pride now. "Thank you for bringing my goats back. I have a suspicion that Steele doesn't latch the gate after he feeds them."

Travis took several steps into the big farmhouse kitchen, his back to her, saying nothing. When he finally turned, she found a very serious expression on his face. "I'm real sorry I indicated that you weren't doing enough to contain your livestock."

Poppy blinked at his formality. "It's...okay. It's not your fault, and you don't get paid to bring the goats back. I wish I could pay you, but." She lifted both hands in the air and let her arms drop to her sides. "I can't."

Travis relaxed slightly and waved her off. "I don't need to be paid. I did just want to let you know that I fixed the roof on your barn, and I can come back with a couple boys from next door and a trailer, and we'll get that moldy hay out of the loft."

Poppy stared, her mind suddenly blank.

Travis gave a single nod and said, "I'm dripping all over your floor." He looked down. "And your dog." He lifted his eyes to hers again. "I'm sorry, Poppy. I just wanted you to know about the roof and that we'll be back as soon as it stops raining to take care of the hay, and I'll bring the goats back any time, a smile on my face." He didn't smile now, nodded again, and walked toward her.

Her mind screamed at her to apologize again. Tell him thank you. Insist he didn't have to come get the hay out of her loft. He'd stepped past her and opened the door, the chilly wind and increased sound of rain pounding on the deck outside jolting her out of her stupor.

"Wait," she said, spinning. "Travis, you—" Their eyes met again, and her mind went on vacation again. What in the world was happening? "You don't have to come back and get the hay out of the loft. I can pay you for the roof."

"Nope," he said. "I already talked to Gray, and it's done." He smiled then, and Poppy reached out to grab onto something to steady her. There wasn't anything nearby, and she stumbled.

Travis lunged toward her and grabbed onto her. "You okay? Have you eaten today?"

"Not yet," she said, holding onto him again, the same way she did in the barn. "You're soaking wet."

"I know, I'm sorry." He didn't release her but stood still, holding her without giving her an inch.

"Elise is coming over," she whispered, the moment between them suddenly intimate. "She's giving me a job."

"That's great," Travis said, his voice just as husky and just as low as Poppy's had been. When the doorbell rang, Cotton barked again, helping Poppy come to her senses. She stepped away from him, noting that her dry clothes weren't as dry anymore, but she didn't care. She wasn't the one who'd been out in the rain for the past ninety minutes, fixing a leaking roof by herself.

"Thank you so much for fixing the roof," she said, as much sincerity as she could muster in her voice. "I mean it. I want to make it up to you."

Travis's eyebrows went up, but again, he didn't say anything. He was an enigma, this handsome cowboy with a soft spot in his heart.

"I'm a really good cook," she said. "I could bring you dinner one night." She put a smile on her face. "Or you could come here with me and Steele."

Surprise marched through Travis's dark eyes, and he reached up to smooth down his black beard. "I do live alone, and dinner for me is usually something from a box or a bag."

"Great," Poppy said, a light laugh coming from her mouth. "I mean, it's not great that that's what you eat for dinner, but...great."

The doorbell rang again, and she twisted to look toward the front door as Elise called over Cotton's barking, "Poppy? It's Elise, and I'm coming in."

She cleared her throat. "Yeah, I'm in the kitchen."

Elise's footsteps came closer, and Travis hadn't left yet. "Morning," she said. "Oh, Travis, what are you doing here?"

"Just leaving, ma'am," Travis said, nodding again. He didn't say good-bye to either of them before stepping outside and pulling the door closed behind him.

Poppy faced Elise fully, the numbness of the situation wearing off. "I just need to wipe up the floor and change," she said. "Then I want to hear all about the job." She hurried from the kitchen while Elise smiled at her the way Elise always did, but Poppy turned back after she'd entered the hallway.

Elise was already tapping on her phone, which meant she'd know why Travis was here before Poppy returned.

Doesn't mean she'll know you invited him to dinner, she told herself, the secret delicious and only one of the reasons she smiled as she went to find another set of dry clothes.

Fourteen

MOLLY HAMMOND SMILED AT THE COUNSELOR candidate on the other side of the desk. She sat with Alex Caswell, their head therapist at Pony Power, and Alex ran these interviews. Molly just sat in to judge character and have a sounding board for Alex should she need one afterward.

In her eyes, the interview had gone well, and a fifth counselor would allow them to bring on five more children each week. Pony Power had a waiting list of over a dozen children, and she wanted to help them all.

She'd quit her teaching job a couple of years ago, and she'd had plenty of similar experiences and feelings in the classroom. She wanted every child to have a warm house, with plenty of food, people who loved them, took care of them, and provided all the services they needed.

She couldn't stand not having horses or counseling space for every child who needed the services Pony Power could provide. She'd learned so much over the past couple of years, including how to get government grants to fund the program, as well as how to offer and screen for scholarships so families who couldn't afford to pay for an expensive service like equine therapy could still enjoy the benefits of it.

"All right, Bea," Alex said, standing. The woman across the desk did too, and Molly realized a moment later, she was the only one sitting. She jumped to her feet, the room spinning as she did. She cried out and reached for the desk in front of her to steady her.

When the world stopped vibrating and circulating like water going down a drain, she opened her eyes.

She saw the ceiling.

"Molly," Alex said, her face coming into view. Concern and worry rode in her eyes, and her hair fell straight down toward Molly

She blinked and reached up to touch Alex's hair. "She's awake," Alex said. "I think she should still be checked out."

"The ambulance is on the way," Bea said, also kneeling at Molly's side. Molly turned her head to look at her, wondering how she'd gotten on the floor. Her back hurt, as did her head.

She reached up to touch her cheekbone, and Alex said, "You hit the desk on the way down. You're not bleeding, though there's a little cut there." She intercepted Molly's hand. "Don't touch it. I called Elise, and she's on her way with ice."

Molly groaned and let her eyes close again, suddenly every muscle in her body shouting at her. Her stomach rolled, and she turned her head in case she got sick. "Did you call Hunter?"

Please, Lord, she thought. *Don't have let them call Hunter.*

Her husband had a very busy week this week at Hammond Manufacturing Company, which he ran as the CEO. A Hammond had always been in control of the family-owned and operated company, and while Molly hadn't wanted him to take the job initially, Hunter had worked tirelessly to make sure he didn't become HMC.

He came home every night precisely at five, and he had dinner on the table by the time Molly returned to their downtown apartment which sat next-door to his office building. The Hammonds owned both buildings, but thankfully, he didn't run the tenant side of things.

He came out to the farm a couple of times a week, and always every weekend. He still went fishing with his father, played with his siblings so Molly wouldn't become their favorite person above him, and was himself.

"I did," Alex said. "Right after I called Elise."

The door to the counseling cabin banged open, and Elise called, "We're here! Where are you?"

"First door on the left," Bea called as she stood. Movement happened, but Molly rolled back onto her back and kept her eyes locked on Alex's.

"Sorry," Alex murmured. "You passed out, Mols."

"How long?" she asked as Elise arrived.

"Oh, you do have a big bruise there," her mother-in-law said. Elise Hammond was the nicest, most loving person on the planet. Hunter adored her with every fiber of his being, and that meant Molly did too. "This is very cold."

Elise pressed an ice pack to Molly's face, and she couldn't help wincing. "Gray is on his way over from the Baird's."

"He didn't have to leave," Molly said. "Will you please call Hunter back and tell him not to come?"

Elise's phone rang in that moment, and she looked at it and then Alex. "It's Hunt now."

Molly put her hand on the ice pack to hold it in place. She closed her eyes. "I'm fine. Tell him not to come."

"The ambulance is here," Bea said.

"Wow, that was fast," Alex said.

"They come from Ivory Peaks," Bea said. "Right in here."

"I'm going to answer Hunt." Elise stood and got out of the way as two paramedics joined the fray. Molly kept her eyes closed as the desk got moved. She answered the paramedic's questions and sat up when they coached her to do so.

"Dizzy?" one asked.

She nodded, deciding not to deny it. "Yes," she said. "I just didn't eat much this morning. I haven't been feeling well."

"How long was she passed out?" one asked, and Alex threw a sorry look in Molly's direction.

"About four minutes," Alex said. "Long enough for us to call Elise and Hunter, and you guys."

"You couldn't rouse her?"

"No," Alex said. "Her eyes rolled back into her head

when she hit the floor. I pressed a tissue to the cut on her face, and it stopped bleeding pretty fast."

Time became fluid then, as Molly had no idea how long it had been since the interview had ended and she'd tried to stand up. She got to her feet with the help of both paramedics, who advised her to come with them to the medical facility in Ivory Peaks just to make sure she didn't have a concussion.

"Hitting the front of the face isn't as bad as up on the skull," one said. "But I'd still come make sure nothing's fractured, broken, or too mixed up." He offered her a kind smile, and Molly nodded.

"All right, but I don't need to go in the ambulance."

Elise turned as she lowered her phone. "I'll take her. Her husband is going to meet us there."

Molly went with the paramedics outside and down the front steps of the cabin. Gray pulled up in his truck and jumped from it. "What's going on? Are you okay?" He swooped right toward her as Elise started to tell him what had happened.

Gray engulfed her in a hug, and Molly's emotions took a dive off a very high cliff. She clung to him and started to cry, because he looked so much like Hunter and acted so much like him too. "I'm okay," she whispered through her tears.

She kept her eyes closed as the ambulance left, Bea was told Alex would call her soon, and the door behind her got closed. She stood at the bottom of the steps with Gray and Elise, feeling weak and wild at the same time.

"I'll call your mom," Elise said. "Gray, she needs to go to the instacare. Help her into the truck."

Gray finally pulled back, his stormy eyes locking onto Molly's wet ones. "Elise said you hadn't eaten."

Molly shook her head. "I don't feel well."

"I have food in the truck," he said, tucking his arm around her. "Come on. We'll call Hunt on the way. He wants to talk to you."

A COUPLE OF HOURS LATER, MOLLY WAS READY TO go home. Now. "Hunt," she said, and her husband looked up from his phone. He wore his suit and tie, and he'd refused to leave her side to even get a soda or a coffee since he'd arrived at the medical facility. It wasn't a full hospital in Ivory Peaks, but they had enough technology to do certain types of emergency surgeries.

Thankfully, Molly hadn't needed anything like that. There had been no evidence of a concussion either, but she had chipped off a tiny fragment of her cheekbone. The doctor said it could just float around in her face unless it started to cause other problems.

Hunter had grilled him about that for a good twenty minutes, taking notes and firing more questions about the symptoms they'd need to watch for in the future.

Molly's head hurt, and she said, "I want to go home. Can you ask them again when we can go?"

Gray and Elise hadn't stayed for long after Hunter had

arrived. He must've gone terribly fast, because it took a solid hour from downtown to Ivory Peaks, and he'd arrived only ten minutes after Molly had. She'd clung to him and cried too, and he'd told her he'd take care of everything.

He'd been texting and emailing for hours at her side, and she just wanted to get him to a computer so he could work.

"Yeah." Hunter got to his feet. "Your mom says she and your dad brought dinner to the farm. We'll stay there tonight."

"I'll text her," Molly said, but she didn't reach for her phone. Her parents were probably still at the farm, and Molly would have to talk to everyone. Explain again that she didn't feel well and just hadn't eaten. Yada, yada, yada.

She hated being the center of attention, and she didn't like making others worry about her. She sighed as Hunter opened the door, her attention already somewhere else.

"Oh," he said. "I was just coming to get you." Hunter re-entered the room, a nurse and a doctor following him.

Molly pushed herself up with her hands, her head twinging slightly as it throbbed with pain. "Can I go home?"

"I put in a prescription for pain meds for you," the doctor said. "But I need to change it." He glanced at the nurse, who simply wrote on Molly's chart. "You can't take that strong of a narcotic when you're pregnant."

Molly blinked and stared, the words English, but somehow not making any sense. "What?" she asked at the same time Hunter said, "I'm sorry. What did you say? She's pregnant?"

"We run a routine pregnancy test when a female patient

comes in," the nurse said. "I didn't look at it, because all of your symptoms seemed to go along with your low blood sugar and a sudden movement from sitting to standing. But when Doctor Yee put in the narcotic, the system flagged it."

"So...I'm pregnant?" Molly wasn't sure why she didn't believe them. "I haven't been sick in the morning."

"You said you didn't feel well the past week or so," Dr. Yee said. "Right?" He looked over to the nurse's chart.

"But I'm not throwing up," she said.

"Not every woman throws up as part of morning sickness," the doctor said. "You definitely need to be eating, though, and you should get into your doctor and get some prenatal vitamins too. Your system has been through a shock, and that's not good for you or the baby."

Molly looked at Hunter, wonder coursing through her. He met her eyes too, his as wide as dinner plates. They hadn't been trying to get pregnant. They'd talked a lot about starting a family, but they'd agreed to wait so Hunter could dedicate his time and energy to just her and HMC. He'd only been the CEO for two years, and neither of them had hit thirty yet.

"A baby," he said, his smile filling his whole face. He reached for her hand and clutched it in both of his. "That's great, Molly." He sounded so happy, but Molly still only experienced numbness.

Hunter leaned down and kissed the top of her head. "So can you put in a different pain med? She wants to go home."

"It's in already," Dr. Yee said, nodding. "They should have it ready downstairs in about ten minutes."

"She can change and get ready to go," the nurse said as she smiled. "I'll bring in a wheelchair."

"Great, thanks," Hunter said, but Molly said, "I don't need a wheelchair."

"You're wearing a fall risk band," the nurse said. "That means you can't leave unless it's in a wheelchair." She raised her eyebrows, her question clear. *Do you want to go home or not?*

Molly looked at Hunter, who smiled at the nurse with everything he had. "She wants to go. Bring in the wheelchair. I'll make sure she's safe."

"Come back if any of the symptoms we talked about get worse," the doctor said. "Though some of them may be pregnancy-related. I'd talk to your doctor about all of that as soon as possible."

"We will," Hunter assured him, walking with the doctor toward the door and shaking his hand, and then the doctor and the nurse left. The moment the door closed, Hunter spun toward her, his face beaming brightness toward her.

"You're pregnant!" He whooped and reached up as if he'd throw his cowboy hat, only he wasn't wearing one. He rushed toward her, which in the small room, only took two strides. He breathed in deep and took her face in his hands. "I love you so much. A baby." He stroked his hands through her hair, sobering. "Are you not happy? Why aren't you smiling?"

Molly wasn't sure why. "I feel...I don't know. What about HMC?"

Hunter shook his head. "No, it's not about HMC. This

is an amazing moment, Mols. This is us starting our family together." He looked down toward her belly, but she wasn't showing at all. "A baby is a huge blessing, not a burden."

He looked at her again, and it was obvious he wanted her to agree with him. She did. Of course she did. She finally let herself taste some of his wonder, and that caused a smile to fill her face. Joy streamed through her, and she cradled Hunter's face in her hands as she brought him closer so she could kiss him.

"A baby," she murmured right before she matched his lips to hers. He chuckled and then kissed her softly and sweetly.

He pulled away after only a few seconds. "A miracle," he said, and Molly nodded, her happiness blooming and growing beyond her wildest dreams.

Fifteen

HUNTER HAMMOND BENT AND LIFTED A STACK OF pavers he had no business lifting. He'd once worked for a moving company while he went to MIT, but it had been a weekend job for a friend. His dad certainly hadn't spared him from farm chores over the years, and Hunter still went out to his family farm and worked alongside his father, friends, and wife every weekend.

But the majority of his time was spent behind a desk, on the top floor of a huge high-rise building in downtown Denver. He didn't run marathons like Dad, and he didn't do a whole lot of yard work either.

Elise, however, needed his help to finish her final yard of the season, and Hunter would do anything for the woman who'd fallen in love with his father and dedicated herself to being Hunter's mother. She'd filled the role flawlessly, at a time Hunter hadn't even known how badly he needed her.

He knew now, and he grinned at her as she finished

giving Dad directions and turned toward him. "Hunt," she said, plenty of chastisement in her voice. "That's too heavy. Molly's going to kill me." She rushed forward with her clipboard as if she could shoulder the pavers on her petite frame.

"She's the one who's pregnant, not me," Hunter said. "Right over here?" He kept moving, because these weren't feathers, and he'd seen where his father was headed.

"If you're injured, you can't help your pregnant wife," Elise said. "Give me two of those."

Hunter did as she said, because he'd learned long ago not to argue with Elise. They took the pavers over to the path that Travis and Matt had leveled, and the pull in Hunter's lower back thanked Tucker and Steele, the two boys that were bent over arranging the rocks.

Elise stayed to direct them now that all of the materials had arrived, and Hunter glanced around for his other half-brother. Deacon was eight years old now, with Tucker almost ten. Jane, the only girl in his branch of the Hammond family, had been working with Gerty that morning on the horseback riding lessons, and they'd stayed at the farm.

It seemed like everyone else had come to help Elise. She'd bitten off a bit more than she could chew with her landscaping projects this year, and Hunter gave a cordial smile to Poppy Harris as she carried a potted fern in each hand toward the corner of the house where Cosette and Boone were putting in the plants.

Molly sat on the front steps, talking to her phone. Her laughter rang out, and Hunter went to see who she was talking to. He knew already—her mother or one of her sisters. She looked up and met his eye. "Lyra says we can name the baby after her."

"Sure," Hunter said, leaning down to kiss Molly's forehead and then twisting to sit beside her. He crammed his face into the small space so Lyra, Molly's sister, could see him. "It's a great name."

"We're not naming our baby after my sister," Molly said. "No offense, Lyra."

"I'm completely offended," Lyra said, clearly joking. "Mama didn't even say when you were due."

Hunter and Molly had just told their families about the pregnancy a couple of days ago, at a combined midweek dinner Molly had made in the penthouse downtown. They'd carted all the food over to the Benson's house, and Dad and Elise had brought the kids in from the farm.

The wind kicked up as Molly told her sister she wasn't due until next June, and the months seemed impossibly far away to Hunter.

"Hunt," Deacon said, racing toward him. Hunter tapped his wife's knee, suddenly feeling beyond blessed, and stood.

"Yep." He looked past his little brother. "Where's the fire, bud?"

"You've got to come see this German shepherd next door. It's just like Uncle Ames'."

"Is it now?" Hunter heard the cowboy twang in his voice, his eyebrows as high as Dad's would be with a question like that. He smiled to himself as Deacon ran ahead of him. He wasn't too worried about becoming a father himself. He'd been playing with kids since he was fifteen years old and Dad and Elise had started having kids.

Hunter was the oldest Hammond grandchild by a long shot, and he normally didn't mind. He thought about his four uncles who all lived up in Coral Canyon, Wyoming, and when Dad would call them and tell them about the baby. He and Molly had gone to Hunter's grandfather's house and told him privately, as Hunter loved his grandfather deeply and wanted him to know.

In all honesty, if the child was a boy, Hunter would love to name him after his granddad. Molly wouldn't mind, as she loved Grandpa too.

"Hey," Hunter said, rounding the corner of the fence and seeing three little boys crowded against the fence. His heart pounded up into his throat. "Back up, guys. That's not your dog."

If Uncle Ames had taught him anything, it was that a dog could seem friendly until poked just the wrong way. He owned and operated a K9 training facility in Coral Canyon, and he put out some of the best police dogs into the workforce across the entirety of North America.

"Will you take us trick-or-treating?" Deacon asked, not upset by Hunter's command at all.

"Let's get out of the neighbor's yard," Hunter said, extending his hand toward his brother. "Everyone." He didn't know who the other two kids were, but they listened to him, happily going along their way down the street. He didn't much care, as long as he didn't have to call an ambulance for a dog bite.

He glanced back over to the German shepherd, finding him beautiful and regal. The animal sat, and Hunter's desire for a dog doubled. He turned away and swooped Deacon into his arms. The little boy laughed, and Hunter joined in with him. "You come sit by Molly," he said.

She wasn't on her phone call anymore, and she said, "We're not getting a dog," as he approached.

"I didn't even mention it," he said.

"You have a look on your face." She looked at him, clearly challenging him to deny that he'd thought about it. He couldn't. But thinking about getting a dog and actually getting one were two different things.

He worked far too much to have a dog, at least the way he wanted to have one. He wanted to take it fishing with him, and he wanted to play fetch every afternoon. If he and Molly got a dog right now, it would be her dog, not his.

"Deacon's gonna sit right here by you," he said, swinging the child onto the top step next to her. "And yes, I'll take you trick-or-treating on Halloween." He grinned at his brother and bopped his nose with his pointer finger. "But we can't go until after work, and I'm not going for more than an hour."

"All right," Deacon said happily. He turned and looked at Molly. "Are you in trouble too?"

"You're not in trouble, sweetheart," Molly said. "Hunter just doesn't want you to get bitten."

He wandered away while Deacon asked her why she had

to sit on the steps while everyone else worked, a smile of joy in his soul. He'd been there while Hunter told everyone about the baby, but Molly didn't look any different on the outside, so Deacon apparently didn't get why she couldn't bend and lift sod and pavers and plants.

Molly had put up a bit of a fight too, until they'd arrived. When she'd seen how much work needed to be done, she'd happily taken her phone and retreated to the front steps. Hunter joined his father, who had moved on to pouring bags of gravel over the now-set pavers. He picked up a bag on the other side of the walkway and did the same.

"Get it in there, boys," Dad said, and Steele and Tucker did just that. "How are you, Hunter?"

"Great," Hunter said, flashing a smile at his dad.

"Thought any more about what you'll do come next summer?" Dad glanced at Elise as she arrived. They exchanged a glance that said they'd talked about it. Hunter didn't mind. He'd told them specifically he was struggling with what to do about his career once the baby came, as transitioning someone else into the role of CEO at a major corporation like HMC didn't just happen overnight.

If he was going to quit, he probably needed at least six months to make that move. Molly was due in seven and a half. That didn't leave Hunter much time.

He'd never been able to work through complex problems very quickly, especially in matters of the heart. He'd felt stunted in that arena for many years, but since marrying Molly, Hunter had been more centered and more sure of himself.

"Go ahead," he said, hefting the half-bag of gravel and pouring it as he moved slowly along the walkway. The sound of rushing rocks filled the air, and the boys stayed out of the way while they settled. He looked at Elise and Dad. "Say it."

"I'm not going to say anything," Dad said.

"Elise?"

She smiled at him in the loving, maternal way she always did. "You're the smartest man in the world, Hunter. You'll know what to do."

"That's not helpful," he said with a frown.

"What are you worried about?" Gray asked.

"Working too much," Hunter said instantly. "Molly and I...we talked a lot about my job before we got married. It's a big job, Dad. It takes me away from her a lot."

"I know that," Dad murmured. "But you guys have done well."

"But now we'll have a baby," Hunter said. He glanced over to the porch, but they were pouring away from it and around the house. "I promised her I'd be a present father. I want to be that dad. I don't want to miss first steps or when he laughs for the first time." He looked back and forth between his parents. "I don't need to work."

"You have to have something," Dad said. "You're twenty-eight years old."

"You're young," Elise said, looking down at her clipboard. She got interrupted while Travis came to get another job from her. "We need all of the rocks from the driveway," she said. "Thank you, Travis. Matt."

The two moved off to get the rocks, and Hunter wadded up the plastic bag he held.

"You didn't work when Elise started having kids," Hunter pointed out.

"That's because I'm an old man," Dad said.

"You retired when you were forty-four," Hunter said, rolling his eyes.

"I run the farm," Dad said.

"You're not even retirement age now," Hunter pointed out.

"I manage to fill my time with something good," Dad said, looking at Elise. "Right, baby?"

She beamed at him, and Hunter did like seeing the two of them in love. It gave him hope that if he kept his promises with Molly and treated her as queenly as Dad treated Elise, he could have the love of his life for decades too.

"That's right," she said. "He might have a point though."

"What point?" Dad demanded.

Hunter wanted to know too, but he remained silent as he took the bag of gravel from Matt and dug his fingernails through the thick plastic to open it. He started to pour again, and Dad did too across from him.

Elise turned to help someone else, and she stopped at the corner of the house to check off the plants. "Sod," she said to someone, and Hunter didn't care much who. As long as he wasn't the one laying the sod across the front lawn, he'd be happy.

"What point?" Dad asked the moment Elise returned to them.

"Hunter is young," she said. "He's got plenty of money. Why can't he take a few years off while his children are little? Then he could go back when they're in school." She moved her clear blue eyes from Dad's to Hunter's. "That's all I'm saying." She left, really committing to her last sentence, and Hunter let her words stew inside his head.

Molly hadn't said anything else about his job since that first time in the medical center out in Ivory Peaks. She'd been to the obstetrician, and she took the vitamins now. There hadn't been any problems with her or the baby since her fall. Hunter could still feel the panic coursing through him after he'd gotten off the phone with Alex. He hadn't been able to get out of the city fast enough, and then no one seemed to be in a hurry once he had.

He and Dad continued working across from one another until every last piece of gravel got poured. With little fingers spreading it where it needed to go, Hunter looked up at his father.

"Nothing? You've got nothing?"

"Let's go fishing this weekend," Dad said. His answer was always fishing, and Hunter loved that about him.

"Okay," he said. "But I have to be back by five-thirty, because I promised the boys I'd take them trick-or-treating."

"Deal," Dad said. "I'm calling my brothers on Sunday. We're going to finalize all the plans for Thanksgiving, and they'll be ecstatic."

Hunter grinned at his father. "If you say so."

"Are you kidding? All I'm going to hear about for days is how I'm going to be a grandfather and still have an eight-year-old son." Dad laughed, and Hunter did too, because he wasn't wrong. All of his uncles had waited and waited to get married, and Dad didn't even have the youngest kids.

"Well, Deacon will be nine by then," Hunter said, bending to pick up the empty gravel bags. Molly joined in the cleanup, and the two of them left while the last strips of sod were being laid.

He drove from the suburbs southwest of the city toward Ivory Peaks, which sat on the west side too, but up north. At some point, his wife fell asleep, and he gazed at her beauty in the soft lines of her face.

"I'm the luckiest man in the world," he whispered. "Thank you, Lord." The truck ate up another mile before he added, "It would be great if You would let me know what to do about my job."

He felt like he'd prayed for that exact answer dozens and dozens of times before. He had. In the end, he'd had to do what he thought best, and it had almost cost him everything with Molly.

"I'm not doin' that to my kid," he vowed in a whisper. At the same time, he couldn't fathom walking away from HMC right now. Or even in seven months.

He turned onto the road that led past the pines that stood as guards to the family farm, a sense of belonging and relief accompanying him. He'd always been welcomed here, and the moment he got past the trees, he'd be able to see the stables and sheds and barns that Molly had put up to build her dream.

Then the pasture in front of the farmhouse, and finally, the place where he grew up. As he trundled past the big red barn that acted as the check-in spot for Pony Power, all the dirt spots out front empty right now, he caught sight of Jane.

His sister giggled with Gerty, and the two towheads twisted to look back over their shoulders. Hunter saw a dark-haired cowboy standing there, a grin on his face. A face that wasn't terribly old, no, but definitely older than Gerty and Jane.

Far older. A decade older. The man might even be Hunter's age, and he was fifteen years older than Jane. He eased the truck to a stop as the two girls faced him. "Howdy, girls," he said, smiling at them while keeping an eye on the other man. He didn't get a bad vibe from him, and he knew Dad had just hired him to build the new stable they needed.

If his father could stop buying rescue horses, he wouldn't need another stable, but Hunter's wife fueled his father's passion for that, and together, the two of them had a real problem when it came to horse auctions.

"Hey, Hunt," Jane said, skipping toward him like the twelve-year-old she was. She'd be thirteen soon, and he looked past her to the cowboy on the path. He'd turned and started to walk away, but Hunter could see the crush on his sister's face.

"Did you get the lessons done?" he asked.

"Yep." Jane climbed up on the runner of his truck so she filled the window. "How was the yard work?"

"Yard work," Hunter said. "Who's that guy you were talkin' to?"

"No one," Jane said, dropping back to the ground.

"Mm hm," Hunter said.

"You started dating Molly when you were twelve." Jane started walking, and Hunter lifted his toe off the brake so the truck would inch forward with her.

"Yeah, but ladies, she was twelve too. That guy's like thirty."

"He's twenty-two," Gerty said, totally blowing their cover.

Jane gave her a dirty look and refused to look at Hunter as she all but marched toward the farmhouse now. He chuckled and let the girls get ahead of him. Gerty stood a couple of inches taller than Jane, and she was straight up and down too. Jane was shorter and petite like Elise, with big blue eyes and all the cornsilk hair.

"Don't let Dad find out," he called after her, the best advice he could give his sister in this situation. Jane just kept going, her and Gerty holding their heads high. Hunter grinned to himself and went around the back of the farmhouse to his grandfather's generational house.

He woke Molly when he opened the passenger door, and she startled. "Are we here?"

"Shh," he said almost under his breath. "Yes, but I'm gonna take you inside my grandpa's place so you can sleep." He lifted her into his arms and took her inside. His grandfather got to his feet as Hunter said, "I'm going to put her in the guest room, okay, Gramps?"

"Yes, of course."

Hunter did that, bent over to kiss Molly's forehead, and then he slipped out of the room and into the living room. He grinned at his grandfather. "How are you?" He laughed again as he grabbed onto the man who'd been right there at Dad's side when Hunter's mother had abandoned them all.

Grandpa seemed a little bonier today than the last time Hunter had hugged him, and intellectually Hunter knew he wouldn't be around forever. But for today, he was, and when he offered Hunter a mug of hot coffee, he took it.

"Gramps," he said. "What should I do about HMC?"

"I raised four boys while I ran the company, Hunter," his grandfather said. "Remember, every morning, every hour, every evening, you get to make a choice. I know you'll make the right one."

Hunter nodded and stirred another spoonful of sugar into his coffee before he took a sip. "Thanks, Gramps." He spied the book of crossword puzzles in front of him "Ooh, which one is that?"

Sixteen

Gray Hammond looked up from his computer as his wife walked into the office. "Thanks for dinner, my love."

"Of course." Elise came around to his side of the desk, and he pushed the rolling chair back to take her onto his lap. He grinned at her, feeling so much like the man he'd been when he'd first met her.

She made him want to be better and do better, and she'd helped him see people through different eyes. "Going over the menu?" she asked.

"Yes," he said, looking past her to the computer screen, where his spreadsheet of foods and names sat. "I meant it when I said you didn't have to cook everything for Thanksgiving." He reached with one hand to jiggle the mouse. "Look, I'm assigning everyone something to bring. They're all able, Elise."

"I know," she said, snuggling into his chest. "Bree never lets us bring anything when they host Thanksgiving dinner."

"And you always want to," he murmured. "This way, they're happy to help, and we're happy to have the help." They were going to need it, he thought but didn't say. He hadn't exactly told her how many extra people he'd invited.

He cleared his throat, and that got his wife to perk up. "Gray," she said in a slow, almost threatening tone. "What have you done?"

"The guest list might be a tad longer than you think," he said.

"Your family alone is a tad longer than I'd like," she said.

"Oh, hush," he said. "You love my brothers and their wives." He grinned at her, and she smiled back at him. He felt young when she sat in his lap, her arms wrapped around his neck, and especially when she leaned down to kiss him.

"I do," she said against his lips. "But my mother and her husband are coming too."

"Mm hm." He kissed her again, so many more names running through his head. He broke the kiss and said, "And Matt and Gloria and their kids, of course. Boone and Gerty. Travis doesn't have anywhere to go."

"We always have a few cowboys around," Elise said. She leaned forward and took control of the mouse. "Who are you hiding down here?"

"Boone's dating Cosette," Gray blurted before she could scroll too far. "He asked if her daddy and sister could come. I said they could. It's just two people."

"And Poppy and Steele Harris," she said.

"She'll be alone otherwise," Gray said. He'd gone to help with Poppy's moldy hay a few weeks ago, and he'd seen the look in her eyes. She'd also recently started working with Elise's landscaping company. "Surely you don't care that I invited Poppy and her son."

"No," Elise said. "But you've got something up your sleeve."

"Molly's family," he admitted.

"All of them?" Elise turned and looked at him.

"The farmhouse holds everyone," he said, confirming without really confirming. "They wanted to be with their daughter this year, and she wants to be out here with us. I told the pastor he should come."

Elise frowned and stopped looking at his screen. "It's just a lot of different families to meld," she said.

"Your mom will be fine," Gray said, stroking her hair over her shoulder. "She likes big parties, Elise. She loves all the Hammond antics. She'll adore Boone." He grinned as he said it, because Boone Whettstein was like a party in a cowboy's body. The man worked hard too, just like Matt, and Gray had struck gold when he'd found the Whettstein brothers.

"You're talking like fifty people."

"It's actually closer to sixty-three," Gray muttered, hoping to distract his wife with a kiss on her neck. She pressed into him, but Elise wasn't as easily distracted as she'd once been.

"You owe me for this," she said.

"Like you owe me for bringing over every cowboy we

employ to help you with that yard work."

She pulled away, her eyes searching his. He could still see her inside that cabin in Wyoming, calling him when she got home alone because she had to walk through the darkness to get inside. He'd changed her lightbulb for her on her porch so she wouldn't have to do that ever again.

"I love you," he said, so many memories swimming through his mind now. "This is just going to be another amazing thing we get to do together."

She sighed and dropped her eyes to his collar, where her fingers fiddled. "You have a big heart, Gray."

"I don't want anyone to be alone on Thanksgiving," he said. "And people want to be with their families. So we're just having them all here."

"How serious are Cosette and Boone?"

"Serious enough for her to bring her daddy and sister to a giant Hammond family Thanksgiving dinner," Gray said. "I don't know. I don't keep track of the relationships out here. That's more your arena, baby."

The doorbell rang before Elise could answer, and she slid from his lap to go get it. He went back to the spreadsheet. He wasn't asking unrelated guests to bring anything for dinner, but Matt had insisted, and then Boone. The two of them had stood right here in this office and said they'd bring anything from soda pop to rolls to butter, but they were bringing something.

Gray had given them charge over the appetizer trays, and he couldn't wait to see what the brothers showed up with. He heard a couple of female voices a few seconds before his concentration broke, so when he looked up as people came into his office this time, he found Poppy Harris entering first, Elise hot on her heels.

"Gray Hammond," Poppy barked at him, waving a paper in her hand. "Tell me the truth. Did you pay my mortgage?"

She looked like she might slit his throat if he said yes. He got to his feet. "No, ma'am," he said, reaching for a pair of reading glasses. His fifties had not been kind to his eyes, and he'd picked up his readers a year or so ago.

"Are you sure?" she demanded, throwing the paper at him. "That just came, and it says I'm caught up through the end of the year." Her voice sounded so shrill and loud in the quiet farmhouse. He'd finished helping Elise in the kitchen after their Sunday dinner before retreating here, and Hunter must've taken the other kids somewhere. Probably over to Boone's or Matt's, as they had kids close to the same age.

Gray picked up the piece of paper, and sure enough, he could see her next payment wasn't due until the first of the year. "It wasn't me, Poppy."

Tears filled her eyes, and he honestly wasn't sure if she was upset or grateful. "Who was it then?"

"Poppy," Elise said. "Come have some coffee. We have cake leftover from Halloween too." She stepped to the woman's side and put her arm around her shoulders, the kindest smile on her face. Elise had always been so good with people, and Gray's more lawyerly side made him too cynical to love them as easily as she did.

"I can't," Poppy said even as she allowed herself to get

led away. "I left Steele at home. I said I'd only be a few minutes."

"Then take some with you," Elise said, guiding her through the door. Gray followed them, leaning into the doorway while his wife packed up enough cake to feed Poppy and Steele for a week not an afternoon. Elise walked her all the way to the front door and then came back down the hall.

"What was that?" Gray asked. Poppy hadn't even taken her mortgage statement with her.

"She thought you'd paid her bills," Elise said, cocking one eyebrow. "Tell me straight, Gray."

"Elise," he said. "I would've spoken to you first had I thought we should do that."

She nodded. "I know. I told her that. She had to see you." Elise moved into the kitchen to put the cake away, and Gray went with her.

"So?" he asked. "Who do you think did it?"

"I *know* who did it," Elise said.

"Did you tell her?"

"No way." Elise shook her head. "Poppy is a wonderful woman, but she needs to learn that accepting help doesn't make her weak." She tucked the cake away on the back counter, and it didn't tempt him the way it did his brother, Colton.

"Who paid it?" Gray asked, still puzzling that piece out.

"Who fixed her roof and then worked late over here because he hadn't gotten his chores done yet?" Elise asked. She leaned both hands into the island across from him.

"Who organized all the men to go help her with that moldy hay?"

Gray's eyes widened. "Who moved to sleepy, slow, small-town Ivory Peaks after being an investment banker in New York City for two decades?"

"Travis," Elise said with a smile. "He's sweet on her."

"You think so?" Gray asked.

"Would you pay a woman's back mortgage if you weren't?" she teased. "You drove hundreds of miles just to change my lightbulb, Mister Hammond."

He laughed as he went around the island. "And you think I did that because I was sweet on you?" He took her into his arms, both of them grinning. He pulled her tighter against him. "I was, by the way."

She giggled and cradled his face in both of her hands. "That's how I know Travis paid those bills," she said.

He'd just leaned down to kiss her when the back door opened and the chorus from a popular song that Jane made them play in the car all the time entered the house. All four of Gray's children sang it at the top of their lungs, Hunter actually leading them by swinging his long arm wildly in a bad imitation of a conductor.

"Oh, brother," Gray muttered though he loved his kids with everything he had.

"Dad," Jane said. "Will you play Haystacks and Hounds with us?"

He would say yes to family game night any day of the week, especially for Haystacks and Hounds. "My children need me," he said to Elise, stepping away from her as she giggled.

"I'll bring over the cake," she said.

"Yes, please," Hunter said, grinning at her. He peeled off from the group and went to Elise, lifting her right up off her feet. "Thank you, Mom." He hugged her, both of them grinning like fools, and Gray's heart melted like marshmallows over open fire. He'd worried so much about bringing another woman into Hunter's life, but Elise had loved his son from the moment she met him.

"Will you all simmer down?" Molly asked, and she appeared from the depths of the couch, where she'd been napping.

"Mols, Mols," Deacon cried, running toward her. "You have to play Haystacks and Hounds with us too."

"No, she doesn't," Gray said. "Leave her be, Deac."

"You just don't want her to play, because she's the only one who can beat you," Hunter said, chuckling.

"No," Gray said, though that might be partially true. "Is my dad coming?"

"Right here," his dad said, entering the house behind him. "I brought some of your mother's craisin white chocolate chip cookies."

A new roar of sound filled the air as all of Gray's children converged on their grandfather. He laughed too, and Gray enjoyed the happiness as it filled his house, his farm, and his very soul.

Elise basked in the spirit here too, and Gray met her eyes

and raised his eyebrows. *See?* he asked her silently. *Thanksgiving is going to be amazing.*

She simply shook her head, opened the drawer, and got out a fistful of forks.

"Hey," Gray said later that night. He could see himself in the video square on his computer. Wes, his oldest brother sat in the top screen, having opened the meeting and sent out the link to everyone.

"There he is," Colton said, who sat next to Wes on the top row. Gray was the second-oldest son, with Colton right in the middle. The twins, Cy and Ames, had already joined too.

"Sorry," Gray said. "I was saying good-bye to Hunter and Molly. They're going back to the city tonight."

"Bree says I have twenty minutes," Wes said, and Gray missed his brother so powerfully. All of them.

"I'll talk fast," Gray said. "I want to go over Thanksgiving. You're all still coming, right? Dad's so excited we're all going to be back at the farm."

"We're coming," the twins said at the same time, then Colton said, "Annie and I are staying with you, right?"

"Yep," Gray said.

"My family is staying downtown," Wes said. "But we'll be at the farm all day on Thanksgiving."

Sure, Gray thought. Wes would go around to all of his friends whose businesses he'd funded over the years, and he'd spend at least half a day training Hunter in the family company. Hunter adored Wes, and he often called his uncle for advice. Gray didn't mind, because he wanted to be his son's friend and father, not his business associate.

"You have that empty cabin, right?" Ames asked. "The boys want to stay there. I told them you'd put them to work, but they don't seem to care."

"There is an empty cabin," Gray said. "I hired a couple of new guys, but they won't be here until the second week of December."

"Bad time to start on a farm in Colorado," Colton said.

"I'm bringing Dad's bike," Cy said. "We're staying with him."

"Perfect," Gray said, getting ready to share his screen. "Wes, make me the host so I can show you what I've been working on."

His brother squinted at the screen, and Wes should probably be wearing reading glasses at his age too. "Give me a sec...."

"While he's doing that," Gray said, his heartbeat slamming against his eardrums and sending the sound through his whole body. "I have an announcement."

Wes stilled, and Colton actually leaned closer to the screen. Gray took a breath, and Colt said, "Gray, tell me Elise isn't pregnant."

"What?"

"Bro, you're sixty," Ames said. "It's time to stop."

Gray glared at him. "Elise isn't pregnant," he said while Cy said something. Wes spoke too, and no one heard him.

"Stop it," he practically yelled. "Enough." He held up both hands, glancing over to the open office door. Elise had put the little boys in the tub as Hunter and Molly had left, and Jane was probably reading in bed.

"You're going to prove Elise right about Thanksgiving," he said. "Come on. She's not pregnant."

Every one of his brothers wore a dubious look, and Gray glared at all of them. "You all have just as many kids as I do," he growled. "Why do you care if my wife is pregnant again?"

"So she is," Colton said.

"No," Gray said. "She's not. Molly is. Hunter and Molly are going to have a baby next summer. That's the announcement, and you know what? I wish I didn't tell you all, and you could be left in the dark." He nodded like that was that, and he could take the announcement back.

Ames grinned first and said, "That's great, Gray."

Ten seconds, he told himself. One of them would make some joke about his youngest's age and his forthcoming grandchild within ten seconds.

"Yeah," Cy said. "That's amazing, Gray. Holy Harleys, you're going to be a grandfather."

Gray lifted his hand and pointed to Wes. "Go on."

"With an eight-year old," Wes said right on cue.

"For your information," Gray said. "Deacon will be nine by the time Molly has the baby. So there."

Everyone not in the room with him burst out laughing, and Gray couldn't help himself. He joined in, beyond glad to see all of them. Sometimes he felt so left out and so alone down here in Ivory Peaks while they all lived in Wyoming.

He took his family north every summer, and he loved his time in the Tetons with his closest friends.

"He'd like some help with HMC," Gray said to Wes. "So schedule that in while you're here."

"Got it," Wes said. "And you're a host now."

Gray could see the button that would allow him to share his screen now, and he said, "Thanks. Okay, I've made a spreadsheet, as we're going to have Elise's mom here, some of our cowboys, a neighbor, Molly's family, and someone's girlfriend's family...."

"I can't even follow that," Ames said.

"Don't bring your K9 trainee," Cy said. "That's what he said."

"I have to bring Goldie," Ames said, frowning. "Gray, I can bring her, right? She's deep in the training."

"Bring her," Gray said, clicking to show his screen. "Look, I even put her on the spreadsheet." He beamed at his beautiful work of art while his brothers studied it. "Okay, let's start at the top...."

Seventeen

Boone relished in the heat pouring through the administration barn, the weather outside today absolutely horrific. He might have misspoken about winter farming in Colorado, and Mother Nature seemed determined to make him eat those words from earlier this year.

He knocked on Cosette's open door and lifted the tiny loaf of banana bread he and Gerty had made last night. "Morning, sweetheart," he said to the gorgeous auburn-haired woman sitting at her desk.

"Hey," she said, smiling at him. "Come in."

"Gerty sent breakfast." Boone stepped into the room and toed the door closed behind him. His heart flipped and slipped inside his chest, and he couldn't look away from Cosette's mouth. He still hadn't kissed her, and Gerty had come on several of their dates over the past couple of months.

He wasn't going to walk Cosette to her front door while

his thirteen-year-old watched through the windshield. They had gone out alone plenty too, but Boone had meant it when he'd said he needed to go slow.

Cosette hadn't been lying about it either. She got to her feet, her smile as wide as the Mississippi River. "She's so sweet."

"I helped too, you know."

Cosette gave him a placating smile as she took the loaf from him. "Of course you did." She swept her lips across his cheek and turned back to her desk. "Thank you, Boone."

He sighed as she moved behind her desk again. He slouched into the chair in front of it, a groan coming from his mouth. She met his eye. "What's going on?"

"It's freezing outside, for one," he said. He didn't want to invite negativity into his life today. "Your office smells nice."

"Raven gave me some of that orange essence oil," she said. "For my new diffuser." She smiled fondly at the lava-lamp-lookalike on the corner of her desk. A thin stream of mist rose from the top of it, and Boone liked that it made her so happy.

Cosette unwrapped the banana bread, spreading out the plastic wrap and placing the loaf on it. "What's number two?" she asked.

"Did you talk to your sister and dad about comin' to Thanksgiving dinner?" Boone had said he and Gerty would drive across the city to her father's place if she wanted them to. He'd said she could do that, and he'd stay here with the

Hammonds. The choice was hers, and she'd been hemming and hawing about it for weeks now.

"Yes," she said. "Raven thinks it'll be more fun here, and neither of us want to put together a whole turkey feast."

Relief ran through Boone. It would be easier for him to have her and her family here. Gerty could run off with her cousins and all of the Hammond children. No one would be looking at Boone and Cosette, not with all five Hammond brothers back in town. The spotlight would be on them, and Boone could find some time to rest and relax.

There would be no lessons. No training. He, Matt, Gloria, Travis, Cody, Mission, and a new cowboy, Cord, would come take care of the horses twice that day, but nothing else. No fences to be fixed. No saddles to be repaired. No lofts to be swept, and no stalls to be cleaned out.

The work on a farm never ended, and Boone normally didn't mind. But the weatherman had forecasted snow for Turkey Day, and Boone just wanted to bundle up, pop popcorn, and drink hot chocolate with his girlfriend.

"I can't wait to meet your dad," he said, though a slip of nervousness ran through him.

"He's excited to meet you too," Cosette said, a false note in her voice.

Boone had let a couple of those slip throughout the months. "Is he?" he asked, deciding not to let this one go.

"Yes." She looked at him, her eyes wide with a hint of nervousness in them. "He just...he's just overprotective. He's...the first person I went to after I left Joel."

Boone nodded, hoping he'd smoothed his face into passivity. Cosette hadn't talked about her ex-husband in a while. "I showed up on his doorstep in the middle of the night," she said. "I had quite a few bruises on my body, and it took some convincing to get him to take me to the hospital instead of driving back to Joel and...." She shrugged and looked at the banana bread. "You know, giving him some of the same bruises he'd given me."

"Cosette," Boone said, leaning forward and taking her hands in his. "He knows I'm not like Joel, right?"

"He does," she said. "I've told him. Raven told him. He's just leery."

He nodded. "I understand that. Is there anything I should do to try to win him over?"

She cocked her head, a smile touching her lips. "Really, Boone?"

"What does that mean?" He grinned back at her.

"You're the most personable man alive," she said, shaking her head. "Do I just go into this? Take a big bite off the end?"

"Yeah, sure," he said. "That's all yours. You don't need to slice it." He watched her pick up the loaf. "I'm the most personable man alive?"

She nodded, didn't elaborate, and stuck the end of the banana bread loaf straight in her mouth. She took an enormous bite, her eyes sparkling like glittering gold. Boone laughed, because his proper, ninety-degree-angle Cosette didn't take ginormous bites from a loaf of banana bread.

She choked as she started to laugh too, her face turning a

shade of red he hadn't seen before. That only made him laugh harder, and she covered her mouth with her hand. "Stop it," she said around the giggles and the gluten.

"You went right in," he said, still laughing.

"You said I could."

"I didn't know you were going to gnaw on it like that." They laughed together again, and in the silence that followed, Boone couldn't stand going slow any more. "There's a third thing."

"Mm?" Her eyebrows went up as she finished chewing and wiped a bit of chocolate from the corner of her mouth.

"We've been dating a while," Boone said, shifting in his seat. He wasn't sure how to blurt out *I want to kiss you. That's the third thing. Can I kiss you? Like, right now?*

He had closed the door. Cosette's office wasn't exactly a high-traffic hub. His stomach clenched, because he hadn't kissed anyone in a while, and he wasn't sure he'd land it right with Cosette. It would require a lot of touching, and while he sure did want that and Cosette seemed to like holding his hand and kissing his cheek, she didn't seem too eager to do much more.

Even that level was more than her telling him not to touch her when he'd tried to save her from falling down. She'd come a really long way since their first interaction, as they were able to have fun and serious conversations now. For a long time, she barely spoke to him. Business only. An invoice here, a receipt there, move the horses over there.

Boone had definitely been the one to push them to go out on Taco Tuesday, and he'd been the one to drive the hard conversations too. Still smiling at her, he decided this was just another of those times.

"Nothing?" he teased. "You don't think we've been dating a while?"

"Yes," she said. "We have."

"Maybe we haven't," he said, leaning back and folding his arms.

"What do you mean?"

"I mean, when I was datin' Nikki, she said if I wanted to be her boyfriend, I'd have to kiss her. Otherwise, she was gonna dance with any cowboy who asked." He grinned as the color drained from Cosette's face. "I kissed her on our first date."

Cosette blinked fast and then blinked some more. "Why doesn't that surprise me?"

"I didn't want her goin' out with anyone else," he said simply. "And Cosette, I don't want you goin' out with anyone else either."

"You don't need to worry about that."

He studied her for a moment. "Do you not kiss?"

"I...kiss," she said, licking her lips as her eyes dropped to his mouth.

"If you're not ready to, it's fine," he said. "I've been thinking about it for a while, and I'm good to go at your pace. You know that. I just figured, maybe...." Heat filled his face now, and he didn't finish the sentence.

He got to his feet, her office suddenly too small and too hot. "I better get back outside. Travis is gonna think I'm tryin' to get out of restringing that carousel."

She stumbled to her feet after him. "What are you guys doing today?"

He'd just said what he was doing that day. "The walking carousel in the third ring is busted," he said, turning back to her. "We've got to restring it, and the wind is a mighty nuisance."

She nodded, reaching up to wipe her mouth with her fingers. "I'll bet. I saw a child lose his umbrella on the way to work this morning."

"Elise said she dropped the kids off at school mere moments before the hail started," Boone said. Thankfully, that had been a quick-moving and isolated storm that had only lasted about three minutes. He could still hear the pounding of the pellets on the roof of the stable he and Mission had run into for shelter.

"Have you heard that there will be something like sixty people at the Hammonds?" he asked. "We really can go to your daddy's."

"I want him to see where I work," Cosette said, a hint of pride filling her voice. She stopped a pace from him, and Boone could easily take her into his arms and kiss her. He wouldn't, not unless she gave him permission. "Plus, one of Gray's brothers is supposed to be bringing his police dog, and I mentioned that to my dad, and he's very excited about that."

Boone grinned at her, reaching to tip his hat at her. "Well, you have a great day, ma'am. I'll see you after the lessons for our cranberry tasting."

"Is that tonight?" she asked.

"Yes," he said. "I texted you about it last night."

"Right." She shifted her feet. "You're going?"

"Back to work?" he asked. "Or to the cranberry tasting?"

She took a micro-step closer to him. "I thought you wanted to...you know." Her cheeks bloomed with spots of pink again.

"Kiss you?" he supplied, enjoying this conversation for some reason. He stepped into her personal space and wrapped her in his arms. "Is this okay?"

"Yes," she whispered. She'd told him that her ex-husband could make a hug into something painful, and Boone was always careful with her, like he was holding broken glass in his bare hands.

He pushed her hair back off her shoulder, revealing that slender, sexy neck. "This?"

"Yes." Her arms moved around him too, and Boone could hold her like this for a while and really enjoy himself. He finally felt like someone wanted him, and he realized how blind he'd been to Karley for so many months.

Boone bent his head and touched his lips to her earlobe, only the hint of pressure. "This?" he whispered.

Cosette nodded, and he moved his hand up her back as his lips traveled south. He kissed the side of her neck and along her collarbone, not asking if it was okay. It was, and Cosette pressed into each tender touch.

"You're a tease," she whispered.

"You haven't said I can kiss you," he said back, his voice husky and low.

"Boone," she said, and he lifted his head and looked into

her eyes. She wanted him to kiss her, and he lowered his head to meet her mouth with his.

He paused a hair away from her, giving her one last chance to say no. He'd learned that Cosette really liked being in control of things. Her situation. Her schedule. Who touched her and when. What she ate and when. All of it. Anything outside of her control was hard for her, though she had allowed him to plan some mystery dates. She really had grown a lot in the past couple of months.

She moved slightly in his arms, her top lip meeting his. Everything male fired inside him, but he held himself back. "This?" he whispered, closing that last millimeter between them and pressing his lips to hers for only a half a heartbeat.

"Yes," she said, pulling him down to her for a real kiss this time. Boone's blood felt like it had been liquified in a microwave, and he enjoyed the chocolatey taste of her lips and mouth as he kissed her oh-so-slowly. He didn't want to accelerate things too fast in case she wasn't ready.

He wanted her to lead, but she seemed content to let him. After a couple of seconds, he deepened the kiss, and she went right along with him. Something centered in Boone in that moment, and he felt the world spinning behind his closed eyes as he fell, fell, fell for Cosette Brian.

He pulled back and asked, "Okay?"

"Yes," she breathed, her eyes still closed.

"Will you really be okay with a huge group at Thanksgiving?" he asked, knowing she'd answer truthfully now that she'd softened in his arms.

"Yes," she said again, opening her eyes this time. "I can do it, Boone. I'm okay."

"You'll tell me if you want to leave?" he asked. "I'll take you home or over to my place so you can have some peace and quiet."

She gave him a shy, small smile. "I'll tell you what I need."

"Mm," he said, smiling at her in a huge way. "What about another kiss? Need one of those?"

She grinned back at him. "Absolutely," she said, and this time she kissed him. Boone had the distinct thought that he never wanted to kiss anyone but her, and that maybe—just maybe—his third try at this love, life, and marriage thing would last longer than eight or nine years.

Eighteen

COSETTE HAD BEEN KISSED BEFORE, BUT IT HAD not been like this. Boone stood taller than other men she'd dated, and he held her like he could not get close enough to her. His mouth definitely explored hers, but he wasn't aggressive in any way. He seemed to be waiting for her to give her permission before moving his hands or kissing her deeper.

She wasn't sure how she gave that permission, but she seemed to, because Boone kissed her and kissed her. When he pulled away the second time, she took in a deep breath through her nose, afraid to open her eyes in case everything that had just happened would poof away into nothing.

"Okay?" Boone asked, and she loved the way he articulated the word just for her.

She opened her eyes, working hard to find the right words to say. They didn't come, so she nodded. He smiled sweetly at her and added, "I'm not going to hurt you."

At least not willingly, Cosette thought, and she supposed that she'd come a long way in her thinking about men. Cowboys in particular.

"Do you like to dance?" she asked.

He blinked, clearly not expecting the question. "What?"

"Dancing," she said, stepping out of his arms. She suddenly didn't know what to do with her hands. "I used to love dancing, but I haven't been in a long time." She didn't need to say why. Dancing required standing in someone's arms, and she hadn't done that until very recently.

"I can do it," Boone said. "Whether I like it or not, I'm not sure."

"You don't know if you like dancing?"

Boone took her into his arms again, his smile lighting up his whole face. "I don't do a whole lot of dancing, sweetheart. I suppose I'll have to give it a whirl to know if I like it or not." He spun her away from him, laughing.

Cosette laughed too, especially when he brought her immediately back to his chest, his arms curling around her waist naturally. He swayed with her, and Cosette inched her hand up his back, smiling with him.

"Yeah," Boone said. "I like dancing."

Cosette laughed, and she pushed her boyfriend away. He stumbled in an over-exaggerated way, crashing into her closed office door. "Go on," she said through her giggles. "You have work to do."

"I'll pick you up later." He bent and picked up his cowboy hat, reseated it on his head, and turned to leave her office.

Cosette ran her fingers through her hair, finding some of it out of place. "All right." She had no idea who she was anymore, because her voice hardly sounded like her own. Boone gave her one last smile and went into the hall, and Cosette turned back to her desk, looking at it like it was a foreign object she'd never used before.

She returned to her chair and sat down, sighing in the process. Her pulse still galloped through her chest and the rest of her body, and she wasn't sure how to get the adrenaline to wear off faster.

She'd just kissed Boone Whettstein. Kissed a man. And it hadn't been horrible. In fact, it was the single best thing that had happened to her since she'd snuck away from Joel in the middle of the night.

The thoughts of her ex-husband didn't stay long, certainly not the way they had in the past. She looked at her computer and tried to remember where she'd been before Boone had entered the office.

COSETTE HAD JUST REACHED THE TOP OF THE HILL, and she put both hands on her hips and looked up into the beautiful sky. It was gray and foaming with clouds this morning, but she didn't care.

"I kissed Boone Whettstein," she said.

Louisa shrieked and danced in front of Cosette. They both laughed as Louisa hugged, and Cosette had no problem embracing her friend and feeling the friendship and love between them.

"When?" Louisa asked. "It better have been like, an hour ago, or I'm going to be so mad you didn't tell me."

"Just yesterday." She smiled at Louisa as her friend stepped back. She'd once found Louisa's light brown eyes all-seeing and too heavy to shoulder, but now, she only found joy when she looked at her.

"And?" Louisa asked, starting to walk again.

Cosette fell into step beside her, their morning walk only fifteen minutes old. "And it was great," Cosette said.

"See?" Louisa asked. "I told you it would be." She laughed again, filling the morning sky with sound. "I'm so happy for you, Cosette."

"Me too," she said. "Now, what about Stan? How did your date with him go?"

"You know, it went okay," Louisa said, her voice pitching up a bit too high."

Cosette wanted to accept her answer, but Louisa had pushed her in the past. "You sure?" she asked.

"He seemed a little clueless," Louisa admitted. "So I just told him—look. I like you, and I think you like me, and let's not pretend like we don't."

"You said that to him?" Cosette marveled at Louisa yet again.

"I did," Louisa said. "I'm older than you, Cosette. I don't have time to mess around with a man who doesn't get dating."

"Wow."

Louisa giggled and said, "The date went far better after that. He held my hand and the conversation was normal and fun. We're going out again after Thanksgiving."

"You never cease to amaze me," Cosette said.

"You're the amazing one." Louisa looped her arm through Cosette's. "Are you taking the tree today?"

Cosette shook her head, her nerves braying at her again. "Not today," she said quietly. "But I've had it for a month, and I'm taking it over on Thanksgiving. I'm eating with Boone and all the Hammonds then."

A FEW DAYS LATER, COSETTE HAD LEFT HER PECAN tarts in the oven while she ran down the hall to finish her makeup. She'd drunk too much coffee this morning, and her heartbeat raced and raced as she lined her lips with a dark pink stick and then filled it in with lipstick.

"Cosette!" Raven yelled just as she put her makeup back in the bag.

"Coming," Cosette called, zipping up the bag and putting it back in the top drawer in her bathroom vanity. She took a moment to look into her own eyes in the mirror, and she noticed that her hair had gotten longer than she usually let it. She touched it and let it ringlet back into place, not sure where her mind was.

"It's beautiful," Raven said, appearing in the doorway.

Cosette turned away from the mirror and her reflection and embraced her sister. "Hey, thanks for going to get Dad."

"I went last night," her sister said. "We closed early for Thanksgiving." She stepped back, grinning. "But we better get out there. Dad's already opening all of your drawers."

Cosette shook her head and led the way. "You told him he can't do that at the Hammond's, right?"

"I told him not to do it here."

Cosette went down the hall and into the kitchen, where her father stirred a spoon in a coffee mug. "Good morning, Dad." The timer on the oven went off, and Cosette shooed her father out of the kitchen. "Those are my tarts. Go. Go."

Everyone cleared the way, and Cosette pulled her treats out of the heat. The crusts looked a little bit too brown, but she wasn't going to worry about it. There'd be so many people at the farmhouse that everything would get eaten.

"I've got the whipped cream in the car," Raven said. "We can whip it there, right?"

"Yes," Cosette said. "Just let me get the other things I said I'd bring." She directed Raven to get out the boxes of stuffing while she loaded up a sheet tray with all the cut-up veggies she'd prepared last night.

"You're making Mom's gourmet vegetables?" Dad asked, and Cosette looked into her father's dark eyes.

"Yes," she said. "Elise asked if I'd make a side dish, and this is my favorite Thanksgiving side dish."

"I love them," Raven said. "We better get going. Are they going to have enough ovens there for all the things that need to be baked?"

"There's a whole bunch of cabins there," Cosette said. "Grab that pound of butter."

Raven put it on the sheet tray, and together, the three of them took out the ingredients they needed for the gourmet vegetables as well as the pecan tarts. It seemed to take forever, with Dad saying he'd ride in the back, and Raven and Cosette arguing with him on every trip in and out of the house.

Finally, Raven stood at the passenger door, holding it open while Dad ducked into the car. Cosette buckled her seatbelt while her sister got in the back seat. A sense of exhaustion pulled through her, and she hadn't even left the driveway yet.

The drive to the farm usually took twenty-five minutes, but Dad kept telling Cosette she was going too fast, and she kept lifting her foot off the gas pedal. After several minutes of this, she finally speared her father with a sharp look. "Dad," she said. "I'm driving, and we're in no danger." She could drive whatever speed she wanted. On this clear, crisp morning, hardly anyone was out. They had their ovens going and their pots bubbling, their friends and family gathered around.

Cosette had been cooking for her sister and father for the last several years, and Raven would bring a store-bought pie and Dad would bring his favorite ice cream, and they'd all have a great time. As she drove past the pine trees and nearly got driven off the road by an enormous motorcycle with a long-haired cowboy holding onto the handlebars and a little girl clinging to his back, Cosette realized she'd entered a whole new world this year.

Dad yelled, and Cosette swung the car wildly out of the

way. The man riding the death trap obviously laughed as he irresponsibly took one hand off the handlebar to give her a wave.

Cosette gripped the wheel as the car came to a stop. Her heart pounded, the rumbling sound of the motorcycle still vibrating in her ears. She squeezed her fingers and then got moving again.

"This is going to be a wild party," Raven said gleefully from the back seat.

Cosette took a deep breath as she caught sight of all the trucks and cars parked in front of the farmhouse. There were so many, a second aisle had been created, and Cosette pulled up next to a black truck that could run over hers and probably not even feel the bump.

Everyone started getting out of the car, but Cosette took an extra moment to settle herself. Before she could get out, her door opened, and Boone said, "You made it."

She stood, and he drew her into his arms. "Who's the guy on the motorcycle?"

"Cy Hammond," Boone said, turning to look down the dirt lane. The engine of that bike couldn't be heard, but he'd be back with the last name of Hammond. Cosette followed Boone's gaze down the road, not realizing that her father had gotten out of the car.

"You must be Jeff Brian," Boone said, releasing her and reaching toward her dad.

Cosette snapped back to attention and followed Boone. "Dad," she said. "This is Boone Whettstein."

"So great to meet you," Boone boomed, pumping her

dad's hand. He chuckled, because Boone always chuckled and was so happy to meet new people. She didn't need to introduce her dad, who likewise shook Boone's hand as he smiled. "It's good to see you too, Raven." Boone moved to hug her sister, and then the four of them stood there.

"Come on," Boone said. "Let's get your stuff inside. It's a little crazy, but since it hasn't snowed yet, Gray and Wes just chased all the kids outside."

Cosette looked up into the sky, which held plenty of gray clouds. "It might snow later."

"Supposed to," Boone said, leading the way up the front steps. Cosette made sure Raven and Dad started after him before she picked up the tray with the pecan tartlets and followed them. A wall of noise hit her when she reached the top of the steps behind the rest of her family, but she kept moving.

"They're here," Boone bellowed into the house, and Cosette seriously considered walking back out. She forced herself to keep going, and when she made it past the formal living room on the right and down the hall, the back of the house opened up into an expansive kitchen, living room, and dining room.

Right when she stepped inside, the group hovering around the island broke into laughter, which filled the whole house with rowdy cowboy voices. Several people had turned toward Boone when he'd called into the house, and Gloria took the tray from Raven, saying, "I'm Gloria Whettstein. You must be Raven." She glanced at Cosette, who smiled at her. Gloria was the nicest person on the planet, and she worked tirelessly around Pony Power, the same way Cosette tried to.

"My sister," Cosette said. "And that's my dad, Jeff." Her dad glanced over, and Gloria gave him the brightest grin ever. "This is Matt's wife," she added. "Matt is Boone's brother."

"He's right here," Gloria said as Matt joined her. "Where'd the kids go?"

"Hunter took them all outside to see the goats," Matt said, his smile genuine and kind. "Howdy, y'all. Come on in. Cosette, Elise made sure you had room in the kitchen for your things."

"Thanks," she said, giving him a smile too. Boone had mentioned going on a double date with his brother and Gloria, but they hadn't done it yet. Cosette told herself she had plenty of time to get to know everyone, and she stuck close to Raven as they trekked into the kitchen.

"Gray," Elise said. "Take that stuff from Boone."

"You got it." Gray Hammond took the items Boone had carried in for Cosette, and he put the tray on an empty spot on the island. When he looked at Cosette and the pecan tarts, his eyes lit up even more. "Oh, Colton's gonna love you."

Cosette grinned and took in the enormity of food on the island countertop. "This doesn't look like desserts."

"Nope," another man said, and he clearly belonged to Gray. "You want to come with me." He gestured for her to come, and he took one of the trays of tarts.

"Don't let him eat those," Gray called after her, and

Cosette finally felt herself relax into the family atmosphere. All of the men wore their cowboy hats indoors, though she'd assumed they wouldn't. Boone said his mother had made them take off their hats the moment they came inside. Of course, he'd followed that up with, "Then she left, and we did what we wanted. Daddy didn't care if we wore our hats during dinner. He wore his."

Cosette admired his resiliency and his optimism, two things she was working on obtaining too.

"Right here," the Hammond brother said. "I'm Colton. The most normal of the Hammonds."

"Cosette," she said, placing the second tray beside the first. "We can combine these. My sister will whip the cream when we're ready to eat them." She hoped Raven hadn't gotten swallowed by the crowd, but she didn't look over her shoulder. She worked quickly to jam in all the pecan tarts onto one tray, and then she slid the extra one underneath the first. "Thanks."

"Sure thing," Colton said, a chocolate cupcake in his hand.

"Colt," someone snapped, and Cosette looked up to see Elise standing beside a dark-haired woman. They both wore daggers in their eyes, and the other woman put her hands on her hips. "You said you wouldn't eat dessert first."

"It's appetizer time," Colton said. "I'm not eating crackers and dip. This is what I eat for an appetizer." He grinned with the wattage of the sun, not caring one whit about the women's glares, and put half the cupcake in his mouth in one bite.

"Disgusting," Elise said, but her light eyes twinkled. She and Colton were clearly friends. Elise switched her gaze to Cosette. "How are you, Cosette?" She stepped right into her and hugged her, causing surprise to dart through Cosette.

"Good," she said, sinking into the hug. In that moment, she realized how much she used to like hugging another person. She'd forgotten, and now she found she couldn't let go. "Thanks for having all of us here."

"No problem," Elise said, stepping back. "This is Bree." She grinned at the woman and linked her arm through the Bree's. "She's my very best friend in the whole world, and she married Gray's brother, Wes."

"He's the one with the big, black hat."

"Is that his big, black truck out there too?" Cosette asked.

"Yes," Bree said, stepping forward to shake Cosette's hand. "I can't tame him and his love of big trucks."

"I understand," Cosette said as Boone laughed loudly a few paces away. "They are who they are, aren't they?"

"Come meet the other wives," Elise said, taking Cosette by the arm now. "Ladies and gentlemen." She tugged Cosette right into the spotlight among all the adults hanging out around the island, which held multiple cheese balls, trays of vegetables, crackers, and pretzel sticks. "This is Cosette Brian. She runs all of the business for Pony Power."

"She's a Godsend," Molly Hammond said, stepping into the circle. Cosette gave her a bright smile, because Molly had hired her and they worked closely together to this day. "These are all of Hunter's uncles."

"Cy's outside with the kids," a woman said. "He's like a child himself."

"Most men are," Bree said. "For example, see how Wes has migrated over to the dessert table with Colton?"

"Hey," another man said, and Cosette knew who he was. Dad stood right beside Ames Hammond, and a German shepherd was getting bits of broccoli with cream cheese on them.

"This is Patsy," Elise said. "Cy's wife. They have four kids around here somewhere."

"Cy had one of the twins on the bike with him," Molly said.

"Annie," Elise continued. "She's married to Colton. They have one daughter who's with her boyfriend this year, and two others who are married."

Cosette smiled and shook hands, glad to see so many shining, happy faces looking back at her. Everyone seemed so...wonderful. She didn't quite know how to describe them. They exuded light, and she wanted to stand next to each of them and ask them questions about their lives. Surely none of them had ever been through anything hard, though she knew that couldn't be true.

Everyone had something hard to endure. The lines around Annie's eyes, even though she smiled, told Cosette that.

"And Sophia," Elise said. "She's married to Ames there, who doesn't think he's just a great big kid."

"I'm not," Ames said, frowning.

"You brought your doggy to dinner," Elise teased.

"She's in training," Ames growled.

"My dad wants to watch you train her," Cosette said, jumping into the conversation. Boone stood on the opposite end of the island with Matt and Gloria, and his eyes shone in her direction. "Right, Dad? You wanted to talk to Ames about his dog."

"Yes," her dad said. "I had a dog in the Army. He worked with us on missions."

Ames swung his attention toward her dad, his eyes round. "He did?"

"Oh, yeah," Dad said, and he'd softened considerably in the presence of the German shepherd. "That dog could smell anything, and he'd bark and bark if there were explosives we couldn't see, people we didn't know were there, anything."

"I'd love to talk about that," Ames said. "I train dogs for police service, but the military, they don't seem interested in my animals."

"They train their own," Dad said, and Cosette's heart filled with love. For him, that he'd agreed to come spend Thanksgiving with all these strangers. For Ames, for being so open and willing to include her father. For Gray and Elise, who stood side-by-side now, talking about something Cosette couldn't hear.

For all the Hammonds, and the Whettsteins, and the Brians, and everyone else who was here.

"This is my mother," Elise said. "Mom, Cosette works here on the farm."

The woman seemed made of clouds and sticks, and she

too grabbed onto Cosette like she couldn't wait to hug her. "So lovely meeting you. I've been enjoying meeting everyone Elise loves."

"It's great to meet you too," Cosette said as the woman stepped back.

"Elise," another woman said, and Cosette blinked out of her gratitude and surprise to find Poppy Harris approaching, a medium-sized cattle dog at her side. "Where do you want this salad? It needs to be cold until dinner is ready."

"Let's put it in the fridge in the garage," Elise said, moving in that direction. Cosette drifted around the island until she stood at Boone's side, her fingers finding his and sliding in between them easily.

He leaned down and put his mouth right near her ear. "You're shining."

"It's Thanksgiving," she said in return.

"I'm glad you're here with me." His hand in hers tightened, and Cosette's joy grew.

"I brought you something," she said, which made him lower his head further to hear her.

"You did? What?"

"Dad," Hunter said as he came in the back door, interrupting them. "We may have a problem."

"A problem?" Gray said, walking away from his brothers and toward the back door. Colton and Wes went with him, as the dessert table flanked the door.

"Where are we all going to sit?" Cosette asked. Only two long tables had been set up in this room, and they'd only seat about sixteen. Maybe eighteen, with people on the end. That was definitely a problem for her.

"They've got tables in the garage," Matt said. "The kids are going to eat out there. Adults in here."

Cosette nodded and turned her attention back to the door, where Gray spoke with his son and his brother. Another man—Travis—crowded into the conversation, and Cosette figured they'd take care of whatever problem had dared to come to the Hammond Family farm this Thanksgiving.

Elise and Poppy returned, and Poppy asked, "Where are all the kids?"

"Out back," Bree said. "Or with Cy on the motorcycle."

She bent down and said something to her son, and Steele headed for the back door, Poppy watching him and their dog leave the house. "What's he doing here?" Her voice sent a chill over the whole group.

Cosette looked at her, and she had her eagle eyes trained on Travis. Her heart bumped out one extra beat, then two.

"His family is back east," Elise said easily. "Anyone who doesn't have anywhere else to go is welcome here."

"You didn't say he'd be here." Poppy trained her eyes on Elise, then flicked them back over to Travis. He was looking at her too, but he quickly dropped his chin.

Her hand in Boone's tightened, but Boone said nothing. Everyone watched as Poppy marched away. Only Elise said, "Poppy," weakly, but the woman wasn't going to be deterred.

She muscled her way into the conversation with the four

cowboys, and she put one palm against Travis's chest and he backed up one step, then two, before turning and leaving the house, Poppy going with him.

The awkwardness and tension that arose went with them, and Cosette breathed out. "Are they dating?" Bree asked.

Elise gave her a look, didn't confirm or deny it, and said, "All right. The turkeys are almost done. Potatoes peeled. Cosette, let's get started on your veggies."

"Yes," Cosette said, already sweating about cooking in front of all of these people. She caught sight of Raven as she sank onto the couch with another cowboy, completely unsurprised that her sister had found someone to pal around with today. She was so very good at that, and she could talk to a fence post and probably get it to laugh at some point.

"All right," a man yelled. "Who wants to see Dad ride his bike?"

The kitchen emptied as they all followed Cy Hammond down the front hallway and out the front door, leaving silence in their wake. It actually rang in Cosette's ears, and she was unsurprised to see Boone had gone. He loved Chris Hammond and if he didn't eat lunch with her, she knew she could find him at Chris's with Matt, Gloria, and Molly.

He'd asked her to join them a few times, but Cosette hadn't felt comfortable. If he asked again, she'd go, because she had new pieces getting put into place every single day.

"What's the problem?" Elise asked, wiping her hands on a towel as she went with Gray. Cosette brought up the rear, everyone else in front of them, stalling as the hallway bottle-necked everyone and slowed them down.

"We have several," Gray said. "The heaters in the garage tripped the breaker, and we can only run one."

"Okay," Elise said. "We can move a table or two inside."

"Poppy knows Travis paid her mortgage," Gray continued.

"Well." Elise blew out her breath. "Nothing to be done about that."

Cosette ducked her head, hating that she could overhear this. She wouldn't say a word to anyone. She worked with Travis, but they didn't have to talk about personal things.

"Britt and Pearl got all muddy out on the farm, so Gerty's taking them back to the cabin to get cleaned up," Gray said. "And my dad might kill himself on this super-souped up motorcycle my brother built for him. Happy Thanksgiving?"

Elise giggled, and Cosette couldn't hold her laughter back either. Gray turned to look at her, a smile on his face. "Sorry," she said. "I didn't mean to eavesdrop, and that was funny."

"Cy doesn't understand limits," Gray said, rolling his eyes. "Or seem to know that our father is in his eighties."

They finally emerged onto the porch, and Boone caught Cosette's eye, reaching for her. She went to his side, glad he tucked her close.

"Okay?" Boone asked.

"Sort of," Cosette said. "You didn't kiss me hello."

Boone grinned and pressed his lips to her temple. "I'll be

sure to kiss you good-bye," he whispered just as Cy Hammond held up both hands.

"All right, all right," he yelled. "Dad's always wanted a bike, and since I build custom bikes, his wish has finally come true." He grinned at the huge motorcycle sitting to his right. It was painted to look like a black stallion, and Cosette had never seen anything like it.

"Start 'er up, Dad," Cy said, and Chris Hammond went down the steps. He paused in front of his son and hugged him, then continued toward the motorcycle.

When he threw his leg over the seat and twisted the key, an enormous roar filled the air. All of his grandchildren cheered, and Cosette couldn't help smiling herself. And when Hunter jumped to his feet from the lawn in front of the porch and started chanting, "Grand-pa! Grand-pa!" and getting all the other kids to do it too, her heart dang near exploded.

Perhaps she did want a family to belong to. A place where she could be her best self and her worst one.

Children....

Her muscles froze, and Cosette told herself to relax. She watched the children down on the grass, and each and every one of them was adorable. Each and every one of them healed a part of her heart that had gone black years ago.

They came in all shapes, heights, and ages, some with deep, dark hair like Matt and some with blonde hair like Elise. They were all different, but they all belonged. They were all loved.

Chris Hammond revved the engine, and his grandkids got louder too.

Cosette leaned into Boone, feeling almost drunk with all of the new growth happening inside her. He held her close and held her up, and she was so very grateful for him today.

Nineteen

BOONE'S FIRST INCLINATION WAS TO JOIN IN THE chanting happening down on the lawn. None of the other adults did, however, and Boone held back. Another reason he kept his voice quiet despite the urge to get into the party was because of how Cosette stood beside him. She seemed to need him, and he cherished the thought of being necessary for someone.

Chris Hammond finally put the motorcycle in gear and sped down the road, Cy and Hunter laughing in the front yard while Wes, Gray, and Colton Hammond all said in tandem, "Dear Lord, don't let him die."

Boone couldn't help laughing then. "Did you guys practice that?"

Gray shook his head and looked at Boone. "He's *eighty-six* years old."

"He handled that thing well," Boone said. He itched to ride the motorcycle, and he would. Later. Just like he'd eat a lot of turkey and mashed potatoes later, and kiss Cosette later. "I hope I can be as spry as him in forty years."

"Not helping," Matt said from beside Boone, and everyone started to drift back inside the house.

"Come see what I brought," Cosette said, leading him down the steps.

Boone went with her easily, because he wasn't really needed in the house, and maybe he'd get to kiss her now and when he said good-bye. She led him to her SUV and opened the back. As the tailgate lifted, a long box came into view.

Boone's breath hitched in his chest. "Cosette," he said, ducking under the lift gate to get to the box. "This is a pine tree."

"For your cabin," she said. "You asked me to get one and help you set it up, and we never did it."

Boone looked at the picture of the pre-lit tree on the box and then swung his attention to the good woman who'd brought it. He engulfed her in a hug, every cell in his body vibrating with gratitude.

"Thank you," he whispered.

She wrapped him in a hug too and said, "Maybe we can go set it up after the feast."

"One-hundred percent." Boone stepped back and bent toward her to kiss her. He kept his lips light against hers, the kiss meaningful and sweet at the same time. "Thank you."

"You'll talk to Gerty about it?"

"Yeah."

She reached up and touched the button to close the back

of her SUV. "Okay, well, we'll just leave it there until we're ready."

Boone went with her back to the porch, where the kids were still tumbling up the steps, from the biggest to the littlest, and Boone grinned at all of them.

"Boone," one of the little boys said at the bottom of the steps. "Carry me."

"Sure thing, bud," Boone said, sweeping the child off his feet. "Have you met Cosette?"

The little boy giggled as Boone put him on his hip. "Wade here is four," he said, grinning at the boy. "Say hi to Cosette. She's with me." He looked at her, and Cosette's hazel eyes shone like polished gems.

"Howdy, Wade," she said. "Who are your mom and dad?"

"Uh." Wade squirmed to look over his shoulder. "Daddy's over there."

"He belongs to Cy and Patsy," Boone said. "Grows apples, right bud?"

Wade nodded, the biggest pair of dark blue eyes on his face.

"Coral Canyon sounds great," Cosette said. She moved a couple of steps away from him, and Boone noted that Hunter and Molly had stayed outside with all the grandkids. Boone supposed Hunter was Chris's grandchild, though he was all grown up. He towered above the other kids, and Michael Hammond never got too far from Hunter.

Gerty, unfortunately, stood right beside Michael. They weren't holding hands or anything, but Boone didn't think for a second that her crush on the boy was over. Oh, no. She'd run from the house yesterday afternoon, yelling, "Mike's here, Daddy! Be back later!"

She hadn't asked. She hadn't said where she'd be. She'd been reading one moment, the wind outside keeping everyone inside as much as possible, and then dashing out the door to see the boy in the next.

He and Gerty had gone to Matt's last night to help with all of the appetizer prep, and Boone hadn't had a chance to ask Gerty if or why she'd forgiven Michael. She obviously had, and Boone could scroll through his social media and see that Michael didn't have a girlfriend. He'd gone to one dance at the junior high with a girl. That meant nothing.

"Are you coming in or staying out?" Cosette asked, and Boone blinked back to the conversation.

"I'll stay out here," Boone said. "Unless you need help with the veggies."

"No," Cosette said, smiling at him. "Raven can help me, and there's plenty of others who will too." She looked at Wade again, her smile growing. "You look good with that boy in your arms, Boone." With that, she walked away, leaving him dumbfounded for several long seconds.

He and Cosette had been moving slow. He hadn't asked her about having children yet. Someone as proper and as polished as Cosette might not want kids.

As he sat on the top step and settled Wade in his lap, a little girl started up the steps too. "Come sit with me, Jilly," Boone said.

Jillian was the youngest grandchild, only a year younger

than Wade. She belonged to Ames and Sophia, and as Boone settled her on his right knee, her mother asked, "Is she okay with you?"

"Absolutely," Boone said as the tiny girl curled into his chest. "You go do whatever. I've got her." He smiled up at Sophia, who thanked him and went back inside.

Boone watched Molly and Hunter organize some lawn games for the kids, and he smiled. Hunter was such a good man, and he was so great with kids. Boone knew then that he wanted more kids, and he saw himself living Gray Hammond's life, with a huge age gap between his oldest and the family he could build with another woman.

With Cosette, he told himself, because Boone knew how he felt about the woman. He'd started falling in love with her, and he wanted to do everything in his power to protect her and show her what real love looked like, sounded like, and felt like.

"Bless me," he said right out loud. "To know which path I should be on, and to take sure steps in the direction Thou would have me go."

"Can we go on a bear hunt?" Jillian asked.

"Yes, yes," Wade said. "Bear hunt. Bear hunt."

Boone looked between the two kids. "What's a bear hunt?"

An hour later, Boone walked slower than he ever had in his whole life. Wade had his fingers wrapped around one of Boone's on the left, and Jilly on the right. They advanced slowly across the back deck and finally into the house, which radiated warmth, life, laughter, and love.

"Is everyone here?" someone asked as Boone kicked the door closed behind him.

"I think Ames is out with Goldie," someone else said. "And Cy's not back from putting the bike away yet."

While everyone else looked around to see who was missing, Boone automatically searched for his girls—Gerty and Cosette. They actually stood next to one another, Gerty dolloping whipped cream onto the tarts Cosette had brought.

They laughed and talked, both of them looking up at him simultaneously. Gerty's grin widened, and she handed Cosette the spoon. "There you are. I called, and you didn't pick up."

"We went on a bear hunt," he said with a smile.

Gerty bent and picked up Jillian. She staggered under the weight of the three-year-old, because Gerty barely weighed seventy-five pounds. She was tall and spindly, and she looked a lot weaker than she actually was. "I think Cosette needs more help with the whipped cream." She took Wade by the hand. "You guys come with me. I'll help you find your spot."

She walked away at a snail's pace, and Boone watched her for a moment. She was such a good girl, and if he and Cosette got married and started having kids, she'd be exactly like Hunter. She'd be their favorite, and she'd be the one they all looked up to.

He approached Cosette as she topped the last tart. "You always show up just as the work is done, Mister." She smiled at him, and Boone didn't care that they stood in a room full of people. All the Hammonds. Her family. Molly's parents and siblings, who'd arrived while he'd been hunting bears between barns out on the farm.

He leaned down and kissed her, seeking for something in the touch only she could give. He found it too and pulled away. "Sorry, sweetheart," he murmured. "I would've come to help."

Cosette looked at him, searching his eyes. "Are you okay?"

"Never better," he said.

"You're good with those kids."

"I love kids."

She ran the rubber spatula along the inside of the bowl, her eyes now trained on it. "Do you want more?"

He saw no reason to lie. "Yes. You?" He couldn't believe they could have this private conversation at the dessert table while other conversations happened around them and on top of them.

"I don't have any," she said.

"You could have Gerty," he said, and she pulled her eyes back to his.

"I don—she is such a great kid," Cosette said, clearing her throat.

"So you do want some kids of your own," Boone said, not really asking.

Cosette's eyes held fear, and Boone was glad he'd handed

off the kids so he could hold her. "Come talk to me," he said, taking the bowl and rubber spatula. He took a couple of steps and handed them to Gloria with, "Can you put this in the sink for me?"

"Sure," she said.

Boone returned to Cosette, who'd started braiding her fingers together the way she did when she got nervous. He put his hands in between hers to calm her. "If you don't, it's fine."

"I do," she whispered, and he only knew she'd spoken because her mouth moved. He threaded his fingers through hers, turned, and took her onto the back deck with him. Cy and Ames hadn't come in yet, and even if they missed the prayer, they wouldn't miss dinner.

"You do, but what?" Boone asked, facing her again. He'd gotten really good at reading Cosette, and he knew when he could push her and when he couldn't. Right now, he could ask and she'd answer.

"I don't know if I can," she said. "Carry a baby to full term."

"Oh." Boone didn't know what to say next. "Did you...? Did you and Joel ever get pregnant?"

"Once," Cosette said, her voice pinching. Tears didn't fill her eyes, and she reached up and brushed her hair back off her face. "I lost the baby."

"I'm so sorry," Boone said.

"It happened after...Joel kicked me in the stomach. He didn't want a baby." She whispered by the end of the sentence.

Boone had no idea what to say, because he couldn't comprehend not wanting a child he'd had a part in creating. He took Cosette into his arms and held her, starting to sway after a couple of seconds where she held him back just as tightly.

"Guys," Matt said, poking his head outside. "We're ready."

"Okay," Boone said, and Cosette stepped out of his arms. She had no tears to wipe, but she wouldn't look him in the eye either. She turned and went back inside, and Boone grabbed her hand and held it tightly so she would know she wasn't alone.

"Thank you all for coming," Gray said, beaming out at everyone. He'd climbed up onto a step-stool, so he was taller than everyone else. "I love having all of my brothers and their wives and families here in Ivory Peaks with me, and it sure means a lot to us to have you all here."

"There will always be a place for someone who needs it at this farm," Chris said from Gray's side. "We're glad we have some of our cowboys with us, and Matt and Gloria, of course. Hunter and Molly, and all of the Bensons. Thanks for joining us out here."

"There's so much food," Elise said. "No one needs to push, and if you're like some of the Hammonds, you can start at the dessert table."

"No kids can start at the dessert table," Wes Hammond said. "At least not mine."

"Mine either," Cy and Ames said at the same time, and Boone smiled at them. They were twins, and while they couldn't be more different as men, they did look alike, and they did seem to know exactly when and what the other was going to say.

"I'm starting at the dessert table," Colton said loudly, and Boone chuckled with several others.

"Dad, can I start at the dessert table?" one of Ames's twins asked, and his father shook his head. Boone grinned at the boy, because Ames had literally just said his kids couldn't eat dessert first.

"We've got two tables in the garage for the kids," Gray said. "All of the adults and our older children can eat in here. There are no assigned seats or fancy china here. Dad's going to say a prayer, and then you can come get a paper plate and get some food." He looked at his father, and cowboy hats got removed from heads. Arms got folded. Younger children got shushed.

With peace and silence raining down on the farmhouse Boone had grown to love, Chris Hammond took a breath and said, "Dear Lord, we're so grateful to be gathered here today, on this Thanksgiving Day. We give glory to Thee and to Thy son, for all of our blessings. For this land, which we love and have tried to honor. For those who come here to work and serve. Bless their minds that they may heal, and their hands that they may work and be safe."

He paused, and Boone simply basked in the spirit flowing through the house. All these tall, tough, loud cowboys stood with their hands in their wives or holding a child's. Their heads bowed in supplication to the Lord.

Boone's chest pinched, and he wished Gerty stood on

his left, so he could have Cosette on one side and his daughter on the other. They meant so much to him, as did Matt, Gloria, Keith, and Britt.

"We're grateful everyone could travel safely from Coral Canyon to be here," Chris said, his voice rougher now. "We ask a blessing on their travel home when the time comes. Bless this food and all who prepared it, and bless us all to be forgiving and kind with one another. Amen."

"Amen," everyone chorused, but it wasn't in a loud or obnoxious way. It was a final punctuation to Chris's prayer, a way for Boone to say he agreed with every word that had been offered.

He put his hat back on his head and looked over as Matt came to his side. "Love you, brother," he said, pulling Boone into a hug.

"I love you too," Boone said, realizing that he and Matt had been relying on one another for a long, long time. He hugged Gloria too, telling her he loved her too, and then he embraced Keith and Britt as well.

Gerty returned to his side, and he hugged her before turning her over to her Uncle Matt. He faced Cosette, and he said, "I'm so grateful I met you this year," before he embraced her.

"I'm grateful we met too," she whispered against his neck.

People had started to queue up to get food, but Boone released Cosette and hugged Raven. "Happy Thanksgiving," he said. "Thanks for coming out here," to which Cosette's sister replied with, "This has been *so* fun, Boone. I want to come every year."

Cosette moved over to the dessert table to help Gray's youngest son with a piece of pumpkin pie, and Boone shook hands with Jeff, who stayed out of the way while people went past them with plates full of salad, potatoes, yams, turkey, stuffing, and those amazing vegetables Cosette had made. "Well, I think I'm gonna get in line," her dad said. He took a step toward the island and then looked back. "I have never seen my daughter so happy," he said. "I don't know what kind of magic you've worked with her, but keep it up."

He nodded, and since Boone had no idea how to tell the man there was no magic involved in his relationship with Cosette, he simply nodded too.

"What did he say?" Cosette asked, having finished with Tucker.

"Nothing," Boone said, deciding to keep her father's words a secret for now. "Should we go eat?"

Cosette watched him for a moment, and he knew he couldn't keep anything from her. "You're happy, right?" he asked. "That's all he said. He said he's never seen you so happy."

She linked her arm through his, and Boone felt like he was the lucky one out of the two of them. "I am happy," she said. "Let's go eat before all of my mom's veggies are gone. I want her to be here with us this year."

They joined the line behind Wes, Bree, and their three kids, and Gerty immediately started talking to Mike about the horseback riding they could do later if it didn't snow. Boone refrained from rolling his eyes, but only barely.

"Be nice," Cosette murmured.

"That *was* me bein' nice," Boone muttered as he picked up a paper plate and passed it to her. Their eyes met, and they both smiled and laughed lightly. "You're still coming with me this weekend for...." He glanced at his daughter, but she'd moved down to the marshmallow-covered yams. "That thing?"

"Yes," Cosette said. "I'm in for *that thing*."

"What thing?" her dad asked from the other side of the island, and that drew Gerty's attention. She looked from Jeff to Boone, her eyebrows raised.

"Nothing, Dad," Cosette said. "Be sure to get some of those gourmet vegetables. They're almost gone."

That diverted his attention, and Cosette grinned while he dished up the roasted cauliflower and broccoli with a layer of stuffing on top, and then a creamy, herb-infused cream sauce on top of all of it.

Boone went through the line and filled his plate to maximum capacity. He, Cosette, her father, Raven, and Gerty managed to find places at the adult table, which had grown from two to three, and as Gerty sat down, she asked, "Do I get to know about the thing, Daddy?"

"No, baby," he said. "It's your Christmas present." He sat too and handed her a napkin. She looked at him, her big, blue eyes so wide and reminding him so much of Nikki. His heart skipped a beat, then another, and he leaned down and said, "I love you, bumblebee, okay? Me and you. I'm so grateful I get to be your dad."

Gerty nodded, tears filling her eyes. "Me and you," she repeated. "I love you too, Daddy."

He spread his napkin over his knee. "Missin' your mom?" She was, he could tell. Gerty had a look in her eye when she thought about her mother. Boone could admit that holidays were hard on him, because his family hadn't been complete since Nikki had passed away.

"A little," she admitted. "Cosette made this huge pan of vegetables for her mom. I should've done something."

"What would you do?" Boone asked, mixing his potatoes and gravy together and scooping up a bite.

"Did your mom cook?" Cosette asked from his other side.

"Not really," Gerty said. "Those frozen lasagnas." Her face lit up then. "But she loved chocolate pudding."

Boone chuckled and nodded, his mouth full of delicious foods and his heart so full it felt like it might burst. He swallowed and said, "We'll make some chocolate pudding for her tonight, baby. The day's not over yet." He glanced at Cosette. "Oh, and Cosette brought us a tree for your mama."

"I'd love to come help with the pudding or the tree," Cosette said. "Or to just eat the chocolate pudding. I haven't had that since I was a girl."

Boone said nothing, giving Gerty the chance to invite her. His daughter's face lit up the way the pre-lit tree would. "You got us a tree?"

"Yes," Cosette said, smiling at her first and then Boone. "Your daddy told me why you had one in Saffron Lake."

"Thank you," Gerty said, leaning forward to peer past Boone. "After this, we can go set up the tree and make the pudding. And you can teach me how to whip the cream like you did for the tarts."

"I would love to," Cosette said, reaching over to pat Gerty's hand, and Boone sent up another silent prayer of utter thanksgiving and gratitude for both his daughter and his girlfriend.

Twenty

COSETTE SHED HER COAT AS BOONE DROPPED THE box containing the tree she'd brought near his couch. She laid it over the back of a dining room chair as Gerty told him where she thought they should put the tree.

"Should we decorate it for Christmas?" The girl looked nervously at her father, and Cosette decided to stay out of the way. She opened her phone and started searching for chocolate pudding recipes.

She wasn't sure if Boone had a family one or not, and she could ask once they got the tree squared away.

"What do you think?" Boone asked, and Cosette looked up.

"Me?"

"Yeah, you." He grinned at her. "Christmas?"

"It is almost Christmas," she said. "And you two don't have a tree here."

Gerty sliced through the tape on the box. "We don't have any of Mom's decorations, Daddy."

"I'll get 'em when I go in January," he said easily. "We can buy some new Christmas stuff here for this year." He looked from his daughter to Cosette, something lit in his eyes. "A new start and all."

"Okay," Gerty said, struggling to pull out part of the tree. "Dad."

Boone lunged toward her and together, they pulled out the three sections of the tree. Cosette abandoned her search for a chocolate pudding recipe and went to help them. She held the cord while Boone set up the stand, and then she plugged in the bottom third of the tree as Gerty tightened the screw holding it.

Another slide, and then one more, and the other two sections of the tree went on smoothly. Gerty found the plug for the second section, and Boone had to dig around on the tallest section to get it lit.

Then, as a single unit, the three of them stood back to look at the pre-lit tree.

"I got all white lights," Cosette said into the silence. She slipped her hand into Boone's, and he put his arm around Gerty on his other side. "Because that seemed the most reverent." She frowned. "Maybe that's not the right word."

"White, like angels," Gerty said quietly. "I get it."

"It's perfect," Boone said. "Not too tall, and it's slim, so it doesn't take up too much room in here." His cabin wasn't overly large, though it did have two bedrooms and two bathrooms. Cosette hadn't been here too many times, but right now, the cabin felt like exactly where she belonged.

"Okay," Boone said, and he took a great big breath. "Chocolate pudding? " He stepped away from his daughter, but he kept his hand in Cosette's. "I hope we have milk."

"Do you have a family recipe?" she asked.

"Nope," he said. "I have a boxed mix."

Horror stole through Cosette. "A boxed mix?" She wrinkled her nose. "Really?"

"How else do you make pudding?" Gerty asked, climbing up on a barstool and leaning over the kitchen island.

Cosette looked at her in surprise. "You boil cream and add egg yolks," she said. "Chop up chocolate and melt it in." She looked from Gerty to Boone. "You don't need a mix."

Boone opened a cupboard and took out two large boxes of instant chocolate pudding. "Or," he said, his eyes twinkling like the lights on the new tree they'd just set up. "You just whisk in some milk and let it sit in the fridge for five minutes."

Gerty giggled while Cosette shook her head. "Okay, fine," she said. "You guys knew Nikki better than I did." She sounded like she'd be perfectly happy with boxed instant pudding, and that meant Cosette was too.

"She loved this stuff," Boone said. "Sometimes she'd add chocolate chips and graham crackers."

"Mm, that sounds good," Gerty said.

"There will be pie at the homestead in a couple of hours," Cosette said.

"But this is for my mom," Gerty said. "Can we add chocolate chips, Daddy?" She got down from the barstool. "And Cosette, you said you'd show me how to whip the cream."

"Yes, ma'am," Cosette said. "We just need a mixer."

"A mixer?" Boone asked, and he so wasn't the type of man to own a stand mixer. But most people had a hand mixer.

Turned out, Boone didn't. So Cosette got out a bowl and poured in the extra cream she hadn't used on her pecan tartlets. "This is so much easier with a mixer," she said, grinning at the two of them. "But we can do it by hand too." She started whisking, and then she added, "Get a bit of sugar, Gerty. Vanilla too, if you have it."

After quite the search through their cupboards, Boone and Gerty came up with vanilla, and Cosette instructed Gerty to put in one teaspoon, along with a couple of the sugar.

Several minutes later, the cream finally peaked, and Boone pulled the pudding out of the fridge too. He added a handful of chocolate chips and stirred them in, then divided up the pudding into three bowls.

"Here you go," he said, and Cosette added a dollop of whipped cream to their pudding.

"Done," she said.

"Let's eat it by the tree," Gerty said, leading them all over to the single couch in the living room. She sat on one end, leaving the other two spots for Boone and Cosette.

She sat first, grinning up at the gorgeous cowboy who'd

invited her into his cabin, his family, and his life, and dug into her chocolate chip pudding.

"Mm," she said as the first cold bite touched her tongue and Boone sat next to her. "This isn't half-bad."

Boone took a bite too, looked at the tree, and said nothing. The feeling of acceptance and peace in the cabin overcame Cosette, and she took another bite of her pudding with the hint of tears burning in the backs of her eyes.

"Thanks for this," she said after several minutes of silence. They'd all finished their pudding, and she got up. She turned back and took their bowls, both Gerty and Boone looking up at her as she did.

"Thanks, Cosette," Gerty said with a smile, and Boone stood and followed her into the kitchen.

She put the bowls in his sink and stood still as he slid his arm around her waist. Leaning into him felt natural and wonderful, and he pressed a kiss to her temple. "Thank you," he whispered. "This means so much to me, and to Gerty."

A smile touched Cosette's mouth and infused her soul, and she snuggled further into Boone's chest. "Happy Thanksgiving," she said, her gratitude for a great many things expanding faster than she could catalog it.

COSETTE PULLED ON HER BOOTS, TUGGING THEM all the way up to her knees. She zipped up the sides, feeling the chill of the new winter weather though all of her doors and windows remained closed.

She stood and reached for her coat, and thankfully, the snow had stopped overnight. She'd waved to the teenage boys who lived down the street as they'd finished up with plowing her driveway and shoveling her walk. She could pay them electronically, and she didn't have to freeze while she tried to lift the heavy, wet snow.

She sipped her coffee and made toast and eggs for breakfast, buoyed by the fact that Boone would take her to lunch after they went to look at the horses for sale at a farm about an hour away from Ivory Peaks.

Her doorbell rang, and Cosette grabbed her purse from the kitchen island and turned toward the door. "Coming," she called, beyond excited to see the man on the other side of the door. That was such a new feeling for her, and Cosette took a moment to enjoy the feathery, fluttering way her pulse moved through her body as she walked to get the door.

She opened it, but Boone didn't stand there. "Oh," she said, hitching her purse higher up on her shoulder as she stepped back. She brought the door back toward her, but it bumped against her boot. "Can I help you?"

She didn't need to be afraid of every male she came in contact with, but her pulse had started to act weirdly at the sight of this one on her step. She gripped the door and edged her boot behind it slightly.

"Yes," the man said, his smile instant. "I see your driveway is cleared already. My wife and I just moved in around the corner, and I have a couple of slipped disks in my back. Did you do this, or do you hire it out?"

Relief sang through Cosette, and she returned the man's smile. "There's a couple of boys three houses down," she said, hooking her thumb to the left. "They come do it for me after every big snowstorm. Pretty reasonable too. They have an ATV and they get it done in about twenty minutes."

The man nodded, his phone out as he typed. "Can I get their names?"

"The oldest one is Ricky Rogers," she said. "I pay him and text him the most."

"Would you mind giving me his number?" The man looked so hopeful, but Cosette hesitated. She wouldn't want someone giving out her phone number, but she reasoned through the discomfort before jumping to a conclusion.

"Sure," she said. "He's only fifteen, so I'm pretty sure his mom checks his phone." She gave the man the number, and he thanked her. He started down the steps as the grumbling engine of Boone's truck arrived in her driveway.

Cosette waved to him, then quickly pulled her phone from her purse and sent a message to Ricky about the new person in town.

"Howdy," Boone said outside on the sidewalk, clearly undisturbed by the stranger leaving Cosette's house. Their lower male voices mingled as they chatted for a moment, and Cosette got a confirmation from Ricky, as well as an expression of gratitude for passing along his name and number, and she stepped out onto her porch.

"Good morning," Boone said at the bottom of the steps.

Cosette practically skipped down them toward him, that humming feeling returning at the sight of him. He wore blue jeans, cowboy boots, and a dark brown leather jacket that had to be tinted the exact same color as his cowboy hat.

"Wow, you look amazing," she said. "I thought we were going to look at horses." She reached him and ran one hand up the front of his jacket. He grinned down at her and received her into his arms effortlessly.

"We are," he said, leaning down to kiss her.

Despite the cold, Cosette could stand outside and kiss this man for a good, long while. She didn't need to give her neighbors a show, so she stepped back after hardly any time at all.

"You look pretty today too," he said, taking her hand and going with her down the sidewalk to his truck.

"Thanks," Cosette said, because she had put some effort into her clothes and makeup that day, and it was nice to hear.

"You ate breakfast?" Boone asked.

"Yes, sir," she said. "You told me we had a drive, and then the horses, and then we could go to lunch." She looked over to him and found that hint of mischief in his eyes. "Boone," she said, her voice full of warning.

"I was just thinking that there's all this glorious snow, and they're doing two shows today for the horses...." He lifted one shoulder in a shrug as they continued around the front of his truck. "Maybe we could do something else this morning, and see the horses this afternoon."

"Don't you have one you want for Gerty?"

"They're going to hold it for me," Boone said.

Cosette blinked at him, sure she hadn't heard him right. Then, she realized that men like Boone Whettstein simply possessed charm and charisma that allowed them to go play in the snow, take their girlfriends to lunch, and *still* get the horse they wanted.

He seemed touched with gold and magic, and Cosette took in a deep breath of him. "You sweet-talked the owner."

He grinned. "Maybe," he said, opening her door for her. She climbed into the truck and set her purse on the floor at her feet while Boone crowded into her side. "You don't want to go see if we can take a sleigh ride? They started those today, out in Goldendale."

He put his hand across her lap, then ran it up her arm, finally curling it around the back of her head to bring her closer to him. "Sounds fun, right?" He spoke with the low, husky voice that caused shivers to run down Cosette's spine.

"You have tickets already, don't you?"

"Maybe," he whispered just before he kissed her. Cosette told herself the truck concealed them, and she didn't need to worry about anyone seeing her kiss Boone. When he deepened the kiss, that sexy groan coming from his throat, she stopped caring who saw. She matched Boone stroke for stroke, telling herself it was okay to enjoy kissing him, it was okay to spend the whole day with him, it was okay to fall in love with him.

He pulled away, and when Cosette finally opened her eyes, he was already gazing at her. "I sure do like kissing you,

Cosette," he said, that mouth able to say so many things she couldn't.

"You like me too, right?" she asked, her voice a tad higher than normal. She couldn't believe she'd asked him that, and she didn't have to look for longer than half a second to see how he felt about her, right there in his eyes.

"I adore you," he said, and her smile spread across her face and through her whole soul.

She kissed him again, hoping she could show him how much she adored him. He chuckled against her lips, breaking their connection. "I do have tickets for that sleigh ride. You can't just kiss me all morning." He started to back up, his confidence one of the things she liked best about him.

"Boone," she said, and he turned back to her. She swallowed, those brown eyes of his waiting, open, ready. "I adore you too." The words very nearly scraped her throat on the way out, and she was lucky she'd been able to vocalize them.

He grinned wider than any other time she'd seen him, and he ducked his head in the most adorable way ever. "I'm glad, Cosette." He closed her door and walked toward the front of the truck.

Cosette watched him, wondering when she'd become someone who could feel and love again. Things had gotten so messed up inside her mind and heart, but because Boone could whisper to horses on their own level, and he didn't have a mean or aggressive bone in his body, he'd somehow been able to coax Cosette out of her shell, away from the cave where she'd buried herself, and back out into the light.

She bent to get out her sunglasses as the man swung into the truck, and she put them on as she turned toward him. "Ready?"

"So ready," he said. "And if you didn't eat a big breakfast, they'll have hot chocolate and scones with raspberry butter on the sleigh ride." He flipped the truck into reverse and eased out of her driveway.

"I swear, Boone," she said, plenty of teasing in her voice. "Only you could make riding around in frigid temperatures sound fun."

"If you don't want to go," he said. "We don't have to." He brought the truck to a stop. "I'd just hang out here with you." He reached over and took her hand in his. "I got Gerty off to that riding camp today, and I just want to spend the whole day with you." He brought her wrist to his lips. "Is that so wrong?"

"No," fell from her mouth. "Not wrong."

He cocked his head to the side, waiting.

"It's just...." She exhaled and looked out the window, gently pulling her hand back from his. "I'm not used to anyone wanting to spend all day with me."

"Well, I do want that," Boone said. "So sleigh or no sleigh?"

"I'm not going to say no to hot chocolate and scones with raspberry butter."

Boone laughed, and Cosette put a smile on her face. She looked away from him as he started to drive again, wondering why she felt so awkward. Everything with Boone had been easy, and Cosette had truly been surprised several times over the past few months they'd been dating and getting to know one another.

Surprised at herself. Surprised that her heart hadn't been completely shriveled and blackened by her experiences with Joel. Surprised that her spirit hadn't been totally crushed, and that she'd been able to recover as much as she had.

"Boone?" she asked.

"Hmm?"

She turned toward him. "Can we spend Christmas at my house? Just the three of us?"

He glanced over to her. "Me, you, and Gerty?"

"I guess there will be four," she said. "With the horse."

Boone smiled and nodded. "We can definitely do that."

"Gerty won't be upset? I could come to your house." He'd be keeping the horse at the farm already, and she certainly had nowhere to house the equine for Gerty to find on Christmas morning.

"Why don't you come over in the morning?" he suggested. "I'll make breakfast, and we'll do the present thing." He looked at her again. "I already know what I'm going to get for you."

"You do?"

He smiled as wide as the sky again. "Oh, yeah."

"I have no idea what to get for you," she said.

"What?" he asked. "I'm easy. Just put together one of those gift baskets I've seen you hand out to parents. I'd love that."

Horror shot through Cosette. "A gift basket? You're joking."

"I am? Why?"

"Gift baskets are what realtors give to their clients when they sign all their documents. It's what we give out to people as a token of appreciation. It's not what a girlfriend gives to her very serious boyfriend for the biggest gift-giving holiday of the year." She shook her head, disgusted with the very idea.

"Very serious boyfriend?"

"Come on," she said without looking at him. "You know where I'm coming from. You know you're the first person I've even considered dating in over a decade. If this isn't very serious, you better take me home right now."

Boone didn't so much as let up on the accelerator. "It's very serious," he said in a very serious voice.

"Yeah, you're just very serious about the scones," Cosette said in a dry tone.

Boone laughed again, and she did love the easy, free sound of his voice in her life. "It's actually the hot cocoa, Cosette. I'm a sucker for that stuff. Put together a hot chocolate gift basket for Christmas, and I just might ask you to marry me."

Cosette shook her head while he laughed again, and when he reached for her hand, she willingly slipped her fingers between his.

He drove them west, further into the mountains, along the plowed road until they reached the trailhead for a hike Cosette had never done. A few people milled about, and when Boone opened her door for her, he stayed back to let her out.

He said, "I brought gloves and a hat for you." He retrieved them from the back seat and handed them to her. "Look, they even match." He smiled as she put them on, because there was no way she could get in an open-air moving vehicle without something to keep her hands and ears warm.

"You're amazing," he said, taking her into his arms. "And so cute in that hat." He touched his lips to her cheek. "One serious question before we go check-in."

"All right," she said, holding onto him as they stood beside his truck.

"If you met the right man and fell in love with him, you'd want to get married, right?"

Cosette stepped away from Boone, finding a river of uncertainty and anxiety in his eyes that she rarely saw on the man's face. "Joel didn't ruin you completely to the idea of marriage, home, family? Did he?"

"Yes," she said.

Boone's eyebrows went up on the edges and down in the middle, his frown deep. "Yes? He did?"

"I mean, no," Cosette said, frustration and a flustery feeling filling her. "If I met this amazing, handsome, charming cowboy with a seriously cute, smart, and loving daughter, and I fell in love with him, and he loved me, and we wanted to grow our family...I'd think about marrying him."

"Oh, boy," Boone said, everything about his expression lightening. "I'm gonna have to figure out how to be amazing, handsome, and charming."

Cosette laughed, her heart growing wings and taking off into the sky.

"Boone," someone called behind them, and he turned.

"That's us, baby. Let's go get our sleigh-ride on."

Still giggling, Cosette went with him, collected her hot cocoa and warm scone with raspberry butter, and climbed into the sleigh. "Ooh, the seats are heated," she said.

"And look." He pointed with his mug. "Cup holders and a tray." He leaned forward and put his boxed scone on the tray which had been fashioned over the seat on the opposite side.

With a warm blanket covering both of their legs, the driver yah'ed at his horse, and the sleigh started swishing through the snow. Cosette closed her eyes and turned her face heavenward, feeling the warmth of the sun but the cold bite in the air on her skin at the same time.

Help me to heal enough to keep Boone in my life, she prayed. *Help me to be enough for him, and for Gerty, though I'm nothing too special.*

She opened her eyes, the last of her prayer dissipating into nothingness. She had the overwhelming feeling that she was special—very special—and she needed to stop thinking she wasn't.

Help me with believing and knowing that too, she thought just before Boone handed her a plastic knife so she could slather the raspberry butter all over her scone.

Twenty-One

Matthew Whettstein hefted another bag of feed out of the back of the truck and turned. He went past Mission and Cord, both of whom were lined up to get their loads too. In the storage room, Travis held a clipboard in his hand, and he checked off the chicken feed and pointed to the far corner. "Over there, Matt, thanks."

The muscles in Matt's back and arms felt like wet noodles, but he got the feed where it belonged. Cord brought in a couple of sacks of horse pellets, as did Mission. Cody brought up the rear with more chicken feed, and by then Matt headed out again.

Back and forth the four of them moved, unloading their supplies for the next six weeks. That would get them through the holidays and all of January, and Matt wasn't looking forward to this job again, that was for sure.

Though he wore gloves, his fingers felt like blocks of ice,

and the wind whistled at him every time he had to take the two steps outside of the barn to pick up his load. Finally, Cody hauled in the last two bags of hay cubes, which a couple of the horses down the aisle could seem to smell from a mile away. They'd nickered as he'd gone by, and Travis led the men back outside to the truck.

He signed the work order, and the truck driver signed his clipboard, and the job finally finished. Matt's day still held plenty of things to do, but he took the water bottle offered to him by Travis, and the five of them stood in a huddle in the heated stable to take a much-needed break and rehydrate.

"What are y'all doin' for the holidays?" Cord asked. He was new on the farm, and Gray had originally hired him to build the stable in which they now stood. He'd done a bang-up job of it too, and Matt had never seen anyone work as fast as Cord Behr did with a hammer in his hands. He hailed from Texas, as evidenced by his stronger cowboy drawl than anyone else on the farm.

"I'm staying here," Matt said. "Travis is too, I believe." He looked at the other cowboy for confirmation.

"Thanksgiving was such a riot, I figured why not?" Travis smiled around at the group.

"Yeah, I think Poppy Harris was the thing keepin' you in town," Mission said before throwing back the last of his water like it was something else.

"No," Travis said, though he ducked his head, minimizing the power the word could've had. He raised his head again and gazed around at everyone. "She doesn't like me all that much, trust me. Took me outside and chewed me up one side and down the other."

Matt said nothing, but his mind moved through scenarios that would warrant that. It was Mission who asked, "Why'd she do that?"

"Because," Travis said simply, no elaboration in sight.

"You stayed," Matt said. "You could've taken your plate of food back to your cabin, but you didn't."

Travis nodded a few times. "There's something about being all alone on major holidays," he said. "I don't like being alone much."

"Really?" Cord asked, his eyebrows shooting sky-high. "That's not what you bellowed at me yesterday morning. I seem to recall somethin' about how you used to enjoy yourself in the mornings before I moved in." He grinned at Travis, who looked back at him stone-faced.

"I believe I said I used to be able to get ready on time," Travis said with zero inflection in his voice.

Matt grinned at Cord and shook his head. "All right, boys," he said, remembering that he'd put Travis in charge of the unloading but he was the acting farm manager. "We just have our evening feed, and we're done for today."

"Elise is doing the doughnuts tonight," Cody said. "For anyone who wants to come." He held up his phone. "We just got a text reminding us of the Sweet Treats event."

Matt's heart warmed at the way Gray and Elise included everyone who worked on the farm in their family activities. Molly and Hunter would likely be at the farmhouse, as would Chris. Matt wanted to go, because he wanted his kids to have the familial experiences of a big family like the Hammonds had.

"Great," Mission said. "Let's get these chores done and get dinner over with. I can't eat a mountain of doughnuts on an empty stomach." He and Cody went to tend to their assigned animals, and Cord followed them.

Travis hung back, and Matt glanced at him. "Everything's okay with Cord, right?" he asked almost under his breath.

"Yep." Travis handed the clipboard to Matt, who didn't look at it. Gray would want it on his desk, but Matt didn't think he'd look at it either. Unless there was a problem. Then Gray would handle anything. "He's great. I was just teasing him the other morning. He does take forever to trim his beard."

Matt chuckled and nodded. "You should see Boone. He thinks that beard is his saving grace."

Travis's stoic demeanor finally cracked, and he too smiled and shook his head. "Boone. That guy's a real character." He met Matt's eye. "He seems to be gettin' on well with Cosette."

"Yep," Matt said, because he didn't want to divulge details of Boone's private life. Not that he knew many. Boone had been particularly tight-lipped about his relationship with Cosette, and though he'd mentioned going on a double-date several times, Matt and Gloria still had not gone out with them.

His kids made that harder than it might be otherwise, as did Gerty. If the two couples went out, someone would have to take all three kids. In all honesty, Keith could stay home and make sure the girls didn't burn the house to the ground while the adults went out. He could drive them to the medical center if there was an emergency, and Keith was very responsible when it came to Britt and Gerty.

"Good for him," Travis said. "I've known Cosette a while, and she's a bit of a tough nut to crack."

"True," Matt said. Boone had mentioned that she had some hard things in her past, and Matt had kindly pointed out that so did he. Their mom leaving when they were younger. Their dad withdrawing even though he'd stayed. His wife dying. Leaving Saffron Lake. Boone hadn't even sold the place yet, and Matt had stopped asking him about the ten acres in Montana that his brother still owned.

His phone chimed several times in quick succession, and he pulled it from his coat pocket. "It's Gloria," he said, frowning at the multiple messages that said the same thing. "I might be in a dead zone."

"Matt," someone called. "Matt?"

Molly's voice sounded on the outer edge of panic, and Matt looked up from his device at the same time he started toward the sound of her voice. "I'm here," he called, Travis right behind him. "What's wrong?"

Molly exited the hallway in a jog, which definitely meant something was wrong. "Gloria needs you," she said.

"Is it Britt?" he asked, reaching her. "You don't need to run. If Hunter finds out, he'll fillet me."

"I'm fine," Molly said, though she definitely breathed harder. "She's in the front barn."

"Did she go rollerblading?" Matt asked, already walking away from Molly at a good clip. "I told her it was too cold." Gloria loved to get out on the open road, nothing but the open sky in front of her, a dog and a horse trotting at her side, and Britt in the running stroller in front of her.

Britt loved it too, and Matt wouldn't deny his wife or his daughter anything if he didn't have to. Gloria had taken other children from Pony Power on her rollerblading excursions, and everyone seemed to love it.

He burst out of the back barn and kept going. Thunder crashed overhead, but he didn't care. He barely heard Molly and Travis behind him as he yanked open the door to get into the next barn. "Gloria?" he called as he ran down the aisle.

Where are you? had come through his phone twice. *I need to talk to you* had as well. He made it past the stalls to the big open area where they unloaded new horses when they got them. In front of him, a row of washing stalls were usually occupied by horses and Gerty, who was in charge of making sure everyone was clean when they needed to be.

Right now, Gloria stood in front of one of the stalls, and when she turned at the sound of his footsteps, he saw instantly that she'd been crying. "Hey," he said, jogging toward her still. "What's going on? I was in the back barn and didn't get your texts until Molly had found me anyway."

He reached her and took her into his arms, searching her face. "Did you fall? Where's Britt?" Gloria didn't seem to have a scratch on her, and Matt held onto her shoulders as he looked at her. His heart pounded in the back of his throat and behind his eyes. His wife didn't cry. Very rarely, at least.

"Britt's okay," Gloria said, her voice nasally and her eyes filling with tears again. "The kids are fine."

Matt waited, his hands moving up and down his wife's arms. "Gloria," he said. "You never cry."

She looked down at the ground, her tears splashing her cheeks as she did. She shook her head and looked up into his eyes again. "Matt, I'm pregnant."

His eyes widened as his spirit soared. "You are?"

She nodded, her smile matching the one filling him from head to toe and back to the very tippy top of his skull. He grinned too, his hands tightening on her biceps. "You are." He wasn't asking this time, and his heart raced through his ribs for an entirely different reason now.

He started to laugh, and he leaned down to press a sloppy kiss to his wife's lips. "I'm so happy," he whispered, leaning his forehead against hers. He wasn't the whooping, throw-his-hat-up-into-the-air kind of cowboy. Boone would've done that, but Matt held his wife in his arms, closed his eyes, and swayed with her, imagining what their child would look like.

"Me too," Gloria whispered. "Do you want a boy or a girl?"

"Both," Matt said, straightening again. He couldn't wipe the smile from his face.

"One at a time, cowboy," she said, and he wiped her tears from her cheeks gently.

"You're crying out of happiness," he said. "Yes? Or shock?"

"Both," she said. "I took two tests, because I didn't believe the first one."

"He found her," Molly said, arriving in the barn. Matt turned toward her, the news wanting to burst from him. He should tell Boone first, however, and the children, so he slipped his hand into Gloria's as they faced their boss.

"I found her," he said, joy spilling from him in waves. Travis was hot on Molly's heels, his concern written in his eyes. "We're fine. Everything is okay."

Molly nodded, her eyes flitting from Gloria to Matt and back. "Okay," she said. "Are you sure? Anything I can do?"

"Just make sure they don't run out of doughnuts tonight until we get back," Matt said, squeezing Gloria's hand. They hadn't discussed who they'd tell if she ever did get pregnant. He was no spring chicken, and neither was she. They'd decided not to wait to try to have children, and they'd only been married for about four months.

"Do you need me to take care of your horses?" Travis asked.

"No," Gloria said, sniffing and wiping her face. "We can do it. Really, I'm okay." She nodded at both of them, her usual demeanor sliding right back into place. Matt exchanged a glance with her, and they both nodded at Molly and Travis again.

"Thanks for coming to get me," Matt said. "That back barn is like a nexus of no service." He grinned at the two of them and tugged on Gloria's hand to get her to come with him. "We'll be down the aisle for a bit."

They got to work, and Matt said nothing while Molly talked to Travis for a couple of minutes. Only when they'd both left, and he and Gloria were alone, did he sneak into the stall where his wife spread out new straw, and say, "I love you, sweetheart."

He kissed her, beyond glad the Lord had brought them back together after many years apart. He'd now trusted them with a brand-new life to raise, nurture, and love, and Matt prayed with all the energy of his soul that he could be the father and husband the Lord wanted him to be.

"Should we have Boone for dinner?" Gloria whispered. "Tell him and the kids together?"

"Sure," Matt said, kissing her again. "When?"

"Whenever," Gloria said, leaning back against the wall in the stall. "Maybe when we have our Christmas dinner together." She smiled as she looked into his eyes, her fingers tracing down the side of his face in a tender, loving way.

Matt nodded, touching his lips to hers once more. Boone, Cosette, and Gerty were slated to come for dinner next weekend, which was the last before Christmas. Matt hadn't known how happy he'd be to have family in the area, but being able to celebrate Whettstein-style with Boone and his family had brought him more satisfaction than he could describe.

"We'll tell them next week," he whispered, and then he kissed the woman he loved one more time.

"We'll definitely be late for doughnuts if you keep this

up," she whispered, but she tilted her head back to give him clear access to her neck. He couldn't just walk away from kissing her there.

"Mm," he said. Doughnuts were nothing when compared to kissing Gloria, and he decided they could be late to the farmhouse for the Sweet Treats event.

Twenty-Two

BOONE PULLED UP TO HIS BROTHER'S HOUSE, THE front windows aglow with beautiful Christmas lights. He grinned at them as he put the truck in park. "Britt got her way," he said, as the multi-colored lights cast greens, blues, and reds onto the snow piled out front.

"She always does," Gerty said. "Uncle Matt can't tell her no." She opened her door and swung out of the truck, reaching back to grab the container of cookies she'd baked that afternoon.

"Sounds like someone else I know," Cosette murmured as she too started to slide from the truck. Boone watched her, not sure if he should defend himself or not. She hadn't said the words with any ill intent, so Boone remained silent as she slammed her door and met Gerty at the front of the truck.

Cosette put her arm around Gerty and smiled at her. His daughter actually smiled back, and Boone was once again

275

reminded of how powerful it was to have two parents. When all he wanted to do was gripe at Gerty for making a huge mess in the kitchen, Cosette told her how amazing her baking skills were.

They went into the open garage and up the few steps to the small landing before entering the house. More light peeked out as they entered, and then the door closed again. Boone sat in the silence, his heart beating out a steady rhythm. He closed his eyes and listened.

"Lord," he finally said. Nothing else came to his mind. He floated in all the darkness, just the hint of Christmas lights outside his eyelids. He sure had enjoyed the past three weeks since Thanksgiving, and he needed to be here at Matt's tonight. They hadn't shared Christmas together in a while, and he finally got out of the truck and followed Gerty and Cosette inside.

"...and then you put on the eyes," Britt said from her position on the kitchen counter. The girl was a waif at best, and Boone could always find her on top of something, usually with Pearl nearby. Tonight, Boone didn't see the golden retriever, and he supposed someone else had taken her home with them.

"Uncle Boone," Britt said, looking up at him. "Come make your pizza."

"We have to make our own pizzas?" He handed the six-pack of soda he'd brought to his brother, then hugged him. "Merry Christmas, bro."

"Everything's practically done," Matt said, grinning as he stepped back. "Merry Christmas to you too." Matt wore something calculating in his eye, and Boone didn't want to talk about anything serious tonight.

He wanted pizza and cake; he wanted to exchange stockings; he wanted to sing carols around the piano. Both he and Matt played, and he'd texted his brother about who would be on the bench tonight.

Matt had volunteered, of course, claiming that Boone was better out in front of the crowd, getting them "hyped up" and waving his arm around like a fool pretending to be a conductor.

Tonight, Boone didn't feel like being out front. He wasn't sure why. He'd been looking forward to tonight's dinner for a couple of weeks now, since Gloria had invited him, Cosette, and Gerty.

Gray and Elise had been having family events all month long, and the big Christmas party for the farm would be on Sunday evening, two nights from now. Then the Hammonds were going to Coral Canyon for Christmas, something they did every year. Matt and Gloria were taking the kids north with Gray and Elise this year, because Gray had spent so much time talking about the tree cutting and decorating that happened at a lodge in Wyoming.

Boone wondered what it would be like to have so much money he didn't have to worry about his farm. He could leave whenever he wanted, for as long as he wanted, and he could afford to pay someone else to look after everything.

He thought about his farm up in Montana, and he wondered if he and Gerty should take a trip north too. He glanced over to Cosette, wondering if she'd ever leave Ivory Peaks and the Denver area.

Probably not, he thought, his mind whispering the words. Raven and her dad lived here, and Cosette did need a very strong support system.

Boone didn't really want to return to Saffron Lake anyway. While the place held plenty of amazing memories for him, it was also a site of great loss and tremendous heartache. He didn't want to explain anything to the people in town, and he thought it was probably time to let go of Saffron Lake and Montana.

He just didn't know how. He wanted to talk to Matt about it, but his brother had been extraordinarily busy with all the bad weather, his kids and the end of their term at school, and getting ready to go on a road trip with his family.

Not only that, but Matt had to make sure the farm was taken care of in his absence too, and Boone couldn't simply leave because he wanted to. He'd committed to Matt to help out while he and Gray were gone, and his fantasies about taking time off to travel dried right up.

"Boone," Matt said, and Boone blinked.

"What?" He glared at his brother, who stood maybe a foot from him, his voice loud and still echoing through Boone's head.

"You zoned out on me," Matt said.

"Sorry," Boone mumbled while Matt asked, "Did you want to build your own pizza or just eat the combination we made?"

"Combination is fine," he said, looking over to Britt.

Her big, blue eyes tugged at his soul, and he changed his mind. "I mean, I want to build my own." He obviously couldn't tell his niece no either, and he didn't blame Matt for a moment.

"Come look at mine, Uncle Boone," Britt said. "I made a reindeer."

Boone took the couple of steps to the counter where she sat and looked at her dough, sauce, cheese, and toppings. He couldn't find any semblance of an animal, deer or not, but he smiled at her. "Look at that."

"Did you want olives?" she asked, lifting the bowl.

"I need some dough first," he said, looking at Gerty's pizza. "Maybe I could share with you."

"Nope," his daughter said, her teen superiority voice employed. "Cosette and I are building one together." She looked at him, her blue eyes cold like winter ice. "Sorry, Daddy." She didn't sound sorry, but Boone only nodded.

"Dough right here," Gloria said, pressing in beside him to put a personal-sized circle of dough in front of him. "Two types of sauces. All the toppings. Pizzas are going in the oven in two minutes. Build fast."

Boone took the challenge seriously, because he knew Gloria, and when she said two minutes, she meant one and a half. He threw on sausage, olives, green peppers, and plenty of pepperoni with his red sauce and handfuls of cheese.

"Uncle Boone," Britt said. "What in the world?"

"You sounded just like Dad," Keith said, sliding his pizza onto a tray and handing it to Gloria. "Didn't she, Dad?"

"Sure did, baby." Matt grinned at his daughter.

"Mine's a snowstorm," Boone said, sweeping his hand across all the white cheese scattered everywhere. "This is how a small town looks at night, when the snow is really flying."

Gerty gave him a look that said *You're ridiculous,* but Cosette smiled at him and Britt tilted her head as if really trying to see the snowstorm. Her face lifted, and she grinned at him.

"It does look like a snowstorm, Uncle Boone."

"Thank you, sweetie." He scooped her into his arms, causing her to squeal, and left his tray for someone else to put in the oven. "Come sing with me." He took her over to the piano in Matt's front room and settled her onto the bench beside him.

His fingers moved across the keys, finding chords. "You start," he said, feeling the weight of Gerty's and Cosette's eyes on him. He didn't care. Gerty had left her chores early and then proceeded to leave a massive mess in the kitchen they'd have to clean up after they got home from this party. He'd had every right to be upset with her after he'd walked in late, because he'd had to finish her jobs.

"Is this *Away in a Manger?*" Britt asked.

He nodded, and played the opening notes again, giving her a strong nod when she was meant to come in. Her sweet, high-pitched voice filled the air, and the tension inside Boone's chest released.

Keith wandered closer, as did Gerty and Matt. The three of them came in on the second verse, and Boone smiled to himself as he looked at the ivory and ebony keys. He hadn't meant to start the caroling right now, but the sound of his family's voices had healed the fissures that had started in his heart.

They finished the song, and Boone lifted his fingers from the keys. He looked up at everyone and said, "Merry Christmas," in a throaty voice. "Sorry, Matt. I know we were going to do that later."

"We still can," Matt said. Gloria came to his side, and they exchanged a meaningful look. "We have something we want to tell everyone."

Boone stayed on the bench with Britt as Matt took his wife's hand in his. They smiled like they'd learned the best news ever. "We're going to have a baby," Matt said, his glow suddenly making so much sense.

Britt screamed, a joyous, loud squeal that had her scrambling to the end of the bench and right off of it. "A baby, a baby!" she yelled. Gerty and Keith laughed at her, and even Keith looked really happy about this news.

Gerty hugged her aunt and uncle, and Boone was glad their exchange from earlier this evening hadn't spoiled her whole attitude. Even Cosette embraced Matt and Gloria, saying, "Congratulations, you two. How exciting for you."

Boone sat on the piano bench, wondering why his first reaction wasn't pure, unadulterated bliss for his brother. Gloria was perfect for him, and they'd waited a long time to be together. Gloria didn't have any biological children, and he should've expected this news to come any day now. Or earlier than tonight.

He got to his feet, a numb feeling spreading through him, and hugged his brother. "Congrats," he said with his voice, but his heart had emptied completely. He kissed Gloria's cheek, his smile fake and plastered onto his face strangely. "To you too."

He retreated to Cosette's side and grounded himself by putting his hand in hers. She squeezed, and when he looked at her, he saw that she knew something was wrong. He didn't know how to hide it, and he wouldn't ruin Matt's good news with his sour attitude.

He wasn't exactly sour, and he searched for the right descriptor. Jealous. He was *jealous* of his brother and all Matt had managed to do in the past couple of years. He'd uprooted his kids and moved to Colorado. He'd found the perfect woman for him and married her. They lived in this picture-perfect house, with double ovens so they could bake several pizzas at the same time.

And now they were starting a family. All of the above were things Boone wanted in his life, and it seemed like every one of Matt's accomplishments only served to showcase Boone's failures.

He pushed against the feelings, because they were neither new nor true. He'd felt like this often with his older brother, and if he could just figure out how to breathe and then swallow, he'd be fine.

"Pizzas are done!" Britt chirped, and Boone blinked as he finally heard the timer. The kids went into the kitchen, followed by Gloria, and that left Boone and Matt looking at one another, with Cosette holding Boone's hand.

"I'll go help them," Cosette said, delicately removing herself from the awkward situation.

"Me too," Boone said, not wanting to let go of her hand. She anchored him, and he didn't want to be alone in the stormy seas of his jealousy.

"Boone," Matt said, and Boone let Cosette's fingers slip out of his as she stepped around him and walked into the kitchen.

He sighed and looked at Matt. "Congrats, brother," Boone said, not trying to put a false smile on his face this time.

"You don't sound happy," Matt said, stepping into Boone's arms.

"I am," Boone said. "Sure I am. You and Gloria wanted a family, and now you're going to have it."

Matt pulled away, but he didn't remove his hands from Boone's shoulders. "What's eating at you?"

"Nothing," Boone lied. He told himself it was a little white lie, and it didn't hurt Matt. He would not ruin this joyous moment for his brother. "Just a little thing with Gerty tonight is all."

Matt looked into the kitchen, and Gerty happened to look over her shoulder at the same time. "All right," Matt said. "You send her over here if she's really bugging you."

"She's not," Boone said. "You're going to be gone anyway." He gave his daughter a smile, and she turned back to the counter as Gloria slid a tray of pizzas onto it. "I'm thinkin' of going to Saffron Lake over the holidays."

Matt whipped his attention back to Boone. "Really?"

Boone shrugged. "Maybe."

"Is the water even on?"

"No," Boone said. If he left the water on in Montana, all of his pipes would be busted by now. He didn't like his brother's tone of voice, though he should probably listen to Matt. "There's nothing in Montana anyway," he said.

"That's not true," Matt said quietly. "But I don't know about you goin' up there for the holidays." He looked over his shoulder, his dark eyes coming back to Boone's. "Aren't you and Cosette spending Christmas morning together?"

Yes, they were, and Boone nodded, glancing over to the gorgeous redhead he'd been falling for fairly steadily. "Yeah."

"And you'll go in January to see Nikki anyway," Matt said, clearly saying Boone didn't need to go to Saffron Lake for the holidays.

"Let's go eat," Boone said as Gloria glanced their direction. He looked at Matt fully now. "Really, I'm thrilled for you."

He hugged his brother again, adding an extra squeeze so Matt would know Boone would work through his own issues and not bother anyone else with them.

"We're okay?" Matt asked, putting his hands on either side of Boone's neck.

"Yes," Boone said. "I'm just being stupid. I'll be fine."

"Maybe we shouldn't go to Coral Canyon."

"No," Boone said quickly. "Matt, really. I'm fine."

His brother searched his face and then nodded. "I know you're not, but I believe you will be."

"Daddy," Britt called. "Gloria wants to pray."

"Yes," Matt said, dropping his hands and turning. He walked away from Boone and into the kitchen. "Let's pray."

Boone hurried to join his family, because he didn't want to stand on the outside looking in, and he'd learned over the years that the best way to make sure he wasn't doing that was to insert himself into conversations and the things going on.

So he stepped to Cosette's side and slid his hand along her waist. She looked up at him and leaned into his side, making him feel strong and sure, just as Matt bowed his head and started to pray.

Help me be happy for my brother, Boone prayed while Matt asked for good health and safety for all who were traveling that holiday season. *Rid me of this jealousy, and guide me with parenting my daughter.*

He wanted to pray for himself and Cosette, but he didn't quite know what he needed when it came to his relationship with her, and Matt finished his prayer before Boone could find the threads of his thoughts and put them together.

"Uncle Boone," Britt said. "Your snowstorm covered everything." She giggled, and Boone grinned—a real grin— as he took in the solid white melted cheese topping on his pizza.

"Let's eat," Gloria said. "At the table, kids. Go on. Move your stuff over there." She herded everyone toward the dining room table. "Then we can do the stocking exchange. I can't wait for you to see what I got for everyone." She smiled, her eyes shining with fool's gold, and Boone couldn't help grinning back at her.

His questions hadn't been answered, and his prayers still existed, but relief filled him as he realized he wasn't nearly as on-edge or jealous as he'd been only five minutes ago. He met Cosette's eye, and she leaned over and kissed his cheek.

"Okay?" she asked, something he'd asked her plenty of times. It sure felt nice to have someone on his side, taking care of him. It was something Boone hadn't had in a long, long time, and as his emotions surged, he nodded.

"Yeah, okay."

Twenty-Three

Cosette listened to Raven say "Hey, Cosy," through the speaker phone as she took the candied ham out of the oven.

"Why are you calling me?" she asked. "Won't you be here in like eight minutes?"

"Yes," Raven said. "I just wanted to ask you about Boone before he shows up. Then you won't say anything."

Cosette set the heavy pan on the stovetop and slid it toward the back of it. She didn't feel like saying anything about Boone even when he wasn't here. Raven had been digging at her for days now. Weeks.

"What?" Cosette asked.

"I'm just wondering how serious it's getting," Raven said. "I've asked you a bunch of times, and you won't say."

"There's a reason for that."

"Must be because it's getting serious."

Cosette didn't know how to deny it—or confirm it. "I... don't know," she said truthfully.

"But you really like him, right?"

"Raven, why do you care?" Cosette asked, her patience hanging by a thread. That wasn't a good sign considering her sister and father would be arriving in a few minutes, and Boone had texted to say he and Gerty were on their way.

"Because, Dad and I want to know if we'll have to be ready for a wedding soon." Raven's voice held plenty of coyness, and Cosette reached up and rubbed the back of her neck.

"I don't know," she said. She couldn't imagine getting married again, but Boone had asked her a similar question recently. She'd said she'd think about marrying the right man again. And she would.

She did like Boone. A lot. She loved Gerty. With them working at the same place, and all of the holidays, they spent a lot of time together, getting to see each other's families, traditions, and more.

"Promise me you're not going to tease me about this tonight," Cosette said. "And promise me you won't ask Boone anything about what he got me for Christmas." Her gaze traveled over to the eight-foot pine tree Boone had carried into her house three nights ago. They'd decorated it together, and his gift sat underneath it.

It was not a gift basket, thankfully. Cosette had gotten a couple of things for Gerty too, as well as Raven and her father. They were doing a small dinner and gift exchange, just the five of them, on this Christmas Eve.

Tomorrow morning, Cosette would make the drive out to the farm and spend Christmas morning with Boone and Gerty. Boone had promised her pecan maple waffles and candied bacon, and she hoped he could cook as well as he could do everything else.

Surely he could, because Boone seemed to be amazing at a lot of things, and those he wasn't, he learned quickly.

"I promise," Raven said. "Dad?"

"I promise," her father said, and Cosette nodded though they couldn't see her. She couldn't even believe she was having this conversation with her dad on the line.

"Listen," she said, tossing the oven mitts on the counter in front of her. "You guys like Boone, right? I'm not missing anything, am I?"

Raven said nothing, and Dad remained quiet too. Cosette suspected they were looking at one another, hoping they didn't have to be the first to speak.

"You're not missing anything," Dad finally said. "He's a great man, Cosette. But what I think about him doesn't matter. You're the one who'll have to live with him every single day."

Live with him every single day.

Cosette blinked, hearing what marriage was in a different way than she'd thought of before. Intellectually, she knew when people got married, they lived together every day. They talked every day. She and Boone conversed every day right now. He stopped by her office all the time, or she wandered outside to watch him work with a horse for a few minutes.

He took her to dinner, and they brought Gerty along about half the time.

Her life had been intertwined with Boone's at this point. She couldn't even imagine what her day would look like without him in it.

She pushed the thoughts away, because she'd once thought the same thing about Joel. She hadn't been able to fathom what her life would look like without him in it. He decided everything for her, including what she ate for breakfast, lunch, and dinner, as well as what times those meals happened. He'd isolated her from Raven and her father, and she hadn't been sure they'd even recognize her if she somehow broke away from Joel and showed up on their doorstep.

She knew now how irrational that was, but her emotional and physical abuse had gotten so deep inside her head that she hadn't been thinking clearly. She and her therapist had worked for a few years to get through all of the erroneous beliefs Cosette had adopted during her marriage.

"I agree with Dad," Raven said. "I think Boone is a great guy. He's smart and funny. He's a good dad. I don't think he'd be able to hide much from all of the people he works with. I don't think you have anything to worry about."

Cosette nodded and said, "Thanks," in a voice that barely reached her own ears.

"We're almost there," Raven said. "We'll talk to you in a minute."

"Okay." The call ended, and Cosette checked on the potatoes bubbling away on the stove. A fork went right through them, and she switched off the flame beneath the pot. She didn't drain the potatoes yet, because she didn't need to have dinner on the table the moment everyone showed up.

They'd be bringing in gifts and shedding coats, and Cosette hurried to plug in her Christmas lights and start the carols on the record player she'd bought for herself.

A car engine rumbled outside, and she peeled back the curtains to see a car she'd never seen before. Raven sat behind the wheel, and it wasn't surprising to see her driving a different car every time Cosette saw her. In fact, Cosette wasn't even sure if Raven owned her own car at the moment.

She and Dad started to get out, and they both opened the back door on the sedan to start getting things out. Dad carried a laundry basket with way too many gifts in it, and Cosette moved away from the window to go open the door.

Raven and her father came up the steps and Cosette said, "Merry Christmas, Dad." He beamed at her, and she took the basket from him. "Why do you have so many gifts?"

"He went a little overboard with the online shopping this year," Raven said, grinning at the back of their dad's head as he continued inside. She lifted three gift bags, obviously proud of herself for consolidating her presents.

"Smells good in here," Dad said.

"Thanks," Cosette said, checking outside to see if Boone was almost here. She didn't see any headlights, so she hastened to close the door to keep the cold out. The furnace kicked on, and she followed her family around the couch to the Christmas tree. She and Raven unloaded the gifts, and

Cosette took the laundry basket down the hall to her bedroom so it wouldn't be in the way. Her house wasn't huge by any means, and she'd had to borrow a chair from the church so she had five for tonight.

She hugged her father, and when she tried to step back, her dad held onto her shoulders. "We don't mean to put any pressure on you," he said, his eyes earnest and filled with concern. "We just wanted to know how you're feeling so we can support you in the best way possible."

Cosette smiled at him. "Thanks, you guys."

Raven created a group hug, and Cosette's heart filled with love for her family. "Merry Christmas," she said in her enthusiastic voice. "Maybe next year, I'll have to host Christmas Eve at my house when I have a hot boyfriend."

Cosette laughed and shook her head. "This year is a fluke," she said. "Obviously."

"I'm totally going to find a husband next year," Raven said.

"Yeah?" Cosette stepped back. "Do you have a plan for that?"

"Not really," Raven said, following her into the kitchen. She picked up a cracker and swiped it through the hummus Cosette had made that morning. "But I think this amazing guy is going to come into the dealership, looking for a killer car...and an amazing wife." She grinned almost maniacally, and Cosette laughed again.

"Boone's here," her dad said, as he'd gone into the living room while Cosette and her sister had gone into the kitchen.

She turned toward the door, but her dad had already

gone around the couch. He opened the door and stepped out onto the porch, calling to Boone and Gerty. Cosette exchanged a look with Raven, who just shook her head.

So Cosette didn't go join her dad on the porch. It was obvious he really liked Boone, and that meant a lot to her. A chill seeped into the house, but neither her nor Raven went to close the door. Half a minute later, Boone's booming laughter filled the sky, the porch, and the living room as he entered. He carried various gifts in his arms, as did Gerty, and her father had a pie in each hand.

"Wow," Cosette said, not moving a muscle to help them. Dad kicked the door closed behind him, and Boone's gaze latched onto hers.

"Wow is right," he said. "Look at that sweater."

Cosette looked down at her sweater, though she knew what she had on. The dark blue yarn held cheery Christmas lights weaving all over, with Snoopy wearing a Santa hat and lying on top of his house.

"You didn't dress up," she teased.

"I missed that memo," Boone said. "Gifts under the tree, it looks like."

"Yes," Cosette said, feeling the sparkling magic start to move through her bloodstream that always came when Boone showed up. She watched him bend to put the presents in place, twisting to take them from Gerty. A flash of pain crossed his face, and Cosette pushed away from the counter.

"You okay?" she asked.

"Yeah," he said, but he groaned as he straightened.

"He hurt his back this afternoon," Gerty said.

Boone's eyes flashed with irritation and darkness. "Traitor."

"Well, you did."

"I'm fine," Boone said, switching his eyes from his daughter to Cosette. "I took some pain pills before we left."

"I have more," Cosette said.

"I think I have to wait a bit before I can just swallow more," he said with a smile. He glanced over to Raven, then to Dad, and then he took Cosette into his arms. "How are you, baby?" He lifted her right up off her feet. "It smells amazing in here. Thanks for having us to dinner."

He set her on her feet and kissed her quickly and chastely on the mouth. A peck, really, and Cosette couldn't really make out with him in front of her father and his daughter. Embarrassing. The fact that he'd kissed her at all felt like a major step in their relationship.

"Of course," Cosette said, stepping back from him. "It's meat candy, and I just need to whip the potatoes and we can eat." She slipped her hand into Boone's and looked at Gerty. "You and Raven can get out the rolls and salads, okay?"

"Sure," Gerty said, giving Cosette a smile. She joined Raven in the kitchen, and they started unloading the fridge of all the things Cosette had prepared over the past couple of days. She heated cream and butter, then whipped the potatoes into fluffy deliciousness while Dad and Boone set the table.

"Okay," Cosette said. "Thanks for coming, everyone." Her emotions surged, and she had no idea what had triggered them. She couldn't look at Boone or her father, and one glance at Raven had tears entering her eyes.

"Should I say a prayer?" Gerty asked, and Cosette blinked as she looked at the thirteen-year-old. Her eyes were so clear and so blue, and she obviously knew Cosette was struggling.

Cosette nodded, and Gerty did too. "Dear Lord," she said, almost before her father could sweep the cowboy hat from his head. "We are grateful to be celebrating Christmas with Cosette, Raven, and Jeff Brian this year." Gerty paused, and Cosette took a peek at the girl.

Boone reached over and put his hand on his daughter's back, something gentle and kind, and Cosette's heartbeat leapt and skipped as Gerty started to cry.

"I'm sorry," she said, her voice cracking.

"I'll finish it," Boone said. "Okay?"

She nodded, and turned into him. He wrapped her in a hug and dipped his head. "Lord, bless us here tonight to have Thy comforting spirit with us. We're grateful for Cosette and all of her hard work on this meal, and bless us to get along all right." He cleared his throat and simply said, "Amen."

"Amen," Dad said, but no one else echoed the sentiment back to Boone.

Cosette reached to wipe her eyes, hoping she hadn't ruined her makeup. Gerty still clung to Boone, and he gave her a kiss on the top of her head and then smiled at Cosette. She had no idea what was going on in his family, but she wanted to.

"Could you slice the ham, Dad?" she asked. "It's cut, but I haven't taken it off the bone."

"Sure." Dad got busy doing that, and Raven queued up with a plate in her hand. Gerty stepped back from Boone, who dropped into a crouch to look at her. He spoke in a voice Cosette couldn't hear, and only a few seconds later, Gerty nodded, and the two of them faced the kitchen.

Cosette picked up a plate and handed it to Gerty as the girl approached. "Okay?" she asked, taking a leaf from Boone's book.

"Yeah," Gerty said. "I don't know what happened. I just sort of lost it."

Cosette understood that on a deep, personal level. She smiled at Gerty. "Just like I did."

Gerty smiled and clutched the plate to her chest. "I guess so."

"Why are you emotional tonight?" Cosette asked, taking a plate for herself and moving into place behind Gerty.

"I think it...it just feels so homey here," Gerty said. "It feels good."

"I'm glad," Cosette said as Boone's warm hand landed on her lower back. She twisted to look at him. "Even you didn't seem to have a lot to say."

"I have no defense," Boone said with a smile. "Why are you emotional tonight?"

"I—" She cut off, because she didn't want to say she didn't know. She did. "I feel very blessed this year," she said. "I feel different. It's usually just me, Raven, and Dad, and I really like having you here." She smiled at him, glad when he leaned down to kiss her.

She couldn't believe the human heart's capacity to love, but she was so, so grateful for it.

"LET'S OPEN MINE FIRST," DAD SAID AN HOUR later. Dinner had been delicious, and all of the dishes sat in the sink. Cosette didn't care. She could take care of things later. They'd gathered around the tree, and Dad had converged on the tree and started pulling his gifts out.

"Oh," Boone said as Dad gave him a long, rectangular box. Then a small one. And finally one that was clearly something made of fabric. "Three gifts for me?"

"My dad likes to give presents," Cosette said. "Should we hand them all out, Dad? Then we can open them one at a time."

"Sure," he said, and he continued to play Santa's little helper and handed out all of the gifts until everyone had a little pile near them. "Gerty," he said, grinning at her. "Do you want to go first?"

"Sure," Gerty said, smiling at Dad. She really was an adaptable child, and Cosette appreciated her more and more as she continued to get to know her. She ripped into the gift in her lap, which happened to be from Cosette.

Her heart pounded in her stomach, against her ribs, and up into her throat. She fought the urge to yell out that Gerty could get something else at the equine equipment store. The gift wasn't even in the box—only the fact that it had been paid for.

"No way!" Gerty yelled, her eyes widening in a second. "The Tina Herman boots!" She ripped off the last piece of paper and held up the box. "Daddy, look!"

"I see it, bumblebee," he said, chuckling.

"They're not really in there," Cosette said, pleased by Gerty's reaction. "Open the box."

Gerty did, and she pulled out the gift certificate.

"It's enough to get the boots," Cosette said. "But the saleswoman said it's best if the rider comes to try them on. Since I wanted it to be a surprise for you, I just got the gift certificate." She twisted her fingers around one another, but Gerty looked at her with pure joy on her face.

"Thank you, Cosette." She leapt up from her chair and threw her arms around Cosette. The girl was all muscle and bones, and she hugged Cosette firmly before pulling away. "Will you take me to get them?"

Cosette nodded, her voice lodged somewhere in her throat.

"I don't get to go?" Boone asked.

"We can go on Boxing Day," Cosette said.

"You can come," Gerty said. "It's just her gift, and I want her to come with."

Boone wore such happiness on his face, which was the complete opposite of the Christmas celebration at his brother's house. Cosette had asked him about that, but he hadn't answered, and she hadn't pressed him on it.

"Boone, you're up," Dad said.

"I thought Gerty was opening all of hers."

"Nope, we go around."

He lifted Raven's gift bag, his eyes shining with joy. He pulled out the red-and-white striped paper and then an all-in-one tool. "Wow, thank you, Raven," he said. "I use stuff like this all the time on the farm."

"That's what Cosette said," Raven said. "She said you've lost two of these since you started at the farm."

Boone swung his attention toward Cosette, his eyebrows high on his forehead. "Oh, is that what she said?"

"You have," she said matter-of-factly.

"I think *one* of us lost a whole shipment of horse blankets just last week," he said, their eyes locked.

Cosette couldn't help laughing, which seemed to give everyone permission to do the same.

Twenty-Four

BOONE'S GIFTS FOR JEFF AND RAVEN HAD BEEN received well. He hadn't brought anything for Gerty, obviously, but he had found something casual for Cosette. When it was her turn, and she only had the one gift left, she looked at him with questions in those amazing eyes. "I thought we were doing gifts tomorrow."

He lifted the one from her, which still sat in his lap—his last gift too. "Should we wait until tomorrow?" He had something else for her to open in the morning, something he didn't really want to have opened in front of her whole family. Something he'd planned to give her while Gerty rode her new horse, when it was just the two of them watching her from the house.

"Open it," Jeff said, and Cosette threw him a look. Boone could tell her patience and energy were waning, and he wished he could offer her some relief.

Cosette started to peel back the paper on the somewhat

large box, and he watched her face light up. "Boone," she said with appreciation in her voice. She revealed the gift and looked up. "Thank you."

"It's for your office," he said. "You're always saying how cold it is in there."

"She even tells me that," Raven said. "Good gift, Boone." She smiled at Boone, and he basked in the praise. Sure, it was just a space heater, and he didn't normally subscribe to giving a woman a gift that plugged in, but this one meant something.

"Your turn," she said, still smiling. "You're the last one."

Jeff had brought several gifts for everyone, and Boone had new gloves, a new hat and scarf, and three gift cards to restaurants, all courtesy of Cosette's father.

"It doesn't feel like a gift basket," Boone said, grinning at Cosette as he lifted his gift. He shook it, but nothing rattled.

"Just open it," she said as she folded her arms and crossed her legs.

Boone found her incredibly sexy in that moment, and he couldn't wait to talk to her alone. At the same time, his heart fell into his stomach. He had no idea how Cosette would react to his personal gift, nor the subject of conversation he wanted to talk to her about.

He told himself he'd know in about fifteen hours, and he prayed he'd be able to sleep tonight. Right now, he peeled the glittery green paper off a slim package to reveal a cookbook with the words *Saffron Lake Neighbors Recipes*.

He read the words again, and then again, wonder

pouring through him. He finally looked up, unable to say anything.

"I saw that on a Facebook group," Cosette said quietly. "It's from your hometown in Montana, and I thought you'd like it." She swallowed, but her hands didn't go round and round one another.

"Wow, cool," Gerty said, taking the recipe book from him. She flipped it open and leafed through a couple of pages. "Look, Daddy, it has a dark orange marmalade recipe in it from Lizzie Whettstein." She looked up. "Isn't that Great-Grams?"

"Yes," Boone said, the word scratching his throat as he spoke. He couldn't look away from Cosette, who also couldn't seem to look anywhere but at him. He got up and took the couple of steps toward where she sat across from him.

He leaned down as if to kiss her. "Thank you," he whispered just before he did. This wasn't the peck from when he'd arrived, nor the kiss he'd given her while they'd waited in line to get food.

This was a heartfelt, appreciative kiss that he hoped told her exactly how much her gift meant to him. He didn't carry on long, and he straightened and turned back to Gerty. "Can I see it, bug?"

She handed him the cookbook, and Boone scanned the pages, finally landing on the marmalade one from his grandmother. "We should make this for tomorrow," he said. "We can have it on toast or something." He looked up from the book, wondering what time the grocery store closed on Christmas Eve.

"Oh, just a sec," Cosette said, and she jumped to her feet. She hurried into the kitchen and opened a low cabinet. When she stood, she held a brown paper bag.

"What have you got there?" he asked, sauntering over to her.

"Look." Cosette stepped back, smiling.

Boone kept his eyes on hers for an extra moment, and then peered into the bag. Oranges. Gelatin. A lemon.

"I don't think you can make it tonight and eat it in the morning," Cosette said. "But we could make it together tomorrow after breakfast and have it the next day."

He looked at her, falling more in love with her with the addition of a dozen oranges and a lemon.

"Okay?" she asked.

He nodded. "Okay."

THE NEXT MORNING, BOONE BUSTLED AROUND THE cabin kitchen, getting out plates, silverware, and napkins. The bacon-wrapped party sausages rested on the stovetop, the brown sugar all melted and caramelized. The oven still sat on the lowest temperature possible, and he had three waffles waiting there already.

He pulled a gallon of milk and a carton of orange juice from the fridge, and then surveyed all of the things he'd gathered. "Syrup," he muttered. "Butter. Candied pecans." He nudged that bowl closer to the whipped cream, which he'd infused with sugar and vanilla extract. "Looks good."

Someone knocked on his door, and Gerty got up from the couch. "It's Cosette," he said.

"I know." Gerty tossed her tablet onto the couch and went to open the door. Sure enough, Cosette stood on the other side of the door, and she'd dressed as festively today as she'd been last night.

Today, she wore a denim skirt with knee-high leather boots, and with her long, wool coat, she looked rich and elegant. She carried more gifts in her hands, and Gerty stepped forward to help her. Boone stayed in the kitchen, out of the way, smiling at his girlfriend.

The presents got put under the tree, and then Cosette shrugged out of her coat. Boone stepped forward to take it, handing it to Gerty and saying, "Take this to my bedroom, would you, baby?"

His daughter went down the hall, and Boone didn't waste a moment before kissing Cosette for a lot longer than just a moment. "Your daughter is on the way back," Cosette whispered, giggling.

"Mm hm." Boone stepped away from her as Gerty returned, his face flaming hot. "Well, breakfast is ready. Or do we want to open presents first this morning? Gerty's been dyin' a slow death for an hour." He tossed a playful look in his daughter's direction.

She rolled her eyes, and Boone almost wanted to tell Molly she could use the horse for her therapy program.

"I don't care," Cosette said, looking back and forth between Boone and Gerty.

"I think we should eat first," Boone said. "Gerty's gonna want to use her present once she sees it, and then she won't eat."

"Fine," Gerty said, coming into the kitchen. The waffle maker beeped, and Boone opened the lid to find a hot, crispy, golden brown waffle. "Can I have that one, Daddy?"

"Sure thing." Boone forked it onto a plate and handed it to his daughter. "There's pecans and syrup, butter, whipped cream. Even strawberries." His nerves screamed at him, and he dang near bobbled the sheet tray of candied sausages.

He managed to refrain from making a fool of himself, and they settled at the table. His stomach wouldn't settle, however, and Boone could barely get anything down. Thankfully, Cosette asked Gerty a couple of questions, and they kept the conversation going.

"You didn't eat much," Cosette said, glancing at his plate as she got up to take hers back into the kitchen.

"Yeah," Boone said, standing too. "I'm just excited about Gerty's gift."

His daughter looked at him, and he grinned at her. "There's nothing under the tree for me," Gerty said as she joined him at the sink.

"That's because your gift is outside," Boone said.

"Outside?"

"Better get your shoes and jacket on," Boone said. "It's a billion degrees below zero this morning." He looked at Cosette, who gave him a quick nod. He'd coordinated with

Travis to get the horse from the barn when Cosette arrived and put it in the back yard, where he'd cleared a spot for it, complete with a bale of hay.

Gerty ignored him and didn't put on her shoes or jacket. She went to the front window and looked out. "There's nothing out here," she said.

Boone leaned back against the counter and folded his arms. When Gerty looked at him, questions in her eyes, he nodded toward the back of the house. She cocked one eyebrow at him and strode toward the back window. He could see so much of himself in her, as well as Nikki.

She paused in front of the window, and then both hands flew up to her mouth as she gasped. "Daddy," she said through her fingers. "Whose horse is that?"

"That's your horse, bumblebee."

She spun toward him, pure electricity flowing from her. "My horse?" She started scanning the kitchen frantically. "Where are my shoes? Daddy, have you seen my shoes?"

Boone started to laugh, and Cosette bent to pick up Gerty's cowgirl boots. "Right here," she said, and Gerty darted toward her.

"Dad, stop laughing and get my jacket, please."

"I told you to get dressed first," Boone said, still chuckling. He got out his daughter's jacket and gave it to her. She only had one arm inside before she ran out the back door, and Boone shrugged into his coat and followed her with a, "I'll be right back, Cosette."

"I'm coming out too," she said. "I can get my coat, right?"

"Sure," he said. "Back bedroom." He ducked outside too, picking up the saddle and blanket he'd stowed beside the door. Gerty had already flown down the steps to the horse, and she stood in front of him, stroking his neck and talking to him. Boone loved watching his daughter interact with horses, and his heart warmed.

"What are you gonna name him?" he asked as he approached.

"I don't know," Gerty said. "I've gotta ride him first."

"Yep." Boone started to saddle the horse, and soon enough, Gerty sat atop him. Cosette stood on the back porch, watching with a wide smile on her face. "Don't go too far," Boone said. "Just down to the farmhouse and back, okay?"

"Okay, Daddy." Gerty leaned down and kissed him on the cheek. "Thank you. Thank you so much."

Boone waved while Gerty rode the horse around the corner of the house toward the lane out front.

"She looks good on him," Cosette called from the porch, and Boone went toward her. They went back inside, and his palms turned slick. He took off his coat, because he was already sweating.

"I got you something," he said, moving into the kitchen and opening his junk drawer. He drew in a deep breath, his shoulders lifting high. He took out the jewelry box, feeling like he was about to blow everything wide open.

He turned back to Cosette, who'd just hung her coat on the back of a chair at the table. "I, uh, got you this." He thrust the box toward her, and she froze.

Everything froze.

Boone breathed, and he blinked, but Cosette didn't take the box. She looked from it to his face and back. "Boone," she said. "Is that a diamond ring?"

He looked at the ring box too. "Would it be a problem if it was?"

"Yes," Cosette said.

His stomach pinched. "Why? I thought you said you'd marry—" He cut off, because he couldn't say she'd said she'd marry him. She hadn't, not really.

"I'm not ready to get married," she said, actually taking a step back.

He frowned, so many synapses in his brain firing at him. How could he have read their relationship so wrong? Panic started to stream through him, because he hadn't seen things clearly with Karley either.

"I thought...I don't know what I thought." He withdrew his hand and shoved the box back in his junk drawer.

"Boone." Cosette came closer to him. "I thought we were goin' slow."

"We've been dating for a while," he said. "We've talked about kids and marriage, and I don't know." He hung his head, unable to look at her.

"Tell me what's going on inside your head."

"First," Boone said, not quite able to sort through so much so quickly. "That's not a diamond ring. It's jewelry, but not an engagement ring. I wouldn't just hand it to you without a proposal. Second, I feel...." He sighed and closed his eyes. "I don't know how I feel."

"Yes, you do," she said quietly.

He looked at her, trying to be brave. "I'm falling in love with you. I want to get married and have more kids, and with Matt and Gloria already down that path, I feel so left out. So far behind."

Cosette put her hand on his arm, and the weight of it comforted him. "We're on our own path, Boone."

"I thought you were almost ready," he said.

"Healing isn't linear," she said quietly. "I still need to go slow and take time to think about things."

"You said you could marry me."

"I said I'd *think* about marrying you."

Boone had no idea what to say, but the desperation swimming through him crushed him from the inside out.

"I think things between us are going well," Cosette said. "Can we just keep doing that?"

"Sure," Boone said, his voice too high and too bright. "Sorry all I got you was a lame space heater."

Cosette opened the drawer in front of them and took out the jewelry box while he stood there, mute and unmoving. She opened it to reveal the silver band inside. It had a trio of gems along it, and she pulled in a breath. "Boone, it's lovely."

"Yeah?" He looked at her, and he could've sworn she wore love in her expression. He wasn't sure of anything now, because he'd read so many things wrong already.

"Yeah." Cosette touched her mouth to his, and he couldn't misread the slow, sensual way she kissed him. Could he?

She pulled away and handed him the ring box. "Will you put it on for me?"

He'd do anything for her, so he took the ring out and slid it onto her finger—on the right hand, not her left. It still looked beautiful, and he found himself smiling.

Cosette gazed at it too, and when she lifted her eyes to his, she said, "It's great. I love it." She kissed him again, and Boone took her face in his hands and really enjoyed the tenderness between them. He pulled away and pulled in a breath.

"We're okay, right?" he asked, his voice slightly wounded. He felt the gash all the way down from his eyes, through his throat, and straight into his heart, and he had no idea what to do about it.

"Yeah," Cosette said, her eyes still closed. "We're okay if you're okay."

"I'm okay," he said.

She opened her eyes, smiled at him, and said, "Let's go see where Gerty got to, then we can start on that marmalade."

Twenty-Five

COSETTE TUCKED HER GLOVED HANDS IN HER pockets as she walked outside. Mother Nature had brought snow for the New Year, but she didn't mind. She loved living in a place that could show her the wonder and beauty of all four seasons, year after year, and she couldn't wait for the rebirth of the trees, grasses, and plants when spring arrived.

For now, she'd put up with the negative temperatures and brisk winds, and she actually smiled as she turned her face into the breeze. She let it pull and twist at her hair, and then she reached up and tucked her locks behind her ear.

She went past the first ring outside the administration barn where she worked, her goal the third one down, where Gerty sat atop Snickers as the horse plodded along the outer edge of the circle.

Cosette had never met anyone like Gerty, at least not in a thirteen-year-old body. She held wisdom and maturity far past her age, and her face brightened when she saw Cosette approaching.

"Look," she called. "He doesn't even care about the rail today."

"I can see that." Cosette grinned at Gerty. "He's got his head down and everything."

"No fight in him," she said.

Cosette reached out and took Gerty's hand in hers as she started by. She went slow enough that Cosette could squeeze briefly before she continued past, and she leaned against the metal railing of the ring as Gerty's back arced toward her.

The sun had already started to lower in the west, though the clock had barely passed four. She didn't love the darkness that came with the winter, but she also didn't have to feed goats, chickens, and horses before dawn or after dusk.

"Did you get your chores done?" she called to Gerty.

The girl looked over to her. "Not yet."

Cosette nodded. "I have to finish up the schedule texts and meet with Molly, but then I'll be ready to go."

"I'm only doing one horse tonight," Gerty said. She reached down and patted Snickers along the side of his neck. "I guess we better be done, Snicky."

"Didn't your daddy ask you to do those two stalls today?" Cosette asked, knowing full-well what Boone had asked his daughter to do that afternoon.

Gerty's face blanked, showed panic, and then fell. "Oh, shoot. Yes, he did."

"I can wait for you," Cosette said. She had no idea how to clean out a horse stall, so she couldn't help much.

"I'll hurry," Gerty said, swinging out of the saddle like a pro. Of course she was. So much of Boone's blood ran in her veins, and he'd spent countless hours with her, teaching her what he knew about horses, farms, ranches, and how to tend to all of it with precision.

He loved animals and the land, and he held a great respect for both of them. Cosette warmed just thinking of him, and when her mind flew back a couple of weeks to Christmas Day, a thin line of ice cut through that heat.

No, the ring inside the deep blue jewelry box hadn't boasted diamonds, and Cosette ran one gloved finger around the line of the ring on her right hand. She wore his ring every single day, and when someone at church or the grocery store asked her about it, she said, "My boyfriend gave it to me," without hesitation. Usually with fondness in her voice, and a few seconds lost where she gazed lovingly at the trio of gems.

All of that made everything confusing for her hesitancy to take their relationship another step down the path they were already on. She'd asked if they could just keep doing what they were doing, and Boone had said yes.

But Cosette knew now that he didn't want to stay where they were. Of course he wouldn't. He wanted more kids; he wanted a wife; he wanted everything his brother had, what Gray and Elise Hammond had, all that Hunter and Molly had.

What do you want, Cosette?

She'd been asking herself that question for fifteen solid days, and she still had no answer. As Gerty opened the gate and led Snickers out. Cosette moved closer to the aisle and watched the two of them go, adoring the way they moved together with no resistance. Snickers loved Gerty as much as she loved him, and watching the girl connect to the rescue horse had made Cosette see that everyone had some internal wounds that needed to be filled and fixed.

Tears pricked her eyes, and she turned away from the blonde teenager who had showed Cosette that she too could be resilient and strong while still being moldable and vulnerable. She'd had no idea that she could learn so much from such a young person, and she pressed her eyes closed to keep the burning at bay.

She tilted her head back and breathed in the terribly cold air. "Help me know what to do," she whispered. "I am willing to go wherever You want me to go. I am willing to take a step in the dark. My will is Thy will."

She wanted to beg the Lord to please, please, *please* enlighten her mind. Turn on the light and illuminate the path in front of her. She wanted to push away the fear and leap in faith, but....

She didn't know how.

You do, a voice whispered in her head. *You do know how.*

She opened her eyes, sniffed, and headed back to the administration barn. She puzzled over the answer she'd just received, her initial response frustration and then anger. Could the Lord be any more vague?

She did? She did know how? How to do what?

Back in her office, she finished all the scheduling and reminders, got out her folders for the meeting, and went down the hall to the tiny kitchenette Travis had put in the front of the administration barn.

He'd brought in an electric kettle which could heat water and put a variety of instant coffees, tea bags, and hot chocolate beside a stack of disposable, recyclable cups. Sometimes someone brought in mini muffins or doughnuts, and on days Cosette had forgotten her lunch or the one she'd planned to spend with Boone, Matt, and Chris Hammond at his home got canceled, she'd been grateful for the assortment of carb-loaded treats behind the check-in desk.

Today, she fixed herself a cup of tea and wandered back down the hall to her office. She knew someone had been there in the few minutes she'd been gone the moment she stepped inside. Her eyes landed on the package on her desk, and her heart somersaulted up into her mouth.

She backed up a step and glanced down the hall, both ways. She didn't see anyone, and no lingering colognes or scents hung in the air. Only the hum of the furnace in the administration barn met her ears, and she swallowed as she looked back to her desk.

As the fear rose up, choking her, she actually stamped her foot. No. She would not be afraid of this. She moved into her office with purpose and picked up the package, which was simply a brown box. No bow. No writing on the outside.

Her fingers shook, but she fisted them. She lifted the lid on the box, not sure what she'd find inside.

A bookmark sat there, a pressed lilac showing. Her adrenaline ran in circles with her confusion. She lifted the bookmark from the box, noticing the paper clip holding something to the gorgeous flower.

She'd only told one person that the lilac was her favorite flower. She adored the purple and the scent, and she removed the paperclip and lifted the pressed lilac to her nose, as if she'd be able to smell it.

She couldn't, and she lowered her hand to see she was holding a couple hundred-dollar bills with a tiny sticky note attached to the front one. *For Gerty's clothes today. Thanks for taking her.*

No name, but then again, Boone didn't need to sign his name.

Cosette drew in a deep breath and pressed the bookmark and cash to her chest. She hadn't asked him for a bookmark, and she had no idea when he'd had time to leave the farm and find this for her. Perhaps he'd bought it online.

It didn't matter. She rounded her desk and picked up her phone. *Thank you for the bookmark.* Her fingers hesitated as a set of words moved through her mind. There was no way—not a chance on this earth—that she'd text him that she loved him.

No way.

I love you.

The words hung in her head, making her immobile and a bit numb.

"Hey," Molly chirped, breaking through Cosette's self-induced freeze. She dropped her phone without sending her text, and embarrassment flooded her.

"Hey." Cosette scrambled after her phone, and she

needed to tuck away the money, and shove the bookmark into a drawer so Molly wouldn't notice it. Her face flamed with heat, and Molly would see that for sure. The woman had the eyes of a bird of prey, and she said that came from her years in the classroom.

No matter where she'd learned to have eyes in the back, sides, and front of her head, Cosette didn't want her boss to see how flustered her thoughts about Boone had made her.

"You okay?" Molly asked, and Cosette opened her drawer and put her phone, the money, and the bookmark inside.

"Yes." She ran her hands through her hair and sighed as she sat down. "Are you ready to go over all of this?" She flipped open a pink folder, which she and Molly had agreed would hold their big, scary plans for Pony Power. The lemon-yellow folder held more reasonable objectives, and the forest green one held their in-progress plans as they brought them to life.

Molly groaned as she sat down too. "I'm ready," she said. "Let's just do one idea from the pink folder today. I'm not sure I can handle too many Big Concept things."

Cosette understood that on a whole new level, and she nodded. "Okay." She scanned the top page in the pink folder, where she kept all of the notes from previous months' meetings. "I think one thing that's been on our list for six months and keeps creeping to the top is this idea of doing a summer camp."

She looked up, noting some exhaustion lines around Molly's eyes. "I think that could be something I can start working on. We could do a girls-only camp; five days, four nights; and house them in those three little cabins along the far north fence."

"Four in a cabin?"

"Yes," Cosette said, noting the number. "Gerty's here, and I think girls would connect to her. We have the manpower with Cord and Gil, even though he's not on-site and full-time. For this camp week, he could be."

Molly nodded, and Cosette kept writing. "Pricing?" she asked.

"I'll do some research on what other farms and ranches do for weekly camp fees," Molly said.

"Okay." Cosette noted that. "I'll work on creating a list of activities? This is separate from the counseling and therapy, right?"

"Yes," Molly said. "We'll continue our main focus on equine therapy outside of this."

Cosette nodded and put a checkmark next to that idea, which they'd talked about previously. The conversation continued, and they moved through a few more details in the pink folder before moving onto the yellow and then green ones.

Gerty still hadn't appeared in the office doorway, and Molly didn't immediately get to her feet to leave. Cosette tucked all the folders back into her desk drawer and looked over to Molly.

Her mind fired at her, and she blurted out, "How did you know you should marry Hunter?"

Molly didn't react with any shock. She blinked and smiled. "Hunter and I have a very long past," she said.

Cosette nodded, because she knew Hunter and Molly had dated as teenagers. She had no history with Boone before last spring when he'd come to visit Matt, and then getting to know him slightly after he'd moved here and started to work the farm.

And then Taco Tuesday.

Everything had changed when he'd set up the perfect date in that barn, even if it was just hard-shell tacos without enough sour cream.

Still, only five months had passed since then, and Cosette's heart needed a lot longer than that to become whole again. Didn't it?

Do you?

"When he came back to town," Molly said. "The spark was still there. It grew and grew, and he became the light by which I see who I really am and know what I really want." She shrugged like this amazing gift came into everyone's lives. "So while we have our challenges, and I thought for sure him taking the CEO job at his family company would break us, it didn't. We work hard to stay close to each other, and that's not one-sided, you know? I work hard at it; he works hard at it."

Cosette let the enormity of what she'd said sink into her ears, her mind, and her soul. Finally, she nodded. "Did he decide to stay on as CEO?"

Molly nodded as she smiled. "For now, yes. We live in the high-rise right next door to his office. He'll be close, and we'll keep working at being the family we want to be." She got to her feet and turned just as Gerty appeared in the doorway. "Hey, Gerty. Wow, it looks like you had a fight with the washing stall today."

Molly laughed as Gerty did too, and then she left the office. Cosette opened her drawer to collect her phone, the money, the bookmark, and her purse. When she looked at Gerty, the girl wore apprehension on her face.

"I have to go home and change," Gerty said, indicating her soaking wet clothes. "I was afraid I'd freeze to death if I walked. Will you drive me?"

"Of course, sweetie," Cosette said, much of her confusion and hesitancy gone now. She wanted to work on her relationship with Boone. She wanted to keep him in her life, because she wanted Gerty in her life too. "Let's go."

Gerty's phone rang, and she pulled it from her jacket pocket. "It's Michael," she said, looking up. Her blue eyes held surprise and desire at the same time. "Should I answer it?"

Cosette didn't know how to advise her on this situation. She knew Boone didn't like Gerty's crush, or as he called it— her "infatuation" with Michael Hammond. She wasn't Gerty's mother, and she'd never been a mother.

"Up to you," she said.

"Will you tell my dad?" The phone rang again.

"Yes," Cosette said. "I can't keep that from him. If he asks, I'll tell him." She'd probably tell him anyway. She didn't know how to keep things secret, and she didn't want anything coming between her and Boone.

Gerty let the call go to voicemail, and she said, "We're already late. I'll text him later," as she turned and left the office. She didn't sound upset, and Cosette followed her out the front door of the administration barn and to her car.

She drove back behind the farmhouse and along the lane with the family stable and barn to Boone's cabin. Gerty ran inside, and Boone came out. "Hey," he said, jogging up to the driver-side window. He wasn't wearing a coat, or even a long-sleeved shirt, and he smelled like soap and something salty.

"Hey," she said. "My meeting ran a little long, and Gerty had trouble with Junior in the washing stall."

"She told me," Boone said. "Did you get my present?"

"Yes," Cosette said, realizing she'd never sent her text. "I was texting you when Molly came in. Sorry, I never sent it."

"It's fine." He leaned in to kiss her quick. "What do you think?"

"The bookmark was amazing," she said.

"So do you want to go?"

"Go where?"

"To Montana with me," he said, a hint of confusion running through his expression. "That's where the lilac came from. From Saffron Lake. I want to take you."

Cosette leaned her head back against the head-rest, her mind screaming *no* at her. "When?" she asked.

"I'm going in a couple of weeks," he said. "Nikki died in the winter, and I always go visit her grave. Talk to her a little. I thought we could go together...." He trailed off, probably because Cosette wasn't even looking at him.

"Is Gerty going to go?" she asked.

"No," he said. "She has school and her work here, and I told her I'd loop her in through video."

Cosette's heart beat very fast. Something loud and obnoxious rushed through her ears. Before she knew it, Boone was striding away from her car and back toward his front steps. He took them two at a time to the porch and disappeared inside. The door slammed closed, and Cosette definitely heard that.

The horrible *bang!* made her flinch, and it cut through the clutter in her ears. She blinked, becoming aware of how amazing the human mind could truly be.

Never mind, ran through her head in Boone's voice. He hadn't yelled. He hadn't sniped or snapped at her. He'd just said it, the tone in her head almost resigned. *I'll go myself.*

Cosette rolled up her window, the cold from outside penetrating her soul and making her numb. A few minutes later, Gerty came bounding down the steps. She got in the front seat and said, "Ready."

Cosette couldn't smile at her, but she did her best to force her lips to curve upward. "All right," she said as happily as she could. She hated this version of herself. The woman who pushed aside uncomfortable things and acted like nothing had happened to make her heart turn inside out. Who accepted that she wasn't good enough, and she didn't deserve any better than she was currently getting.

She backed out of the cabin driveway, her discomfort and anger growing. But not with Boone.

With herself.

Yes, her heart sat in her chest wrongly, but that wasn't Boone's fault. It was hers.

He hadn't treated her badly; he'd been disappointed she didn't want to take the next step in their relationship. He was ready; she was not.

What was she supposed to do about that?

"Cosette?" Gerty asked. "Can I ask you something?"

"Sure," she said, her voice falsely bright again.

"Are you gonna marry my dad?"

Cosette's fingers tightened around the wheel, and she glanced over to Gerty, who wore a carefully placed mask over her expression. "I don't know, sweetie," she said, turning the corner and continuing past the farmhouse. She looked out her window too, where Boone had leaned in and kissed her only five minutes ago. "I don't know."

Twenty-Six

TRAVIS'S HEART SHRIVELED INTO THE TIGHT CAGE he kept it in whenever he went next door. He muttered to himself as he brought his truck to a stop, his eyes glued to Poppy's front porch. Sometimes she came outside to talk to him, as if letting him inside her house would leave a bad taste in her mouth.

He knew what he wanted to do with that mouth, and it wasn't listen to her talk. Fine, that too, as she had a melodic voice he could sometimes hear while he laid in bed at night, desperate to fall asleep.

Most of all, he wanted to kiss her. He wasn't even sure why. She didn't treat him all that nicely, despite his many and varied attempts to make up for being unkind to her a few months ago. He'd paid her mortgage for a few months, and she'd berated him for it. He'd ordered groceries the day before Christmas, and she'd sent him a text that she didn't need the food.

Thank you, but we would've been okay. We're coming to the farmhouse again.

He'd known that, but he'd sent the bags of produce, protein, and pound cake anyway. She'd told him once in one of her nicer texts that she loved pound cake.

"I can't believe you're doing this," he said to himself as he put the truck in park. The New Year had rolled over a few days ago, and he wanted to make sure she didn't lose her farm. She'd said she didn't have anywhere else to live, and Travis had more money in his bank account than he knew what to do with. He wasn't going to do nothing while she suffered.

"Lots of people are suffering," he muttered. He opened the door and got out, gazing left and then right before focusing on and committing to walking toward the house. Poppy didn't appear, and he wondered if she'd be home.

Of course she would. This was where she lived and worked, and her rusted, forest green minivan sat ten feet from his truck in the driveway. He forced himself up the steps and onto the porch, the sound of Cotton's barks already coming through the door. Yep, they were home. He rang the bell and fell back a couple of steps.

"Coming," Poppy called, and Travis swept his cowboy hat off his head. Poppy—pretty Poppy Harris, with all that gorgeous strawberry blonde hair and those eyes that could render him mute—opened the door and held onto the doorknob as she met his eyes. "Travis."

"Hullo, Poppy," he said, clearing his throat. So he hadn't had a girlfriend in a while. It wasn't like he'd *never* had one.

He'd dated quite a lot in the city, actually, but it felt like someone had removed his memories and brain and stuffed his skull with cotton.

"What can I do for you?" she asked, her voice formal and guarded.

Travis wondered if she could feel the electric current running between them. He wasn't sure if it was actual attraction or the most extreme awkwardness that made his skin sizzle.

"Travis?" she asked, and his name in her voice would torment him tonight. He should've texted her.

"Yes," he said, blurting out the word as Cotton came out onto the porch with him. "I don't want to get into another...thing like we did at Thanksgiving, but I...." He tilted his head to the side as if he'd be able to determine her wealth that way. She had been working for Elise over the past couple of months, and she hadn't had to pay her mortgage.

"You what?" she asked.

Travis decided not to beat around the bush. He'd dealt with far surlier personalities in New York City, and he could handle this woman who wore warring emotions in her eyes. He couldn't quite name the one, but fondness fit the best, which didn't go with the annoyance he could plainly discern.

"I wanted to make sure you're okay with the mortgage for the next little bit," he said, delivering the line evenly, without any emotion at all. "And I thought I'd ask to see if there's anything you need help with around the farm." He dang near choked on the last word, making himself sound like a blasted pirate.

Poppy's eyebrows went up. "Really? It seems like you're aiming for another thing like what happened at Thanksgiving."

"I don't want you to lose your house," he said. "And I know how overwhelming a farm can be." He indicated the land past her huge trees, as if she might have forgotten where she lived. "I don't even own that one. I'm not even in charge of it, and most days, I feel like drowning."

He saw the flicker of appreciation in her eyes. It got covered quickly by the pure hopelessness he'd seen on her face in that leaky barn when he'd stumbled upon her crying.

"I have enough money to pay the mortgage," she said. "The job with Elise has been really great."

"I'm glad," Travis said.

"How do you have so much money to be payin' my mortgage?" Poppy asked, those deep, blue eyes squinting at him.

"I already said I'd rather not say." Travis shifted his feet. Only a couple of people knew he'd once dressed in designer suits and shiny shoes to go to work.

"Yes," Poppy said without moving her lips. "You did say that."

"So you're okay?" he asked. "The driveway is getting plowed?"

"I can do that myself," she said.

"I thought you sold your tractor," he shot back.

Poppy's face turned a bit pink, and she reached up to pat

her hair. "Yes, it's getting plowed," she said like a true diplomat. "Thank you, Travis."

"How's Steele? He doesn't need anything?" Travis told himself to stop asking her what she needed. She had his phone number, and she had to know by now that he'd drop everything and come over here to help her. He hadn't been shy about that, and in fact, he'd inserted himself into her life whether she wanted him to or not.

"He's fine," she said. "We had a great Christmas...." Her voice trailed off as she dropped her gaze to the ground. "Thank you for the food and the wrapping paper. I thought I had some, but it turned out I didn't."

"Sure," he said easily. For some unknown reason, he took a step forward. "Poppy...."

She looked up and Travis froze. She broadcasted innocence and pain at the same time, and he wanted to take her into his arms and tell her the same thing he'd said in the barn. *It's all going to be okay.*

He rocked back on his heels, stumbling backward as he started to tip. After righting himself, and with heat firing through every muscle in his body, he said, "You have my number. If you need anything, let me know."

"Travis." Poppy stepped right to the threshold of her house but didn't come outside. "Thank you for everything you've done for me and Steele this year. Really." She seemed sincere, and Travis's heart started to dance behind his ribs.

"Of course," he said, his mouth filling with his next words. *Do you maybe want to get dinner sometime?*

They streamed through his head, but he couldn't push them out of his mouth.

Poppy offered him a small smile that lit up her eyes. "It's nice to have such a good friend and neighbor."

The words punched him with a fiery fist. *Good friend. Neighbor.*

He scoffed, the invitation to dinner suddenly gone. "Good friend?" he asked without censoring himself.

Poppy's smile slid off her face as her eyebrows rose. "Yes."

"Maybe we've been seein' the same situation differently," he said. "You literally swatted up and down my arms on Thanksgiving. You asked Elise in front of everyone what I was doing there, and you shoved me outside in front of my friends and coworkers."

Not only all of that, but he didn't want to be her *good friend* or her *neighbor*. She might as well have told him he reminded her of her brother.

"You paid my mortgage without telling me," she shot back.

"I apologized," he said.

"I did too." She folded her arms, plenty of fire shooting from her eyes now. "Steele and I are doing okay. We don't need anything right now."

Travis wished he could rewind time just thirty seconds and silence himself from questioning her about the two of them being friends. It wasn't warm standing here on her porch, and she hadn't invited him in. Wouldn't a good friend and a neighborly neighbor do so? Could she afford to be heating the whole outdoors?

He smashed his cowboy hat on his head, using the brim to conceal his eyes from her. "Okay," he said, because he wasn't going to argue with her. Not again. "You have my number." With that, he turned and got the heck out of there.

He didn't look back, and he didn't expect her to text or call. He heard her call Cotton back into the house, and nothing more. No slamming of the front door. No muttering.

As he drove back to the Hammond Family Farm, he muttered to himself about trying to change lanes too late in life. "You've never been happy, Travis," he told himself. "You're a cowboy now, and you don't need a wife or a kid to worry about." He nodded like he could just turn off his attraction to Poppy Harris, but deep down, he knew he couldn't. He also didn't want to.

He simply didn't know what else to do. He'd bounced the ball into her court over and over and over, and she never seemed to catch it to throw it back to him.

"That's your answer," he said as he parked along the fence at Pony Power. "No response *is* a response."

"ALL RIGHT, BOYS," HE SAID A COUPLE OF NIGHTS later. He tossed the huge bag of corn chips into the middle of the table and sat down. "Who's ready to lose all their money?" He grinned at Cord, who sat across from him, then Mission and Cody.

"I think you are," Mission said, grinning back. He shuffled the cards, making the flipping sound fill the air.

Travis shook his head, just glad he didn't have to be alone tonight. Now that Cord lived in the cabin with him, Travis didn't have nearly as many lonely nights. They didn't have to talk to watch TV at night, and Cord actually did all the dishes without being asked.

Now, the man couldn't manage to hang up his bath towel to save his life, but for the most part, Travis could've had far worse roommates. He met Cord's eye, and he nodded toward the freezer.

"Oh, right," Travis said. "We got ice cream." He got up to get out the double-fudge ripple and brought it back to the table. "Everyone want some?"

"Yep," Cord and Cody said at the same time.

Mission nodded and started to deal. "Okay, boys, remember, if you get the killer bunny card, you've got to put in a whole handful of treats."

"I thought it was an exploding kitten," Cord said.

"Nope," Travis called from the kitchen, where he gathered four bowls and spoons. He put everything next to the ice cream as Mission tossed a card to his spot. It flipped over, and everyone looked at the bright pink killer bunny card. Travis rolled his eyes and said, "That shouldn't count."

"Get your handful in the middle," Mission said with a huge smile. He looked around soberly at the other cowboys. "This here is a serious game of Zombie Rabbit."

They all chuckled, and since they didn't play with real money, Travis grabbed a big handful of their currency— crispy M&Ms, and dropped them into the empty bowl next to the softening ice cream.

He did love their weird and wacky card games, and he couldn't wait until the unicorn stash one arrived from that project he'd funded online. He liked feeling like he belonged with a group of people, and the cowboys he'd worked with and met here on this farm in Colorado had been some of his best friends. Even after they'd left, and he'd stayed, Travis kept in touch with them.

The group who worked there now got along great, and while Matt and Boone weren't here tonight, they'd come by to play a few times. Even Gray and Chris had come to card night, ready to lose big with colored candies.

It didn't matter that he hadn't asked out Poppy Harris. He had his friends, and he could try to find someone more... agreeable, who didn't glare at him every time he offered to help her keep the things she had.

"All right," he said, picking up his cards and fanning them out in his hand while simultaneously pushing away all thoughts of Poppy. "I'm in. Let's see whose brains I can eat tonight."

Twenty-Seven

"ALL RIGHT," BOONE SAID WITH A SIGH. "YOU listen to Uncle Matt, and you be on time to get to school." He pierced Gerty with a look that said he'd fillet her skin from her bones if she caused problems this week.

His daughter looked up from her phone, missing most of the fierceness of his glare. "What?"

"Okay, who are you texting?" He reached for her phone, and Gerty let him take it from her fingers. She didn't want to, he could tell that much, but she did.

Michael, of course. Boone's heart boomed in his chest one, two, three times as he read their most recent texts and scrolled up slightly.

He sucked in a breath on *I love you! You're the best!*

"Gerty," he said, wanting to stomp her phone into a million tiny pieces, bury it in the backyard, and then move to an igloo in the middle of the arctic. No cell service up there.

"What?" she asked. "We're just texting. He's coming for

337

Spring Break." She reached for her phone, and Boone let her take it. He needed to talk to her more about boys. He just didn't know how. She needed a mother to soften whatever he said, and he pressed his eyes closed and prayed for guidance.

He was leaving for Montana in the morning, solo. He hadn't asked Cosette again, even when she'd found him out on the farm and said she wanted to talk more about it. He hadn't meant to brush her off exactly, but he was afraid it had come across that way.

He didn't really know. He hadn't spoken to her much in the past several days. Texting, sure. He stopped by her office for coffee or met her at Chris's house for lunch with his brother and Gloria.

To him, they'd taken a giant step backward at Christmastime, and when she'd sat silently in her car after his invitation to Montana, Boone had decided he didn't need to add more gashes to his still-wounded heart.

"Okay," Boone said, taking a deep breath. "Gerty, I just want you to listen to me for two minutes, okay?" He looked at her, her innocence so sweet and special to him. "Can you give me two minutes? Don't argue with me. Don't dismiss me. Just listen, and think about what I say. Two minutes, I swear."

She nodded, the set of her jaw indicating that she'd already dismissed him at least a little.

He nodded too, wishing the words would fall into line and he could just spit them out. "Michael is...honestly,

Gerty, he's a good guy. I like him. But he's a boy, bumblebee, and the truth is, boys are not like girls."

"Okay," she said, but she didn't get it. Boone knew she didn't. And how could he possibly explain the whole of the male species to her?

"I know you like him, and I know he likes you. That's totally okay and one-hundred percent normal. But you can't send him texts that say *I love you* and *you're the best*."

"We're just friends," Gerty said. "He helped me with a math problem."

"I know," Boone said, another sigh slipping from his lips. "But when boys see messages like that, they don't read them as —oh, this girl is such a great friend. She's so happy I helped her with her math. He's thinking about kissing you the next time he sees you." Boone looked at Gerty, who seemed a little surprised.

"He thinks about it every day," Boone said, looking away as his thoughts moved to Cosette. "Most hours, probably. On the way down here for Spring Break, it'll be the *only* thing he thinks about. And it's not because he's gross or perverted. That's how boys think."

Gerty let a few seconds go by, and Boone finally looked over to her. "He did ask me if he could kiss me when he's here in March," she whispered.

Boone's first thought was to chain her in her room. No way was Michael Hammond going to kiss his little girl. As he studied his daughter, he saw her grow up right in front of him. She was gorgeous and kind and absolutely *not* a little girl anymore.

"What did you say?" he asked.

She shrugged. "I don't know. I told him—" She inhaled quickly and blew it all out. "I told him we'd have to see. That if it felt right, and we had the chance, and I didn't want to lie to you—"

She turned and looked at him, and she suddenly morphed back into the scared six-year-old who'd lost her mother only hours ago. He put his arm around her, and she dove into his side.

"I don't want to lie to you, Daddy."

"You never have to lie to me," he said, his voice throaty and whispered. "Ever, Gerty, okay? I'm always on your side, and even if you did something I didn't agree with, even if you got pregnant and weren't married, or you failed all the math tests in the world, or you ran off to join the circus as a horse trickster, I would love you. Always."

Her arm tightened across his abdomen, and Boone gripped her shoulder with all the strength he had. "You're my daughter, and you never have to lie to me. You can tell me anything, and I will do whatever I can to help you."

Gerty cried against his chest, and Boone blinked back his own emotion, silently begging the Lord to allow her to come to him for anything. At any time. And to bless him that he'd recognize her pleas for help and be available to her when she came.

He looked at the tree he, Cosette, and Gerty had put up on Thanksgiving Day. He and Gerty had bought Christmas ornaments for it, donned them all, and then taken them all down. It currently just shone with lights, as Boone was planning on finding Nikki's other decorations when he went to Saffron Lake tomorrow.

After way longer than two minutes, he said, "I know how he feels, bumblebee. I was his age once, and it is very exciting to have a beautiful girl pay attention to you. Kissing is fun, and exciting, and heck, even now, I spend a lot of my time thinking about kissing Cosette." He chuckled, which definitely lightened the mood.

Gerty pulled away from him, her pretty blue eyes watery. She sniffed and wiped her face. "Really?"

"Yes, hon," he said. "It's normal to feel like this about someone you like and care about. But I don't go too far. I know I want to wait to be intimate with Cosette until we're married. *If* we get married." He frowned at his own assumption. They had a long way to go until any sort of proposal or I-do. "Your mom and I waited to be together until we were married, because commitment is something we both believed in."

"I'm not going to...do that with Michael."

"Why aren't you?" Boone asked.

"Dad, gross."

"No," he insisted. "It's not gross, Gerty." He shook his head, unable to find the right thing to say. "It's actually a really beautiful thing between two people who love each other, who have made promises to each other and to God, and are willing to face the storms of life together." He let out his breath, his eyes focused on something blurry on the horizon. Something he couldn't quite see. "I loved being married. I want to be married again, right now."

He looked at his daughter again. "But you and me? It's always you and me, Gerty. Okay?"

She nodded, her eyes filling with tears again.

"So." He kept his arm around her as she leaned into his side again. "Tell me why you like Michael, and then we'll talk about why you might kiss him."

"He's smart," she said, her voice tinny and quiet. "Like, the smartest human you've ever met, especially with math." She took a breath. "He's cute."

"Very important," Boone said, smiling.

"Dad."

"It is," Boone insisted. "You have to be attracted to him, right?"

"He works hard. He loves his family—like, his brothers and sisters and all of his cousins love him. He's so sweet with them."

"Mm." Boone couldn't argue with her, and he didn't even want to.

"I don't know," Gerty said. "He's easy to be with. I like talking to him. We like a lot of the same things."

"All very good points," Boone said. "I gotta tell you, though, Gerty, kissing is pretty gross. I mean, it's his *mouth*, and you have *no idea* what he's put in that thing."

Gerty giggled and straightened. "You just said kissing was exciting and fun."

"Did I?" Boone grinned at her, the moment only lasting for a single breath before he sobered. "Seriously, Gerty. Why do you think it won't be?"

"I don't know," she said quietly.

"Why don't you tell me what you're worried about?" Boone distinctly remembered how Matt had talked to his son about kissing and his girlfriend, but as Boone had just said, boys and girls were different.

"I guess I'm scared," Gerty said. "That I won't like it, or it won't be fun. And then what? I tell him it was gross? Won't he feel bad?"

Boone did his best not to smile. "First, let's go backward through that, okay?" He gazed evenly at his daughter. "It is not *your* job to make sure Michael feels good about things, okay? If *you* don't like what he's doing and *you* don't want to kiss him—or anything else, and let's be clear, you shouldn't be doing anything else but kissing right now. I don't even want you doing that."

His thoughts derailed, and Boone closed his eyes and ran his hand through his hair. He sighed out his frustration and panic. "Okay, let me start over."

"It's not my job to make him feel good," Gerty said. "I know, Daddy."

"Do you?" Boone looked at her again. "Because you just said you were worried about him feeling bad if you didn't want to kiss him."

Gerty blinked and simply looked at him.

"You get to say no," Boone said. "End of story. It's not your job to make sure his feelings don't get hurt. Clear?"

"Yes, sir."

Boone nodded and took another breath. "Okay. Let me think." He pressed his fingers against the bridge of his nose. "I think you'll like it, but if you don't, then you just pull away, make something up, and get on back to me. Use me as a reason you have to go. I don't care. You don't owe Michael anything."

"Okay."

"It's also okay to be scared," Boone said. "He probably is too. In fact, I know he is. Heck, I was terrified to kiss Cosette, and I'm a heckuva lot older than Michael."

"Daddy." She spoke in a scandalized tone.

"Gerty, boys are just as afraid as girls," he said. "I was when I was Michael's age, for sure. I don't think that ever goes away, because he's hoping for the same things you're worried about. He's scared he won't be a good kisser, and he's scared you'll be grossed out." He chuckled and shook his head. "Trust me on this."

Gerty leaned back into his side. "All right."

The tension and pulsating nerves in Boone's chest started to quiet. "You'll come tell me when you kiss him, right?" he asked. "It's not embarrassing, Gerty, and I want to know so I can be a good dad."

"You're a great dad," she whispered.

"I can't be as effective as I'd like to be if I don't know what you're doing." He squeezed her shoulder. "I know you'd probably tell your mom stuff like this, and right now, I have to be her and me. I promise I won't tease you or make a big deal out of it."

"I'll tell you," she whispered.

"Good," Boone said. "I want to help you with solutions should you find you need them. It's hard to be thirteen or fourteen, and I can offer a neutral point of view."

Gerty looked up and smiled at him. "You? Neutral?"

Boone blinked and then burst out laughing. "Fine," he said between his chuckles. "Maybe I'm not that neutral when it comes to you." He leaned down and kissed her forehead. "I love you, Gerty-girl."

She pulled in a breath, and Boone knew precisely why. Nikki had called her "Gerty-girl" as a term of endearment the way he called his daughter *bumblebee*. The last words Nikki had ever said to Gerty before she'd passed had been, "I love you, Gerty-girl."

Boone's emotion rumbled through his body, and his daughter gave him strength as she said, "I love you too, Daddy."

THE FOLLOWING MORNING, BOONE HUGGED HIS brother and said, "Thanks, Matt. I'll be back by Sunday evening."

"I'm worried about you," Matt said quietly, refusing to release Boone. He stepped back and rubbed his hands together. "Are you sure you should be going alone?"

"No," Boone said. "But I am." He glanced over to where Gerty sat with Britt and Keith at the bar. Gloria poured a cup of coffee, not looking in anyone's direction, but Boone knew she had phenomenal hearing. "I'll call you when I get there."

He moved over to Gerty and kissed the top of her head.

"'Bye, bumblebee. I'll call you tomorrow night after the lessons, okay?"

"Okay," Gerty said, giving him another side-hug. "Love you."

"Love you too."

"Travel safe, Boone," Gloria said, her concern written in her eyes. He hated that she and Matt worried about him, and worse, that they talked about him. He couldn't change that, and he supposed he should be grateful that he and his brother were so involved in each other's lives.

"Thank you, Gloria." He gave her the best smile he could muster as he faced the prospect of leaving Ivory Peaks by himself when he'd rather Cosette be in the passenger seat beside him. When he was driving to visit his deceased wife's grave near the seventh anniversary of her death.

He caught Matt's eye again, and his brother followed him out onto the porch. "Boone," he said.

"What, Matt?"

"I know this is going to work out for you," his brother said.

Boone stopped next to the pillar on the porch at the top of the steps and looked out over the frozen front yard. January held a lot of snow in Colorado, as it always did in Montana. He found the landscape white and holy, which was gorgeous and beautiful to him. He didn't mind the cold at all, and winter always reminded him of what he hoped heaven would be like.

His chest felt so deep right now. Like a huge hole that went past his feet and continued into the earth. Down and down and down, and he'd never claw his way back to the sunlight. He'd felt this way when Nikki had died, and he often reverted to this dark place in January.

Which was just another reason he hadn't wanted to go to Montana alone.

"Cosette will be on the call with Gerty," he said when Matt didn't say anything else. He glanced over at his brother. "You were talkin' about her when you said it's going to work out, right?"

"Yes," Matt said quietly. "I know you love her, and—"

"That doesn't matter," Boone said roughly. He spoke too loudly too, and his voice carried too far over all the snow. His fury flamed, and he scoffed. "Listen, thank you for taking Gerty. I appreciate it. I better be going."

"Boone," Matt said as he flew down the steps. "Come on."

"No," Boone said. "I'm not going to come on." He spun to face Matt. "It *doesn't* matter if I love her or I don't. I loved Karley too, and that didn't matter. I *adored* Nikki." He reached up and took off his cowboy hat, his desperation reaching a new high. He started to laugh when he wanted to cry.

He put his hat back on and glowered at his brother, who wisely said nothing. Boone had always been the more emotional of the two of them. Louder and funnier and willing to risk more.

"I loved my wife with everything I had," Boone said, his voice stuck somewhere in his throat. "And it didn't matter. She died anyway. So it doesn't matter if I love Cosette with all I have now. She still gets to choose something or someone besides me. Just because I love her *doesn't* mean it's going to work out."

Matt cocked his head to the side. "Doesn't it?"

"No," Boone barked at him. Had he seriously not heard a single thing Boone had said? Had he missed the reason Boone had uprooted his daughter and moved here in the first place?

He shook his head. "I have to go." He turned and started toward his truck.

"I think she's it for you," Matt yelled after him. "*That's* why it's going to work out. She's not Karley, Boone, and she *isn't* going to choose someone or something else over you."

"Yeah, okay," Boone said, waving his hand above his head. He glared at Matt as he got behind the wheel of his truck. He slammed the door, turned the key, and backed out far too fast.

He contained the pressure in his chest until he hit the highway leading north, and then he pounded his open palm against the steering wheel. His chest heaving, he said, "What you don't know, Matt, is she might not pick something else over me, but she's never going to pick me either."

————

As Boone approached his wife's grave, a small snow shovel in one hand and a vase of flowers in the other, he read her name, her birthdate, and the date she'd died. "Hello, love," he whispered into the night air. He'd checked in at his hotel an hour ago, and then he'd driven around the town where he used to buy groceries and take Gerty to soccer practice in the summer.

He'd video call her tomorrow, but he always came to the cemetery alone first. He crouched down and touched the top of the stone, which sent shivers and ice through his blood. "You look good."

He half-laughed and half-sobbed at his comment, because when Nikki had been so sick those last few months, he'd tell her every day how good she looked when they both knew she looked one step away from dying. He'd hold her in his arms to help her stand in the morning, and he'd whisper how good she looked and how much he loved her.

When she couldn't get in bed by herself, he picked her up and slid her between the sheets, whispering that at least she still looked good. She'd smile or giggle every time, and at that time in their lives where there was absolutely nothing to smile about or be happy about, his ability to make her happy had buoyed them all up.

He stood and used the shovel to clear away the snow so he could leave his flowers. They'd freeze in under an hour, but he didn't care. Nikki had loved sunflowers, and he always ordered a dozen for her from the single florist in town.

"I'm seein' someone," he said as he set down the vase with the bright sunflowers. They stood out so starkly against the white snow and the gray headstone. "Her name is Cosette. I'm not sure if it's gonna work out."

No one asked him why, but he heard the words in the

wind. "I don't know," he said, sighing. He reached up and wiped his eyes, feeling a hint of wetness there. "She's...she's had a rough time with relationships and men, and I don't know if I'm strong enough to help her past that."

Heck, for all he knew, she might not *want* to get past it.

There were no other footsteps in the snow, which meant that Nikki's parents hadn't come yet. They'd likely be here tomorrow, and he'd let Gerty talk to them for a few minutes via the video chat. A pang of guilt hit him for taking their granddaughter from them, but they'd both assured him that he could do what he felt was right.

So he had. "I moved," he told her. "Remember I came and told you I was leaving Saffron Lake? The house?" He sighed and looked out over the cemetery. In the summer, the trees protected the graves from the worst of the sun. "I haven't sold it. I'm not sure why."

Putting the house and farm up for sale had actually been on his to-do list for tomorrow, but now he wasn't sure he'd do it.

"God." He looked up into the cloudless sky. The blackness went on forever, making it seem like the universe could swallow him. "What's the right thing to do here?"

He didn't even know where "here" was. He just wanted to stop feeling like a bulldozer had driven over his chest, ran out of gas right when it was on top of him, and stopped. For days, weeks, months, seven long years, it had been parked on his ribs, crushing him.

He wanted his third try to be his final attempt at finding

the lifelong happiness he'd dreamed about the day he'd married Nikki.

He closed his eyes against the darkness and let himself sway with the wind and the earth. *What's the right thing to do here?* he wondered again, and then again.

He wanted to honor his wife and keep reminding Gerty of her. He'd come visit her every January, no matter where he lived. "I love you," he whispered as he opened his eyes. He knew the capacity of the human heart at this point, because he'd now been in love with three women in his life. "I love Cosette Brian too. What do you think I should do about her?"

Nikki didn't answer, but Boone's instincts told him to go back to Ivory Peaks as quickly as he could. "Gerty misses you somethin' powerful," he said. "I'm doing my very best with her, and she might kiss a boy for the first time in March." He grinned at the letters in his wife's name. "I'll tell you all about it next time I come, okay?"

He stood with his thoughts and the snow for several long minutes, working through the tangled mess in his mind. He didn't want to move backward, break-up with Cosette, or start over with someone new. A scripture popped into his head.

Love is patient. Love is kind. It does not boast and is not proud. It is not easily angered. It always protects, always trusts, always hopes, always perseveres.

Love never fails.

He was pretty sure he'd missed a few things in there, but the important bits hit him right in the chest. He could be patient. He could be kind. He could be slower to anger, be better at protecting Cosette, trusting her, hoping for her, and persevering until she couldn't live without him.

He would not fail her.

He also needed to get back to her as soon as possible.

His phone rang, and he glanced down as he pulled it from his pocket. The brightness of his cellphone screen made him squint, but he saw Cosette's name and face easily. He wanted her at his side. He wanted her here.

He wanted her.

What do you think I should do about her?

He turned away from the headstone as he swiped on the call. "Cosette," he said, so many things becoming clear as he walked away from Nikki. "Hey, listen, I'm on my way back from Montana right now—"

"Are you? Because I need you here. I need you here so badly."

Boone's pulse spiked, and he asked, "What's wrong?"

"My sky is falling," Cosette whispered. "Please hurry, Boone."

Twenty-Eight

Cosette sat up straight at the very distinct sound of a car door slamming. Her face felt like she'd coated it in chunky sea salt and then fallen asleep. She was on the couch and not in bed, and she had been asleep until the noise had woken her.

She got to her feet at the same time someone banged on the front door. "Cosette," Boone called. "It's me, sweetheart."

She realized she was wearing her plaid pajama bottoms and a dingy gray T-shirt about the time she opened her front door. Boone stood there, concern and compassion and caring in his eyes.

"Hey, my love," he said, entering her house and taking her into his arms in one fluid movement. He held her right against his chest and pushed the door closed with his foot. "You're okay? You made it through the night okay? I thought you were going to Raven's." He didn't back up to see her face, for which Cosette thanked the Lord above.

She started to tremble, her emotions on the tip of a dangerous precipice. She couldn't speak, and she had no idea what time it was. Montana was a good eleven or twelve hours from Ivory Peaks, and Boone had made the drive there and back in a single day.

She drew in a deep breath of him, getting the leather from his jacket and the spice from his cologne. "I'm not okay," she finally said.

"I'm here," he said, as if his presence alone would chase out the fear and darkness in her life. Standing in the circle of safety in his arms, she absolutely believed he could. "Do you want to tell me more about your daddy now?"

Cosette stepped back from him, unwilling to let him go completely. She took his hand in hers and turned to lead him into the kitchen. She couldn't remember what she'd eaten for dinner last night, and as she looked over the kitchen island, she saw dried garlic on the cutting board and a pan on the stove. She'd been making dinner when Raven had called and said their father was sick.

The panic still choked her now, as it had then. She saw herself from above, running from the house and racing to get to Raven's. The drive to their father's had taken so long, and he'd said the dreaded word.

Cancer.

"He's got prostate cancer," Cosette said.

"You said stage one," Boone said gently. "Did he say what the doctors said about a treatment plan?"

"He's going on Monday," she said. "Raven and I will go with him." After she'd held everything together for her family—the way they'd done for her when she'd shown up with her own terrible news—she'd gone into her father's backyard and cried.

Alone.

In the dark.

Then, she'd done the one and only thing she'd been able to think of to soothe herself.

She'd called Boone.

"I'll have lunch when you get to the farm," Boone said. "At my cabin. You can lay on my couch, and I'll hold you, and you'll tell me all about it." He smiled at her, which seemed like the exact right thing to do though she couldn't even fathom feeling happiness or joy right now. "You don't have to go through this alone. Is that what you're worried about?"

"Yes," she whispered. "Which is just so stupid. You had to weather much worse with your wife, and—" She cut off, unable to continue. She shouldn't have called Boone. He'd gone to see Nikki, and she'd ruined it with her sky-falling episode.

"Hey, now," he said. "This is a trial for you, and I want to make it easier if I can. What I went through with Nikki...I wouldn't wish that on anyone."

Cosette looked at him, this gentle giant of a man. He had such a good heart, and she couldn't believe that he'd given part of it to her.

"You were supposed to be at Raven's," he said gently,

touching his forehead to hers. "You don't have to be here alone, suffering."

"I went," she said. "I just got back here about an hour ago." She'd laid on the couch and fallen asleep.

"What else is bothering you?" Boone lifted her fingers to his mouth and tenderly kissed her knuckles. He led her to the couch and sat, pulling her onto his lap. "Tell me."

Cosette took a deep breath, finally able to tell him what she'd been trying to say for several days now. "I should've gone to Saffron Lake with you. I wanted to, Boone. You didn't give me the chance to really apologize and allow me to come with you."

"I know," he said with a sigh. "I didn't want to push you somewhere you weren't ready to go."

"I'm ready," she whispered.

"Okay," Boone said, his voice turning a shade deeper. "That's great, because I'm in love with you, and you absolutely are welcome to come with me next time I go. And I'll be right here beside you through everything with your daddy."

Cosette froze by the end of the first sentence, and while her eyes remained open, she only blinked because her body did so involuntarily. Boone's rough yet tender fingers ran up her arm and back down to her wrist. Up and down, silent. Waiting.

She cleared her throat. "You're in love with me?"

"Completely," he said, no embarrassment or qualms in sight. "I shouldn't have let my impatience dictate my actions. I'm a fool sometimes, and I hope you can forgive me."

Cosette pushed away from him and sat up straight. She looked directly into his face. "Me forgive you?"

"Yeah," he said, smiling at her gently and pushing her ratted hair out of her eyes. "For being difficult these past couple of weeks. I was just disappointed about goin' to Montana by myself. I love you, Cosette, and I wanted you to experience the trip with me. I wanted you to see Nikki's grave and try to understand why it's important to me to go every year. Because I'm gonna go every year."

She nodded and swallowed against the dryness in her throat. "I know you are."

"You're okay with it?"

"Of course I am."

Boone's eyes shone with joy and desire at the same time. "Okay, harder question, and any answer is okay." He cleared his throat. "Do you love me too?"

"Yes," she said, again not letting any of her feelings sabotage her mouth. Instant fear reared up, but just as quickly, something inside her smothered it. Her eyes widened. "Yes," she said again. "I *do* love you, Boone. I do."

He chuckled, the picture of happiness and light. "You sound like you're surprised."

"I am, a little," she said. "I mean...yeah." She smiled at him too. "Yeah, I've been trying to deny it, because I'm scared, but yeah."

"This doesn't mean we have to get married right away," Boone said. "I will be patient and kind and hopeful. You'll continue to heal however you need to. And when it's right, we'll get married."

She beamed at him, at the goodness inside him, at the kind spirit and healthy soul he possessed.

"Okay?" he asked, his voice the same throaty one he'd used when he'd first kissed her, months ago.

She leaned toward him, watching his eyes drift closed in anticipation of kissing her. She paused only a hair from touching her mouth to his. "Okay," she whispered, and then she kissed this beautiful man who'd shown up in her life right when she needed him. He was there to shield her as the world crashed down around her, and she did love him with her whole heart because of that.

And he wasn't a bad kisser either.

THE CABIN DOOR BANGED OPEN, STARTLING Cosette from where she stood at Boone's stove. "Gerty," she chastised. "What in the world?"

"Where's Daddy?" the girl asked. She looked like she'd run across the whole farm, her cheeks bright red patches against her normally fair complexion. Not only that, but her cowgirl hat was mysteriously missing from her head.

"He's out back with Matt," Cosette said, watching Gerty run through the house. Full-on run. It didn't take long, what with the size of the cabin, and she yanked on the doorknob there too. She hadn't bothered to close the front door, and with both of them open, the late-March weather had free access to the cabin.

It had started to warm up, but Cosette wouldn't categorize the weather as double-door-open worthy. She shivered as she called, "I'll get the door," after the teenager. Gerty was gone already, and Cosette shook her head as she headed for the front door first.

With that shut, she strode to the back door. She curled her fingers around the door and pulled it open a little further. Boone and Matt had paused their work on the lawn mower Matt had been tasked to fix, and they both looked at Gerty as she gestured with her hands.

Boone's smile grew and grew, and then he looked at his brother, one eyebrow cocked, clearly asking his brother what to do with whatever Gerty had presented him with. She sure had been animated and excited.

Matt shrugged, and Boone laughed. About the moment he swooped Gerty into his arms, Cosette knew what had caused Gerty to come racing inside the cabin in search of her father.

"She kissed Michael," Cosette breathed out as she started outside, now the one leaving the door open behind her.

Boone set his daughter back on her feet, the two of them grinning like fools. She missed the front of his sentence, but she caught, "...did it go? Did you like it?"

Gerty glanced at Cosette as she arrived at Boone's side. She slipped her hand into his, because while he painted the perfect picture of calm, cool father on the outside, she knew this news was slicing away at him quietly inside. He'd confessed his worries to her weeks ago, and again just last night when Michael and Wes had arrived at the farm for Spring Break.

Without school today, Gerty and Michael had spent most of the day together. In fact, Cosette hadn't seen her since breakfast, not even over at Pony Power.

Gerty's eyes glowed with delight as she nodded. "Yeah," she said. "I liked it."

Matt chuckled then. "Good luck, brother," he said quietly before he went back to the lawn mower.

"Where did you go?" Cosette asked, exchanging a glance with Boone.

"Uh, out past the cabins that we're using for that camp this summer," Gerty said, meeting her father's eye again. "He held my hand, and he was really sweet."

"What did you say to him afterward?" Boone said. "Or did you just run straight here?"

"I need that socket," Matt said, and Boone released Cosette's hand to get it for him.

Gerty groaned and spun around. Surprise and alarm coursed through Cosette. "Hey, what's wrong?" she asked, stepping in to give Gerty a female perspective on her first kiss.

"I just ran off," Gerty said, meeting Cosette's eyes with plenty of panic in hers. "He kissed me, and then after, he asked me if it was okay, and I just nodded and scampered away. Ugh!" She paced away from the adults, and Cosette looked at Boone.

He nodded at her to go after Gerty. "She's not my daughter," Cosette said.

"Yes, she is," Boone replied. "I'm going to tell her not to see that boy again, so you better handle this." He gave Cosette a dark look that transformed into something else entirely when Gerty turned back to them.

"Cosette," she moaned, and Cosette stepped in front of Boone.

"All right," Cosette said, moving toward Gerty while her heart panicked. She put her arm around the girl's shoulders and steered her toward the house. "I need help with the steak, and you can tell me everything from start to finish. I'm sure it's not as bad as you think."

They went into the house, and Gerty slumped onto a barstool and started giving more details. "He asked if we could go for a walk after the last wash," she said. "He's *so* cute, Cosette. I knew he wanted to be alone, and I said sure. He asked if I'd been out to those cabins, because his dad and uncle want them cleaned this weekend for the camp. I said I hadn't, but I knew where they were. So we went that way."

"Mm hm." Cosette salted and peppered one side of the steaks and looked at Gerty so she'd keep talking.

"He held my hand after he asked. He *asked*, Cosette. He's seriously so amazing." She sighed, and Cosette smiled at her.

"He sounds like it."

"Is my dad romantic like that?" Gerty asked. "He holds your hand all the time. Does your stomach...I don't know, dive-bomb through your whole body when he touches you?" She looked so hopeful and so lost at the same time.

Cosette grinned at her and nodded. "Yes, ma'am. Your

daddy is plenty romantic." She pointed the tongs at Gerty. "Don't you go tellin' him that. His head is big enough."

Gerty grinned too and made a crossing motion over her heart. "So we get out to the cabins, and we go past them, and I realize he doesn't care about these cabins. He says the sun is bright today, and then he looks at me, and I knew." She stared off at nothing, and Cosette could only relive her first, amazing kiss with Boone too.

"He asked if he could kiss me, if it felt okay. I nodded, and then he just sort of...did it."

"Did it?"

"Well, he sort of fumbled for a second with his hands. It was a little awkward, you know? I didn't know where to touch him either." A look of horror came across her face. "What if I did it wrong?"

"I'm sure you didn't," Cosette said. She glanced toward the back door. "You know your dad is going to ask me for these details. Where...did he put his hands? Where did you put yours?"

Gerty looked down at her hands as if she'd just now realized they were attached to her body. "I think they ended up on his back," Gerty said, looking up. "My arms went under his, and yeah, I had my arms around him and my hands on his back."

Cosette flipped the steaks and reached for the salt shaker again. "And his?"

"He held my face in his hands," Gerty said, reaching up to touch her face. "Right here, along the sides."

"Smart," Cosette said. "And very romantic." She slid

Gerty a smile she hoped would encourage the girl to keep talking and sharing her secrets. "And then?"

"Then he pulled away, and he leaned real close, his chin ducked low. And he said, 'Was that okay?' That's when I nodded, and when he stepped back, I ran off. Literally ran away. I didn't even *say* anything."

"I'm sure it's fine," Cosette said. "Why don't you text him and ask him to come eat dinner with us?"

"It's his first day in town," Gerty said miserably. She laid her head in her folded arms and looked toward the back door. "He's going to dinner with his dad at that burger place they funded."

"I see." Cosette had absolutely no idea what to do now. "You could still text him. Tell him you didn't mean to run off. You were just nervous."

Gerty lifted her head for long enough to give her a dirty look and then she sighed and flopped back into her arms. "He's never going to want to kiss me again. Not now."

"Gerty—" She cut off as someone knocked on the front door. Gerty jerked to attention, also looking toward the front of the cabin. Cosette cleared her throat and wiped her hands on her apron. "I'll get it."

"Cosette," Gerty said, but Cosette ignored her. Everyone on the farm knew she and Boone were dating. No, they weren't engaged yet, but all Cosette had to do was say the word, and Boone would be down on both knees. She got closer and closer to being mentally well enough to picture herself as Boone's wife with every passing day.

She opened the door and none other than Michael

Hammond stood there. He held two hats in his hands. One was clearly his, and he pressed it to his chest. He looked one breath away from throwing up, and Cosette settled her weight on one foot. "Hello, Michael."

"Cosette," Gerty hissed from behind her, but Cosette refused to look at her.

"Gerty, uh, dropped her hat," Michael said, thrusting out the second hat in his hands. "I, um, is she here? I checked at the center, but she wasn't there."

"Yes," Cosette said, smiling broadly at the good-looking teenager in front of her. "She's here." She stepped back and looked over her shoulder. Gerty stood at the end of the couch, frozen. "Gerty," Cosette said gently but with plenty of power too. "This fine young man brought back your hat. I wonder how you dropped it and then forgot it?"

When Gerty still didn't move, Cosette took the few steps to her and stood in front of her, blocking her view of Michael out on the doorstep. "Honey, look at me."

Gerty raised her eyes to Cosette's. "You go thank that boy, talk to him like a normal person, and kiss him again if you can." She stroked the girl's wispy hair off her face and behind her ear. "Your daddy's gonna be done in about ten minutes, so you best be back before then, cowgirl hat and all."

Gerty thawed, started to smile, and then nodded. She stepped around Cosette and went toward the front door. "Mike," she said as she reached him. "Thanks for bringing this. I'm so sorry I—" She pulled the door closed behind her as she left, cutting off the conversation.

Cosette giggled quietly to herself. She didn't need to eavesdrop on the teens. Gerty would tell her everything once they sat down to dinner...if Boone didn't glare her into silence.

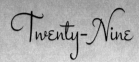

Twenty-Nine

Boone looked up as Gerty entered his bedroom. "I'm ready," she said, folding her arms.

"Glad to see you're so excited to go visit your grandparents." He cocked his eyebrows at her and went back to folding his clothes.

She took her attitude down a notch, her bony shoulders falling as she dropped her hands to her sides. A sigh slipped from her mouth. "I know. I'm sorry."

Boone shoved an extra pair of shorts in his suitcase. "I need your help this week, Gerty."

"I know."

"If it's gonna be me and you, we have to figure out how to get along." They got along just fine—if Boone did whatever Gerty wanted.

"It's not just me and you," Gerty said, and Boone looked up.

"It is," he said, advancing toward her. "Always. We're just adding Cosette, hopefully." He drew his daughter into a hug, glad she wrapped her arms around him too. "You like her, right?"

"Yes," Gerty said.

"She loves you," Boone said. "Just like I do. Just like Gloria loves Uncle Matt's kids." He pulled back and bent his head until his forehead touched Gerty's. Somehow, he didn't have to bend as far, because she wasn't seven years old anymore, and she'd grown at least five inches since they'd moved to Ivory Peaks only a year ago. "I love you. It's always me and you, okay?"

She nodded, her eyes closed, and kept quiet.

"I know why you're mad," he said, moving away from her and adding a touch of coolness to his voice.

"It's not about Mike," she said.

"Sure it is," Boone said. "You're leaving this morning, and he won't be here until this afternoon." He turned and studied his daughter. At least she didn't argue with him when they stood face-to-face. "We'll be back in four days. It's not a long trip. He'll still be here." Michael Hammond would be working at the farm all summer, in fact. He and Gerty would have plenty of opportunities to sneak off behind cabins to kiss, and Boone finished his packing while Gerty watched, trying to distract himself from such thoughts.

He zipped his suitcase and looked at her again. "You've got her ring?"

Gerty stuck her hand into her cutoff shorts pocket and lifted the diamond ring. "Right here." He'd taken it from the box and slipped the white gold band with the glittering diamond atop it inside a tiny plastic bag. "I'm going to put it in my backpack."

Boone nodded, appreciating Gerty so much for who she was in that moment. His daughter would never be caught with a purse, and he'd bought her a small backpack for the trip. She'd loaded it with snacks and drinks, her phone and tablet, chargers, and her headphones. The ring would obviously ride with all of her most important belongings, and Boone's heartbeat tripped over itself.

Gerty left the room, and Boone picked up his suitcase and put it on the floor. It rolled along beside him as he followed her down the hall to the kitchen and living room area of the cabin.

"She's here," Gerty said. "My zipper is stuck." She threw Boone a panicked look. "Daddy, help."

Boone abandoned his suitcase and hurried toward Gerty. "You go say hi," he said, taking the ring from her. "I'll get it tucked in this pocket."

Gerty straightened and wiped her hands down the front of her shorts. She opened the door and stepped outside with, "Hey, Cosette," before she brought the door closed behind her. Boone yanked on the zipper once, then twice, and it finally slid up the teeth. He stuffed the ring inside and pulled the closure down again.

His pulse raced now, and he had no idea how he was

going to get down on his knees and ask Cosette to marry him. He'd thought about doing it at the cemetery, and quickly dismissed the idea. He didn't need to be kneeling on his wife's grave, for crying out loud.

The three of them were staying at his house in Saffron Lake, and Boone was planning to work himself to the bone over the next few days. He'd hired help to get the farm and house in tip-top shape so he could list it for sale.

He wasn't going to return to Montana. Not now that he had a reason to stay in Ivory Peaks. Not when Cosette had mentioned to him exactly seventeen days ago that she thought she was ready to take the next step in their relationship.

Her schedule had become a bit tighter since she'd started driving over to her dad's twice a week. Sometimes Boone took her so she could work on a report or catch a nap, and he was just glad he could help.

Jeff had been through his first round of treatments, and his doctors were pleased with his progress. Right now, he didn't have any appointments or anything urgent, and Raven had said she'd take care of him while Cosette went with Boone and Gerty to Montana.

He never had video-called his daughter at the cemetery, and Nikki's parents hadn't seen Gerty in a year. Boone knew he needed to go, and this trip felt miles different than the one he'd done five months ago.

"Oh, he's ready," Gerty said brightly as she opened the door.

Boone picked up her backpack and handed it to her.

"Yep," he said. "I'm ready. Let's get this show on the road."
His whole body lit up as Cosette entered the house, and he
laughed as he scooped her into his arms. "Hello, love." He
knew exactly what he was saying when he said that, as he'd
said it to Nikki for years and years. When he went to visit her
grave, he still said it.

Now, he had another living, breathing love in his life,
and as he leaned down to kiss Cosette, he closed his eyes and
thanked the Lord for His goodness and kindness in leading
Boone somewhere he didn't want to go and providing for
him a third try at happiness.

———

"Here we are," Boone said many hours later.
The sun had started to arc through the western sky, and his
backside felt stiff from sitting for so long. "Looks like
Grandma and Grandpa beat us," he added.

He killed the engine and got out of the truck, letting
Cosette get out on her own on her side of the vehicle. He
couldn't move past the rearview mirror for some reason. He'd
never frozen when he came to the cemetery before, but
now, he did.

Gerty got out behind him, and as she moved beside him,
she slipped the tiny plastic bag with the diamond ring into
his hand. "Do you see them?" she asked casually, and Boone
wasn't sure if he should be alarmed or impressed by her
acting skills.

"That's their car," he said, nodding to the black sedan a

couple of spots over. He tucked the ring into his pocket, wondering how he was going to ask Cosette to marry him. He'd already decided not to do it here.

They hadn't gone to the house yet, choosing to meet Kyle and Carrie here. As he looked out over the still-greening grass and all the headstones, the most amazing feeling of peace ran through him. Cemeteries usually held so much sadness, but today, all Boone could think about was that these souls had been taken to heaven, where they must be so happy.

Cosette arrived at the corner of the truck, and Gerty walked the few steps to her and took her hand. "I'll show you where she is."

Boone's chest hitched at the strength and maturity in his daughter, and he caught Cosette's eye before she turned to go with Gerty. She bent her head closer to his daughter, her long auburn hair falling down and touching Gerty's bare shoulder. Cosette said something to her, and Gerty looked over her shoulder, slowing her pace.

"Come on, Daddy," she said. "You have to tell her everything that's happened since the last time you came."

Boone cleared his throat and got his legs to work, thankfully. He caught up to his girls quickly, and he put himself between them. "I want to hold your hand," he said to Cosette, slipping his fingers into the spaces where Gerty's had just been. "And yours." He grinned at his daughter and looked up again, the sunshine warming him now.

"There's Grandma," Gerty said, squealing and releasing

his hand so she could run toward Nikki's mother. Boone smiled as widely as he ever had, especially when Carrie jogged toward Gerty too, both of them colliding in their joy.

"Wow," Cosette said. "They miss her and love her."

Boone nodded. "You've met Gerty, right? Everyone loves her. She has this...fire people seem to want to have in their lives."

Cosette bumped him with her hip. "That comes from you, you know."

He looked at her, glad his cowboy hat shielded his eyes from the sun in front of him. "You think so?"

"One-hundred percent," she said.

They were barely moving, and Boone looked back toward Gerty and her grandparents. "Carrie looks just like Nikki," he said. "Gerty is a small version of the two of them."

"She's taller," Cosette said.

"That's the little part I have in her," Boone said as Kyle looked in their direction. He wore a huge smile too, and he started toward Boone.

Something tickled in Boone's soul, and he picked up the pace, starting to laugh as he approached Kyle. "Boone," the older man said. He took Boone into a tight hug and held on as if he let go he'd fall to his death.

Neither of them spoke, and Boone smiled while his emotions stormed through him. He pressed his eyes closed and prayed he was doing the right thing. Finally, Carrie came over, and she wanted a hug from Boone too.

She wept openly, and Boone didn't know how to explain or let go of her. He eventually managed it, his own eyes wet. He wiped them as he turned to find Gerty holding Cosette's hand.

"This is Cosette," Gerty said, helping Boone right when he needed her to. She smiled up at Cosette, who also wore a gorgeous grin on her face. "Daddy's in love with her, and if he can ever get his act together, I think he'll ask her to marry him."

"Hey," Boone said, his smile falling. "I have my act together."

Gerty's eyebrows went up, her smile teasing and taunting him. She glanced at Cosette. "Did he ask you to marry him and I missed it?"

"No, ma'am," Cosette said, giggling. She released Gerty's hand and stepped toward Kyle and Carrie. "It's so wonderful to meet you."

"This is Kyle and Carrie Burgiss," Boone said. "Cosette Brian. We have been seein' each other for a while. Nine months or so."

"Boone and I met on this very day a year ago," she said, giving him a look that said he probably should've known that.

"Is that right?" Kyle asked at the same time Boone did. They all laughed together, and once the handshakes and hugs finished, the five of them stood there awkwardly.

"Daddy," Gerty hissed, and he looked at her.

"What?"

She sighed and rolled her eyes toward the heavens.

Ask her now.

The words flowed through his mind, and Boone resisted them for a couple of seconds. Carrie looked at him, and Kyle stepped over to Gerty.

Boone "got his act together" and dug his hand into his pocket. "Before we go," he said, feeling the slick plastic. Well aware of every eye on him now—and Gerty raising her phone so she could record the proposal—Boone dropped to one knee and then two.

Cosette sucked in a breath, and Carrie said, "Oh, my goodness."

His thick fingers fumbled with the tiny zipper at the top of the bag, and he looked up at his daughter. "Gerty," he said. "Help."

She handed her phone to Cosette, who looked at it blankly. Gerty got the bag open and poured the diamond ring into Boone's palm. She took her phone back and resumed her recording position.

Boone's heart thundered in his chest, making his tongue thick and his mind slow. He met Cosette's eyes, which were wide and glittering in the sunlight. Everything cleared, and he grinned at her. "Cosette Brian," he said in a steady, strong voice. "I'm not sure I've figured you out yet, but I know I'm in love with you. The day I met you a year ago made everything in my life pivot. I want to spend the rest of my life at your side, and maybe one day, I'll know everything that makes you so amazing, special, and beautiful." He held up the ring. "Will you marry me?"

Cosette reached up and wiped her eyes while Gerty

swung the phone in her direction. She giggled and smiled the way children do, and Cosette looked at her first. "What do you think? Was that romantic enough?"

"Yes," Gerty said, and Cosette looked at Boone.

She cocked one eyebrow and took a step toward him. She looked at the ring and then him, her expression filled with adoration and love. Boone almost couldn't believe it was for him and because of him, but it was.

"I love you," she whispered, nowhere near loud enough for the cell phone camera to capture the sound. "I'm ready to marry you. So yes, I'll be your wife."

Boone grinned as he slid the ring onto her left hand this time. He whooped and threw his cowboy hat into the air, put one foot solidly on the ground, then grabbed Cosette and pulled her onto that knee.

With his face only an inch from hers, he whispered, "You are precious to me. I love you."

"Love you too, Boone."

He kissed her while Kyle and Carrie clapped. He kept it chaste, because his daughter had the camera rolling, and when he pulled back, his smile popped back into place. Cosette's did too, and they both got to their feet.

"That's wonderful," Carrie said, weeping again. Even Gerty lowered her phone to wipe her eyes. All the muscles in Boone's face tightened, and he pulled his daughter into his chest.

"Okay?" he asked, looking at Cosette. She sandwiched Gerty on the other side, hugging her too, and Boone finally felt like he'd reached the top of the deep, dark hole he'd fallen into over seven years ago.

He cleared his throat, and their huddle-hug broke up. "Let's go see your momma," he said to Gerty, and they linked hands again.

The five of them made the rest of the walk in silence, and Boone smiled at the headstone as it came into view. "Hello, love," he said the way he always did. He came to a stop in front of his late wife's name. "There's so much to tell you this time." He crouched down and ran his fingers along the letters.

"Gerty kissed a boy," he said in an over-exaggerated whisper not meant to truly keep anything secret. He grinned as he looked up at Gerty. She knelt next to him in the grass, and he put his arm around her. "She'll tell you all about it in a minute."

He cleared his throat. "I brought Cosette, Nik. She said she's gonna marry me." He took a deep breath and blew it all out. "I did it, love, okay? I found someone else who can put up with me." A sob gathered in his chest, and he bowed his head. *I found someone who can help me raise Gerty.*

He didn't say the last part, but he'd fulfilled his promise to his wife. Finally.

He straightened and stepped back, Cosette's hand slipping into his and squeezing. He didn't wipe his eyes before he looked at her, and he let her see every vulnerable thing currently running through him. She didn't say anything, but her smile radiated kindness and acceptance. She moved her other hand to cover his as well, and Boone leaned down to press a kiss to her forehead.

Gerty sniffled and fell back to his side. He put his arm around her as Carrie put down the huge tin bucket filled with flowers, kissed her fingers, and touched the top of the tombstone.

"It's amazing how much love the heart can hold," Boone said, hoping he could vocalize everything they were all feeling. Carrie nodded, and Cosette's hand in his tightened.

He took a big breath and held it. "All right." He looked around at everyone. "Who wants to go get tacos for dinner?"

"I'll go if you're not gonna kiss Cosette the whole time," Gerty said as she turned away from her mother's grave.

"I can't promise that," Boone said, grinning at his fiancé. "She did just agree to marry me. I should probably sneak her over behind that there shed and kiss her."

"I've never kissed Michael behind a shed," Gerty said in a deadpan, her stride not hitching even a little.

"I need to know more about this boy," Carrie said with a frown, and Boone gave her an emphatic nod. She and Kyle left, and Boone turned toward Cosette, taking her into his arms.

"Look at that. We're alone." He kissed her again, this time enjoying a slow, sweet kiss until she accelerated it.

"Daddy!" Gerty called, and Boone had no idea how much time had passed. He chuckled as he broke the kiss, and Cosette buried her face in his chest and laughed.

When their eyes met, they said, "I love you," at the same

time, and Boone risked the wrath of his hangry teenage daughter by kissing the love of his life one more time.

Read on for a sneak peek at the next book in this family saga & Christian Romance series, **HIS FOURTH DATE**, to find out how things are going to go down with Poppy and Travis!

Sneak Peek! His Fourth Date, Chapter One:

TRAVIS THATCHER WALKED INTO THE HOUSE where Chris Hammond lived, the scent of bacon and basil meeting his nose. "Just me," he said.

The older gentleman came out of the kitchen, which sat off to the left of the front door, near the back of the house. Chris smiled, his bright eyes showing Travis that even brown eyes could shine like stars. "There you are," he said, hobbling slightly toward him. He wore a black apron tied around his waist, with a blue golf shirt and a pair of shorts.

Travis couldn't help smiling at the man. "You look like one of your mutual funds had a very good night."

Chris laughed as Travis took off his cowboy hat and hung it on the rack beside the door. The blessed air conditioning reminded him that some people worked without sweating all day. He honestly didn't mind the weather he had to put up with here in Colorado, because anything was better than living in the city.

"Come see," Chris said, turning to go back into the kitchen. Travis followed him, noting the man's desk in the living room still overflowed with papers. Gray, his son, had told Travis that his father had run their family company for decades, and even after he'd retired, he couldn't get rid of some things.

He loved investing, any talk of stocks, bonds, holdings, accounts. He took risks because he was almost eighty-seven years old, and why shouldn't he? He'd been a billionaire since birth, and Travis loved the old man as if he were his own father.

"It's HMC," Chris said, indicating the laptop on the kitchen table. "Didn't I tell you to buy up our stock? I knew they were going to split it. I just knew it."

Travis glanced at Chris and then the laptop. He'd made the text bigger, so Travis didn't even have to get that close to see it. "So now I own twice as much as I used to."

Chris laughed again. "I almost have the sandwiches ready." He bustled back into the kitchen, where the sizzling sound of something frying met Travis's ears. He sat at the table while Chris talked. "Hunter didn't tell me. I know you're thinking that."

"It's a valid thought," Travis said, peering closer at the screen. "It's already going up." Investing in HMC had been a good thing, and while Travis was good with numbers, he couldn't math that fast.

"Boone and Matt are coming," Chris said. "Can you put that on the desk? I don't have room otherwise."

"Sure." Travis watched the decimals tick up, then down,

then fly up for another few seconds. "So what next?" He stood and closed the laptop. After picking it up, he started toward the desk. "Are you going to sell?"

"Not yet," he said, flipping over a grilled cheese sandwich. This wouldn't be just any grilled cheese though. Chris always doctored them up with things Travis had never thought to pair together. "I think the stock will go higher as soon as Hunter announces the new shrink foam." Chris grinned like it was the money he cared about.

Travis knew it wasn't. The man hadn't had to live a day of his life without what he wanted and needed. Chris's joy came from experiencing his children and grandchildren achieving great things, and it touched Travis's heart in a way that reminded him of his own single status.

No children, and no girlfriend since moving to Colorado. From there, his thoughts immediately moved to Poppy Harris, the woman who lived on and ran the farm next door. She had an eleven-year-old son named Steele, and Travis had done his darnedest to help her over the past several months. She didn't seem to want his help, and he could admit he hadn't told her much about himself or why it was so dang easy to help her.

The only person who truly knew that he also had over a billion dollars in the bank was Gray Hammond. Elise too, of course, and Travis wanted to keep that number as small as possible.

The front door opened as Chris said, "These are apple-bacon grilled cheese sandwiches." He put one on a plate and picked up a big chef's knife to cut it into triangles. "With basil dipping aioli."

"...I'm just saying, it would be fun," Boone said, his voice always full of laughter and joy. Travis liked the man a whole lot, because while he worked hard and did amazing things with their therapy horses, he was always the life of the party too.

In many ways, Travis wished he could be more like Boone. The man said whatever was on his mind, to anyone. He didn't hold back in showing his happiness—or his heartache. He felt things, and he felt them deeply.

"A motorcycle is a death trap," Cosette, his fiancé of only eight days, said. "Not fun."

The darker version of Boone came inside and closed the door too. Matt Whettstein, his brother, chuckled and said, "I kind of agree with Cosette."

"Traitor," Boone boomed. He grinned at Travis and clapped him on the shoulder. "Howdy, Trav."

"Hey, Boone." Travis smiled, because no one could look at Boone while he was smiling and not feel the pure radiance from him. Travis was a bit surprised he'd gotten the formal, polished, precise Cosette Brian to even go out with him, and he wondered—not for the first time—if he should ask Boone for some tips when it came to Poppy.

"If you get a motorcycle," Matt said, also arriving at the island in the kitchen where everyone else stood. "Then Keith will want to ride it. And Britt. Then I'm going to be the bad guy who won't let her."

"It's *such* a great deal," Boone said.

Cosette looked up from her phone, and as usual, she wore a pretty flowery dress, perfect makeup, and this time, a smile. "Too bad," she said in a voice that didn't indicate she thought anything was bad. "Raven said the bike sold already." She smacked her lips and shook her head in mock disappointment.

Matt and Chris chuckled while Boone blinked at his fiancé. "You think this is so funny," he said, teasing her. He swooped his arms around her, the two of them laughing, and Travis couldn't help basking in their love.

He couldn't remember the last time he'd been in love with a woman. Maybe he never had been, though he'd dated Jenni for a long, long time. She'd been so focused on her career, and truth be told, so had he. The relationship was so they didn't have to eat alone at night, and he could watch her cat while she traveled for work.

"Where's Gloria?" Travis asked Matt, nodded a silent hello while Boone and Cosette settled down.

"The sandwiches are done," Chris said. "Someone take this one and eat it."

"Don't have to ask me twice," Boone said, claiming the already-cut sandwich before anyone else could even reach for it.

Chris turned back to the stove to get more out of the pan, and Matt said, "She's tired today, so I made her go home to take a nap."

"When is she due again?" Travis asked, picking up a plate and handing it to Matt. He stood around the island, closer to the stove, and he got the next sandwich.

"Uh, let's see," Matt said. "August twenty-fourth." He smiled at Travis, who took the next sandwich and handed the plate to Cosette. The two of them joined Boone at the kitchen table, and Travis waited for Chris to dish up the last two sandwiches. Then they joined everyone at the table too.

"Molly should be having her baby next week," Chris said, his voice once again filled with pride and joy.

"I can't believe they didn't find out what they're having," Cosette said.

"It's a baby, baby," Boone said with a grin. "I know it won't be a chicken." He laughed, and Travis couldn't help joining him. Cosette just rolled her eyes, though she did smile.

"Did you find out with Gerty?" Cosette said. Travis dipped the corner of his sandwich in the basil sauce and took a bite. Salty bacon, sweet apple, and gooey cheese. With the basil, this sandwich was perfection.

"Yes," Boone said. "Nikki wanted to decorate the nursery. We had so much pink stuff, it was unbelievable." He spoke easily of his deceased wife, his smile only growing fonder and wider.

Sitting there with the four of them, and thinking of Molly and Hunter Hammond starting their family in just a few short days, Travis determined he needed to do something more than try to discover himself. He'd left his big-wig finance job in the city and come west, where he'd found this farm and this job to be a safe haven for him.

He'd learned who he was beneath the shadows of the

huge Rocky Mountains, and he knew his place with the Lord.

Now, he needed to find someone to share his life with. Someone who could tease him the way Cosette did Boone, and someone who could help him continue to try to improve every single day the way Molly did for Hunter.

"So," he said in a lull in the conversation. "Has anyone ever gone to the Lazy Summer Days in town?" He put the last bite of his sandwich in his mouth and looked up. Boone and Cosette shook their heads, but Matt and Chris had sort of frozen.

"What?" Travis asked.

Matt cleared his throat. "You know what the Lazy Summer Days is, right?"

"Clearly not," Travis said, already reaching for his phone. "I saw a poster in the window at the grocery store a couple of days ago. It said there were activities and movies in the park."

"Yeah," Matt said. "For couples. It's a dating event."

Travis looked up from his phone, his search forgotten. "Dating event?"

Matt shifted and cleared his throat again. "It's for like, you know, a summer girlfriend. You sign up, and the first event is speed-dating. Hopefully, you find someone, and then you...spend the summer with them, doing all these 'activities' and going to movies in the park." He exchanged a glance with his brother.

Travis wasn't sure how that was bad. "Don't people keep going out after summer ends?"

"Sure," Matt said easily. "I just—well, usually the people who do it are in their twenties. I went the first summer I got hired on here with Gray, while he went up to Coral Canyon. I was one of the older men there."

"You went to that?" Boone asked, chortling.

Travis knew then that should he choose to go, he would not be telling Boone. Cosette whacked him in the chest and said, "Stop it." She looked at Travis, her deep, green eyes partly worried and partly compassionate. She'd always been kind to him, if professional, and Travis did like her.

"That was a long time ago, Matt," she said, dropping her eyes to her phone. "It says here that there are age ranges. Twenty-one to twenty-nine. Thirty to thirty-four. Thirty-five to thirty-nine." She paused and looked at Travis.

"Keep goin'," he said, his voice almost a growl.

"Forty to forty-four, forty-five to fifty." She read out ages all the way to sixty-five, and then said, "And sixty-six-plus." She looked at Matt and Boone and Chris. "So even Chris could sign up should he want to see about finding someone special again."

Chris looked horrified at the thought, and everyone at the table chuckled. Cosette said, "So it's for everyone." She cut a look at Travis again. "Love can be found at any age, anywhere."

Travis gave her a nod and stood up. He picked up his plate and then gathered everyone else's, taking them all into the kitchen. "Well," he said. "I best be gettin' back to work."

"The sign-up date ends tomorrow," Cosette said. "The

speed-dating event is this weekend." She had to be talking to him, and Travis's face heated.

"All right," he said, neither committing to signing up nor saying he wasn't going to.

———

THE FOLLOWING EVENING, TRAVIS SIGHED AS HE sat in front of his computer. The sign-up form for the Lazy Summer Days already open. It had been open since he'd returned home last night, and he'd been stewing about signing up for over twenty-four hours now.

He looked at the screen, his fingers acting almost of their own accord. His name got entered, then his phone number, and email. Before he knew it, his mouse hovered over the submit button, and then he clicked on it.

A breath of air whooshed out of his lungs, and Travis jumped to his feet. He backed up a couple of steps, staring at the computer screen like he'd just committed a heinous crime. He turned away and took a breath.

"No," he said. "It's time, Trav. Time to take the next step in your life." He felt like he'd been on quite the journey in the past few years, and finding a girlfriend who could become a wife was simply the next, natural thing for him.

So it was that Travis showed up at the high school gymnasium the following evening. He'd arrived early, but he wasn't the first person there. After he'd watched the fifth or sixth man walk through the doors, he gathered his courage close and unbuckled his seat belt. No one had been much younger than him, because he'd signed up for the forty-to-forty-four age group of men.

He'd been emailed a time for his speed-dating event, and he still had ten minutes to spare. He walked the short distance to the steps, up them, and through the door without panicking or turning back.

Inside, lines of men waited to be checked-in, but everything ran smoothly. Voices filled the air, but Travis didn't talk to anyone. Nerves ran through him, and he wasn't the only one. It felt like someone had electrified the oxygen in the high school, and then Travis gave a younger man his name.

His got checked off, and he took a number from the guy. "That's your table number," he explained. "In the gym, you'll find a matching one. The ladies are moving tonight." He smiled like this speed-dating event was something Travis should be thrilled to attend.

He managed to smile back, looked at his twenty-eight, and tucked it into his front jeans pocket. Yes, he'd worn jeans, but he'd paired those with a really great blue and yellow shirt. Well, really great according to Hilde, his sister. He'd called her about tonight's activity, and with the help of the camera on his phone, she'd gone through his closet with him an hour ago.

He found his table easily and sat down. Glancing left and right, he saw men his own age stretching in both directions. He barely had time to wonder how there could be so many singles his age in this area before a man stepped over to the microphone up on the stage and started speaking.

"All right, gentlemen," he said. "Our ladies are getting debriefed right now, and then we'll open the doors and let them in." He beamed out his happiness at all of them, and Travis couldn't help searching for a wedding ring on his hand. Sure enough, this guy was already married.

Travis cleared his throat as someone put a bottle of water on his table. He practically lunged for it while the guy on the stage went over the rules. Six-minute rounds. Bells ringing. Women moving.

Travis was the one who suddenly needed to move, and move now. Before he could get up and admit he'd made a terrible mistake, the first bell rang, and the doors in front of him opened.

Sneak Peek! His Fourth Date, Chapter Two:

POPPY HARRIS LOITERED NEAR THE BACK OF THE group of women now entering the gymnasium. She had an assigned seat, and she didn't need six minutes to know if she liked a man or not. In fact, that was about five minutes too long, and she was fine to let the other, more eager, women get into position first.

She'd opted into the male thirty-five to thirty-nine age range, as well as the forty to forty-four. She'd already been doing this speed dating thing for an hour, and she'd struck out spectacularly.

Ten dates, and not a single man in her age range had asked for her number. Even if they had, Poppy wouldn't have given it to them. One of her dates had looked to be the same age as Steele, and Poppy didn't need two eleven-year-olds to mother, thank you very much.

These were men five to nine years older than her, which was still an acceptable range in her book. Other than Eli, her ex-boyfriend, her dating playbook was quite empty, and Poppy had decided she needed to do something about that.

Elora had told her about this Lazy Summer Days event, not that Poppy hadn't known about it. The town of Ivory Peaks had been running it for a lot longer than just this year. She'd never attended, though her sister swore by the event. Elora had met her husband a few summers ago, and she'd managed to get the man to marry her and do things the right way.

Of course. Elora was the younger sister, but she was the far superior daughter.

Poppy pushed her perfect sibling from her mind, reminding herself that she had a brother who seemed to need to move home very other year. No one was perfect, and she didn't have time right now to dwell on all the ways she needed to improve.

She would meet ten more men, and hopefully one of them would become the love of her life, the way Briggs had for Elora.

She went to her left, because she knew where station twenty-five sat. She'd rotated through it an hour ago. Now, she'd start there. She drew in a deep breath and smoothed down her errant curls as the woman in front of her veered toward table twenty-six, leaving her view clear of table twenty-five.

A man she didn't recognize sat there, looking anxious. Poppy knew the feeling, as her stomach tried to vacate her body while her feet kept moving toward him. "Hello," she said just as the bell rang.

"Six minutes," the man up on the stage said. The man at the table didn't stand, not like Twenty-Six had to meet the blonde who'd gone his way. Poppy gave her guy a strike, but kept her smile stitched in place. "Your first date starts now!"

She had no idea how the caller could sound so excited, but he had. With several more age ranges to go, she hoped he had plenty of coffee or a whole case of energy drinks nearby. She'd consumed four slices of turkey from the deli and a Red Bull before making the drive to this high school gym a couple of hours ago, and as she sat down, she cleared her throat nervously.

"I'm Poppy Harris."

"Dwayne Rush." He smiled at her and extended his hand. He wore a cowboy hat, but he clearly didn't work outside. His hands looked like he'd just gotten a manicure, and his skin felt softer than hers. "It's great to meet you."

"You too." She pulled her hand away from his. "So, Dwayne, what do you do?" She could really use a chef or a veterinarian, but Poppy had told herself to be open-minded. She couldn't afford to be picky about who she went out with, and Dwayne was good-looking in a non-cowboy kind of way.

It really was a shame her attraction to true cowboys was so strong, because she'd never met one who could be tamed enough to settle down. At least not by her.

What about Travis? she asked herself as Dwayne said, "I run the cellphone store in town," like he'd single-handedly delivered Christmas gifts to all needy people in the state of Colorado. "What about you?"

"I run a farm," Poppy said as pleasantly as she could. *Two strikes* ran through her mind, though she wasn't sure why. If she ended up marrying Dwayne, she could eliminate a very expensive bill from her long list of them.

The conversation stalled, and Poppy struck Dwayne right on out. She made it through the six minutes, and with seconds to spare, Dwayne asked, "Do you think I could get your number?" He wore hope in his bright blue eyes, and Poppy could admit that pleasure and satisfaction filled her.

"Sure," she said, and she filled out the paper with her name on it and handed it to him. He gazed at it, truly seeming surprised, and he did stand to shake her hand this time.

"Move to the next station," the caller on the stage bellowed into the mic. "You have thirty seconds until your second date begins."

Poppy offered another smile to Dwayne before she turned her attention to Twenty-Six. He was still talking to the blonde. Neither of them seemed to have heard the man on the stage, and Blondie tipped her head back and sent gut-laughter toward the ceiling. The man across from her laughed too, and Poppy stood there awkwardly.

She couldn't go back to her seat, because someone else had already taken it. In the three-foot space between tables, she barely fit, and she towered over both people *still* talking.

"You're supposed to switch," she said. Only a moment later, the microphone squealed, and Blondie finally looked toward the stage.

"Oh," she said, giggling as she got to her feet. "Looks like we're supposed to change."

"Your second date starts now."

She wrote her number on the slip of paper with her name printed on it, tucked it in the man's pocket and moved over to the next station. Poppy rolled her eyes as the guy watched her, completely oblivious to his next date.

Poppy sat in the now-vacated chair and pulled out her phone. She'd taken three breaths before the man across from her sat down. He cleared his throat. "Sorry about that."

"Yeah," Poppy said without looking up. "You know, for future reference." She did raise her head from her mobile social media. "If you're that interested, you can ask the woman to leave with you right then. Then the whole station is taken out of play, and I would've just moved down to that guy."

She hooked her thumb to the right, but she didn't look away from Mister Smitten.

"Really?" He looked over to the next table, where Blondie let loose with another hysterical round of laughter. *Of all the luck*, Poppy thought. Of course she'd get behind the perkiest, funniest woman at the speed dating event.

She already battled a demon who told her she was dull and drab, and following Blondie around for the next hour wasn't going to help one bit.

"Yeah," she said. "But you have to do it in that thirty seconds. Because if you go now, then the whole rotation is off."

"Maybe I could ask her after this round," he said,

looking at Poppy with extreme hope. "Then, this station would be gone."

"And then the one past her won't have anyone. Because I haven't gone out with that guy yet." She shook her head. "Nope. You had to ask her and leave before I sat down here and she sat down there." She went back to her phone. "It's fine with me. I have a couple of comments to leave anyway."

He hadn't introduced himself, and Poppy wasn't about to give him her name. The six minutes passed fast enough, and the bell rang. "Great to meet you," she said as pleasantly as she could, getting to her feet and reminding herself that Dwayne had asked for her number.

Thirty seconds. Third date beginning...now!

"Hello, Sal," she said, smiling at the man who'd once sold her some...overripe fish. She'd driven right back to the butcher shop and told him so, and thankfully, he did think the customer was right. She'd gotten something else for dinner, but of course Steele didn't eat it. The boy only ate dino nuggets and tater tots, boxed macaroni and cheese, and cold cereal.

Poppy supposed that could've been a commentary on her parenting skills—and her lack of cooking skills—but her son hadn't died yet.

"Poppy," he said, smiling at her. "How were those pork chops?" And date three would be six minutes of meat talk.

Ivory Peaks wasn't that big of a place, and Poppy understood she'd likely run into some men she knew at this event. She never looked down the line to see who came next, because that was half the fun of speed dating.

"Thirty seconds to switch."

"Good luck tonight, Sal," she said as she stood up.

"You too," he said, glancing to Poppy's next station and then toward his next date. "And come get that beef roast on Monday. I'll have it wrapped for you."

"I will." She smiled and turned toward station twenty-eight. The man there met her eyes, shock immediately entering his.

Then Travis Thatcher jumped to his feet, knocking the table in front of him a foot or two forward. "Poppy," he said, his voice low and sexy.

"No," she said out loud, but it wasn't to him. It was for herself. His voice was *not* sexy.

Except that it one-hundred percent was.

"I'm sorry?" he asked.

"Nothing," she said, shaking away her surprise. She wanted to say something else, but nothing came to mind.

Travis gave a nervous chuckle, and she realized a flush had worked its way into his face. "I, uh, haven't ever done this before."

"The speed dating?" she asked.

"Yeah."

"Me either." She moved toward the chair and pulled it out a little further. "How's it going?"

"Not great," he said as he retook his seat. He smiled at her from across the table, his big, rough hands clasping together. "You?"

"Not as bad as last time," she said.

His smile faded slightly. "I thought you said you hadn't done this."

"Before this year," she said, clarifying. "I signed up for two age groups. This one, and the one before it. The younger guys."

"Ah, I see."

"How old are you?" she asked, realizing how blunt she sounded. "I mean, that was rude. Sorry." She gave a light laugh. "I actually belong in the younger group, but I figured someone who was forty-four was still only nine years older than me." She shrugged, another horrible giggle coming from her mouth.

Travis's smile brightened again. "I'm forty-two," he said. "And I'm not from here—or any cowboy-dominated region —but my mother did teach me some manners. I won't ask how old you are."

Poppy grinned at him, surprised at how easy he was to talk to. He'd always been fun to be around, and she was the one who'd put up bars and barriers between them. He'd taken her displeasure at him paying her mortgage, and she swallowed just thinking about it.

"Listen," she said, leaning her elbows onto the table and inching closer to him. She told herself it wasn't because his cologne did strange things to her pulse. "I want to apologize for making a big deal about...." She cleared her throat. "My mortgage payment."

"I did say I was sorry for paying it," he said. "I was just trying to help."

"It did help," she said. She wasn't sure why the two

words she needed to say always stuck in her throat. "Thank you."

Travis tilted his head to the side, his dark brown cowboy hat perched so deliciously on his head. He wore a full beard, the darkness of it showing some gray and making his white teeth shine in the bright overhead lights.

"That seemed hard for you to say," he said.

"It is," she admitted, feeling one of her walls crumble to the ground. "I...can I tell you something?"

"I wish you would." He grinned at her, and Poppy realized he was flirting with her. Travis Thatcher. Flirting.

She blinked out of the surprise—this cowboy had plenty of them to throw at her—and said, "It's hard for me to thank people. I'm working on it."

"Why is it hard to tell someone thank you?"

"It just is," she said. "See, I've had to do everything myself for so long, and I hate feeling like I can't do something. I hate requiring help."

"Everyone needs help sometimes," he said.

"True," she said. "My sister says I need to swallow my pride and just let people in."

He leaned closer, a glint in those gorgeous eyes that reminded her of the color of chocolate mousse. "You've let me come help you. I heard you tell Gray and Elise thank you. I listened as he gushed over how helpful Cody was up in the hay loft."

Poppy swallowed, because he wasn't wrong. "Maybe it's just you then."

"Why me?"

"You make me nervous," she admitted.

His eyebrows went up. "I do?"

"Yes." She pulled her arms back and folded her arms as she leaned against the back of the uncomfortable chair. "Happy?"

"Not at all, Miss Harris," he drawled.

"If you're not a cowboy, where are you from?" she asked, the question a clear challenge.

"Raleigh," he said. "You?"

"What makes you think I'm not from right here in Colorado?"

"I didn't say you were from somewhere else. I just asked where you were from." He could hold his own with her, and that made him so much more attractive to Poppy than he already was.

Her pulse pumped out an extra beat, and a certain sense of instability flowed through her. "I'm from Laramie," she said.

He nodded. "Why'd you move here?"

"I came with my boyfriend," she said. "We were to live and work on the farm where I still am."

Travis simply blinked, no judgment filled his face. "I moved here from New York City. I worked in investment banking there."

"No wonder you could find out my private financial information so easily."

He chuckled and shook his head. "It wasn't like that."

"You still haven't told me how you figured out where I bank and how to pay your money onto my past-due mortgage." She raised her eyebrows, wondering if he found her even slightly attractive. She'd been thinking about him for weeks and months, and she really wanted to go out with him again.

"Time's up!" the man screeched into the microphone, and Poppy flinched.

Travis got to his feet while the guy said they had thirty seconds to move. "Hey," he said "What do you think about us getting out of here and continuing to talk somewhere else?" He swallowed visibly, his expression filled with anxiety and hope at the same time.

Numbness flooded Poppy, and she couldn't make sense of his words or her thoughts.

"We could go to dinner somewhere. I'll tell you how I figured out where your mortgage was." Travis glanced to the woman who would be his next date, but Poppy couldn't look away from him. "I guess this is something we can do, but the clock is ticking."

Yes, it was. Every tick seemed to take a very long time, and Poppy couldn't get her voice to work.

Another chuckle, and Travis's eyes bored into hers. "Poppy?" he asked. "What do you think?"

His Fourth Date is available for preorder.

His First Love (Book 1): She broke up with him a decade ago. He's back in town after finishing a degree at MIT, ready to start his job at the family company. Can Hunter and Molly find their way through their pasts to build a future together?

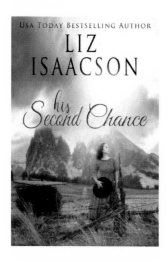

His Second Chance (Book 2):
They broke up over twenty years ago. She's lost everything when she shows up at the farm in Ivory Peaks where he works. Can Matt and Gloria heal from their pasts to find a future happily-ever-after with each other?

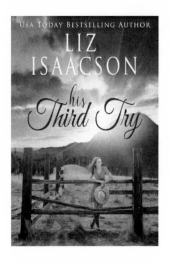

His Third Try (Book 3): He moved to Ivory Peaks with his daughter to start over after a devastating break-up. She's never had a meaningful relationship with a man, especially a cowboy. Can Boone and Cosette help each other heal enough to build a happily-ever-after...and a family?

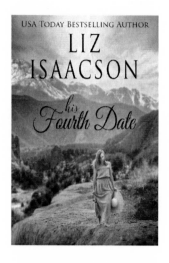

His Fourth Date (Book 4): Their relationship has been nothing but loose goats, a leaking roof, and her complete humiliation after he pays her mortgage so she won't lose her farm. Travis wants to go back in time and start over with Poppy, but he doesn't know how. Can a small town speed-dating event get their second chance off on the right foot?

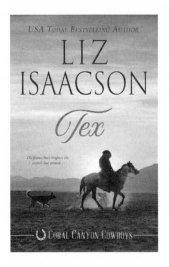

Tex (Book 1): He's back in town after a successful country music career. She owns a bordering farm to the family land he wants to buy...and she outbids him at the auction. Can Tex and Abigail rekindle their old flame, or will the issue of land ownership come between them?

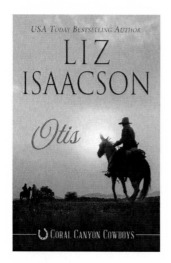

Otis (Book 2): He's finished with his last album and looking for a soft place to fall after a devastating break-up. She runs the small town bookshop in Coral Canyon and needs a new boyfriend to get her old one out of her life for good. Can Georgia convince Otis to take another shot at real love when their first kiss was fake?

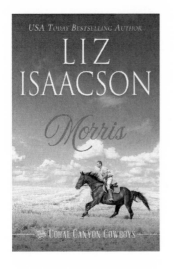

Morris (Book 3): Morris Young is just settling into his new life as the manager of Country Quad when he attends a wedding. He sees his ex-wife there—apparently Leighann is back in Coral Canyon—along with a little boy who can't be more or less than five years old... Could he be Morris's? And why is his heart hoping for that, and for a reconciliation with the woman who left him because he traveled too much?

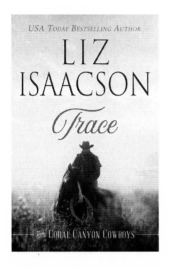

Trace (Book 4): He's been accused of only dating celebrities. She's a simple line dance instructor in small town Coral Canyon, with a soft spot for kids...and cowboys. Trace could use some dance lessons to go along with his love lessons... Can he and Everly fall in love with the beat, or will she dance her way right out of his arms?

The Mechanics of Mistletoe (Book 1): Bear Glover can be a grizzly or a teddy, and he's always thought he'd be just fine working his generational family ranch and going back to the ancient homestead alone. But his crush on Samantha Benton won't go away. She's a genius with a wrench on Bear's tractors...and his heart. Can he tame his wild side and get the girl, or will he be left broken-hearted this Christmas season?

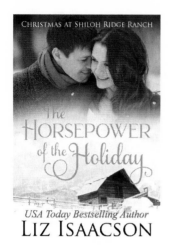

The
HORSEPOWER
of the Holiday

USA Today Bestselling Author
LIZ ISAACSON

The Horsepower of the Holiday (Book 2): Ranger Glover has worked at Shiloh Ridge Ranch his entire life. The cowboys do everything from horseback there, but when he goes to town to trade in some trucks, somehow Oakley Hatch persuades him to take some ATVs back to the ranch. (Bear is NOT happy.)

She's a former race car driver who's got Ranger all revved up... Can he remember who he is and get Oakley to slow down enough to fall in love, or will there simply be too much horsepower in the holiday this year for a real relationship?

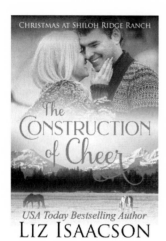

The Construction of Cheer (Book 3): Bishop Glover is the youngest brother, and he usually keeps his head down and gets the job done. When Montana Martin shows up at Shiloh Ridge Ranch looking for work, he finds himself inventing construction projects that need doing just to keep her coming around. (Again, Bear is NOT happy.) She wants to build her own construction firm, but she ends up carving a place for herself inside Bishop's heart. Can he convince her *he's* all she needs this Christmas season, or will her cheer rest solely on the success of her business?

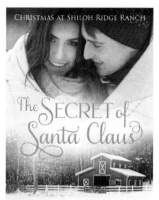

The Secret of Santa (Book 4): He's a fun-loving cowboy with a heart of gold. She's the woman who keeps putting him on hold. Can Ace and Holly Ann make a relationship work this Christmas?

CHRISTMAS AT SHILOH RIDGE RANCH

The HARMONY of Holly

USA Today Bestselling Author
LIZ ISAACSON

The Harmony of Holly (Book 5): He's as prickly as his name, but the new woman in town has caught his eye. Can Cactus shelve his temper and shed his cowboy hermit skin fast enough to make a relationship with Willa work?

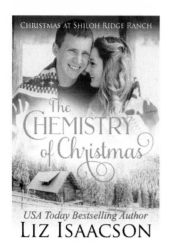

The Chemistry of Christmas (Book 6): He's the black sheep of the family, and she's a chemist who understands formulas, not emotions. Can Preacher and Charlie take their quirks and turn them into a strong relationship this Christmas?

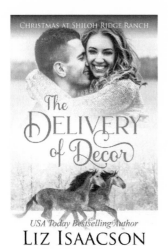

The Delivery of Decor (Book 7): When he falls, he falls hard and deep. She literally drives away from every relationship she's ever had. Can Ward somehow get Dot to stay this Christmas?

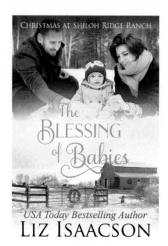

The Blessing of Babies (Book 8): Don't miss out on a single moment of the Glover family saga in this bridge story linking Ward and Judge's love stories!

The Glovers love God, country, dogs, horses, and family. Not necessarily in that order. ;)

Many of them are married now, with babies on the way, and there are lessons to be learned, forgiveness to be had and given, and new names coming to the family tree in southern Three Rivers!

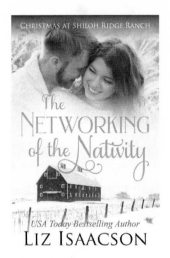

The Networking of the Nativity (Book 9): He's had a crush on her for years. She doesn't want to date until her daughter is out of the house. Will June take a change on Judge when the success of his Christmas light display depends on her networking abilities?

The Wrangling of the Wreath (Book 10): He's been so busy trying to find Miss Right. She's been right in front of him the whole time. This Christmas, can Mister and Libby take their relationship out of the best friend zone?

CHRISTMAS AT SHILOH RIDGE RANCH

The HOPE of Her Heart

USA Today Bestselling Author
LIZ ISAACSON

The Hope of Her Heart (Book 11): She's the only Glover without a significant other. He's been searching for someone who can love him *and* his daughter. Can Etta and August make a meaningful connection this Christmas?

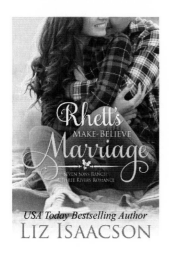

Rhett's Make-Believe Marriage (Book 1): She needs a husband to be credible as a matchmaker. He wants to help a neighbor. Will their fake marriage take them out of the friend zone?

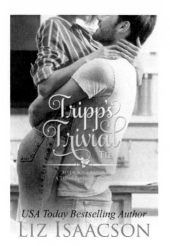

Tripp's Trivial Tie (Book 2): She needs a husband to keep her son. He's wanted to take their relationship to the next level, but she's always pushing him away. Will their trivial tie take them all the way to happily-ever-after?

Liam's Invented I-Do (Book 3): She's desperate to save her ranch. He wants to help her any way he can. Will their invented I-Do open doors that have previously been closed and lead to a happily-ever-after for both of them?

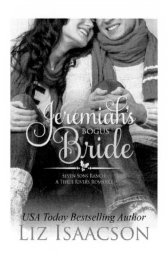

Jeremiah's Bogus Bride (Book 4): He wants to prove to his brothers that he's not broken. She just wants him. Will a fake marriage heal him or push her further away?

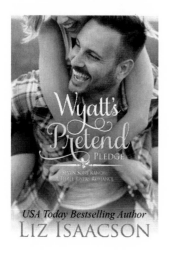

Wyatt's Pretend Pledge (Book 5): To get her inheritance, she needs a husband. He's wanted to fly with her for ages. Can their pretend pledge turn into something real?

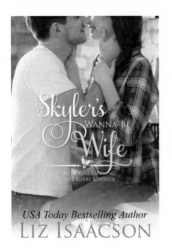

Skyler's Wanna-Be Wife (Book 6): She needs a new last name to stay in school. He's willing to help a fellow student. Can this wanna-be wife show the playboy that some things should be taken seriously?

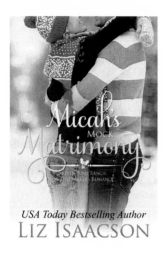

USA Today Bestselling Author
LIZ ISAACSON

Micah's Mock Matrimony (Book 7): They were just actors auditioning for a play. The marriage was just for the audition – until a clerical error results in a legal marriage. Can these two ex-lovers negotiate this new ground between them and achieve new roles in each other's lives?

About Liz

Liz Isaacson writes inspirational romance, usually set in Texas, or Montana, or anywhere else horses and cowboys exist. She lives in Utah, where she writes full-time, drives her daughter to her acting classes, and eats a lot of peanut butter M&Ms while writing. Find her on her website at lizisaacson.com.

Made in United States
North Haven, CT
19 May 2022

19311070R00262